Praise for the novels of Brenda Novak

"Novak delivers another expertly crafted work
of suspenseful intrigue heightened by white-knuckle danger
and realistically complicated romance."
—*Booklist* on *The Perfect Couple*

"I guarantee *The Perfect Couple* will keep readers on the edge
of their seats. Each character is completely developed, from
Tiffany and Colin to Zoe and Jonathan. The story line sizzles."
—*Romance Reviews Today*

"Realistic and gritty, this story grabs the reader
by the throat on the first page and never lets go."
—*RT Book Reviews* on *Watch Me*

"Gripping, frightening, and intense...a compelling romance
as well as a riveting and suspenseful mystery...
Novak delivers another winner."
—*Library Journal* on *The Perfect Liar*

"Two emotionally damaged protagonists find
much-needed healing and unexpected love in a chilling,
sensual tale that features a host of skillfully developed
characters and intricate, multilayered plotting.
Sacramento-based Novak (*The Perfect Liar*) writes gripping
romantic thrillers. This is the latest in her Last Stand series."
—*Library Journal* on *The Perfect Murder*

"As always, Novak's plotting is flawless, and her
characterizations are rich and multilayered. What sets this story
apart from the rest is the intensity of the romance between the
two wounded protagonists—it simply sizzles. A keeper."
(4.5 stars, Top Pick)
—*RT Book Reviews* on *The Perfect Murder*

"Strong characters bring the escalating suspense to life,
and the mystery is skillfully played out.
Novak's smooth plotting makes for a great read."
—*Publishers Weekly*

BRENDA NOVAK

WHITE HEAT

MIRA®

Recycling programs
for this product may
not exist in your area.

ISBN-13: 978-0-7783-2795-0

WHITE HEAT

For questions and comments about the quality of this book please contact us at
Customer_eCare@Harlequin.ca.

www.MIRABooks.com

Printed in U.S.A.

To Dara Favero...
Someone as sweet as she is beautiful.

Dear Reader,

It's time to turn up the heat! I'm really looking forward to sharing my three "Heat" titles with you (*White Heat, Body Heat* and *Killer Heat*). Although each book stands alone, they all revolve around a private security company called Department 6 and the retired special forces personnel, private investigators and police officers who make their living working as "hired guns." These men and women face some diverse and unusual circumstances—and some very frightening challenges.

Another common thread is that all three books are set in Arizona, a place I find fascinating. While growing up, I lived in Chandler for eight years, back when it was still a farming community and not the sprawling metropolis it has since become. I miss those days, especially the long days of summer, which is probably why I've chosen to set each of these titles in a small town during the hot months. If you've never experienced an Arizona summer or one of the infamous monsoons, you're really missing something....

Arizona has more than its share of ghost towns. Paradise, the setting of this book, is one of them. I took a little (or a lot) of artistic liberty when I settled my fictional cult in Paradise, but it's a unique place that really exists. With such a perfect name, I couldn't resist.

I love to hear from my readers. Please feel free to contact me via www.brendanovak.com. There you can also enter my monthly draws (I give away all kinds of things), learn more about my annual online auction for diabetes research (we've raised over $1 million so far!), download a free 3D screensaver, get the latest info on my annual FAN convention (which I do with #1 *New York Times* bestselling author Christine Feehan), or check out any new books on the horizon (you can even read a sample). If you don't have a computer, you can write to me at P.O. Box 3781, Citrus Heights, CA 95611.

Here's wishing you many hours of reading pleasure!

Brenda Novak

1

Beware of false prophets, which come
to you in sheep's clothing, but inwardly
they are ravening wolves.
—*King James Bible, Matthew 7:15*

"This guy is *dangerous?*" Rachel Jessop studied the glossy black-and-white photograph her manager slid across the table.

Nate Ferrentino's leather chair squeaked as he leaned back and locked his hands behind his head. "He doesn't look dangerous to you?" One eyebrow arched, telling her he found her reaction amusing, but she couldn't begin to guess why, and she'd worked with him long enough to know he wouldn't explain even if she asked. With short dark hair and green, gold-flecked eyes, he had the face of a sensitive man who'd become cynical and the body of a soldier. Nate was a tempting physical specimen. But he wasn't one to reveal much about his thoughts.

Rachel wished that was *all* she knew about her boss. When she'd first started working at Department 6 eight months ago, she'd been so convinced she'd met the one man she could love with all her heart, she'd made a humiliating miscalculation. The embarrassment of that incident still burned so intensely she could barely look at him.

Ignoring the way his T-shirt stretched over his clearly defined pecs, she kept her focus on Ethan Wycliff, the man in the picture. Wiry and with the appearance of some height, Ethan had polish to spare—high cheekbones, black hair, black eyes and a beguiling smile. "He's too pretty to seem dangerous. He could be on billboards, modeling suits for Armani. What's he done?"

Except for possibly height, Nate was Ethan's opposite. Although he wasn't overweight by any stretch of the imagination, slender wasn't an adjective that came to mind. Pretty and polished didn't fit, either. He was handsome, but not in the classic sense of movie stars and models. His forehead was a bit too wide, his jaw too square. And he had too many scars—both from when he was a navy SEAL and from working for Department 6 after he'd left the military.

"Depends on who you talk to," he said. "There's a chance that none of it's illegal, but the secrecy surrounding him and his group is making some important people nervous."

Rachel shoved the picture back in Nate's direction, but he didn't move to reclaim it. He let Ethan Wycliff's image remain on the table, eyes staring sightlessly at the ceiling of the small conference room—one of several in the L.A. office. Unlike other security contractors, Department 6 rarely handled military operations. They specialized in undercover work, generally inside the U.S.

"What's he *suspected* of doing?" she asked. "Laundering money? Smuggling drugs? Working in the sex-slave trade?"

"He's the leader of a religious cult about two hundred members strong."

That was the last thing she'd expected Nate to say. Judging by Ethan's elegant business suit, he had taste. He wasn't sporting a scraggly beard, wasn't beggarly or odd-looking in any way. Neither did he appear smarmy like some televangelists she'd seen. Not in the photograph, anyway. "What kind of religious cult?"

"A Christian cult. Sort of. It seems to be a compilation of whatever Ethan wants it to be. He and his followers call their organization the Church of the Covenant. One thing they believe is that the world is coming to an end very soon. Only those who are properly branded—"

"You mean, tattooed?" she cut in.

"No, I mean, *branded*—and baptized and living within the gates of their little commune—will rule with God."

"That's not particularly creative." She'd heard plenty of the same rhetoric in her own house growing up. For most of her life her father and the leaders of his small sect had claimed that the world was in its "last days." They'd named date after date when Armageddon would arrive. Every one had come and gone. "How'd he get his start?"

"Five years ago, he was a popular frat boy at Cornell. I guess he and a few roommates went out in the woods and devised their own religion, loosely based on the Old Testament's patriarchal order. Our intelligence report indicates that it was originally meant to be a joke. Drugs were involved. They called it the 'antireligion.'

But when they began meeting regularly, word spread among the kids at Cornell and other colleges in nearby communities, somehow generating support, and it became real."

"Power is tough to resist, especially for an Ivy League frat boy who's used to being on top of the world."

"That's my take, too."

She glanced away from Nate so she wouldn't squirm in her seat at the memories that overwhelmed her whenever their eyes met. "How many of his roommates still belong to this so-called religion?"

"The original four are still with him. They're known as 'spiritual guides' now and they're part of the Brethren, the twelve men who form a close circle around him. A fifth roommate, one who joined a bit later, is dead."

"Dead?" she echoed. "At twenty-something?"

"He was killed in a drunk-driving accident after a meeting. There are a few unanswered questions but no real proof that it was anything other than that."

She considered what she'd just been told. "What's so appealing about his religion that others are interested in joining up?"

"It's mostly familiar stuff but with a modern twist. It includes extramarital sex and drug use. And Wycliff has a few assets—*besides his looks*—that make him more dangerous than most cult leaders."

She ignored his reference to her appreciation of Wycliff's appearance and scooted closer to the table. But the instant she caught Nate's scent, that mix of clean male and leather that would forever differentiate him from every other man, the memory of slipping into his bed to "surprise" him came to her as vividly as the night she'd done it. Would the mortification *never* go away?

He gave her a speculative look, as if he could suddenly sense an added level of discomfort, but she was determined to pretend she'd forgotten all about her terrible faux pas. As a child, she'd been sheltered so long she hadn't grown up with the usual interplay between the sexes and, apparently, hadn't read his signals correctly. She'd thought he wanted the same thing.

Keeping her gaze steady, she struggled, once again, to forget that night. "And those assets are…"

"More charisma than any man has a right to, at least a man who once idolized Charles Manson."

"Charles *Manson?* Are you serious?"

He chose a file from a stack he'd brought in with him, and thumbed through it while he talked. "Dead serious. Wycliff corresponded with Manson regularly while he was in high school. I've got copies of some of those letters here."

"Was their correspondence a joke at first, too?"

"He played it that way, used to read Manson's letters aloud to various people he knew, including his parents. His mother said he liked the shock value. His father claims he's always been fascinated with killers. Especially Manson, because of the brutality of the Tate murders and the power Manson held over those who committed them."

"Why would they allow him to correspond with someone like Manson?"

"It started out as what Ethan called 'a psychological study.' He said he wanted to major in behavioral science when he went to college."

She shivered. "But couldn't they see where it was going? These letters make me more than a little nervous."

"They should've made everyone nervous." He offered the file for her perusal.

Careful not to brush his hand, she accepted it but merely placed it in front of her, because he was still talking.

"At first his parents saw only what they wanted to see and hoped his interest was professional, as he'd claimed. He didn't read them what *he* wrote to Manson. He kept that private, so the bits and pieces they heard of Manson's letters made it sound as if Manson was the only crazy one."

"So how did we get copies of the letters?"

"You know how closely prison mail is monitored. Once his father finally became uneasy, he paid a correctional officer to keep an eye on the budding relationship. It was that guy who made copies. But he worked certain days and shifts, of course, and the letters that came and went on someone else's watch were lost."

"Why didn't dear old dad put a stop to the letters once he saw what they contained?"

"His wife insisted it was just a 'phase' Ethan was going through, that he was purposely trying to provoke Manson, the same way he tried to provoke everyone else. And then the problem seemed to solve itself. Ethan grew disenchanted with Manson, quit writing him and the relationship ended."

"But that was a pretty ominous start, and it led to a bigger problem."

"Exactly. Now Ethan's set himself up as a prophet,

the Holy One, the man to lead all Christians to enlightenment."

"And let me guess—enlightenment happens *after* this life."

"With your background, I knew you'd be familiar with the dogma."

Far more than she wanted to be. She'd tried hard to distance herself from the brainwashing she'd undergone as a child, but it wasn't easy to put all those hours of religious "instruction" behind her. Not when there were so many lasting effects, some of which she blamed for the embarrassing blunder she'd made with Nate six months ago.

"Sounds as if he's as whacked as Manson," she mused. Or, like her father, his teachings and devotions could be similar enough to mainstream religions to fall within what society deemed "normal." Not that her father's "normal" was normal to most people. From the moment she got home from school every day, Fredrick Jessop had kept her under lock and key, forced her to read the Bible for hours on end and go to church three or four times a week. Until she'd left home at seventeen, he'd had complete control. Even after she was on her own, she'd been so well trained she was twenty-five before she lost her virginity; at that point she'd finally slept with a man just to punish her father after an argument. That had turned out to be such a bad experience, so cheap and unsatisfying, she hadn't had sex again until she met Nate. But, for different reasons, her encounter with Nate had been even more disappointing than the original one.

"He might be crazy," Nate said. "But making up

your own religion isn't a crime. You know that better than most."

Her father and his cronies had done it, hadn't they? "So what law has Ethan broken?"

Nate's broad shoulders lifted in a shrug. "That's the reason for this assignment—to find out."

She'd already assumed as much. But she wasn't comfortable with the religious element. Her background dealing with religious zealots had taught her there was no way to win, no way to argue any doctrine logically because people like her father always referred to the illogical to back up their beliefs.

"Do you think I have the experience for this?" she asked. Before coming to Department 6, she'd worked undercover for the LAPD, pretending to be a prostitute, as well as helping in some drug busts. Since hiring on at Department 6, she'd continued with drug enforcement, generally contract labor for the DEA. Bottom line, she'd specialized in something that was more straightforward, easier to fight. And she liked it that way.

"You have as much experience with this type of thing as anyone else at Department 6," he said.

That was probably true. They all did more drug work than anything else. "There must be *something* besides his affiliation with Manson that's brought this man to our attention," she said. "I'm guessing there are a lot of whack jobs who've contacted Manson over the years."

"A woman by the name of Martha Wilson recently escaped from the commune," Nate explained.

Now they were talking. "Another interesting word choice, seeing that *escaped* has the connotation of being held against her will."

"*Her* word," he said. "She claimed Wycliff punished her for sleeping with her own husband."

"I thought sex was dealt with in a more liberal fashion in this commune."

"It is. But she was on 'restriction.'"

Because it was beyond awkward to talk about sex with Nate after what had occurred between them, Rachel tried to cover her anxiety by toying with the edge of the file in front of her. "You're kidding."

"Nope. Otherwise, sex is open to anyone, married or unmarried, as long as both people are consenting and of age."

"Now I see why Ethan's attracting converts. Religious endorsement of drugs *and* sex. No willpower required. What's not to like?"

His lips quirked in a wry smile. "It's not quite as simple as it might sound."

"With religion, it never is," she muttered.

"Only those who live according to various 'higher laws'—" he made quotation marks with his fingers "—gain that benefit. But there's a cost. Once you join, you begin a process that culminates in embracing certain rituals that go with these laws. We're not sure what these rituals are. We got most of this information from what was reported in the papers. Martha was vocal about the group's abuse, but less so about their beliefs."

"And Milt can't get more information?" Milton Berger owned the company. Slightly eccentric, he was basically a wealthy businessman who'd never spent a day in the field. At forty-five, he drank and smoked so much he couldn't possibly run the forty-yard dash. But he had an eye for talent and a talent for making money.

"He's relying on us to figure out the rest."

"Do you know what the prize is?"

"The prize?" he repeated.

"What do the people in Ethan's religion get for living these supposed higher laws? There's always a prize for good behavior. It's usually called salvation."

"They're admitted into 'the Holy One's' inner sanctum and become sanctified like he is. Or something like that. Again, there might be more to it."

Remembering what she'd been taught regarding the few elect who would rule with God, she made a face. "How do people fall for this crap?" She'd been steeped in it and still couldn't buy it, although there'd been plenty of times she'd wished she could. It would've made her life so much easier.

"I think psychologists say they're not happy with the world in which they're living. Some want to prove how unique and special they are. Others are just hoping to feel as if they belong." He drummed his fingers on the table. "But who really knows? Motivations are as individual as people."

"Doesn't sound to me like the world they're building will be any better than the one we've got." No matter how hard her father and brother had tried to convince her that the afterlife was all that mattered. "How badly did Ethan Wycliff beat the woman who escaped?"

"She says it wasn't him. It was a public event—a stoning modeled after those in the Bible."

She stiffened. "Stoning is a death sentence in the Bible."

"Martha managed to escape."

"How?"

"We don't know exactly. But according to her, Ethan's getting crazier by the day. She says everyone in the church will wind up dead if someone doesn't do something soon."

Rachel glanced at the photograph again. This time, Ethan's black eyes appeared far colder than they'd seemed before. "Looks like my job's about to get interesting. Again." Interesting and potentially dangerous. The dangerous part never changed. But she didn't mind. It kept her fully occupied, kept her from having to acknowledge the fact that she had nothing in her life except the satisfaction of doing a job most people couldn't. "When do I leave?"

"We leave in the morning."

She riveted her eyes on his face. They never worked the same case. He made sure of it. And they both knew the reason. So why the sudden change of heart? "You don't think I can handle it on my own?"

"Milt's decision, not mine." His response divulged nothing of his own reaction. But she could easily guess how displeased he'd been when he heard the news. He probably feared she'd try to seduce him again. He'd made it very clear that he didn't want that.

"What about Rod?" she asked, trying to control her voice so it wouldn't reveal her panic. "He could go with me." More than just a coworker, Roderick Guerrero was one of her best friends. She'd feel far more comfortable with him.

"Rod's on another job. So are Jonah, Drake and Kellen."

"Then maybe Angelina would be a better choice for—"

He shook his head. "She's too new."

And had no more business in this line of work than Rachel did. He didn't have to say that; Rachel knew he didn't approve of having females taking on the dangerous stuff. "Then I can handle it alone," she argued. A homicidal maniac, drunk on his own power, would be easier to face than daily association with Nate. "It'll be more difficult for *two* strangers to gain the trust we'll need."

"Milt wants us to go in as a couple."

"What?" This went beyond going undercover together as…say, friends or acquaintances. What did it mean? Would she be sharing a room—a *bed*—with Nate?

She couldn't do it. Not after the way she'd thrown herself at him six months ago. "How will we get them to accept us?"

"They hold meetings they call Introductions. I'm not sure where. But they're open to the public. Once we find out where to go, you'll attend one, feign interest and drag me to the next one. We'll go from there."

The plan already seemed set in stone, but surely there had to be a way out. "Where is this cult? Not here in Southern California…"

"No. Paradise, Arizona."

Allowing his response to distract her, she frowned. "That's the name of the compound?"

"That's the name of the town they've taken over and has been since it was founded more than a century ago."

"They bought a whole town?"

"Every parcel, and since no one else wanted it, they got it cheap."

"They actually came across one named Paradise? Ironic, to say the least," she said. Especially because it certainly wouldn't be Paradise for her.

"Arizona and paradise are an oxymoron, at least this time of year."

"So it's as barren and hot and dry as the last place we worked?"

"Nevada? It's just as barren. But it's even hotter and dryer. I'd describe it as more of a white heat."

"It's *that* hot?"

"It's *that* hot."

He lowered his voice. "And there are a lot more snakes."

The guys she worked with would never let her live down her fright at the pet boa constrictor Drake had put under her desk a few weeks ago. In a group of hard-asses, any weakness was to be exploited, if only for the sake of entertainment. But she got the impression Nate wasn't needling her for fun. He didn't like the idea of working together any more than she did. He wanted her to fight this assignment, to go outside the chain of command, if necessary, straight to Milt.

For a moment, she considered doing that. But she was relatively new and still trying to prove herself. She couldn't risk getting fired, not with her mortgage. Besides, if there was any way to change Milt's mind, Nate would've already tried it.

"I can put up with snakes," she lied. "I just wasn't expecting one to come slithering up my leg."

"I'm not talking about *pet* snakes. I'm talking about rattlers."

"Doesn't matter."

His jaw tightened. "This will be dangerous, Rachel."

"Our job always is." That was how she liked it. She didn't have to worry about heaven and hell, her father's disapproval or anything else—just surviving from one day to the next.

They stared at each other in a virtual standoff. She wasn't sure what to do about this, but she wouldn't let him manipulate her into causing trouble inside the company. That would only convince everyone that she was as whiny and hard to please as the guys were afraid a female would be. "I'm not quitting. Or getting myself fired," she said.

He cursed under his breath, but she ignored it.

"So where are we going *exactly?* Paradise must be south of Flagstaff if—"

"It's in the southeast corner of the state, not far from the Mexico and New Mexico borders. Used to be a ghost town. Until Wycliff decided to revive it, there weren't more than a handful of people living in the area."

"Are those people still around?" Or did they leave when the Covenanters moved in the way *she* wanted to flee at any mention of prophecy, scriptures or the end of the world?

"For the most part, he either converted them or bought them out."

She wiped damp palms on her jeans. She was the only female operative at Department 6 with any field experience. That was why Milt had chosen her. They were just beginning to hire women. But who said this assignment required a woman or even a couple? Maybe Nate could go in alone. "Where's Ethan getting the funds to buy land and build a town?" she asked, stalling.

"Like any cult leader, he requires converts to forfeit all their wealth for the greater good. And he makes everyone work. They sell cheese, for one thing. He also has other resources."

"Like…"

"A trust fund."

She sat up straighter. Now Ethan's suit and polish made sense. Apparently, he hadn't attended Cornell on student loans. "He comes from money?"

"You could say that. His father is Robert Wycliff."

The name meant nothing to her. "It's not as if you said Bill Gates. Who's Robert Wycliff?"

"The owner of the eighth-largest engineering firm in the country. Gets big government contracts, makes the *Forbes* list every year."

She whistled. "I see. So…who wants to know what little Ethan is up to? The government? Or Daddy?"

"If you heard your son was amassing weapons and explosives, and you knew he once had a relationship with Charles Manson, wouldn't *you* be concerned enough to find out what's going on? Mr. Wycliff doesn't want anyone hurt. And he'd rather not see his only child in prison."

"He has to have a security contractor? Wouldn't a PI work just as well?"

"He tried that. Ethan's group is isolated and very cliquish. The PI he hired couldn't get close enough. And because of the potential danger, Wycliff senior wanted people who could defend themselves—and others—if necessary."

She wondered if part of Robert's concern stemmed from a desire to protect his family name. It would certainly be a consideration for her own father. He was forever asking her to make him proud. She'd just never been able to do it. "How'd he lose track of junior in the first place?"

"He said there's always been something different about Ethan. Their relationship was strained almost from the beginning, but it's gotten worse with time. They've been completely estranged for more than a decade. Ethan dropped out of college, wouldn't work, never applied himself. Robert says he did what he could to turn his son into a productive individual. I get the impression he would've done more if Ethan's mother hadn't stood in his way. She insisted their son was fine, that he just needed to be himself and live his own life."

"Classic denial," she said, but she was intrigued in spite of herself. "So Robert backed off?"

"He immersed himself in his work and let her deal with Sonny, until Ethan started to preach in their neighborhood and town. They finally drew the line, so he left to take his followers to a place where they'd be 'unmolested.' Robert was confident he wouldn't be able to make it work. He thought Ethan would eventually be forced to come home, hoped he'd quit with all the oddness and be the son they wanted him to be."

"That didn't happen."

"No. For months, they had no idea where he'd gone—until an assistant Robert hired to follow the money flowing from Ethan's trust fund sent a clipping from a Tucson newspaper. It was an article about the Church of the Covenant taking over Paradise."

She opened the file and flipped through photocopies of several letters, all written in the blocky print so typical of males. But because she figured there might be a chance to duck this assignment, she closed the file without bothering to read them. "Are the Wycliffs aware of the woman who claims she was stoned at their son's command?"

"I can't speak for Valerie. Robert is. The PI he used could tell him that much. But Robert's also aware that the police have visited Paradise and found nothing to substantiate Martha's claims."

"So he's still hoping for the best."

"Yes."

Rachel tucked her long hair behind her ears. "What did Martha's husband have to say to the authorities?"

"His name's Todd. He said the same thing Ethan did. That she wanted to watch the children instead of work in the cheese factory and became more and more unhappy when she was denied. He told the police he was disappointed in her, that she wasn't worthy of enlightenment if she could become disaffected so easily and make up such terrible lies."

"She had to sustain those injuries somehow," Rachel mused.

"No one in the compound seems to know anything about how she might've been hurt. And unless someone's willing to talk, there's not a whole lot the police can do."

A growing sense of injustice, the kind that had fueled her desire to get involved in undercover work, began to percolate in Rachel's blood. Society had to take a stand before these cancers grew out of control. And she was willing to be part of the solution. At least in this fight she wouldn't have to hold anything back, the opposite of what she'd experienced with her father. That call to duty tempted her. She wanted to infiltrate the Covenanters and seek justice for the woman who'd been stoned, put an end to Ethan's reign of terror—if that was indeed what it was. But she couldn't do this assignment pretending to be Nathan's wife. There was too much residual emotion between them. "Why do we need two people on this?"

His eyelids lowered. "If you don't want to do it, you should talk to Milt."

Of course. They were back where he'd been trying to lead her all along. "Why bother? You've already tried, haven't you?"

He didn't respond.

"I'll take that as a yes. What did he say?"

Stretching out his legs, he crossed them at the ankles. "He said Ethan likes women. Pretty women. He said you're the bait that'll get us both in."

Here was the difference between Milt and Nate, Rachel thought. Milt would send his own wife undercover if there was something to be gained by it. But it was Nate's job to make sure everyone remained safe, which was why he wasn't thrilled when Milt began using women in the field. He came from a conservative family where he'd been taught to protect "the fairer sex." And his SEAL training supported his upbringing.

"That's a pretty unequivocal no," she said.

Nate's eyes nearly drilled holes into her. "You could always quit. Someone as qualified as you would have no trouble getting back on the police force."

And lose her house to the bank? No, thank you.

She leaned forward to prove she wasn't intimidated by him. "Sorry to disappoint you, but it's my life and I'd rather get paid well for the risks I take." She also liked having a clearly defined target for the legacy of anger her father had left her, and she had more latitude working for Department 6. "If you're afraid you can't effectively manage me or Angelina or any other woman Milt might hire, maybe *you* should be the one considering a career change."

Silence. He definitely wasn't happy with her challenge.

"Sorry to disappoint you," he said when he'd let her squirm long enough.

He wasn't leaving, and it came as no surprise. As Milt's first operative, Nate had all but built Department 6 into what it was. Rachel couldn't see him moving on anytime soon.

"Then we're stuck. But you don't need to worry about me, so spare yourself the headache."

When he simply stared at her, she sat back. Glaring at each other wasn't going to help. "What names will we use in Paradise?"

A muscle flexed in his cheek, but he revealed no other outward sign of anger or dissatisfaction. "We'll keep our first names. Our last will be Mott."

"Mr. and Mrs. Mott."

"That's right."

Still intent on creating a situation more to her liking, she blew out a sigh. "We don't have to say we're married, you know. We could go in as brother and sister."

"That wouldn't allow us to share a room. I need to be close. Just in case."

Close was precisely what she wanted to avoid. *Close* would bring turmoil. "Just in case…what?" He hadn't been there to protect her on the last drug job. No man had. And she'd done fine.

"Just in case," he repeated.

Obviously, she wasn't going to get a better answer. "How long have we been married?"

He shoved a manila folder at her. "Here are the details Milt's provided so far."

Grabbing both files, she put them in her leather satchel and got to her feet. "The Arizona desert in the middle of July. White heat. Sounds great. When do we head out?"

His eyes glittered with frustration. "First thing tomorrow."

Rachel felt some of the determination drain out of her. "That soon?" Usually they had a few days to gather facts, get into character, make travel arrangements. Milt established the infrastructure and provided what he could to support their covers—like fake ID and other documentation—but they had the freedom to add the finishing touches themselves.

"Robert Wycliff has offered a hefty bonus if we make quick work of it. Milt knows he's already late on this one."

And far be it from Milt to let any consideration outweigh money. "I see."

Nate collected the remainder of the documents he'd brought into the room. "I'll pick you up bright and early. Six sharp."

At five foot seven inches and one hundred and twenty-five pounds, she felt dwarfed as he stood. It was all she could do not to keep her mind from flashing back to how the difference in their sizes translated horizontally. "We driving or flying?"

"Driving. It's a good ten hours from L.A., but having a rental car in such a remote area will be too conspicuous. I figure we'll want a vehicle that's broken in, one that doesn't scream Hertz."

"Your truck?"

"My truck."

The very mention of it evoked the scent of engine grease and pine air freshener. It also brought back her acute sense of shame when he'd curtly explained that she'd assumed too much and took her home the morning after their night together.

"I'll be ready." With a mock salute, she started out of the room, but he called her back.

"I almost forgot." He skirted the table to hand her a small, crushed-velvet box he'd pulled from the front pocket of his jeans.

Rachel didn't need to open it to know what was inside. As much as she told herself she'd learned her lesson, she still sometimes dreamed of getting a ring from him.

But not in any of those dreams had it happened like this.

Without even looking inside the box, she dropped it in her satchel.

"Don't you think you should see if it fits? You'll have to wear it tomorrow."

Feeling as though a vise was squeezing her chest, she dug out the box and peered inside.

The diamond was tiny, the band plain. A similar ring could've been bought at any number of stores for around five hundred dollars, even less at a pawn shop. But she would've been happy to receive a plastic ring from a gum-ball machine, if only it held any of the usual symbolism.

"Well?" he asked.

She took it out and slid it easily onto her finger. The fit was loose but with a little tape she could fix that. "This is the best you can do?" she said with a grimace as if she hated the ring as much as the thought of wearing it.

He gave her a grin that wasn't meant to be sexy but managed to look that way. "What can you expect from a lowly cement contractor?"

She supposed his cover would have to involve a job that required manual labor. How else would he explain all those muscles? "Can you actually pour cement?"

"I can do anything," he said.

She knew he was teasing but, from what she'd seen, that was true.

2

According to the dossier Milt had created, they'd start this job by moving into a mobile home in Portal, Arizona, a small town five miles east of Paradise. Not only would Rachel keep her first name, she'd keep her age—twenty-eight. But that was about it. Under her assumed identity—Rachel Mott—she came from Utah instead of California. She had four siblings living in and around Salt Lake City. She'd married Nate three years ago, after meeting him at a Jazz game.

There was a little more—her schooling, her previous job at a child-care facility, information about their families and backgrounds. But as Rachel studied the dossier, she felt her anxiety increase. Going undercover with Nate would be even more difficult than she'd thought. How would they pull it off? There were details husbands and wives knew about each other, intimacies shared, that couldn't be faked. And what about body language? Ever since the night she'd surprised him in his bed, Nate had been careful not to come within three feet of her.

"Crap." Finding the remote on her nightstand, she muted the television and sat in silence for several seconds. Should she call him? See if she could convince him to postpone the trip for a day or two? With more time, maybe they could talk Milt into letting her infiltrate Ethan's cult on her own.

If she didn't make her argument now, Nate would be at her door, packed and ready to go, in six hours.

"I've got to try." Safety was a concern Nate would listen to. He always looked out for his team. It wasn't just his SEAL training; it was part of his makeup. He'd fight Milt on those grounds if no other.

Feeling a fresh burst of confidence, she reached for the phone and dialed his number.

He answered on the first ring.

"He won't let us off the hook," he said. "And I'm sleeping. Don't bother me again."

He didn't sound as if she'd awakened him. His voice wasn't the least bit gravelly. But the *click* and subsequent dial tone told her he'd said all he was going to say on the subject.

Angry that he'd known the reason for her call before she could even say a word, she slammed the phone down and went back to the dossier. "This won't work," she mumbled. For instance, she might say that her brother was gay and he might call the same brother a womanizer. What then? There was no way they could script every detail ahead of time. Going undercover was all about ad-libbing. Trying to do this together could make it unravel. And Ethan was a dangerous man. Those letters to Manson confirmed it.

Rachel glanced at the stack she'd set to one side. The hero worship exhibited in Ethan's earlier writing gave her chills. Had he really admired a man who'd used others, mostly women—except for Tex Watson—to brutally murder seven people? A lot of psychopaths admired killers because they themselves fantasized about com-

mitting the same kinds of acts. Was Ethan capable of
such heinous crimes?

Putting the dossier on her nightstand, along with her
fake ID, which had been tucked inside it, she picked up
the letters and read them again. They were more than a
decade old. She had no way of knowing if they still re-
flected Ethan's thoughts and attitudes, but they gave her
a glimpse into the psyche of the man he'd once been.
He talked about Spahn Ranch, where Manson had lived
when he ordered the murders. He compared it to a place
he'd find for his own "spiritual family," a place where
he could "operate beneath the awareness of the outside
world." Except for one letter, he ignored Manson's
fascination with the Beatles and their music, but he
quoted several of Manson's favorite verses from the
Book of Revelation 9:2, 3.

> And he opened the bottomless pit…. And there
> came out of the smoke locusts upon the earth: and
> unto them was given power, as the scorpions of the
> earth have power.

"I have this power," Ethan wrote. "I can feel it taking root in me. I can make scorpions of locusts. What
would you have me do?"

Wishing she had Manson's reply, she flipped to another letter, this one dated August 4, 1998. Here, Ethan
began by thanking Manson for his latest response and
quoting Revelation 9:4.

> And it was commanded [that the locusts] should
> not hurt the grass of the earth, neither any green

thing, neither any tree; but only those men which have not the seal of God in their foreheads.

"I have the mark," Ethan informed Manson. "My people will freely take it upon themselves. They will be God's avengers against the wicked. They will avenge *you*."

That was where the brand came in, Rachel mused. He went on to quote verse 17.

And thus I saw the horses in the vision, and them that sat on them, having breastplates of fire, and of jacinth, and brimstone: and the heads of the horses were as the heads of lions; and out of their mouths issued fire and smoke and brimstone.

"You will be free," Ethan promised Manson. "I will make you free." He'd closed that particular letter by quoting one last verse.

And the fifth angel sounded, and I saw a star fall from heaven unto the earth: and to him was given the key of the bottomless pit.

"You have passed that key to me."

"'You have passed that key to me,'" Rachel repeated. What did he mean by that? Did he feel as if he was taking over where Manson had left off?

That was a terrifying thought....

She chewed anxiously on her lip as she read the only letter in the pile that had been written by Manson.

"You know, a long time ago being crazy meant something. Nowadays everybody's crazy. And you're crazier than them all."

Some sort of drink had been spilled on the bottom half, making the rest impossible to read. That was disappointing, especially because Ethan's next letter revealed growing frustration. It seemed to be in response to Manson's rebuke, or maybe there'd been a letter or two in between; the dates were three months apart. The gist of what he'd written suggested that Manson wasn't living up to his prophet status, wasn't guiding young Ethan as he wanted to be guided. Ethan was getting angry.

"You and all those Beatles songs, man. What was with that? What did the Beatles have to do with God? You're full of shit, you know? Yellow Submarine, my ass. Where were you when Helter Skelter started? Safe at the ranch."

Did that mean Ethan would be a different kind of leader? One who actively participated instead of watching from afar?

"The only thing you had right were the women. The women are where it's at."

Twisting her new wedding ring around her finger, Rachel read that line for the third time. Ethan had a fascination with women, probably because he felt more capable of bending them to his will. His mother had defended him and protected him against his father's criticism, hadn't she? Maybe he thought he could manipulate all women as easily as he'd manipulated his mother.

That was why she should do this job by herself. She had a better chance of appearing pliable without a hulking male at her side. And once she gained Ethan's trust, it'd all be over. She'd bust him like she had so many drug dealers, shut him down as quickly as possible, so none of the other women in his commune would suffer as Martha Wilson had suffered.

She could imagine victory, but the satisfying image dissipated as the clock on the wall continued to tick. Five hours and counting…

It was too late to fight Milt's insistence that Nate go with her.

In this part of the desert, night was nearly as hot as day. And the air hung heavy. There wasn't so much as a slight breeze or a rustle—just the scrape of Bartholomew's shovel. His efforts, sounding abnormally loud because of the silence and the rockiness of the soil, made him wince with each scoop. A tent filled with his fellow Covenanters stood only a few yards away. If someone woke and heard him, came to investigate, he'd have an even bigger problem on his hands….

But he wasn't accustomed to this type of labor, and at forty-seven he was no longer young. Digging strained his back and made his arms feel so weak he could hardly keep going.

Taking a break to conserve his strength and catch his breath, he leaned on the shovel and gazed toward the little cemetery on the hill, half a mile or so away. It'd been established when Paradise was built as a mining town back in the early 1900s and it still had some of the old headstones jutting out of the bare soil beneath a paloverde tree. Thanks to a bright moon, Bart could almost make out the largest one. Except for the fact that the ground would be even harder, he wished he could dig this grave out there.

But burying Courtney Sinclair beyond the fence that

encircled the commune wasn't safe. It would be much more difficult to keep track of who came and went. What if someone noticed the disturbed earth and told Courtney's parents? They'd already come to Paradise several times, looking for their daughter. Ethan had covered well, but Bartholomew had a feeling the situation was far from over. The Sinclairs weren't going to give up and go away. Maybe Courtney claimed to have been unloved, that her parents were the worst parents ever, but her mother, at least, seemed quite devoted.

That just went to show that the girl didn't have a clue about people. She was—*had been,* Bartholomew corrected as he glanced with distaste at the limp figure wrapped in a blanket at his feet—barely seventeen.

But he'd tried to warn her. She wouldn't listen. The Sinclairs no doubt had the same problem with her. The black lipstick, fingernails and clothing, the earrings lining the rim of each ear and the metal rod through her nose—they all designated her as a rebel. And the scars from the cutting she'd done on her arms took it to a rather desperate level. She'd been deeply unhappy, hadn't acclimated when her family moved from Texas. A lot of children, forced to take a backseat to a step-parent, resented it. Bart had been raised with a step-father himself, knew what it felt like to deserve more yet receive less. But he'd left that old identity behind. There was no more Francis Williams. He was simply Bartholomew now. An apostle to the Holy One.

Courtney had been offered a home in Paradise. She could still be here, as alive as he was, if only she'd played by the rules.

A light went on in the Enlightenment Hall where he lived with the Holy One. Twisting around, he stared up at it. Was Ethan worried? Was he frightened by what had occurred with Martha and then Courtney?

He hoped not. Ethan needed to remain stable or they'd both lose everything.

Drawing his exhaustion and concern inside himself, he returned to his digging.

3

Ethan paced inside his room. The Brethren were still meeting in the pit. He'd put in an appearance earlier, but he'd been too anxious to stay long. Watching them argue wasn't any fun. It made him feel as if this was the beginning of the end of everything he'd created. Were they right? Was the paradise he'd built about to come tumbling down? With all the bad publicity, it felt that way. The rest of the world seemed to be pressing closer, crowding him, banging at the gates. The Brethren, the twelve he'd designated as Spiritual Guides for his people, had tried to tell him that a local girl going missing on the heels of what Martha had told the press wouldn't be good. But he hadn't listened. Sometimes he felt as though he could get away with anything. Other times...

What had he been thinking? Of course they'd been right! The attention his actions had drawn would only hasten the confrontation he'd been preparing for from the start. That was what the Guides were discussing now. They were hashing out plans for the final battle. But had it really come to that?

He wasn't ready. He should've left Martha and Courtney alone. He'd screwed up, indulged himself one too many times....

It was the drugs, he decided. When he was tweaking,

he made mistakes, and he tweaked too often these days. But the thought of getting high only made him want to do it again.

Crossing to the bureau, he found the quarter gram of meth he kept close at hand, took his pipe from the same drawer and lit up.

When that first anticipated rush of euphoria hit his brain, he dropped onto the bed and stared up at the ceiling. Courtney came to him immediately, like a ghost. Or a memory. He knew what he was seeing wasn't real, that he was hallucinating, because there was no lust, no anger, no betrayal. He was completely objective, an indifferent bystander observing the unfolding of their relationship—until the final moment when he'd strangled her.

Another memory surfaced—the day he caught his father grimacing when someone said, "The apple doesn't fall far from the tree." The person who'd spoken hadn't been able to see past their physical similarities long enough to realize they couldn't be more different if God had intended to make them enemies. Conservative and self-disciplined, Robert loved sports and business and took great pride in his financial success. Ethan preferred music, art, literature, fashion. Nothing he did could ever match what his father had accomplished. Even worse, he was emotional and high-strung, which irritated and angered his father.

Oddly, the differences hadn't really bothered Ethan until the day he'd heard his father tell his mother that he planned to order a paternity test. Robert hadn't doubted her fidelity; he'd been teasing when he said it. But Ethan's mother had laughed with him and that was when Ethan knew Valerie was in on the secret. She preferred her husband to her son; she felt as embarrassed and ashamed of Ethan as Robert did.

Wincing at that memory, he took another hit on the pipe and then another.

Soon he seemed to be floating above his own body. Then the room began to spin and he could no longer remember what upset him so much. He had nothing to worry about. Look at what he'd become. His father had told him he'd never amount to anything, but he'd been wrong. Ethan had money *and* power and he hadn't had to work for any of it.

Suddenly, the silence seemed to press in on him like an invisible hand, holding him down on the bed, smothering him. Nearly dropping his pipe, he staggered to his feet, knocked over a lamp and cut his arm. He was standing in a stupor, watching the blood drip onto the carpet when Bart walked in.

"Holy One, you've hurt yourself," he cried. "What happened?"

Ethan's mouth moved and words came out, but they sounded garbled, even to his own ears. Was he making sense? Somehow that didn't matter. The only thing that mattered was that Bart had come to take care of him.

Just like always.

The sun was up when Nate pulled into Rachel's driveway. Her house sat on a cliff overlooking the ocean a little south of Los Angeles. With one whole side made of glass, it was different—far more modern than the home of any other woman he knew. But Rachel was different, too. She tried to be so damn tough. In ways, she *was* tough. She could fight. She could play whatever part she needed to play. She'd gravitated to the polar opposite of her sheltered upbringing and wielded a gun instead of the Good Book. But for all that, she didn't have the ability to protect her heart. He'd never forget the night he'd come home to find her waiting in his bed.

Working this closely together wasn't a smart idea. He saw how she looked at him when she thought he wasn't paying attention, could tell how she felt about him. Hell, she'd said as much when they were making love. What she wanted from him reminded him too much of Susan. He still heard from her on occasion and he knew that, in some ways, he'd never really be free of her or the memory of rushing to the hospital that cold January night....

But Milt was adamant he take this assignment, so Nate would have to protect Rachel—not only from the Covenanters but from himself.

"Just do it," he said, and shoved the gearshift into Park.

He was getting out to ring the bell when she appeared, wearing a simple peach-colored sundress beneath a cardigan sweater and carrying a small suitcase.

"You can't take that case to Portal," he said without a greeting. He didn't recognize the label, but he didn't need to know the designer to realize it had cost a bundle. "That's a dead giveaway. You're the wife of a cement contractor, not Paris Hilton."

"I'm aware of that. But I tossed my crappy luggage after the last job. It was completely shot. We'll have to stop at a secondhand store along the way."

"What will you do with this one?"

"Ship it home," she said with a shrug. "The clothes I wear when I'm not working are too sophisticated, too 'single woman supporting herself.' The ones I wear on other jobs are too 'I'll do anything for my next fix.' I need something in between if I'm going to build the illusion of a sweet wife who recently got married and is trying to eke out a productive life with her husband. So we would've had to do some shopping, anyway."

Maybe she needed additional clothes, but the dress she was wearing right now worked, he admitted grudgingly. The color brought out the golden tones in her hair and skin and contrasted nicely with the ice blue of her eyes. But he didn't tell her that. He knew better than to lead her on and still kicked himself for not sending her home when she'd let herself into his condo six months ago.

"This is all, then?" he asked.

"Except for my computer." She reached in to get the satchel she carried almost everywhere, but he stopped her.

"Leave it behind."

"That's like asking me to leave my gun!"

"No, it's not. Where we're going, there probably won't be Internet service. And when we need a computer, we can use mine."

"What about other gear?"

He motioned toward the truck. "I've got everything we might need."

"Fine," she muttered, and he put her bag in the truck while she locked the house.

Rachel was seven years his junior, but today she looked even younger. With her hair pulled into a messy bun and minimal makeup, she could pass for twenty. Had he spotted her on the road, he might've mistaken her for a teenager heading down to the beach.

But she wasn't going to the beach. She was wearing his pretend wedding ring and packing a gun so Milt could thrust them both into the middle of a potentially dangerous situation.

"Why do you do it?" he asked as she climbed in.

She blinked. "You mean, the bag? I told you. I had to bring it. I didn't have another one."

"I'm not talking about your suitcase. Why are you in this business?"

She slammed the rusty door of his old truck. "It's a living, isn't it?"

A good living. They'd only have to devote ten years to their work to be set for life. But he knew Rachel's involvement wasn't entirely about the money. According to what he'd read in her file, and the bit of information she'd revealed, she'd had a difficult childhood with an overbearing father. That made him suspect her attraction to undercover work had something to do with slipping in and out of character, of being anyone she wanted to be except the child who'd known almost nothing of the real world until she was seventeen. She wasn't comfortable in her own skin, didn't know who she was or who she wanted to be.

"The danger doesn't bother you?"

"No more than it bothers you."

He almost told her to get out. She didn't need to be mixed up in Ethan Wycliff's twisted world. The auto accident involving Ethan's former roommate had left skid marks suggesting he might've been run off the road. There were no witnesses to say if he'd swerved to avoid an animal or another car. So the possibility of murder was there. For all they knew, Ethan was as bad as Charles Manson, which made this assignment worse than usual. "Maybe we should try talking some sense into Milt," he said, suddenly second-guessing his decision to comply with his boss's orders.

She flashed him her wedding ring. "Too late. You already tried that, anyway. Let's go."

His thoughts gravitated to a former Department 6 employee. Enrico had lost his right eye when someone he knew in regular life happened upon him while he was on the job. After that friend inadvertently blew his cover, Enrico had been forced to fight for his life. Nate didn't want something like that to happen again—to any member of his team, but especially one of the women.

"This could be unpredictable," he warned.

"They're all unpredictable."

"You're sure you're up for it?"

"I'm positive."

"You didn't seem so certain when you called me a few hours ago."

"How would you know? You didn't give me a chance to talk."

"I'm giving you a chance now."

"Someone's got to do this. Might as well be me."

She was right. Someone had to do it. He doubted Milt would change his mind, anyway. As she'd just said, Nate had already argued with him about it, to no avail.

Ultimately, this was Milt's decision. And Rachel's. Not his.

Taking a deep breath, he backed down her long drive. She'd chosen this line of work, applied of her own free will, knowing full well the dangers she'd encounter. And she'd proven herself effective.

While he made the turn onto the winding road that would take them to the highway, she dug through her purse. He had no idea what she was searching for until he smelled the distinctive scent of fingernail polish.

"Hey, that stuff stinks," he complained.

She pulled off her sandal and hugged her left knee to her chest so she could paint her toenails. "I need to get into character. Rachel Mott is the kind of woman who likes her nails a delicate pink."

"How do you know?" he countered. "That wasn't in the dossier."

"There wasn't much in the dossier. So I figure the role is subject to interpretation. I've got to sell it, make it real." She moved to the next toenail. "And the way I picture her is sort of sweet and naive and madly in love with her nice but none-too-bright husband."

He shot her a dark look. Where was she going with this? "Did you say 'none-too-bright'?" he grumbled, but it was really the "madly in love" part that disturbed him. He didn't want to get anything started.

"It's just a role."

"I don't mind playing dumb as long as you remember I'm the boss here. Milt's sending me with you for a reason."

"I think Milt is sending us together because there's safety in numbers, not because he expects you to exert your authority while we're there."

"He doesn't need to specify that because I'm already your boss."

"And I'd never question that." She gave him a saccharine smile to take the edge off her sarcasm, and he seemed to accept the statement at face value.

"Glad we're on the same page."

"Back to that incomplete dossier." She waved one hand rapidly over her toes. "What was Milt thinking, being so vague?"

"He said he didn't have a lot of time. He thought we could finish strategizing today while we drove."

"I'm glad to hear I'll have some input, because we need to come up with ways to seem more like a *real* couple."

What was she up to? He narrowed his eyes as he looked at her, speculating on what it could be. "Such as…"

"I don't know. Something that makes it appear as if we've been together for more than, say…a *day*."

He decided to go along with her. "Like what? Like… getting my name tattooed on your neck?"

She didn't argue as he'd expected; she frowned in contemplation. "Exactly. Only…not on my neck. That's too…overboard. But maybe my arm."

"No way! I was joking, and you know it. There's no telling how long we'll be there. A fake tattoo might wash off."

"Which is why it would have to be a real one. Right here." She indicated her deltoid. *"Nathan's woman."*

She was pushing his buttons. After the way she'd avoided him the past several months, it seemed out of character, but now that they'd been forced into this situation, he wondered if she was overcompensating. "That might be just the thing," he said, refusing to take the bait.

"As long as it's designed to be turned into something else when this is all over," she murmured. "I've been meaning to get one, anyway—maybe a skull to impress the drug dealers I usually work with."

His name—turned into a *skull?* The kiss of death. The image hit far too close to home. But, of course, she wouldn't know that. "Tattoos take time to ink and to heal. And they hurt. Are you sure you want to go through all that pain just to put your manager's name on your arm for one assignment?"

"I could use it afterward. The skull, I mean."

"Right. You mentioned that."

"Besides, they can't hurt too badly if everyone's getting them."

He slung one arm over the steering wheel. "They hurt badly enough. Why put yourself through it?" *And mar that soft skin,* he added silently.

"Good point. Since you're so tough, you should get the tattoo—*my* name on *your* arm."

No way would he etch a woman's name on his skin. The permanence of that scared the hell out of him and she knew it. That was partly what told him this was a setup. "Sorry, ain't gonna happen."

They reached the highway, and he accelerated as they headed toward Interstate 10, which would eventually take them through Riverside and into Arizona, almost all the way to Portal. "We don't need tattoos."

"It'll take more than simply telling everyone we're married to make them believe it."

"You've got a ring, don't you?"

"A ring only signifies that we once exchanged vows. It doesn't mean we have a close relationship. So…you tell me. How do you want to play this? Do you want us to seem sort of…estranged? Regretful that we tied the knot? On the brink of divorce?" She poked the tiny brush inside the polish and changed feet. "I could win an Oscar I'd be so good at *that* performance."

He'd hurt her six months ago, and now she didn't like him. It bothered him, but it was better to have her not like him than like him too much. At least, that was how he felt most of the time. "That won't work, not for this. We need to act as if we're close." Otherwise, he'd be less capable of protecting her.

"That's what I thought you'd say. Or you would've gone in as my brother, like I wanted you to in the first place."

So *that* was what all this was about. She was punishing him, or trying to spook him into changing the nature of their pretend relationship before they arrived in Phoenix and found themselves locked into the arrangement.

He would've been more than happy to accommodate her, but he wasn't sure it'd be any easier to play brother and sister. There was too much sexual tension between them. They ignored it, of course. When he'd rejected her, he'd cut her pride so deeply she'd go without air before she'd ever admit to wanting him again. But since that night in January, the energy that flowed between them had only grown stronger. When they were at the office together, he was aware of every move she made, and he was afraid others were beginning to sense what they both so categorically denied. That kind of interest would hardly seem appropriate between siblings.

"We'll have a close relationship, but no tattoos," he reiterated.

She dipped the brush again. "So you're suggesting we let it all hang on a ring?"

"Works for me."

Finally dropping the manipulative tactics, she

straightened. "Oh, come on. Let's just say you're my brother! We don't even want to get close enough to rub up against each other. How convincing will body language like that be?"

Want had nothing to do with it. He glanced over to tell her they'd just have to improve their acting and caught a glimpse of her dress bunched up around her hips, bare legs plainly visible. Another inch or two and he could've spotted her panties.

Rachel wasn't trying to entice him. That was obvious from her careless attitude. She was so sure he wasn't interested, she saw no point in being cautious, which wasn't very wise if they were going to be living together. Maybe he wasn't in love with her, but that didn't mean he was blind. He could appreciate her physical assets the same as the next guy.

"Convincing enough, I hope," he said. "And one other thing."

She made a careful swipe with the polish, then another. "What's that?"

He waited for her to look at him. "Unless you want me to knock down that invisible wall you've constructed between us, I wouldn't tease me if I were you. That's not a punishment I'll tolerate."

Her jaw sagged. "*Tease* you?"

When he shifted his gaze to her legs, his meaning finally seemed to register.

"I'm painting my toenails!" she said. "You think I'm trying to punish you? That I'm trying to do it by *arousing* you?"

She didn't have to *try.* That was the problem. "Just put your dress down," he said with a scowl. "And leave it there."

4

She wasn't the only one nervous about sharing a bedroom. Nate's grumpiness made that clear. He probably wouldn't refuse a quick lay if he was in the right mood—he hadn't refused last time, had he? But he didn't want *her,* and he couldn't be any more obvious about it. She wasn't willing to get burned a second time. She'd already offered him her heart and soul, and he'd tossed them right back at her. Hell would freeze over before she ever made him that offer again.

Ignoring his order to keep her dress down, she raised it again and proceeded to paint the rest of her toenails. Without shifting her dress she couldn't do it comfortably. If he thought ordinary behavior constituted teasing, that was his problem. They'd be "married" in name only. Until they moved into the commune, they wouldn't even share a bedroom.

Soon after she'd finished, the scenery outside changed from the green and brown of the rolling hills surrounding L.A. to the monochrome beige of flat desert. By afternoon, they couldn't get a radio signal and Rachel lamented the fact that she hadn't brought her iPod. The only sound, other than the warp of their tires on asphalt, came from the fan of the air conditioner. It hummed at full speed but pumped hot air into the cab. According to Nate, they must've lost their coolant somewhere along the highway because he couldn't get the AC to work any better.

"Why do you still have this old truck?" she grumbled.

"Because I like it. It has character. And it comes in handy for work—and play."

Besides using it on various undercover jobs—jobs like this one—he sometimes took it four-wheeling with the guys. But she never would've agreed to ride with him if she'd thought they'd have to travel without air-conditioning. She would've flown into Tucson and had him pick her up there. At least that would've eliminated this extended trek across the hottest desert in North America. It had to be one hundred and twenty degrees outside. The truck felt like an oven.

"I can't believe this," she complained. "We're in the Sonoran Desert. It's the middle of July. And we don't have air."

"Roll down your window."

She did as he suggested. The wind caused strands of her hair to come loose but did little to cool her off. Drops of perspiration rolled down her back and between her breasts. She'd abandoned her sweater long ago. Now she kept raising her skirt over the closest air-conditioning vent to funnel the air up under her dress, which clung miserably to her if she didn't.

"Do you want me to drive?" she asked, suddenly so restless she felt she couldn't tolerate another mile.

"I've got it," he said, but when she continued to shift and squirm, he pulled to the shoulder and turned off the engine.

"Change your mind?" she asked.

"No, I'm getting you a cold drink."

He was hot, too. She could see the dampness of his T-shirt, could smell the slight tang of his sweat—and wished she found it distasteful.

A moment later, her door opened, and he stood there with a bottle of water he'd taken from the cooler in back.

"Thanks." She reached out, but he twisted off the lid and squeezed it down the front of her dress.

Gasping at the cold, she grabbed hold of the bottle and fought to turn it back on him.

"Hey, I'm just trying to help!" he said, laughing at her futile efforts.

Mad enough at his surprise attack to scramble out and get her own bottle, she flung water at him while he circled the truck to avoid her. She got him by acting as if she'd given up, then pivoting abruptly when he made a move to get in. But he didn't seem to mind. He merely removed the cap from a third bottle and poured it over his head.

"Better?" He grinned as he dribbled the last few drops over *her* head.

Knowing she looked bedraggled, she glanced down at her soaking dress. She wasn't willing to give him any credit, but she did feel cooler. "A water fight. That's your solution?"

"*I* enjoyed it," he said. Then, in a motion that seemed as impulsive as it was unexpected, he used his thumb to stop a drop of water from rolling down to her cleavage.

Rachel caught her breath at the contact. Looking up

to see him watching her intently, she stepped out of reach. "It's my turn to drive," she said, and hopped in before he could protest.

This was the way Nate liked Rachel best—completely undone. Her hair was a mess, her face devoid of what little makeup she'd put on, her dress damp and wrinkled and hugging every curve. He could even appreciate the thin sheen of sweat on her smooth skin. The dampness caused the soft tendrils of hair at her nape to curl.

God, she was pretty. At times she took his breath away.

"What?" She glanced over as if she could feel his scrutiny and didn't like it.

"Nothing." He turned his attention to the rocks, soil and cacti flying past his window. During moments like these, he was so tempted to act on the attraction between them it was all he could do to keep his hands to himself. He wouldn't have bothered to fight the impulse if she was half as resilient as she pretended to be. But her desire to love him showed in those wide blue eyes every time she looked up at him. He couldn't take advantage of her vulnerability; he wouldn't break her heart. He, of all people, knew what could happen if he did.

"We haven't talked about Portal," she said.

He adjusted his seat belt. "There's not a lot to say about Portal. It's a very small town."

"How small?"

"Maybe fifty people, mostly ranchers, artists, birdwatchers and nature enthusiasts. Paradise used to be even smaller than Portal, until the Covenanters moved in."

"Why aren't we starting off in a bigger place?"

"The closest town with any significant population is Willcox. They have about thirty-five hundred people, but it's an hour and a half from Paradise. I felt that was too far and we'd have trouble making contact with the cult."

She fought the wind whipping at her hair by anchoring several loose strands behind her ears. "But how can a cement contractor expect to earn a living amid fifty ranchers, artists and bird-watchers? I doubt they're the type to pay for a lot of concrete work."

"I'm actually playing an out-of-work contractor. With the downturn in the economy, I've decided to go after my real aspirations—photographing wildlife. I'll be taking pictures for a coffee-table book I hope to sell."

Her eyebrows slid up. "Did you bring a camera?"

"Of course."

"Nice thinking. Except that doesn't explain to others where we get the money to eat and pay rent."

"We've recently inherited a small sum from your grandfather."

"That wasn't in the dossier, either," she pointed out.

"I just made it up before we left. We have this inheritance and we're using it to spend a year in Portal to take photographs for my book, hoping to recoup expenses when we sign a big deal."

"Okay, so you're an aspiring photographer. What am I going to say *I* do?"

"You'll be my assistant." That would keep her at his side all the time. It was perfect. But she didn't seem convinced.

"Don't you think this might seem kind of random?"

"No one says we have to be the most responsible couple in the world. Reckless can be believable, too."

She bit her lip as if contemplating what he'd said, but his explanation must've pacified her because she changed the subject. "How much farther do we have to go?"

He checked his Swiss Army watch. "Another four and a half hours. But we'll hit Phoenix soon. We'll stop there to buy your wardrobe and other supplies."

"Are we planning to get the air conditioner fixed in Phoenix, as well?"

"We don't have time if we want to reach Portal before dark, which is advisable considering there'll be no city lights. I'll fix the air-conditioning myself once we take up residence."

"If Portal is an hour and a half from Willcox, which is the closest population center to Paradise, how far is Tucson?"

"About three hours."

"This is sounding *very* remote."

"There's no mall."

"Forget the mall. I'll settle for running water."

"We'll have an outhouse."

She wiped the sweat from her upper lip. "Great. Snakes *and* an outhouse. My two favorite things."

"Don't worry. I'll be there to look after you." Confident that it would provoke her feminist tendencies, he gave her a satisfied smile and she didn't disappoint.

"I can look after myself," she snapped.

"Aren't you at all concerned that we'll be so far from help, should we need it? I mean, say one of us did get bitten by a rattler. Tourniquets aren't an attractive option if you plan on using that leg again."

"I'm not worried."

He could tell it was a lie. The fact that they'd be so out of touch bothered him, too. But he wouldn't let her get hurt—by a rattler or anything else.

Pulling the bodice of her dress away from her body, she fanned herself, even though she must have known it was a futile gesture. "I'm anxious to see what these little towns are like. Especially Paradise."

"I'm surprised you didn't look them up on the 'Net."

"Last night? I had too much to do to get ready."

He covered a yawn. "Like trying to talk me out of taking you."

"Actually, I was trying to talk you out of coming along," she admitted.

"You wanted to do this alone."

"That's how I prefer to work."

"Milt would never have gone for that."

"Milt's totally indifferent to what's best for us. He didn't even give us a chance to prepare."

"He knew we'd have a long drive, plenty of time to flesh out the details."

She narrowed her eyes. "How long have *you* known about this?"

"A couple of days."

"That's long enough to do some research."

"And I did a little. What do you want to know?"

"How about what I would've found if I'd done my own?"

"Portal sits at one end of a large canyon, with the Chiricahua Mountains to the west and New Mexico to the east. Paradise is an old mining town, five miles up the mountains."

"Mountains? You mean, *real* mountains—in the desert?"

"Real enough. The highest peak is almost ten thousand feet."

She nodded. "I'd say that's a real mountain."

After driving in silence for several miles, she glanced over at him again. "It won't be easy keeping our stories straight. The longer we live in Portal or Paradise or wherever we wind up until this job is done, the more we'll get to know other people, and the more we'll talk and share anecdotes. We'll seem strange, reclusive, if we don't make friends. That'll make folks uncomfortable and less likely to trust us. Yet the more we open up, the greater our risk of exposure."

"We'll manage."

"But we won't even be sleeping together. How do we fake intimacy that's not there?"

She was putting him on notice, drawing the line at her bedroom door. But he had some ammunition he could use, too. "It's not as if we haven't made love in the past, Rachel."

Her knuckles turned white on the steering wheel. That was the first time he'd ever referred to the night he'd found her waiting in his bed. He generally chose not to embarrass her, but what had happened sat so awkwardly between them. If they were going to play husband and wife for the next few weeks, they needed to address the issue and get it out of the way. Then maybe they could both relax.

"That was a long time ago," she said, but he wasn't about to let her off the hook that easily.

"Not *that* long ago. I know your body, and you know mine. We'll go by memory."

Her chin jerked up. "I *don't* know your body. I—I can't remember a thing. I was drunk or...or I never would've been so bold."

She hadn't been drunk at all. As a matter of fact, he'd only ever seen her drink one glass of wine, even at company parties, where most employees drank much more. "You're saying that wasn't the real you."

Unwilling to meet his eyes, she kept her head at a jaunty angle. "Not at all. You know what it's like. Sometimes you have too much to drink. You get a wild idea like 'hey, why don't I surprise my boss?' and you act on it. Then you wake up feeling like an idiot, wondering what on earth possessed you to do something so stupid and normally unappealing." She glanced over to see if he was buying her act, so he pretended to believe her.

"Normally unappealing."

"Yes."

"And the details are...gone. You've forgotten them all."

"Every single one."

"Bullshit," he said with a laugh.

She blinked. "Excuse me?"

"You remember the details as well as I do." And for him, they remained in sharp focus, including the taste and texture of her skin, even the smell of it. He'd never forget how greedily she'd responded to his touch, how she'd given herself so artlessly, so honestly—then brought all pleasure to a screeching halt when she told him she loved him. Talk about getting sucker-punched.

Her grip on the steering wheel grew noticeably tighter. "No, I don't."

He waved a hand. "Fine, if that's what you want me

to believe, I'll play along. So…you'll just have to fake the attraction."

She tossed him an overconfident grin. "No problem. I'm a pro at faking."

Now she'd gone too far. "You weren't faking anything when you were with me," he said simply.

Keeping one hand on the wheel, she yawned and stretched. "Like I said, I wasn't myself. I didn't know what I was saying or doing. Or saying," she added again. "It doesn't matter, anyway. I was going through a rough patch, so you were just one in a long line of screw-ups. I mean, men."

"You were sleeping around?" That statement took him off guard.

"Not a *lot*, but…I live on the beach, you know? I have my share of men."

Nate sincerely doubted it. The woman he'd had in his bed had been exciting as hell, but not because she was well practiced. Part of the fun had been introducing her to so much she found completely new. And, considering her background, it made sense that she wouldn't be particularly experienced. "Taking strangers in off the beach isn't a safe thing to do," he commented. Especially because she didn't know how to pick one who wouldn't break her heart. Take him, for instance…

"I keep a few condoms on hand just in case. What's wrong with having some fun once in a while?"

Fun… The strap of her dress had fallen off her shoulder. He stretched his arm across the seat to slide it back into place, but she flinched and ducked away before he could touch her.

"Whoa! For someone who sleeps around, you're pretty skittish."

"I'm not skittish. I'm…I didn't know what you were doing, that's all."

This time he moved more slowly. She sat perfectly still as he slid that strap up, but she wasn't as unaffected as she wanted to appear. His touch had created a swath of goose bumps. "If you're so free and easy with everyone else, I guess there's no need for me to be any different, right?"

"I'm afraid I'm on hiatus right now," she said. "It all got to be a bit boring and stale…you know."

"No, I don't know."

A furrow formed between her eyebrows. "That happens when you do it too often."

"I've never reached that threshold. But then…I don't live on the beach."

"That must be it."

"You're not remotely tempted? Even though we're sort of married?"

"Not remotely. If we were any good together, I'm sure I'd remember more than I do about the last time."

"Let me get this straight. You were drunk. You weren't yourself. You don't remember making love with me. *And* it stank?"

Her lopsided smile finally righted itself. "Now you've got it."

5

Where was Courtney Sinclair? Sarah Myers paused in the doorway of the tent where the children attended classes. After the glare of the early-afternoon sun, it took her eyes a moment to adjust to the dimmer light, but even when she could see clearly, she saw no one resembling her young friend. Courtney hadn't shown up at the cheese factory this morning, either. And when Sarah had visited her tent to ask her roommates, everyone said Courtney hadn't even rolled out her bed last night.

Had she gone back to her family in Portal? If so, why? She'd been terribly unhappy there....

Still, the girl's parents wanted her to come home. Maybe they could salvage their relationship. If Courtney wasn't going to stay in Paradise, she needed their help and support. But Sarah didn't think Courtney had gone home. Something didn't feel right. A hush had settled among the Brethren, an uneasiness Sarah had never sensed before—except during the first few days after Martha got away. Once again the men scurried through Paradise with their heads bowed, going to or from the Enlightenment Hall, as if they were deeply worried.

Earlier, Sarah had dared to approach Brother Titherington to ask about Courtney, and he'd barely paused long enough to mumble, "Haven't seen her."

"Sister Sarah? Is there something we can do for you?"

Patricia Sellers had spotted her. Patricia was the administrator of the children's programs and one of the nicest people Sarah had ever met. "I just…I was wondering if Courtney was here."

"Courtney…?"

"Sinclair. The new girl. She wears black and has lots of piercings?"

"Oh, you mean, Trix."

Sarah had heard the nickname, knew it was the girl's own preference, but she hadn't used it herself. Somehow it didn't fit Courtney. She wasn't sure why Courtney thought it did. "Yes."

"She doesn't usually come by until after she gets off at the cheese factory."

"She didn't go to work," Sarah explained.

"Perhaps she's ill."

"I've checked her tent, spoken to the other women who share it with her. They don't know where she is. They say she never joined them for dinner last night and never rolled out her bed, either."

"She might've stayed at the Enlightenment Hall with the Holy One. He's been taking a special interest in trying to help her, praise be to God."

"Yes, praise be to God," Sarah echoed. But after what she'd witnessed with Sister Martha, Sarah didn't think she wanted another friend to draw so much of the Holy One's attention. Although Sarah had been a devout follower of Ethan Wycliff since she'd first heard him speak on the Appalachian Trail near her hometown, he seemed different. Changed.

Or was that her broken heart talking? She couldn't deny how much it hurt that he scarcely noticed her these days. She supposed now that the church had grown so large, he had other things to worry about than an ugly, scarred woman. But he'd been able to see past her appearance before. At least, he'd made her feel as if he could. And what about the stoning? The bloodlust that'd overtaken the Covenanters when Ethan ordered Martha stoned still horrified Sarah. How could Ethan be the man she'd thought he was, a man she'd compare to any of the great prophets, if he was willing to resort to such violence? Was it true that his actions were sanctioned by God, as everyone said? That God's punishment was righteous punishment?

Maybe. She didn't pretend to know God's mind. But sometimes Ethan didn't seem Christ-like at all. To Sarah, Martha had been no more deserving of public slaughter than anyone else in Paradise. What had happened to acceptance, tolerance and love? To providing a refuge from the dangers of the world?

Those questions had swirled in her mind ever since she'd helped Martha escape, probably because the answers were so unsettling. If Ethan was wrong in ordering Martha stoned, he wasn't really holy and the foundation for the religion she'd gladly embraced was a false one. And if he was right, she'd rebelled against him and therefore rebelled against God.

"Is there anything else?" Patricia asked when Sarah didn't leave.

"No. If you see Courtney, would you tell her I'd like to talk to her? I'd really appreciate it."

"Of course." Patricia reached out to squeeze her hand. "You look lovely today."

"Thank you," Sarah murmured, but she knew it was one of those kind lies designed to lift her spirits. She hadn't been pretty since she'd been injured in the house fire that had killed her mother and taken the lives of her younger sister and brother. The terrible burns she'd sustained trying to rescue them had destroyed too much of her face and hands. The skin grafts made her look like a monster. Even the children were frightened of her.

"She'll be okay," Patricia called after her.

Sarah had to catch the tent flap so it didn't hit her in the face. "How do you know?"

Patricia widened her eyes. "Because God will mend her broken heart the way He's mended yours. The way He mends every heart that turns to Him for solace."

Embarrassed, Sarah nodded. Patricia hadn't been speaking of Courtney's physical welfare. That the girl might be in danger hadn't even crossed her mind. But it had crossed Sarah's, and the resulting fear sat like a lump in the middle of her chest. Although she kept telling herself she was crazy to suspect her beloved leader of harming anyone, she kept recalling the triumphant expression on Ethan's face at the stoning, when Martha's husband had thrown the first rock and hit her so cruelly on the temple. Martha had become so disenchanted with him that she'd been very vocal about her doubts, only to be stoned days later. Courtney had also been talking, saying things she shouldn't. Sarah had heard her tell others that Ethan couldn't be a prophet. She accused him of being a sexual deviant who preyed on the weaknesses of others to cover his own inadequacies. She claimed she had proof that he wasn't superior to anyone else.

What that proof might be, Sarah didn't know. She hadn't asked because she didn't want to get involved. She was trying to rebuild her faith, not demolish it entirely. She wasn't convinced Courtney would've told her, anyway. When the others had asked, she'd merely laughed and said she'd discovered a secret Ethan wouldn't want her sharing with the world, and that he'd pay dearly to keep her silent. She said it would be her ticket to the good life somewhere outside Arizona.

Had she gotten what she wanted from Ethan and left?

Sarah happened to pass Bartholomew as she walked back to the cheese factory. He didn't seem to be in any better mood than the other Spiritual Guides. He was moving slowly, obviously in pain. She had to call to him three times before he looked up.

"Brother Bartholomew!"

As if reluctant to be interrupted, he glanced at the Enlightenment Hall but stopped to address her. "What is it?"

"Have you seen Sister Courtney?"

"Sister who?"

His response surprised her. Unlike Patricia, he'd been heavily involved in Courtney's indoctrination and should have recognized her real name. "Trix. The new convert."

"Oh, yes. I think she went back home to her parents."

"She did?"

"That's what the Holy One told me."

"When?"

His scowl was always unsettling, with his lazy eye drifting off to the left. "Does it matter? Why are you asking?"

"I'm..." Her voice trailed off beneath his glower, and suddenly she felt silly for being worried. Ethan was a man of God. He gave beautiful, moving sermons about being true to oneself, about being generous in spirit, about becoming a better person.

"It's nothing," she said. "She didn't come to work so I was afraid she might have fallen ill."

"She's not ill. She's gone. Hopefully, for good."

Sarah's fingers curled into her palms. "You didn't like her?"

"I like everyone," he said, even though his expression suggested just the opposite. Aloof and difficult to read, he dogged Ethan's every step, and had ever since she'd joined. But he wasn't like Ethan at all. Sometimes, he was downright unfriendly. "I just didn't appreciate some of the lies that came out of her mouth," he added. "Not everyone is capable of upholding the covenants we make. This was clearly not for her."

Sarah could understand. She was the first to admit that living in the commune wasn't easy. She herself sometimes struggled to trust her leaders. This was a perfect example. "Yes, Brother."

He waved toward the cheese factory. "Aren't you supposed to be at work?"

Her chin nearly hit her chest as she nodded. Not only was she questioning her faith and doubting God's anointed, she was being derelict in her duty. "I'm on my way."

"Make it quick." He started off again but turned back. "Before Courtney left, she mentioned to several people that she'd learned something shocking, something—or so she claimed—that would destroy us all. Did she tell you about it?"

Sarah didn't know how to respond. Courtney hadn't really *told* her anything. Sarah had merely overheard what the others had said. She opened her mouth to say as much but that irrational fear she'd been feeling welled up inside, and it was powerful enough to silence her. She didn't want to be thrown out. She had friends here who'd become more like family to her than her own emotionally aloof father. And she had nowhere else to go. "No, Brother."

"Well, if you do hear anything, it was all a pack of lies. Courtney was a lost soul, as you know. We did our best to redeem her, but one must be repentant and willing to be cleansed."

"I agree."

Why was he bothering to explain this to her?

"It would be wise to remember that anyone spreading gossip or falsehoods will be shunned. God will not stand for His prophet to be mocked."

Was Ethan worried about being mocked—or questioned? Sarah got the impression he refused to allow either. "I'm aware of God's laws."

"I'm happy to hear it," he said. "Peace be with you."

Having an explanation for Courtney's disappearance helped. Sarah felt relieved as she hurried to work. It made her sad that Courtney hadn't bothered to say goodbye. But that didn't matter as long as her friend was safe. Sarah was used to being forgotten.

"Self-pity is a sin," she reminded herself as soon as the "forgotten" thought passed through her head. Then she said a prayer of thanksgiving for a Savior who made it possible to repent and change. As she stepped inside the cinder-block cheese factory, she decided she didn't care what her leaders did. As long as her heart was pure, her soul would be saved.

Or was it a little more complicated than that? Did she have more of a responsibility to make sure her leaders were being honest than she wanted to acknowledge?

Rachel rubbed her temples as she stared through the windshield at a white single-wide trailer. Judging by the dents and the rust and the broken picket skirt, it had to be at least thirty years old. There was a dog pen on one side, also broken in places, and a rock pile in an area Rachel couldn't even call a yard. It all sat at the end of a dirt drive. They'd actually been driving on dirt for a while. The only way to reach Portal was to go around the mountains or over them, and the road over was dirt. Taking the pass meant you risked running into one of the thunderstorms that could happen so suddenly during monsoon season, but Nate had insisted on the direct route, and Rachel hadn't been surprised. He was in his beloved ramshackle truck; that was what he felt such a vehicle was for. "This is *it*?"

"It is if we can trust our directions." Nate didn't sound any more enthusiastic than she was.

"Wow." Thanks to her job, she'd lived in plenty of dumps. She'd tolerated soggy, water-damaged ceilings, threadbare carpet, cockroaches, cigarette smoke clinging to drapes, bedding and furniture, leaky plumbing and paper-thin walls in motels where she could hear headboards banging, courtesy of her prostitute neighbors. But she'd always had electricity and running water. This place had a generator, if it worked, and an outhouse made of sun-bleached wood that listed to one side.

Taking a deep breath, she studied the surrounding area. As Nate had promised, the Chiricahuas were close by. They rose like islands from the desert "sea," which was why, according to Nate, these mountains and others like them were called "sky islands." Rachel was happy that this part of the state wasn't quite as flat as the land they'd crossed coming from L.A. In addition to creosote and cacti, they now saw some oak and pine.

The sunset resembled taffy melting on the mountain peaks in stunning layers of red, orange and gold. It was one of the most spectacular displays Rachel had ever seen—but all she could do was gape at the remote outpost she'd be sharing with Nate for God knew how long.

"How much is Milt paying in rent?" she asked.

"*I* lined this up. I knew I was getting taken even at the time, but…shit," he grumbled. Then he was gone, carrying their luggage to the front door as if they might as well get on with the task at hand.

Nate had mentioned snakes. If Rachel had her guess, there were plenty of scorpions, tarantulas and lizards, too—not to mention the odd mountain lion. She could picture the Apaches who'd holed up here with Cochise and Geronimo in the 1860s and '70s. Two of the last bastions of the Old West—Tombstone and Douglas— weren't far away. Nate had talked about the area's history as they'd passed the grocery store/café constituting the center of town. Apparently, there wasn't even a gas station in Portal. You had to drive seven miles to Rodeo, New Mexico, in order to fill up.

If Wycliff had wanted a remote spot, and if Paradise was anything like Portal, he'd certainly chosen well.

"You coming?" The door of the trailer hung open as Nate waited on the landing.

"I'm coming," she called back, and got out.

Nate hadn't told Rachel that only one bedroom was furnished. There weren't many rental options in Portal; he'd had to take what he could find. He'd figured he could always sleep on the couch. But as he studied the short, lumpy sofa in what passed for a living room, he decided he'd rather lie awake night after night suffering from sexual frustration at Rachel's side.

She stood in the hallway, gazing into one bedroom and then the second, which was empty. Eventually, she turned to glare at him.

"What?" He spread his hands in mock innocence.

"You know what."

"Don't worry. I'll let you bunk with me, at least until we can get a mattress for the other room."

"You're going to *let* me sleep with you."

He wondered if she was remembering the last time she'd been in his bed. "Just until we can get you a mattress. That won't be any problem, will it?"

"What do you think?"

"I know you're on a sexual hiatus and all, but you said yourself that I'm no temptation. And even if we get a little hot and bothered, what's one more hurrah after entertaining all those beach bums?" He chuckled at her stricken expression as he went out to collect the rest of their supplies. But he'd underestimated her resistance. When he returned, he met her going in the opposite direction, carrying the cheap secondhand suitcase they'd bought for her in Phoenix.

"I'm finding my own place to stay," she announced. "Consider us estranged and on the brink of divorce."

He put down the groceries in his arms and moved to cut her off. She had the keys. "There's no need to over-react," he said, sobering in an effort to calm her. "We can't be estranged when we approach the Covenanters. And there's nothing else around here. Do you think I would've picked this place if I'd had any other choice?"

"I think you feel it's a big joke that I'm going to be without any personal space—but I'm not laughing."

"It's not a joke. I—I'll sleep on the floor, okay? It's a job, Rachel, like any other. You can't tell me you haven't been in compromising situations before. What makes this one any different?"

That wasn't hard to answer. He knew working with him was what made it different. But he also knew she'd never admit it.

"I just don't understand why I couldn't have handled this alone," she said. "I work better that way."

"So you've said. But sometimes you have to adjust."

"That doesn't include sleeping with my manager!"

He could've mentioned that it was a little late to worry about that. After all, *she* was the one who'd let herself into *his* condo, removed her clothing and offered him everything she had, including her heart. But he knew the reminder wouldn't help. It was the fact that they'd been together before that was causing all the trouble now. "Hey, this isn't about us," he said. "Our work never is. It's about doing what we have to. Period. You know that."

She remained stiff, resistant, so he tried another tack.

"Look, I didn't set you up, okay? You've seen what's available in Portal. This place was all I could get, unless you'd rather camp out under the stars. I figured we'd make improvements when we could—and we will. Until then, I'll sleep in a bag in the spare room. Nothing's changed. There's no problem."

Her forehead rumpled as she kicked at the dirt, but it wasn't long before she let him take her suitcase and the keys.

"Lightweight," he muttered.

"I'm not a lightweight," she snapped. "It's the damn heat. It's insufferable."

Although it was no longer the hottest part of the day, they were still sweating. "Whatever you say. Sit down while I get the generator going."

"I don't need to sit down. I can carry stuff, too," she said. Then she helped him unload and, using water from two metal barrels provided by the landlord, they began to clean.

By midnight, the temperature hadn't dropped more than a few degrees. Rachel felt as if she couldn't breathe in the sweltering heat. L.A. could get warm in the summertime, but the breeze coming in off the ocean generally made for comfortable nights.

The generator whined out back. Supposedly, it was large enough to run the swamp cooler in the hallway, but she'd needed to put some space between her and Nate so she lay in bed with her door shut, praying for the slightest breeze to carry through her open window.

Those prayers went unanswered. The desert stretched beyond the trailer on all sides, quiet and still. But with her drapes open, she could see the night sky.

The stars had never looked quite so close or so bright. She supposed this place could get in a person's blood. Although it was a far cry from her glass-and-chrome house on the ocean—she doubted she'd ever be able to give up her proximity to the sea—the desert had a stark beauty she found appealing, if lonesome.

What would tomorrow bring? She and Nate had to start talking to people in town, make their presence known and build their cover. Maybe they'd take some pictures around Paradise. They couldn't wait for Ethan and the Covenanters to notice them. They had to draw the attention of someone in the group, get an invitation to one of the Introduction Meetings. She hated the thought that Ethan might be stoning people while they settled in, completely unaware, in this trailer.

Would gaining admission to the group be difficult?

Rachel couldn't even guess. Like every job she did, this one was filled with unknowns....

The creak of Nate's footsteps in the hall told her he was up. She tensed, waiting to see what he'd do, but she wasn't worried that he'd try to come into her room. He hadn't really wanted to be with her the first time they'd made love. Why would he feel any different now?

She heard the front door open. He was going out.

Leaving her bed, she went to the window to see what he was doing. He appeared to be heading to his truck, but it didn't look as if he planned on going far. He wasn't wearing anything except a pair of basketball shorts.

The cab light went on when he opened the passenger door. He got something out of the jockey box, then started back.

Because she didn't want him to catch her watching

him, she climbed back into bed. *Forget Nate!* Obsessing about him was what had gotten her into trouble before.

She cringed as she remembered all the signals she must've misinterpreted to wind up in his bed, naked. The way he'd sometimes looked at her at the office, she'd assumed…well, she'd assumed too much, obviously. Without the experience most women had in dealing with men, she hadn't known how to take their relationship from colleagues to lovers and had gone too far, too fast.

Getting into his bed had been her first mistake. Not getting out of it when he reacted with such surprise had been her second. And not leaving his house right after they'd made love had been her third. But by then she'd known deep inside that she'd have only the one night with him. So she'd stayed, secretly treasuring every moment.

The crushing disappointment that'd come in the morning—with his polite explanation of why he'd lost control and how sorry he was for not sending her home—still made her cringe.

God, what a fool! Why couldn't she have salvaged her pride?

Because she'd been lonely too long. And because she'd let him mean too much to her. When she realized that feeling wasn't mutual, she simply didn't have the skills to shrug it off or act indifferent.

He'd taught her a good lesson, though. One most people learned in their teens, but better late than never…

At least she'd never make that mistake again. She'd demand more from any lover she took in the future.

But there were times she was tempted to lower her standards. Times like now, when she lay in bed, remembering Nate's hands on her body and craving them there again.

6

Every Wednesday, Ethan called his entire church together for morning prayer. Then Bart and his guards took over for two hours with armory drills. In the summer, they met in the courtyard outside the Enlightenment Hall as the sun came up, like they were doing now. It wasn't Wednesday, but the sudden disappearance of Courtney Sinclair had to be addressed. At Bartholomew's urging, Ethan had called for a special prayer so he could handle the issue via public announcement. This would enable everyone to hear what he had to say on the matter. But he hated that this was the second time he'd been forced to convene a meeting for the sake of damage control within the past two months.

He could feel Bartholomew behind him, keeping silent watch, as always. Bart took his job as head of security very seriously. The way he'd supported Ethan after that fight with Courtney, how he'd hidden the body and then buried it, proved he could be trusted with anything.

Ethan had been lucky the day Bart had attended one of his first Introduction Meetings. Claiming she couldn't live with his sexual dysfunction—which probably had more to do with his orientation than his impotence—Bart's wife had recently left him. Days later, he'd closed his failing chiropractic practice. He'd been in the middle of a full-blown midlife crisis, had been searching for an anchor of some sort, a devotion that felt worthwhile, and Ethan had been there to offer him that. Bart was so grateful to have a purpose, to be valued that he'd become one of Ethan's most loyal followers.

But he hadn't tracked down Martha, and that grated on Ethan. He couldn't abide the thought of a Covenant member leaving the group and then spouting off about him to the outside world. Martha was a Judas and would suffer God's wrath, just as traitors like her deserved.

The other Spiritual Guides stood behind him, too, but Ethan wasn't as completely sure of them as he was of Bartholomew. Some had been with him since college, but whether they stayed because of loyalty or self-interest, he couldn't say. He protected himself by telling them only what he wanted them to hear.

Unfortunately, he couldn't keep this particular situation between him and Bart, as he would've preferred. Harry Titherington knew he'd been with Courtney the night she went missing. Ethan had spent an hour trying to convince the entire group that she'd been alive when she left his apartment, but he wasn't positive they all believed him. Especially Harry...

Head bowed, Ethan waited for the prayer to come to a close. It was beneath him to have to reason away doubts and accusations, but he had to put the rumors concerning Courtney to rest. He also had to prep his people so they'd know how to react if Courtney's parents reappeared at the gate or, God forbid, sent the police. He wasn't sure Paradise could tolerate another media onslaught, not on the heels of the botched stoning.

The sudden silence notified him that the prayer, said by one of the Spiritual Guides, was finally over.

"Thank you for your eloquence, Brother White-head," he called out.

A resounding "Praise be to God" rang loud and clear in response.

"Yes, praise be to God," Ethan said. "And now, before you go about your day, I have an issue of some importance to discuss."

A ripple of expectation filtered through the crowd. The last time he'd said those words, he'd had to tell them that Sister Martha had escaped God's justice and could not be found. As a defensive measure, he'd also had to exhort them to speak to no one about the incident, to pray that she could be caught before her evil tongue destroyed the work of God and to remember their covenants to put God's work and glory above all else.

"Many of you celebrated with me when Sister Courtney Sinclair was saved from the cesspool of the outside world two short weeks ago. As you remember, because she was underage, we voted on whether or not we would take the risk associated with accepting her into our family." In a private meeting before that, several of the Guides had voted against it, but he'd wanted her in his life and forced the issue. Now he was paying the price.

"We took a great deal into consideration," he went on. "But, envisioning her with us after the world is cleansed of pride and iniquity, we took that risk and re-joiced at having reclaimed another lamb of God." He changed the inflection of his voice. "Unfortunately, as sometimes happens, she has already lost her way."

This time a groan sounded from the crowd and Ethan thought he heard someone mention Martha, but he ignored that and the disapproval he felt from the Brethren who hadn't wanted him to admit Courtney in the first place, and talked over the noise. "She informed me of her decision to leave over the weekend. It was with a sad heart that I listened to the news. But I did not attempt to persuade her to stay. Not one so young. We can't afford trouble with the authorities. They don't understand us and those who don't understand prefer to destroy."

"They persecute and belittle!" someone cried.

"That they do," Ethan responded. "Thus, I allowed her to make the choice on her own and then I escorted her to the gate that very night. Several of your Spiritual Guides saw me do it," he added, even though, other than Bart and Harry, there wasn't a soul who'd seen him with Courtney on Monday. Everything had happened in the pit and only the Brethren had direct access.

Murmuring arose. "I saw her go, Holy One." "Me, too." "How could she?" "Why would she do it?" "We loved her." "We accepted her into our family."

Slightly relieved by the response, he raised a hand to indicate silence. "Bartholomew tells me that many of you have expressed concern about some of the things she was saying before she made the decision to leave. I assure you, those were the words of Satan. He grabbed hold of her heart when it was at its most vulnerable, and he'll grab hold of yours, too, if you do not watch and pray constantly."

"We will watch and pray" came the echo.

"And to stop the poison from spreading further, we will speak no more of her," Ethan continued. "We won't so much as mention her name. She is to be shunned completely and, here in Paradise, it shall be as though she never existed."

"All betrayers deserve to be shunned," Sister Titherington called out.

"That's true," Ethan agreed. "It says in the scriptures, 'If thy right eye offend thee, pluck it out…and if thy right hand offend thee, cut it off, and cast it from thee: for it is profitable for thee that one of thy members should perish, and not that thy whole body should be cast into hell.'"

"Praise be to God!" everyone cried. "We will cast out the devil."

Ethan raised his voice even louder. "Yes, cast out the devil, cast out all evil, my brothers and sisters. Be strong. Fret not about Courtney's sudden withdrawal. As with Martha, God will punish her and justify us in the end."

"We will pray for her soul!" the woman standing next to Sister Titherington yelled.

"As will I," Ethan said. "Pray also that the Lord will provide us with others who seek the truth. Others who are more sincere in heart and more capable of taking on His covenants and promises. That way, we will have many hands to build up His Kingdom and plenty of friends with whom to rejoice in the enlightenment we have received."

"Amen!" they called.

"Guard even your thoughts," he cautioned, "lest ye be ensnared by the devil and dragged down to hell."

"Amen!"

Warming to his role, Ethan stepped forward, once again feeling invincible in their worship. "And although it greatly pains me, I must broach another part of this issue. When we decided to accept Courtney, we decided to protect her from discovery and removal."

"I remember," Roger Lamkin shouted from the back.

"We sheltered her from the parents who'd been so unkind to her." Ethan shook his head. "And now she will betray us, put us at risk. I have no idea what details of our lifestyle she might twist, but she could cause problems for us. I have made this a matter of much thought and prayer and it has been revealed to me that we are to stick with what we told her parents initially. Courtney was never here. The Lord would rather have us maintain that as the truth than to admit a lie that would cause the innocent among us to suffer."

"The Lord will protect us."

"He has shown us how to protect ourselves," Ethan added, wanting to drive that point home.

"We only lied to make her free!" someone else called out. "We only lied to protect her. For the greater good of truth and freedom."

"And in that we are justified." He rubbed his hands together. "As we are justified, according to His word, in this—if outsiders come to call, you will say nothing of Courtney. You will come directly to me, and I will handle all inquiries. Do you understand?"

"Yes, Holy One," they cried.

Cupping a hand around his ear, he spoke louder. "What did you say?"

"Yes, Holy One!"

The unified response satisfied him. "Good. Now, go on about your work and don't worry. All is well."

"All is well," they echoed. "Praise be to God."

Bartholomew came up behind him as the crowd dispersed. "You have led them in the right way," he murmured.

Ethan turned to study his friend's haggard face. He had bags under his eyes and a gray tinge to his skin that made Ethan suspect he wasn't entirely well. But Bartholomew wouldn't go back to bed even if ordered to do so. He was on guard, waiting for this latest problem to blow up or blow over. "It's the only way."

"We'll be fine so long as we're consistent. She came to a meeting here. That is all we admit. We never saw her after that. We cannot undermine our credibility by changing our story. The Lord will protect us if we hold our tongue on all else."

The belligerence on Courtney's face during their argument flitted through Ethan's mind. He was shocked that she'd tried to blackmail him. Or had he been hallucinating about that, too? That was what really frightened him. Maybe she'd posed no threat and he'd killed her, anyway.... "Another scandal so soon after what happened with Martha is regrettable."

"All will be well," Bartholomew said. "Leave it to me."

"I've left Martha to you, and it's been weeks," he complained to deflect attention from his own mistake.

"I'm working on it. I know she's in Willcox."

"If you know she's in Willcox, why haven't you been able to bring her back?"

He lowered his voice. "She's not exactly listed in the phone book, Ethan. But I'll find her. I have two men there as we speak."

"Not with the mark—"

"Of course not! Do you think I'd send men so easily identified as belonging to us?"

"No. You're too smart for that."

"Thanks be to God I have never let you down. And I don't plan to start now."

"But by the time you recover her, the damage will be done."

"The damage was done the moment she escaped and opened her big mouth. What more can she say now that she's told the world we tried to kill her?"

"She knows details about the way we worship that I'd rather she didn't share. What we do here is sacred. I won't throw pearls before swine, won't hold our beliefs up for the world to judge."

"She's probably already told. But we'll get her back, and it won't be too late. It's never too late to punish the deserving."

Ethan watched the crowd disperse. "I can't believe she slipped through the hands of two hundred people."

Bart lowered his voice. "She had to have help, as I said from the beginning."

"Who helped her?"

"That's what I want to know. And I won't be satisfied until I find out."

They'd called in at least two dozen people who'd been there that night, but all denied any knowledge of what had occurred.

"Once the fuss dies down, we'll quietly reclaim her," Bart said. "It'll be safer then."

With a sniff, Ethan nodded. It was going to be another hot day. After last night, he'd rather not be wandering around. And he didn't want to be so close to Bart. Sometimes his head of security made him feel…

strange. "Cancel my meetings this morning and send me three women," he said. Then he searched his pockets for the meth he'd put there and hurried to the Enlightenment Hall, where the privacy of his room awaited. He wanted to get high and experiment with the women who were always so eager to please him.

But it was only an hour later that a knock on his door interrupted them.

"Holy One!" a breathless voice called from the hallway.

Ethan was pretty sure it was his housekeeper, Sister Maxine, but the sound came to him as if through a synthesizer. It took several seconds for him to realize he hadn't imagined it, and even longer to bring the response swimming around in his head to his lips.

"Yes?" He'd had the women tie him to the bed so he couldn't move. He didn't want to leave the room, anyway. He'd been fantasizing about a most erotic encounter, one that didn't include women at all.

"Holy One!" The second call came with enough urgency that his companions sat up.

"What is it?" he managed to ask.

"Courtney's mother is at the gate!"

Rachel stood just inside the entrance of Portal's store/café with Nate at her side, waiting for someone who worked in the restaurant portion of the establishment to seat them. They wouldn't have any trouble getting a table. The place was almost empty. Apparently, even birders avoided this part of America at the height of the summer.

"You're quiet today. You okay?" Nate asked.

"I'm fine," she replied, but she already felt tired and

dusty. She'd had only a few hours' sleep and had to settle for a rudimentary bath. With such a limited water
supply, a shower had been out of the question.

Somehow, Nate looked none the worse for wear.
Dressed in a loose pair of khaki shorts that fell low on
his lean hips and a T-shirt tight enough to delineate his
rock-hard pecs, he hadn't shaved and he hadn't showered. But acknowledging that he could rough it far
more gracefully than she didn't make Rachel feel any
better.

An elderly woman with white hair piled on top of
her head and turquoise teardrop earrings smiled when
she noticed them waiting. "Hello. Two for breakfast?"
she asked, scooping up menus.

Rachel smoothed her pink cotton blouse and—
thanks to the dust—ill-advised white shorts as Nathan
nodded. Resting a hand at the base of her spine, he
guided her to a booth along the perimeter. There were
ten tables in the restaurant, but only one was
occupied—with two ranchers, judging by their cowboy
hats and weather-beaten faces.

Once they were seated, the hostess presented them
with menus. Glancing out the window, Rachel could
see heat rising from the earth in shimmering waves. The
temperature here was exactly as Nate had described
it—white-hot, hot enough to bleach anything. But with
wood paneling and deep awnings, the restaurant provided a cool, shady respite. An oasis.

Thank God.

Of course, they'd have to contend with the heat later
on. But in the meantime she accepted a glass of ice
water from a young girl of about twelve.

"Thank you." Rachel tried to catch the girl's eye so

she could get a clearer glimpse of her delicate features, but the child ducked her head and scurried away.

"Abby's deaf," the hostess explained. "She can't hear and she can't talk, but she's the sweetest thing in the whole world."

"Is she any relation to you?" Rachel asked.

The deep wrinkles on the woman's face easily accommodated a smile. "She's my grandchild. Unfortunately, her daddy isn't up to much, so I take care of her every summer. I'd keep her over the winter, too, but she goes to a special school."

Rachel guessed that the girl was part American Indian. Her bronze-colored, dewy skin was especially beautiful. "Maybe when she gets older."

"Maybe." The woman straightened their flatware. "This your first time in Portal?"

Rachel held her menu at the ready but didn't open it. "Yes."

"Where you headin'?"

Expecting Nate to enter the conversation, Rachel hesitated—but he was already perusing the list of entrées and didn't seem to be paying attention.

"Nowhere," she replied. "At least, not anytime soon. We're renting the Spitzer place about three miles from here."

"You've moved in? You're new?" she asked in surprise.

"Yes. We plan to be here for a while. My, um, husband—" she stumbled over the word but made an effort to cover her gaffe by hurrying on "—is a wildlife photographer."

"Really! Well, you've come to the right corner of the

earth. We have one of the most biologically diverse areas in America here."

They were sure hiding it well. So far, Rachel had seen nothing diverse about it. Hot and dry, more hot and dry, and desert scrub mixed with a few other plants that looked about the same. That was it. But she pretended to agree. "So we hear," she said, and kicked Nate.

Lifting his head, he set his menu aside. "From what I've read, you've got more than eighty species of mammals."

"I wouldn't doubt it," the woman responded. "I hear people talk about the wildlife all the time—hooded skunks, mountain lions, black bears, javelinas, raccoons. We even have quite a few different kinds of bats. One of 'em has these really big ears," she said with a laugh.

"You have a lot of snakes, too, don't you?" The expression on Nate's face suggested the question was in earnest, but Rachel knew him too well. He was needling her.

"Oh, yes. Lots of snakes and lizards."

"What about spiders?" he asked. "I'd really like to photograph a tarantula—a tarantula crawling out of an old outhouse would be a great photo."

Suppressing a shudder of revulsion at the thought of such a creature living in *their* outhouse, Rachel kicked him again. "If you want to get started today, we should probably order, *honey,*" she reminded him.

The woman took the hint gracefully. "Heavens, yes. Don't let me hold you up. I'm a talker. It's because of living in such a small community." She laughed again. "I'll be back after you've had a few minutes to look over the menu."

"*Sure* you want to photograph a tarantula coming out of an old outhouse," Rachel muttered when she was gone.

"I'd rather capture a snake slithering across a woman's bare stomach, but I only have one woman at hand, and I doubt my trusty assistant would cooperate."

"Damn right."

He chuckled under his breath.

"You could've jumped into that conversation a little sooner," she whispered.

"Why? You were doing just fine. No need to overact. As long as what we say makes sense and appears to be true, the less detail, the better."

"There's nothing wrong with making friends and opening up, Nate."

"Except that we're lying, right?"

He had her there. "Except for that," she reluctantly agreed.

"So…are you going to ask this woman about the Covenanters, or should I?"

"I will."

"When?"

Her stomach growled. "After we eat."

7

The woman who'd seated them also waited on them through breakfast, eventually introducing herself as Thelma Lassiter. Abby, her grandchild, came around once or twice to fill their water glasses.

After the ranchers left, Nate and Rachel were the only patrons in the restaurant. But they weren't the only people in the building. Voices drifted over from the store section, Thelma's chief among them as she greeted her customers like the old friends they probably were.

It wasn't until they'd finished eating and Thelma had come to get their plates that Rachel brought up the Covenanters. "We've been hearing about a cult that's moved into the area. Do you know anything about them?"

Losing some of her cheerfulness, she frowned. "A little. They live about five miles from here and have occasional meetings where they invite folks in to see the place. But they're very unfriendly if you show up any other time. Even if you attend the Introduction, you get the feeling you're just seeing what they want you to see and hearing only what they want you to hear."

"So you've been there? You've been to an Introduction Meeting?" Rachel asked.

Thelma cast a serreptitious glance over her shoulder as if she was afraid she'd be overheard. But she couldn't be worried about Abby. Was there someone else who wouldn't like her talking about the people of Paradise? "I took Abby about six weeks ago. That Ethan fellow who claims to be a prophet saw her in the store one day and told me he could heal her—that he could make it so she can hear."

Nate leaned back in the booth. "That's quite a claim."

"Chaske—my husband—was skeptical, too. He still is."

Chaske was obviously the person in back, the one she didn't want overhearing the conversation. Maybe he was the cook.

"He thought I was crazy for hoping," she went on. "But...I believe in miracles. There's got to be more to this life than the tangible things we deal with every day. I thought maybe one reason God sent the Covenanters here was to help Abby."

Kicking off his flip-flops, Nate found Rachel's feet under the table and began to play footsie with her. Under the guise of their cover, he could get away with goading her in any number of ways, and messing with her made this assignment a lot more fun. "Did they? Help her, I mean?"

He suppressed a chuckle at the sharp *stop it* glance he received from Rachel as Thelma shook her head. "No. Once I got out to the commune, Ethan told me I'd have to leave her there if I wanted him to heal her."

"Leave her for how long?" Rachel kept trying to move her feet out of reach, but he wouldn't let her. Although he knew he'd pay for it later, he was enjoying getting her riled up.

"A few weeks, at least. But...I couldn't do that. As far as I was concerned, there was no one to look after her. No one I trusted, anyway."

Nate thought Thelma's practical side had served her better than her spiritual side. "So you took her and left."

"Yes, but...I've gone back once since then."

Pointedly clearing her throat, Rachel moved her feet again. "What happened?"

"They wouldn't even let me in until I mentioned Ethan's offer to heal Abby. Then they checked with him, and he gave me an audience. But he told me the same thing as before. We couldn't come for brief visits. I'd have to trust him, have complete faith, or he could do nothing."

He was tempted to tell Thelma about Ethan's correspondence with Charles Manson. Nate also knew a little about Ethan's mental health or lack thereof—tidbits his father had shared with Milt. But as much as Nate longed to convey the danger, he couldn't reveal his true interest in Paradise. The best way to protect Abby and Thelma, and everyone else, was to get inside that compound and figure out what was really going on. And that required him to be judicious. "You can't leave a child in the keeping of someone you don't know," he said. "You made the right decision."

Thelma cast another glance over her shoulder. "It was my *only* choice. Chaske would've gone up there with a shotgun if I'd left Abby. He says there's no way he'll ever let her fall into the hands of a cult."

Rachel finally resorted to pulling her feet up and

tucking them under her, effectively ending Nate's game. "You *considered* leaving her?"

"More so the second time," Thelma admitted. "I wish Chaske had been there with me. The Holy One—that's what Ethan's worshippers call him—introduced me to several people who say he's done miraculous things. One said she had cancer until he cured her. Another was in a wheelchair, suffering from multiple sclerosis. Three members of that man's family told me he couldn't even feed himself when he first met Ethan. You should see him now."

"But MS is a strange disease," Nate said. "It can advance and recede. Maybe his miraculous improvement had nothing to do with Ethan."

"Then how do you explain the woman with cancer?"

Nate had heard the peddlers of various health tonics claim they had the answer to a whole list of incurable maladies. That didn't mean it was true. It just meant they had a vested interest in making others believe, and it might be the same here. "There could be a lot of explanations," he said, "a flat-out lie being the most obvious."

"Why would they lie?" she countered.

"Because they *want* to believe what Ethan is telling them, and it builds the group's credibility to outsiders."

Rachel frowned. "Did it seem to bother Ethan that you wouldn't leave Abby?"

"Of course. He told me he could give her a much better life." Tears filled Thelma's eyes. "That's all I want for her—that she'll be okay when I'm gone. He was disappointed, maybe even a little disgusted, that I wouldn't trust him." She blinked several times.

"But there are all those rumors about their sexual practices…."

"What rumors?"

"He has some very…liberal ideas. People say orgies go on up there. But who knows? That might be a witch hunt. Most folks around here don't like him much. The Covenanters are all I've heard about since they moved in, and none of it's been good."

"Maybe they *are* having orgies," Nate said.

"If so, he certainly didn't talk about it at the Introduction Meeting. And he denied it when I told him that was why I couldn't leave Abby. According to him, it's just superstitious folks bein' scared and talkin' about things they know nothing of. He said that sex and drugs aren't part of the religion, freedom and acceptance are. But—" she sighed "—my husband is one of those superstitious people."

Nate saw Abby going between the restaurant and the store. "Did Abby know he wanted her to stay?"

Thelma straightened her apron. "Oh, yes. She's very smart. But she wouldn't have any of it. She clung to me and kept signing that she was fine and wanted to go home to Grandpa."

Hoping to add a little support to what her husband believed, Nate spoke up again. "Someone else told us about a woman who left the commune. Sounds as if she had it pretty rough when she was with them. Have you heard about her?"

The dishes clinked as she stacked them. "Oh, yes. Her name's Martha Wilson. She's not from around here. She came with Ethan from back east somewhere—like most of the Covenanters. Chaske's mentioned her several times. So has everyone else who hates the church. I think she's the source of most of the rumors. But who knows if she's being truthful?"

Nate turned his water glass around and around. "Has she been seen in Portal lately?"

"No. I guess Martha went straight to the police. She's staying in Willcox now. From what I hear, she's getting a lawyer so she can fight for custody of her son."

Nate considered that good information. Maybe they could have a talk with Martha....

"You think she's lying?" Rachel asked.

Thelma pulled their dirty plates toward her. "I can't say one way or another. I only know that everyone I saw in the commune looked busy and peaceful. There was no hint of violence or sexual impropriety. Ethan preaches Christian values. He told me so."

Rachel shoved the salt and pepper and sugar packets against the wall. "Hard to imagine a Christian preacher, at least in this day and age, ordering a person stoned."

"Chaske doesn't think it's so hard to imagine. He keeps saying that what Ethan shows the world and what he does behind those closed gates could be two different things."

"That's true," Nate agreed. But she didn't seem to be convinced. The dream of fixing her granddaughter held too much allure.

"But he's never been up there," she argued, "never seen it for himself. And the police looked into the matter. If Martha was telling the truth, they would've done something about it, wouldn't they? The sheriff and his deputies came in here for lunch not long ago. I asked them about Martha's accusations and they said they couldn't prove a darn thing."

Nate knew police work from the other side. "Investigations rarely occur overnight. There's the truth. And then there's proof of the truth. Truth without proof won't build a case."

"I guess." She jingled the change in her pocket. "Chaske keeps talking about Jim Jones and David Koresh and what they got away with. He thinks Ethan's no better."

Abby approached with a pitcher of water, distracting Thelma. She touched the child's face with such love, Nate worried that Thelma's desire to see Abby healed would eventually overtake her good sense.

"You're a wonderful child. Aren't you, Abby?" she said.

The girl smiled up at her grandmother, then refilled their water glasses.

"I'd heard Paradise was a ghost town," Nate said. "Before we learned about the Covenanters, I was planning to go up that way, take a look around, maybe get some shots."

"They won't like you taking pictures," Thelma said. "They're very private. They know what other people are saying about them. When I was there, they definitely seemed a bit…defensive."

Abby, who'd refused to look at him or Rachel since they'd come in, was watching them both closely. Gone was the shyness and reluctance he'd witnessed in her mannerisms and bearing so far. Not only was she staring at him directly, she was shaking her head.

"You don't like it up there, Abby?" Rachel asked.

She shook her head again, even more adamantly.

"She doesn't want you to go to Paradise," Thelma

said. "She thinks her grandfather is right, that Ethan is dangerous."

Nate leaned toward the child to let her know he was talking to her. "As long as we don't bother him, we should be okay taking a few pictures, don't you think?"

The child's eyes widened and she jerked her head again.

"Don't listen to her," Thelma said. "She can read lips better than you can imagine and picks up on far too much. Richard and Lynne Sinclair have scared her, that's all."

Rachel placed her napkin on the table. "Who're Richard and Lynne?"

"They own a ranch between here and Rodeo. They've been stopping in almost every day, spouting all kinds of accusations against the Covenanters."

"Like?" Rachel prompted.

Abby didn't leave. She tapped her grandmother's arm to get her to turn so that she could see her lips; she seemed to be closely monitoring the conversation.

"Courtney, their teenage daughter, went missing last month," Thelma said. "They swear up and down she's been kidnapped by the Covenanters."

"You don't believe it," Nate said.

"No. That girl was always a handful. Cutting herself and thumbing rides with anyone who came through town. She dressed in that gothic garb. You know, the black pants and black T-shirts with black boots. She even wore black nail polish and lipstick. They actually caught her propositioning a couple of old birders! She'd gone out to their campsite to trade you-know-what for the chance to 'get out of this dump' as she put it." She waved a hand in apparent disgust. "She musta run off. She's done it before."

Nate rubbed the condensation on his glass. "What makes her parents believe otherwise?"

"She went to one of the Covenant meetings a week or two before she disappeared and came home gushing about Ethan. She thought he was—" she made quotation marks with her fingers "—'hot.' That's all. It's not much to go on, which is why the police haven't been able to help. They can't force the Covenanters to let them search without some evidence that she might be in the compound."

Rachel took a sip of water. "No one's seen her since?"

"No one."

"How many Covenanters attend the Introduction Meetings?" Nate asked.

"Quite a few. Fifteen or twenty. Ethan usually officiates—him or one of the Spiritual Guides."

"Aren't there any women in the leadership?" Rachel asked.

"No, the men hold all the power."

Nate could almost hear Rachel's spine snapping straight with indignation. She'd come from a church with a strict patriarchal order where that power had been abused. "That doesn't bother you?"

"Isn't that the way it usually is?"

Nate cut in before the conversation could drift away from what he was interested in learning. "So once people join the commune, can they maintain relationships with their former friends and family?" If so, it might be possible to gain more information from those on the outside. That was his hope in asking, but Thelma's answer didn't surprise him.

"They're not allowed to see them again, unless Ethan sends them on the Errand of God."

"I take it the Errand of God isn't just getting supplies."

"No, the Spiritual Guides get all the supplies. Right after a convert is baptized, he's sent to warn his family that they're risking God's wrath by rejecting the truth. That's the Errand of God."

Sounded more like Ethan's errand. The more people he converted, the more it would increase his power and enrich his coffers. "Otherwise, they sacrifice all association with their friends and family?"

"Yep."

"And you think that's okay?"

"Not exactly okay, but I can understand why they do it. Ethan says Covenanters are *in* the world but not *of* the world. They offer spiritual peace and prosperity, and you can't do that if you're always looking at the person you used to be before being born again."

So, like any good cult leader, Ethan made the most of isolation and alienation. *Very convenient.* "I see."

A noise by the entrance distracted Thelma. A woman and two middle-grade boys had come in. "I'd better get to work," she said. "It was great chatting with you. We're happy to have new folks in town."

"I'm sure you'll be seeing a lot more of us," Rachel said. "Breakfast was delicious."

"I'm glad." Taking their empty plates, she paused by the door on her way to the kitchen. "I'll be right with you folks," Nate heard her say. Abby followed her grandmother but returned a moment later with a sheet of paper she'd taken from a stack at the register. She thrust it at him, then stood resolutely beside the table as if she could communicate her thoughts simply by glaring at them.

Nate glanced at the sheet. It was a Missing flyer for the girl Thelma had been telling them about—Courtney Sinclair.

"Do you know where Courtney might be?" Rachel asked.

Shaking her head, the child made several darting hand signals.

"I'm sorry…I don't sign."

She made the same signals again, more slowly this time, then hurried off.

The flyer had a picture of a girl that reminded Nate of the character Lily on *The Munsters*. "What do you suppose that was all about?"

Rachel shrugged, so he took the flyer and tossed twenty dollars on the table to cover the bill plus a tip.

Thelma was busy seating her new patrons as they started across the restaurant, but a grizzled Indian with bowed legs and a black cowboy hat stood in the kitchen doorway, watching.

Rachel must have assumed he was Chaske, because she paused the moment she spotted him and mimicked the child's motions. "What does this mean?"

"Bad people," he answered, and turned away.

8

Bartholomew took one look at Ethan and quickly clasped his arm, then turned him around. His hair was mussed, his pupils dilated, and he smelled as though he'd walked out of a massage parlor. Ethan was doing too many drugs. Normally, Bartholomew didn't mind. He believed in freedom of choice and expression as much as Ethan did and wasn't opposed to running the compound when Ethan was indisposed. But Ethan needed to be coherent in times of trouble, and that meant now.

"You're not well, Holy One," he said when Ethan tried to yank his arm away.

"Didn't you hear? Courtney's mother is at the gate."

"I know." Bartholomew encouraged him to return to the Enlightenment Hall, but Ethan tried to shake him off again.

"I need to tell that bitch to get lost!"

"I doubt she'd react favorably to that. But don't worry. I'll handle it."

"What will you tell her?"

When Ethan stumbled over his own feet, Bartholomew had to keep him from falling facefirst in the dirt. "I'll tell her what we agreed to say."

They finally reached the Enlightenment Hall and walked through the front doors. "What was that?"

"You'll remember when you can think straight."

Sister Maxine stood in the doorway to the kitchen. "Is everything okay?"

Bart waved her away and led Ethan toward the stairs. He didn't want her or anyone else to see the Holy One in such a state. Despite his open acceptance of drug use, he had an image to uphold. He could not appear to be letting it get the best of him. "It's fine. Go back to your dishes."

"Maybe you should invite her in." Ethan was still talking about Mrs. Sinclair. "Maybe if we give her an audience, we can convince her Courtney was never here."

"No." Bart wasn't willing to even consider it.

Ethan's voice dropped to a whisper. "We could take her to the pit, teach her to mind her own business."

The pit was used for their most sacred, and secret, rituals. There was one key to the heavy metal door; Ethan held it. Only the Brethren, their wives and select Covenant members knew what went on there, and they'd all taken an oath not to divulge the smallest detail. It was part of the Covenant of Brotherly Love. So far, they'd been able to maintain absolute secrecy. Each person knew what would happen if he or she talked. But a greater deterrent than the threat of harm was the fact that they were all involved. Telling would incriminate the whistle-blower as much as the rest.

"That would just make the problem bigger," he said, and helped Ethan up the stairs.

"She won't leave us alone. She'll keep coming."

"No, she won't." Hoping to distract him, Bart changed the subject. "I'm afraid this isn't any happier news, but I received notice from the investigator we hired a few weeks ago that Martha's suing the church."

Ethan stumbled again. "*What?* Where's she getting the money to do that?"

Bart stabilized him until he could recover his balance. "Who knows? Donations, maybe. Or she's made friends with some sympathetic and overzealous lawyer. She's got the whole outside world feeling sorry for her."

At last they reached the landing. "You told me you were going to bring her back!"

"I am."

"When?"

"As soon as I can."

Ethan seemed to lose direction until Bart gently guided him toward his room. "What does she hope to gain?"

"The return of her property."

They hesitated outside the door to the suite where they each had a room. "She deserves to lose the small amount she gave up when she joined us," Ethan said. "She's the one who broke her covenants. She's the one who disobeyed. That whore's possessed by demons."

"When we get her back, you can cast them out." The idea of an exorcism excited Bart. He loved watching Ethan in action. It was a sight to behold. And, as the only woman who'd ever defied them and lived to tell about it, Martha was the perfect candidate for this painful and degrading process. It galled Bart to think she was in the outside world, walking around, saying anything she wanted, after the effort they'd exerted to keep their actions, thoughts and practices to themselves. Eighty percent of the compound didn't know as much as she did. Besides taking the Covenant, she'd participated in some of the rituals in the pit.

Bart lowered his voice to a whisper. "You should know that several of the Brethren disagree with bringing her back here."

"Who cares? I'm the only one who matters."

Bart swung the door wide. Fortunately, the women were dressed and leaving. He waited until they were gone to continue. "You and I know that. But they might make trouble. And we can't risk a division. Internal strife leads to self-destruction."

"What do they expect me to do?"

"Nothing." Bart pushed Ethan down onto the bed. "They prefer to let the scandal die."

"The only way it will die is if she dies with it. What we've built is too good to allow Satan to destroy it. We'll use the minds and hands God gave us to protect His work."

"Of course you're right, Holy One. I'll see that it happens."

Ethan had been whispering, too, but in his current state his whisper was loud enough that anyone within ten feet could hear. Sister Maxine was around. As a frequent visitor to the pit, she was almost as trustworthy as Bart, but this wasn't something Bart wanted *anyone* to hear. Not yet.

Searching for the dope that was all too tempting for Ethan, he went through the dresser. When he found it, he shoved it in his pocket.

"What are you doing?" Ethan cried. "Why are you taking that?"

"So you can sober up. When your mind's clear, we'll call another meeting with the Brethren. They need to feel included. They're getting upset thinking you've gone rogue."

"*I'm* the Holy One. This is *my* church. I can do whatever I want."

"We have to at least pretend to listen to their opinions. You're the one who made them Guides, granted them a voice."

"Half of them would've left if not for that."

"And now we've got to consider their input, that's all I'm saying. We'll enlist their help and then we won't have to worry about internal problems. About unity. We need unity more than ever."

Ethan shook his head. "But we won't be able to convince them to act. They're too scared."

"Now that she's filed a suit, things will be different. This will rekindle their anger. They can't afford to be dragged into court any more than we can."

Ethan fumbled with the bedding as he tried to cover himself. "Martha will ruin us if we don't do something."

Maybe Ethan was thinking more clearly than Bart had assumed. It was amazing what he could do, even when he was high. "We'll put a stop to her," Bart said.

"Wait…" Ethan's lucid moment gave way to confusion. "What will we tell everyone when she goes missing? The police will come here first."

"We'll say we haven't seen her. They can't do anything unless they can prove otherwise. The Lord will stand by us and so will our people."

"Right. We don't know what happened to her. Like Courtney," he said.

"Like Courtney," Bart repeated and hurried to the

gate, where he told the hysterical Mrs. Sinclair that she had to leave or he'd call the cops and have her forcibly removed.

Willcox seemed like a big city compared to Portal, but it was infinitesimally small by L.A. standards and looked like the set of a John Wayne movie. According to some trivia Nate had mentioned, the building designated as city hall had once been a train depot for the Southern Pacific Railroad. Not far away, on Railroad Avenue, sat several Old West-style buildings with plank walkways and wood overhangs. In this cluster of buildings Rachel saw the Willcox Cowboy Hall of Fame—A Tribute to Rex Allen, the Singing Cowboy. She supposed he'd either been born in Willcox or he'd died here—maybe both.

"Interesting place," she said as Nate slowed the truck to a crawl in accordance with the new speed limit.

"Warren Earp was shot in this town, outside a saloon," he responded.

"You mean, Wyatt Earp?"

"No, Warren—his little brother."

"How do you know?"

"Same place I learned the history of city hall. I saw it on the official Web page for Willcox when I was trying to figure out where we'd stay."

She gazed around, noting the Chiricahua Mountains in the distance, the farms in between and the heavy ranching influence. "Not that I'm criticizing, but I wouldn't have minded staying here. It would've been better than a trailer with an outhouse. It doesn't even seem as hot."

"It's not. This is high desert—about four thousand feet."

"I like it."

"What's not to like? Willcox is home to the world's largest hothouse tomato grower." He winked at her. "Now *that's* something."

She frowned. "Smart-ass."

"Hey, I have nothing against tomatoes," he said with a laugh.

"I'm more interested in these small, clean-looking motels." She indicated a mom-and-pop motel with about twelve units. "Why don't I stay here until you infiltrate the cult? You can send for me when you're ready."

"Nice try." He motioned to a much more modern building than the ones hunched together on Railroad Avenue. "There's an AutoZone. Let's stop and get some coolant, see if the clerk's ever heard of Martha Wilson."

Normally, Rachel would've laughed at the notion of pulling into some business and asking about a citizen without knowing of a prior connection. But in a town this size, it was entirely possible that word of Martha and her claims had circulated widely enough that they might succeed with a random inquiry.

Bracing as they rolled over a speed bump, she climbed out as soon as Nate cut the engine. "So what are we going with here?" She kept her voice low as they met near the entrance. "Newspaper reporter? Husband and wife out to photograph nature? Or what?"

"Curious people passing through should work. If not, make up something that seems to fit."

"God, I love my job," she muttered but she wasn't entirely serious. She loved the money and the freedom it would eventually afford her. And she loved putting bad guys away. It made her feel that what she did was worthwhile. In this case, she even loved the idea of taking an ax to her father's "you will do as I say or go to hell" type of religion. But she did not like suffering the heat of an Arizona summer while fighting the mixed emotions she felt whenever she looked at her boss. The combination made her irritable.

An electronic squawk announced their entrance. Hefting a body that was at least a hundred pounds overweight from a stool, the guy behind the counter waited to assist them. With a buzz cut and a face as full as a baby's, he looked young—maybe eighteen or nineteen.

Rachel thought he might be the only man in town, besides Nate, who wasn't wearing a cowboy hat and Wranglers. "Hello."

The clerk smoothed the front of the Led Zeppelin T-shirt that hung over his black pants. "Can I help you?"

Nate strode down the aisles, searching for the coolant while she approached the register. "Our air conditioner went out on us. We need some coolant."

"Aisle five." He spoke up so Nate could hear and pointed. "Right over there."

While Nate followed the clerk's directions, Rachel stood where she was. "How long have you lived in Willcox?" she asked, as if merely striking up a conversation.

"I was born here."

"Nice place."

"Thanks."

Someone older might've asked if she was visiting or

what had brought her to town. This boy, who seemed very shy, gave her nothing to work with, so she forged ahead on her own. "I hear there's a strange cult in the area."

"*This* area?"

"In Paradise."

"Oh, you must be talking about the Covenanters."

"I think that's the name. You don't know anything about them, do you?"

He smoothed his shirt again—apparently a nervous habit. "Not really. I've never even met one."

"How would you know if you had or not?" she asked.

"Most of 'em have a *C* on their foreheads. With a little mark in the middle."

"A tattoo?"

"I guess."

"Really! On their foreheads."

"Right in the middle." He indicated the spot between his own eyes.

"That would certainly make someone stand out," she said with a laugh.

"Yeah, I'd like to see it."

She leaned on the counter. "Why not go there?"

He rearranged a display of key rings and some deodorizers. "Paradise isn't that close. It's about an hour and a half. And from what I've been told, they're not very friendly. There's a woman running around who says they tried to stone her." He lowered his voice. "*To death.*"

"That's what I've heard. That's actually why I'm here. I'm this close—" she formed an inch with her fingers "—to getting my doctorate in psychology. I'm doing my thesis on cult behavior. You don't know where I could find this woman, do you? I'd love to interview her."

"I'm pretty sure she lives here in Willcox now. There was an article in the paper about her not too long ago. But I don't know exactly where she is." He straightened his shirt again. "There've been lots of people asking about her, though. I heard someone talking to the gas station attendant just the other day."

"Someone?"

"A man. I'd never seen him before."

Who else was looking for Martha? And why? "What did the gas attendant say?"

"He didn't know where to find her, either."

"Where do you think she *might* be?"

"You're asking *me?*" He pressed a hand to his chest, which gave like a sponge beneath the pressure.

"I figure you grew up here. Surely you know who's privy to town gossip and who isn't."

"Not really. But—" he shrugged "—maybe the cops do."

That was possible. Maybe even likely. But Rachel preferred not to involve the local police, who'd be all too interested in finding out why she and Nate were searching for Martha. "Right. Thanks."

She turned to see if Nate was ready to go and, suddenly, the obvious occurred to her. The clerk had mentioned a newspaper article, hadn't he? If the police knew Martha's whereabouts, it was possible the local press did, too. The press usually kept close tabs on such sensational cases. And that wouldn't be too hard in a town this small.

"What about the local newspaper?" she asked.

"What about it?"

"Do they have offices here in town?"

"Yep." He gestured to the west. "Just down the street."

Nate, who'd been listening, came over with the coolant and the clerk rang it up.

Rachel eyed the bag as they walked out of the store. "You sure that's all you need to fix the air-conditioning? What about tools?"

"I've got tools. You don't own a badass truck like mine and not have tools."

"The question is—do you know how to use them?"

He scowled and shook his head as if he was disappointed in her. "Babe...I can do anything, remember?"

She rolled her eyes. Anything but fall in love.

According to Jay Buckman, the editor they met at the newspaper office, a single woman in her early thirties named Laura Thompson had written the article on Martha Wilson. Although she occasionally submitted pieces to the paper, mainly to see her name in print, she worked at the drugstore across the street. Fortunately, they happened to catch her during her lunch break. They talked to her standing outside the store. She promptly gave them Martha Wilson's address as soon as Nate mentioned his "sister's" imaginary thesis.

The fact that Laura kept giggling and gazing up at Nate, eyes wide, told Rachel the woman's willingness to accommodate them had a great deal to do with Nate's appearance and charm. But Ethan was handsome, too. What would she do if the Holy One ever came to call? The Auto Zone clerk had said that some-one was asking after Martha at the gas station a few days earlier. Rachel couldn't imagine it'd be a good thing if the Covenanters had Martha's address....

"Don't tell anyone where you got the information," the would-be journalist added as they left, but fear of exposing someone to danger was definitely a lesser concern than impressing Nate.

"So much for protecting a source," Rachel said. She'd noticed her demotion from "wife" to "sister," but after asking Nate to do this undercover assignment as brother and sister, she couldn't complain, even if it did seem rather convenient in the face of Ms. Thompson's adoration.

"Don't be too hard on her," he said. "This is a small town. The mentality is different. And it's a weekly paper with a volunteer staff. She doesn't know the meaning of privacy—or danger. What can you expect?"

"Is a little common sense too much to ask? I mean, you heard the clerk. We're not the only ones looking for Martha. It wouldn't be any fun for Laura to learn that Martha got hurt as a result of *her* loose lips."

He twirled his keys around the ring. "You sure Laura Thompson's loose lips is all that's bugging you?"

Hearing the hint of suggestion in his voice, she stopped and narrowed her eyes. "What else could it be?"

"I don't think one of us slept very well last night."

"I can't imagine why." She smiled sweetly. "It was so nice and cool in that tin can you call a trailer."

"You could've left your bedroom door open."

"That wouldn't have helped."

"It helped me."

She had no response to that. Shooting him her best glare, she donned her sunglasses. As long as they were together, it was going to be too hot no matter where they were.

9

They found Martha Wilson's address easily enough; she lived in an apartment at the edge of town. But Martha didn't come to the door when they knocked. Nate was about to break in when Rachel caught the back of his shirt and called out, "Martha? My name's Rachel Jessop. I'm an ex-cop who works for a private security company, and I'd like to see what I can do to help you get your son back. Will you please let me in so we can talk?"

"Why don't you just tell her who we really are?" Nate whispered sarcastically, but Rachel didn't have time to reply. The door opened the width of the safety chain, which was still in place, and the dove-gray eyes of a small woman stared out at her. Rachel knew she was looking at Martha because of the brand on her forehead.

"Who did you say you were?" she asked.

Rachel had had a feeling Martha was home, and she'd been right. "I'm Rachel Jessop," she repeated. "I've been hired to find out what's going on with the Covenanters, and I need to ask you some questions."

The door closed and they heard a chain slide. Then Martha poked her head out and looked both ways. When she saw Nate, she started.

"It's okay," Rachel told her. "This is my colleague. He's trying to help, too."

"I'm sure they're looking for me. I—I can't take the chance that you're lying."

While Rachel was contemplating whether or not to tell her that there were indeed people in Willcox searching for her, Martha began to close the door. "They tried to kill me," she murmured. "They want me dead."

Nate blocked the door with his foot. "If *we* wanted you dead, you'd already be dead."

Rachel sent him a dirty look and hurried to smooth over his rough edges. "We know Ethan's background, Ms. Wilson. We have copies of letters he once wrote to Charles Manson. We're aware that he's been...violent. We agree with you that he's dangerous, that he has to be stopped."

"Charles Manson?" she echoed weakly. "The Helter Skelter Charles Manson?"

"One and the same."

She fingered the *C* on her forehead. "Ethan never mentioned Charles Manson, not that I ever heard."

"It's been ten years since those letters. By the time you met him, he'd probably distanced himself from that earlier behavior."

The hesitation that followed made Rachel nervous that they'd be refused entry, but as Martha stared down at Nathan's foot, she seemed to realize he could've forced his way in but hadn't.

Thank God for small favors. Commando style wasn't exactly the best approach to enlisting a woman's help.

"Can you show me any ID?" she asked.

"Not ID that tells you who we really are," Rachel said. "We're undercover."

"So...wait. You're cops?"

"We're from the private sector but we fulfill basically the same function."

Her expression revealed a conflict between her desire to believe them and the memory of recent betrayal.

"If you want to get your husband and son out of Paradise, we might be your only chance," Nate said.

"I know you're frightened, but you've got to trust us," Rachel added.

Tears glistened in Martha's eyes as she stepped back and waved them in.

The apartment was a mess and so was Martha Wilson. Her uncombed hair and wrinkled clothing indicated she'd just rolled out of bed. The blinds were drawn tight, blocking the sunshine. Dishes cluttered the counters of the kitchen and spilled into the living room, some with food that had been left out so long it'd hardened.

Depression seemed to be taking deep root.

Trying to ignore the stench of rotting food and cigarette smoke, Rachel opened the blinds, cleared away some newspapers, as well as several bowls, which she stacked on the coffee table. Then she sat down on the sofa; Nate apparently preferred to stand. For all his rugged ways, he was meticulous about hygiene and probably repelled by the filth, but she knew he could deal with germs if he had to. He'd been through a lot worse when he was a SEAL. "Are you okay?" she asked Martha, and pulled him down beside her.

Martha shook her head. "No, I haven't been okay for a long time. But...how'd you find me? No one's supposed to know where I am." She gestured at the room around them. "This is some stranger's apartment, someone who lives in Minnesota during the summer. My attorney arranged for me to stay here. It's not even in my name."

"Willcox is a small town," Rachel started to say. "So it's not hard to—"

"If you're truly concerned about your safety, you need to move," Nate broke in.

"I can't move," she complained. "I have nowhere else to go. My—my husband turned on me. Just like the rest of them. Even my son—" her throat worked as she wrestled with her emotions "—even my son turned on me."

Rachel softened her voice. "I'm sure he didn't understand what he was doing."

"I want to see him," she whispered with desperate entreaty.

"We're hoping to make that happen."

Her eyes darted to Nate. "Who hired you?"

"Someone who's concerned about the situation," he replied. "We plan to infiltrate Ethan's cult and put a stop to any illegal activities, but in order to be successful, we'll need some help."

She reached for a pack of cigarettes and a lighter. "There's nothing I can do. I can't go anywhere near Paradise. I—I told you. They tried to kill me."

"We don't need you to take us there. We just need information. When was it that they tried to stone you?"

"Six weeks ago."

No wonder the bruises were gone. "You told the police you thought other people in the church were in danger."

"It's true. He's got weapons, explosives."

Rachel exchanged a look with Nate. "He does?"

"A whole cache."

"What are they for?"

"The Final Battle, when Satan's army comes against the people of God. He says that God's warned him to be prepared and that we must be valiant in resisting evil."

"Where does he keep the weapons?"

"Locked up. In an old shed."

"Does everyone know about it?"

"Yes. There are…rituals that are essentially drills on how to respond to an outside threat."

Ethan was serious about protecting what he'd built.

"What else can you tell us?" Nate asked. "Who or what should we watch out for? How can we gain Ethan's trust?"

"That takes time." She tried to light her cigarette, but her hand shook too badly.

Taking the lighter, Nate held it for her. "Time is the problem," he told her. "That's why we need you. Do you know anyone on the inside who might be able to get us in, to act as a sponsor of sorts?"

Smoke curled out of her mouth as Nate closed the lighter with a snap. "No one I could contact," she said. "All my former friends would be terrified to hear from me. Even if I could reach them, no one wants to get on Ethan's bad side."

"What will happen if they do?" Nate asked.

"They'll be punished."

"Stoned?"

She studied her cigarette. "He'll take away little privileges at first."

As inconspicuously as possible, Rachel slid a plate

with a hard yellow substance that looked like egg yolk farther to the left, away from her foot. "Like?" She could tell Nate hadn't missed the movement, but then... he didn't miss anything.

"Like being put on restriction."

"Which means..."

"Being denied the opportunity to socialize with others, being denied contact with loved ones."

"That happened to you?"

She nodded. "I couldn't be with my son anymore. When I tried to fight that, I was told I couldn't have sex with my husband. But I fought that, too. So Ethan ordered me stoned."

Rachel grimaced. "Isn't that a bit harsh?"

"I'd been involved in the most sacred rituals, yet I'd dared to stand up to him." She touched the brand on her forehead again. "He couldn't tolerate it for fear others would do the same. He wanted to get rid of me, or he wouldn't have left me in the same tent with Todd. How long did he think I could deny my husband—or myself?"

"What started this string of punishments?" Nate asked.

She took another drag. "I thought James was too young to fast. Ethan demands that everyone go without eating for twenty-four hours once a week. To show that we can master our bodies. But my son's only two years old. I could see that he wasn't growing like he should, so I began slipping him food on fast days. Rosie Lester, someone in my tent, caught me, so he took away some of my privileges."

"How could he keep your son from you? Weren't you living with your husband and son?"

"Each tent houses about twenty people, equal numbers of men and women, all married couples, unless someone's been widowed. The children are in a nearby tent, with a caregiver who stays there during the night. My son was removed from the tent next door and placed in another one across the compound."

"And you still made an effort to see him."

"Yes, but the women in the other tent wouldn't allow it. They didn't want to get into trouble. My husband could visit James in the evenings and on weekends, but I couldn't. When I tried, and wouldn't quit trying, they told Ethan." She grimaced. "The women are especially watchful. They get small rewards for helping Ethan and they'll do anything to gain his favor. They're all hoping to become the Vessel—the one to bear him a son."

At this, Rachel's fingernails curved into her palms. "Even the ones with husbands?"

Martha held her cigarette to her lips. "It's a privilege," she said through the smoke. "Like the Immaculate Conception."

Only there wouldn't be an immaculate conception. Rachel was quite sure this pregnancy would be accomplished the old-fashioned way.

Leaning forward, Nate rested his elbows on his knees. "How did he find out that you had sex with your husband? Did you confess?"

"No, someone told. I thought the others were asleep. We were very careful not to make any noise. But…"

Nate's eyebrows shot up. "There's no privacy?"

"None. A Covenanter is never alone. We believe that only those who have reason to be ashamed need to hide what they do."

Rachel tried to mask her own horrified reaction. "What does the brand signify?"

"That I've taken the Covenant of Brotherly Love."

"Which is…"

"A promise to live closer to God. It prepares you for rituals and worship the others cannot partake of."

"What kind of rituals?"

She grew morose. "I can't say. They're sacred. Or, at least, I thought they were at one time." She rubbed her face. "I don't know anymore."

"What if someone in the commune is unwilling or unready to accept the Covenant of Brotherly Love?" Rachel asked. "Can they still be part of the group?"

"Of course. For as long as they like. They're learning and progressing toward that ideal. You should never take the Covenant until you're ready. Ethan says it's too sacred to do it lightly. Even if you decide you are ready, you first apply to the Spiritual Guides and get their approval."

"They're the governing body."

"Sort of, although Ethan has the most say."

"How does the application process work?"

She put out her cigarette in a slice of cold pizza and managed to light another one. "You go in for an interview. They bring it before the Lord. Then they vote."

"What if they turn you down?" Nate asked.

"You keep trying to purify your soul, hoping you'll be accepted at some point."

Rachel cleared her throat. "Sounds as if everyone's very serious about it."

"They are. They have to be. If you take the Covenant and aren't able to live up to it, the consequences are dire. That's what this little line signifies." She pointed to the small dash that cut through the *C* on her forehead. "If you break the oath of secrecy or your promise to keep the faith, you accept death as the punishment. Ethan claimed I broke the Covenant. That's why he felt justified in having me stoned. That's why the others went along with it."

Rachel wanted to say, *You've got to be kidding,* but she bit her tongue. From all indications, this woman had taken the covenant of her own free will, so she must've agreed with the commune's practices at that time, even if she'd become disenchanted since.

Fortunately, Nate spoke up, giving Rachel a chance to control her reactions. "Does sex have anything to do with these rituals?"

"Sex is the ultimate spiritual manifestation, a celebration of life and the procreative power. But that power is not to be abused."

"Is that a yes?"

She didn't respond.

"That's a yes," he said.

Apparently, Ethan got to designate how the procreative power was used.

"What about any babies that might be conceived?" Rachel asked.

"Babies are considered a gift from God. You raise that child with your husband and with the rest of your group."

Ethan had thought of everything....

"What happened after Ethan learned you had sex with your husband?" Nate asked. "How did he pronounce his punishments?"

"Three of the Brethren showed up at the cheese factory where I worked and told me they were going to hold a council, which is like a…a trial. But my council didn't last long. After they brought the accusations against me, they turned me over to Ethan to see if he could gather proof of…of my crime. At that point, he took me to his room."

"He doesn't sleep in a tent?"

"No, he has a whole wing in the Enlightenment Hall. Sometimes he invites members to stay with him. Or he visits various tents, spending one or two nights in each."

"Availing himself of other men's wives?"

"If that family is lucky and he's willing to spill his holy seed into the female vessels prepared for him." She spoke dully, as if by rote.

"So there could be more than one Vessel."

"Lesser vessels. We're still waiting for him to name the one who'll be mother to the whole church and bear the son he'll call his heir."

To Rachel, it sounded as if the families were merely concubines for Ethan. He allowed the other men to co-exist with him, probably because he couldn't support so many women and children. He needed the men to work, if nothing else. "You said he was going to 'gather proof' that you'd had sex with your husband. How did he plan to do that in his room? He already had a witness or he wouldn't know about it."

Her jaw hardened. "He took me to his private rooms for 'prayer.' Only…"

"Only…" Rachel watched Martha carefully, try-ing to figure out who'd she'd been then and who she was now. She'd actively participated in the cult's sexual practices. That was clear. But it was just as clear that she'd thought she was living a "higher law" when she did.

"He did more than pray. He tied me down. Then he...he did some...other stuff."

"Can you tell us what?" Rachel asked.

She stared at her smoldering cigarette. "No. It was too painful. I—I can't even think about it. I tried to confess so he'd stop, but it didn't help."

Was Ethan sadistic? Or just ruthless in administering "punishment"?

Nate took over the questioning. "What happened next?"

"He decreed that I'd have to wear a chastity belt and be shunned until I could prove myself worthy by obeying God's commandments." Tears slipped down her cheeks. "But I couldn't bear a punishment like that. I knew then that he hated me, that he'd keep me in that belt forever, which meant I'd have to live as an outcast. I wouldn't be able to participate in the rituals, couldn't bear any more children. In a commune where a woman's main purpose is to give pleasure and raise up seed unto the Lord, that would be worse than death."

"So you refused," Rachel said.

"That's right. I thought my husband would support me, that we'd leave. Especially once I told him what Ethan did to me, how badly he hurt me and the joy he got out of it. But..." Her hand was shaking again when she lifted the cigarette to her lips. "But Todd accused me of lying to pull him away from the truth. He told me I was speaking with the voice of Satan. And when Ethan and the Guides came for me and dragged me out into the public square, it was Todd who threw the first stone. Ethan even had my s-son join in."

Of course, such a young child wouldn't realize that throwing rocks at Mommy was anything more than a game. But the image Martha's words created brought bile to the back of Rachel's throat. What had her husband been thinking? "Have you talked to Todd since?"

"No."

"I'm guessing he eventually helped you or...how'd you escape?"

"I—I started picking up rocks and throwing them back. I was hurting, throwing blindly. I had to defend myself. That was all I could think. I could not let Ethan take my life, or take my son and my husband from me." Her cigarette dangled from her lips as she gazed past them, obviously experiencing the stoning again. "I accidentally hit Ethan. Then everyone panicked. They cried out that I'd attacked the Holy One and swarmed over to see if he was hurt. In the middle of the uproar, I felt a pair of hands yanking me away, sheltering me behind a body no bigger than my own. I have a feeling it was Sarah Myers, a widow from my tent, who's a burn victim and often ignored by the men because of her scars. While Ethan was tending to his daughter and calling for Dominic, the closest thing we—*they*—" she corrected as if still not quite sure that she didn't belong "—have to a doctor, Sarah or whoever it was shoved me toward the fence, and I ran and ran and ran. I don't know how I got through the gate. I just know I stumbled in front of a car on the first road I encountered, and an older gentleman and his wife picked me up in their RV." She took another long drag. "It was freak luck," she finished. "If that couple hadn't been there, Ethan would've come after me. And I wouldn't be around today."

"I'm sorry," Rachel said. As misguided as Martha

had been to get involved with such a group, no one deserved to be treated so cruelly.

"What made you join the Covenanters in the first place?" Nate asked.

Martha continued to smoke without answering, but Rachel could tell she was considering the question. It was one she'd no doubt asked herself many times. Apparently, she was still searching for the answer. "I think it started out as awe—Ethan moved me when he spoke, filled me with rapture. And then it was fear. If Todd and I went with him and the others, we wouldn't have to be responsible for ourselves anymore. Todd had just lost his job, and he had no idea what he was going to do. What I was earning wouldn't support us. With the Covenanters, we'd have a guaranteed home, food, friends. Even salvation. I wanted to live a better life than what we'd known."

"You didn't mind sleeping with other men during the rituals?"

"Mind? I considered it a spiritual experience to connect on such a primal level with so many. It made us one as a group. That's powerful."

And perfect for the spread of infectious disease, Rachel thought, but remained silent as Nate spoke.

"What if you were caught having sex with someone other than your husband outside of a religious ritual?"

"That's out of bounds. You'd be punished."

"Like you were punished."

She tapped the ash from her cigarette onto the floor. "You'd be restricted and then, if you wouldn't quit, shunned."

Nate rubbed his right fist in an absent manner, his body language speaking volumes beyond what he actually said. "Three weeks ago, a girl from the Portal area went missing. Courtney Sinclair. Are you familiar with her?"

"No."

"You're sure? She was only seventeen." He pulled out the flyer they'd been given at the restaurant. "This is her."

Martha accepted the flyer with a frown. "I don't recognize her. Is there a reason I should?"

"She had some contact with the Covenanters before she disappeared."

"She wasn't around when I was there."

"This is more recent." Nate took back the flyer. "Is it conceivable that Ethan might have abducted her?"

"Anything's possible with Ethan."

"So how do we get in and get accepted?" Rachel asked.

Martha's cigarette had burned down to the filter. She stubbed it out in the same pizza she'd used before. "You'll have to go to an Introduction Meeting like I did, I guess."

"Where are these Introduction Meetings?"

"At the compound."

Rachel scooted forward. "When are they held?"

"It depends on what Ethan has planned that particular week. What kind of mood he's in. The Covenanters' entire world revolves around him and the other Spiritual Guides."

"They must have some way of alerting the public when they hold their meetings," Rachel said.

"There is. They post notices at various places."

"Where?"

She seemed too tired to think, almost too tired to

care. "I don't know. I never did the posting. I couldn't leave the compound. Only the Spiritual Guides can enter Satan's domain and be allowed to return. Only they are deemed strong enough. Anyone else would be contaminated."

According to her own words, she was now living in Satan's domain. "We have to wait until Ethan posts a notice?" Rachel asked. "A lot could happen before then. We're worried for this girl. And we want to help your son. Please think. There's got to be another way."

"There's not. You have to go to a meeting—" Her head snapped up. "Wait. There's a bulletin board at the Museum of Natural History in Portal."

During the few times Rachel had passed through town, she hadn't seen any museum. "In *Portal?*"

"It's up the canyon a bit. I heard Sister Maxine talking about it. Her husband works on the flyers and distributes them. He used to be in marketing. If there's a meeting coming up, the information might be posted there."

"How do they appeal to nonmembers?" Nate asked.

Martha's expression grew sad. "They promise to love you no matter what. They say, 'The great Alpha and Omega opens his arms and his heart to you.' But it's a lie."

"Aren't they supposed to mean God when they refer to the great Alpha and Omega?" Nate wanted to know.

"Once you join, you're taught that Ethan *is* God. 'By me or my messengers, it is the same.'"

Rachel and Nate exchanged concerned glances. Ethan held the ultimate power, just as they'd suspected. "We'll check at the museum, see what we can come up with," she said.

Martha stood and reached out for her, then clung to her hand. "If you get in, if you see James, please tell him…" She fell silent.

How could a mother even begin to explain a situation like this to a child so young? Rachel wondered.

"Tell him Mommy loves him."

That was about all that could be said, all he might understand. "We will," Rachel promised. Then they showed themselves out.

When they got to the truck, Nate slid behind the wheel but didn't start the engine. Instead, he turned to face her.

"You realize what the situation could be like if we infiltrate this group," he said.

"I do."

He squinted against the glare bouncing off the buildings in front of them. "It could be worse than anything either of us has ever faced. Could be a *lot* worse." He finally started the engine. Then he pinned her with a frank stare. "Especially for you."

Rachel knew what he meant. She'd read or heard about the most notorious cult leaders, was fully aware of the atrocities they'd committed. She now believed Ethan was as twisted as any of them and that he was particularly focused on women.

"Milt knew, didn't he?" she said.

Nate didn't answer, but that muscle flexed in his cheek, the one that flexed whenever he was unhappy.

"That's why he sent us down here as a married couple," she went on. "He'd found out enough about Paradise to know we'd have to be married to take the Covenant of Brotherly Love. And only if we do *that* will we learn any of the secrets that could bring Ethan down."

"You don't have to go through with this," Nate said. "I can drive you to Phoenix, put you on a plane and finish this myself."

But then he'd have much less chance of infiltrating the group, of finding Courtney Sinclair....

Blowing out a sigh, Rachel looked up at the apartment they'd just left. The blinds had been drawn again. Behind those blinds was a woman who'd nearly been killed by Ethan because she'd wanted to see her son and sleep with her husband. Rachel felt obliged to help Martha get James back. She also felt obliged to find Courtney and stop Ethan. He was drunk on power and running unchecked, which meant a lot of people could be hurt. And what about Ethan's stash of weapons?

But if she joined the Covenanters, she'd be treated like the other women in the commune, would be expected to make the same sacrifices. If she didn't, she and Nate might never gain the trust necessary to be effective.

"This is the question we face every time we go undercover, isn't it?" she said.

He jammed a hand through his hair. "What question is that?"

"How far are we willing to go to make it seem real?"

"Infiltrating the Covenanters could compromise your safety. I say you go home."

Somehow she knew he'd suggest that. But every job "compromised her safety." She wouldn't let Ethan scare her away. Neither would she let him continue to use religion to manipulate others. "His days as Alpha and Omega are numbered. I'm staying."

"Rachel—"

"You need me on this one, Nate," she interrupted. And for the first time since she'd received this assignment, she was willing to admit she needed him, too.

10

Nate had had a bad feeling about this assignment from the beginning. After hearing what Martha had to say, he knew why. He wouldn't have brought Rachel into this volatile a situation had he known. Milt must've guessed as much or he would've been more forthcoming.

The fact that Milt would hold out on him made Nate angry, but it shouldn't have surprised him. Milt generally had a good reason for what he did, but that didn't mean Nate always approved of it.

Still, Ethan had to be stopped, and that wasn't going to happen without significant effort *and* risk. It made no sense to leave two hundred people—virtually everyone in Paradise—in danger in order to protect one woman. He and Rachel had come this far. They had to finish. But he'd have to be more diligent than ever before, or this assignment could go terribly wrong.

As they approached a fast-food joint only a few blocks from Martha's apartment, Rachel pointed at it. "You want to grab lunch?" Although she'd mentioned lunch when she spoke to the Auto Zone clerk, they hadn't yet visited a restaurant in Willcox. They'd eaten a late breakfast, which made this meal late, too.

"Might as well," he said. "We need to send a quick

report to Milt, let him know what's going on. And while we're on the Internet, I'd like to check Mapquest to get directions to the museum. I'm sure we'll have a better connection here than at the café in Portal."

"Have you ever looked up the Covenanters on Google?" she asked as he pulled in.

"I did. The only thing that I got was information on the Scottish Covenanters of the seventeenth century."

"Who were…what? Another group of religious zealots?"

He parked, climbed out and waited until she came around to meet him. "Not really zealots." He held the door for her. "I just skimmed the information to find out if their theories and practices had any relation to Ethan's group. From what I read, they formed a fairly important movement that was one of the precursors of Presbyterianism, but I don't think there's any similarity in theory or practice."

She chose a table in the far corner and he sent an e-mail to Milt, telling him they'd arrived and were already at work. Then, while Rachel ordered, he began searching for "Natural History Museum, Arizona." A whole page of links appeared, but most were for a museum in Mesa, which wasn't anywhere close to Portal.

"Wow, there are a lot of natural history museums." Rachel was back, holding the receipt for their food. Instead of sitting down, she leaned over his shoulder so she could see the screen.

"Could be the one we want is named something slightly different." He added "Portal" and "Southeastern Arizona" to the keywords but that didn't help.

"This isn't related to the museum, but what do you get when you search for Paradise?" Rachel asked.

"A homemade Web site giving a few paragraphs of information on the town and a couple of pictures. Nothing about the Covenanters or Ethan. I get the impression the site predates him by a few years and hasn't been updated."

"Maybe the museum is closer to Rodeo," she mused.

The pimply faced boy behind the counter called out a number that must've corresponded to their order because Rachel headed back.

Nate had found what he was looking for by the time she returned with their food. "I got it," he said. "They call it the Southwest Research Station."

She put the tray on the table. "So...is there an Introduction Meeting in Paradise in the near future?"

"With any luck, we'll soon find out." He closed his laptop and had just picked up his sandwich when Laura Thompson came in. She scanned the restaurant, spotted them and hurried over.

"I guessed that was your truck in the lot."

Nate put his lunch down. "You were looking for *us?*"

"Yes. I—I thought you should know you're not the only people asking about Martha Wilson."

"We're not?" Rachel said.

She didn't even glance at Rachel. "Just after you left, another guy came by, asking where he could find her. Isn't that *weird?*"

It *was* weird. But thanks to what they'd gleaned from the Auto Zone clerk, not really surprising. Apparently, there'd been people asking about her all over town. "Did he say who he was?"

"He said his name was Simon Green. He told me he'd read my article in the paper and wanted to know if I could put him in touch with her."

Nate sensed Rachel's alarm but didn't react to it. "Did he give a reason?"

"He said he feels bad about her situation and wants to help."

The concern on Rachel's face might've revealed that they had more than a passing interest in Martha but, fortunately, Laura wasn't looking at Rachel. "And did you tell him where he could find her?"

"No. I asked for his card and said I'd pass it on if I happened to see her again. When he made up some lame excuse about why he couldn't give it to me, I got suspicious." She leaned toward their table with a conspirator's glint in her eyes. "And you know what else?"

Nate waited for her to go on.

"He was driving a rental car," she said. "Why would anyone who lives in *this* area need a rental car? Around here, a car breaks down, we borrow from a friend or neighbor, you know?"

"Did you ask him where he was from?" Nate asked.

"No, I let him go. But he said he'd check back with me in a few days, so I might see him again."

Nate pictured Martha, miserable and defenseless, in that apartment. "Have you told the police about this?"

"Not yet. I was on my way to the station when I saw your truck."

She'd wanted to use what she knew to finagle a second conversation with him. Her motives were pretty transparent. But Nate wasn't interested in her romantically. "That's probably the best thing to do. They need to offer her some protection. Make sure you tell them that, too."

"Right." She hesitated long enough to let him know she was reluctant to end the conversation.

"Thanks for telling us," he said, hoping that would elicit a goodbye.

"You bet."

When she still didn't leave, Rachel jumped in. "If the Covenanters are trying to reclaim one of their own, it might make an interesting tidbit for my thesis," she said. "I think my brother owes you dinner since you've been nice enough to help me. What do you say, Nate?"

Responding swiftly, just in case Laura accepted before he could derail Rachel's suggestion, Nate forced a sheepish grin. "Come on, sis, you know I've always been a sucker for a gorgeous lady. But you also know I'm practically engaged. You're going to get me in trouble if you're not careful."

The hope that had flashed across Laura's face vanished. "Oh, I don't expect dinner or anything," she said with an awkward laugh. "I was just…trying to help. Thought you'd be interested."

"We were. Thanks again." He maintained the same appreciative but dismissive grin, and she finally moved out the door.

"'I think my brother owes you dinner'?" he repeated under his breath to Rachel.

She shrugged. "She obviously has the hots for you."

He cocked an eyebrow at her. "Stay out of my love life."

"Or…"

"Paybacks are a bitch."

She drank some of her shake. "What kind of pay-backs are we talking about?"

"For starters, you'll be the one sleeping on the floor tonight."

Once they arrived at the museum, the flyer was right there on a billboard, just as they'd hoped. It began with the heading Church of the Covenant. Beneath was a quote from Matthew 11:28. "Come unto me, all ye that labour and are heavy laden, and I will give you rest." A picture of the scenery surrounding Paradise, beautiful with the Chiricahua Mountains in the distance, came next, along with a promise of the joy to be found in living a Christ-centered life, "where every man is equal, every woman eagerly fulfills her role as a nurturer and children are brought up in love and industry."

"I have a problem with that 'every woman eagerly fulfills her role' crap. Who decides what her role will be?"

"Men, of course," Nate said. "As it should be."

She had to know he was teasing but she gave him a dirty look, anyway. He smiled and continued reading. "God is no respecter of persons. Why wait? Know God. Know Paradise." On the very bottom they found a list of meetings, one of which was being held the following night.

"I think we have our wish," Rachel breathed.

Nate nodded but his mind had already moved on to other concerns. They'd likely have to go in without weapons. And even if phones were permitted, there wouldn't be any cell service. Once they went in, they'd be on their own. Cut off from the rest of the world.

* * *

"What do you see?"

Nate was squinting at Paradise through a Sigma 50-500mm supertelephoto lens on a handheld Nikon D1. He had two shorter lenses in a pouch slung across his body. The gear would've cost the company a fortune if they'd had to purchase it. Fortunately, he had a buddy, a talented sports photographer, who owned several cameras.

"Nate?" Crouched beside him wearing sunglasses, a tank top, cutoffs and tennis shoes, Rachel also had a backpack, but hers was filled with water and snacks. It sat nearby, where she'd dropped it when they'd established their position on a plateau overlooking the compound. "Did you hear me?" she prompted when he didn't answer.

"I don't see a lot." He adjusted the bill of his cap for more shade. "The saloons are gone. I can tell you that much."

"*Saloons?*"

"On the Web, it said there used to be thirteen saloons."

"You mean, from when it was a mining town."

"Yep."

"I'm not surprised there were so many. People would have to be drunk 24/7 to want to live out here in the middle of nowhere," she muttered, reaching for the camera. "Especially before modern transportation, which would make it easier to get out."

Nudging her hand away, he brought the Nikon back up to his own eye. "No, you don't, sweetheart. Not yet. I don't even have it in focus yet." But a second later he had a perfect view. There was a ten-foot fence with razor wire on top enclosing the whole town. Not many of the early twentieth-century buildings remained. There was just one that still had a roof—the old post office. According to the Web site, that post office had been built around 1900 and was discontinued forty years later. Considering the mine had closed in 1907, Paradise had died a slow death.

"There we go…" he murmured.

"There we go, what?"

He handed her the camera. She put her sunglasses on top of her head, and he helped her hold the Nikon steady while she gazed through the lens. "Wow. Looks more like a prison than Paradise."

"Question is—are they trying to keep people in or out?"

"*In.* They don't have the saloons anymore, remember?"

She had a point. But it sounded as if they had weed, meth or other drugs. "According to Martha, they're not teetotalers," he said, and took back the camera to shoot a few pictures he hoped to enlarge later.

"They must live in those large white tents."

"There wouldn't be enough housing otherwise." He spotted a brown building behind a patch of trees. "They have some permanent construction. And it appears they're building more…" He got a picture of that, too.

"Can't be easy to drag lumber all the way up here."

"Or cheap."

"Hence the big tents." She squatted closer to him. "Can you see any of the people? I couldn't find a single soul."

Neither could Nate. There was no movement in Paradise. "Feels sort of deserted."

"It's late afternoon. Maybe they're inside, having a siesta."

Waves of heat bounced off the rocks all around. "Or some sort of prayer meeting in an air-conditioned building." Lowering the camera again, he pointed to the Chiricahuas, which rose from the desert directly across from them. "Maybe we should hike over to those hills, try to get some shots of the town from a different angle." Even if the second vantage point afforded them no new details about Paradise itself, it couldn't hurt to familiarize themselves with the land. Depending on how relations with the Covenanters went, that information could come in handy if they ever had to sneak out at night or slip away unnoticed—although how they'd get out of the compound except through the gate remained a mystery. That razor wire looked daunting.

Rachel stood and grabbed her backpack. "Sure, why not hike for the rest of the afternoon? It's only a hundred degrees out here."

Nate raised his eyebrows at her sarcasm. "We can go swimming later."

"In the nice swimming pool behind our trailer? Or at the resort?"

"What a smart-ass. I was thinking of the creek."

"Not *Cave* Creek."

"Why not?" He shrugged. "It runs year-round."

"It's *July,* which makes 'year-round' a matter of interpretation. The water barely covers the boulders."

He'd seen that for himself. They'd driven along the creek on their way out of Portal earlier. But he was so hot he would've been happy with a trickle. "It's water, isn't it? Are you done griping yet?"

"No," she snapped, but she didn't complain again.

"Wait up and give me a drink," he called. She'd gotten ahead of him while he'd been packing the camera equipment.

She came back but didn't bother handing him her Camelbak. She passed him the mouthpiece at the end of the long rubber tube.

He drank, then watched her drink from the same mouthpiece. Her skin, naturally golden to begin with, had tanned quite a bit since the beginning of summer. She spent a lot of time on the beach when she wasn't working. He doubted she had to worry about burning two months into summer. But this wasn't another hour on the beach in L.A. Anyone could fry out here. "Time to put on some more sunblock," he told her.

"I'll get it out for you if you want, but I'm fine."

"You haven't put any on since before we left the trailer."

"So?"

"You're not in California anymore." He slid the strap of her shirt off her shoulder. "You're burning."

"It'll fade by tomorrow."

"Put on some more sunblock or I'll put it on for you."

She yanked her strap back into place. "Excuse me, but I'll make that decision. I'm not a child."

"Then start acting like an adult." The heat was getting to them, making them both irritable. But Nate wasn't willing to let the issue go. "If you get burned, it could become a problem and might even interrupt this assignment. That's a pointless risk."

With an exaggerated sigh, she dropped her backpack, dug out the sunblock and applied it so thickly to her face and arms that she left white streaks. "Happy?"

"That's a good wife," he said with a wink. "Now give it to me."

She passed the bottle to him and stalked off. With his T-shirt covering his shoulders, and his ball cap protecting his face, he wasn't as worried about himself, but he put some on, anyway. Then he dropped the tube into the camera bag and strode after her.

They hiked to the other side of Paradise, where they finally saw people moving about. It looked as if they'd just come out of some kind of church service. There were vegetable gardens in this part of the compound, too. And animals. A pen with two dogs. Cows. Pigs. Sheep. Goats. But the rest of the view was similar to what they'd seen before. They could make out more of the brown building Nate had pointed out—he guessed it was a meeting hall or mess hall or maybe the cheese factory Martha had mentioned—and another two or three buildings, one under construction. There were more tents on this side, and the fence with the razor wire looked just as tall and impenetrable. He took pictures of all of it.

Damp with sweat and nearly out of water, they walked back to the dirt road where they'd parked. The sun had begun to set but the temperature hadn't fallen yet. The fruity scent of the sunblock filled Nate's nostrils, along with the more astringent odor of the creosote bushes surrounding them. Although it was peaceful, Rachel's mood hadn't improved. She wasn't complaining, but she'd grown quiet. And she'd abandoned him again while he was putting away his camera equipment.

It wasn't until he crested a slight rise that he caught sight of her. She wasn't walking away from him anymore. She'd stopped, but she didn't seem to be waiting for him. He was a little confused as to what she might be doing until she shifted and he could see past her. Then he realized she was no longer alone.

11

Rachel got the impression that the meeting with the man she'd just stumbled across hadn't been as accidental as he was pretending. She could tell by the brand on his forehead—a C with a slash—that he was a Covenanter. He'd probably noticed their car. Otherwise, it was too coincidental that he'd be wandering around out here without so much as a backpack or a water bottle.

Obviously, he felt far more comfortable, since he was closer to home, than she did. It was also obvious that he didn't like them nosing around the area. She hadn't expected that anyone associated with Paradise would. But when she and Nate had gone all afternoon without seeing a single person, she'd assumed they were in the clear. She'd been surprised to find this man standing on the ridge as she trudged back to the truck.

Somewhere in his late forties, he wasn't wearing a shirt, just a pair of leather sandals and handmade Middle Eastern-style pants. From the look of him, he could've hailed from Biblical times.

"What are you doing here?" he asked. Tall and rail-thin, with only three or four gray hairs growing from his sunburned chest, he had a lazy eye that drifted to his right.

Smiling brightly, she focused on his beaklike nose to avoid being distracted by his eyes. "We're checking out the area. My husband and I are new. We moved in yesterday."

"Moved in...*where?*"

She made the mistake of lifting her gaze to meet his eyes, then blinked and returned her attention to the center of his leathery face. "Portal."

"I see." He fingered a gray straggly beard as he saw Nate coming up from behind. "That's your husband?"

"Yes. Nate."

"What is it you're looking for?"

Although his tone was mild, she could sense his displeasure. "A few good shots. My husband's a wildlife photographer."

"He's a big man...for a photographer," he added.

"What does his size have to do with his work?" she asked.

"He looks more like a soldier, athlete or bodyguard."

"He's really a cement contractor. But that's such hard work. He's been having trouble with his back and would like to get out of concrete before we have children. We're hoping some of the pictures he takes while we're here will help."

"You said he photographs *wildlife?*"

"Yes."

"Did you happen to see something...unusual that brought you up here?"

There was an awkward silence during which Rachel could hear Nate's footsteps. "Not really," she said. "Today we're mostly getting familiar with the area. We'd like to see an ocelot, but I know that won't be easy."

He seemed to be looking at Nate, but that lazy eye

made it difficult to tell. "You won't see an ocelot before sundown. They're nocturnal wildcats."

"Good thing I wasn't planning on photographing one today," Nate said as he drew even with them.

"I can guarantee you won't find one in Paradise anytime."

But they might find something far more dangerous. Rachel was pretty sure that was what this gentleman was worried about. She had a feeling he knew perfectly well that they'd paid more attention to the town than anything else. He'd been keeping track of them somehow.

Were the Covenanters even less social toward outsiders than she'd supposed? Those Introduction Meetings created a sense of warmth and hospitality, but she suspected it was a carefully crafted illusion.

"Is that the name of the town we came across?" she asked. "We couldn't figure it out. Our map says it's a ghost town, but there are all kinds of tents and buildings and—"

"Those tents and buildings constitute a special place," he interrupted. "A sort of Zion to all who seek refuge."

Nate adjusted his ball cap. "Zion? It's a religious group?"

The older man continued to stroke his beard and scrutinize them but didn't answer right away. Eventually, he said, "It's home to me and others like me."

"And you are…" Nate said.

"The Church of the Covenant. My name is Bartholomew."

Nate moved his camera bag to the other shoulder and

stuck out his hand. "I'm Nathan, Nathan Mott. Nice to meet you," he said as they shook hands.

Bartholomew reminded Rachel of the self-proclaimed prophet who'd kidnapped Elizabeth Smart. Or maybe Charles Manson himself. The mark on his forehead appeared crudely made, as if it had been carved with a hunting knife.

Taking hold of Rachel's arm, Nate encouraged her to go around the man. "It's getting late. We'd better head home."

Bartholomew stopped them. "You don't think you'll be coming back, do you?"

Nate froze. "I don't know. We might. Is there anything wrong with that?"

"This is private property."

Other than the square mile or two that made up Paradise, the desert seemed to expand in all directions without fence, post or no-trespassing signs. "Every acre?" he asked.

Bartholomew's right eye seemed to focus before drifting off again. "Most of what surrounds the town."

"I didn't know that."

He gave them a thin-lipped smile. "Now you do."

Rachel pulled away from Nate's grasp. "Who owns it?"

"Alpha and Omega."

"That's sort of what I thought," Nate said with a grin. "I doubt God will mind if we take a few pictures."

Bartholomew didn't appreciate the joke. His nostrils flared as he answered. "I was referring to Ethan Wycliff."

"Who's Ethan Wycliff?" Rachel asked.

He blinked at her. Was it credible that she hadn't

heard of him? She hoped so. "God's anointed. The prophet who will usher in the Second Coming," he answered with a slight bow.

She wanted to say, *Oh, him,* but swallowed the sarcastic response. She'd heard dope addicts claim a lot of different things—from being abducted by aliens to being able to fly—but she'd never had anyone look her in the face and call another man Alpha and Omega as if he were God Himself. She might've found it merely bizarre, except for the menacing air that surrounded this guy. His body language sent a very clear warning signal to her brain: *Steer clear.*

"We're only taking pictures," Nate said.

"Still, we'd appreciate it if you took them elsewhere."

Nate stepped closer to Bartholomew. It wasn't like him to allow anyone to push him around, and his resistance to that showed, even when he was in character.

Rachel jumped into the conversation, hoping to stop it from escalating into a fight. "Sure. No problem."

She expected Bartholomew to move out of the way, but he didn't.

"And if you'll delete the pictures you've already taken, I can let you pass," he added.

Let them pass? Rachel felt Nate stiffen.

"There's no need to delete my pictures," he said.

Bartholomew reached for the camera. "It'll only take a moment."

Nate couldn't turn over his camera. Then this man would know they hadn't been shooting photos of wildlife at all.

Obviously as aware of that as she was, Nate didn't budge. He set his jaw instead, and Rachel knew, unless he acquiesced, no one on earth would get hold of that equipment. "I'm telling you no."

Rachel held her breath.

"And if I insist?" Bartholomew asked.

Beneath the bill of the Diamondbacks hat they'd purchased in Phoenix, Nate's expression grew even more determined. "You don't want to know the answer to that question."

His fingers forming a steeple, Bartholomew inched back and bowed his head, continuing more cautiously. "We have a right to our privacy."

"So do I," Nate said.

"The media has no respect for people who believe differently from mainstream America."

"We're not the press."

Now the other man hesitated. Rachel could almost see him considering the question: *Do I push any harder?* "You see, Ethan—"

"Has nothing to worry about," Nate finished. "I haven't taken any pictures of him. I don't even know who he is. We thought there was a ghost town out here and we figured that might be interesting. But we came to photograph the wildlife in the area. That's it."

Bartholomew looked over his shoulder at their vehicle, which wasn't parked far away, and Rachel knew he had to be wondering why, if they'd come to see a ghost town, they hadn't driven up to the gates instead of turning off on some random road leading into the desert.

Or did Bartholomew already know the truth?

Her mind reverted to what she'd divulged to Martha. Had it been a mistake to trust her? Had Martha compromised their cover before they could infiltrate the com-

pound? If so, this would be a much shorter assignment
than Rachel had envisioned....

She waited for Bartholomew to mention Martha, but
he didn't. His Adam's apple bobbed as he swallowed.
"Fine," he said at length. "Keep your pictures. Just
don't come back."

"*Now* we're off on the right foot," Rachel said as she
got in and slammed the truck door.

"I had no choice," Nate responded. "I couldn't turn
my camera over to him without giving us away. Every
picture I took is of Paradise. I even got close-ups of the
security gate, for crying out loud."

Rachel agreed. She hadn't been criticizing him. She
was frustrated that their first encounter with the Covenanters hadn't gone smoothly. She wasn't sure how
they'd compensate for that later on. And she was afraid
she might be to blame for Bartholomew's suspicion.
"You don't think Martha somehow alerted them, do
you?"

"No. They're still searching for her. You heard what
Laura Thompson said." Nate twisted around to look
through the rear window. They'd left the truck where a
jeep trail converged onto a footpath so narrow and so
filled with rocks and cacti on either side that they'd
decided not to drive any farther. He had to back down
the hill before he could turn around.

"Maybe they found her. And maybe she thought
she'd have a better chance of reuniting with her family
by using what she knows about us to curry favor with
someone important inside the group."

"They haven't found her. If Laura went to the police,

like she said she was going to, they should be watching over her."

"Maybe Martha reached out to Ethan." Rachel had assumed that anyone who'd been stoned by the Covenanters would be too disillusioned and fearful to do that. But it was possible Martha had tried to find a quicker method of reclaiming her son than relying on the help they offered.

"It's unlikely," he said. "If the Covenanters know who we are, Bartholomew would've arrived with some reinforcements. He wouldn't have attempted to stop us on his own."

That made sense, but Rachel had found the man they'd met strangely unsettling. The gleam of fanaticism in his normal eye was far too familiar. "I hope you're right."

"I am."

"I wonder if Bartholomew is even his real name," she mused.

"Why wouldn't it be?"

"It's not very common. Considering his religious persuasion, he could've taken it from the Bible."

"There's a Bartholomew in there?"

She rolled her eyes. He'd had it so easy growing up. He hadn't been dragged to church several times a week, hadn't been forced to proselytize for two hours a day, longer on weekends. For years, the Bible was all her father would permit her to read, other than textbooks. "Bartholomew was one of the disciples of Jesus." Although it'd been ten years since she'd cracked the cover of the Holy Scriptures, she remembered that much.

Nate scowled. "Right. I knew that."

"No, you didn't," she said with a laugh.

"Okay, I didn't," he admitted. "So what does failing to read the Bible mean? Am I going to hell?"

"In my father's religion, they don't embrace the concept of hell, at least the kind with fiery torments. Like the Jehovah's Witnesses, they believe in the 'common grave,' from which you'll never escape if you're not worthy."

"I guess that's hell enough."

"It's a lonely prospect, at any rate."

Sobering, he drove for a few minutes before speaking again. When he did, he surprised her by trying to reassure her. "You won't end up in the common grave, Rachel. You're a good person. You haven't rebelled against God."

According to her father, she had. At seventeen, she'd been cast out of his church, ostracized by all their friends and disowned by her family for protesting when someone in their congregation had refused medical treatment for cancer and subsequently died. She'd felt that loss of life was so senseless, so…confusing. She couldn't go back to church after that.

Although she still considered herself a Christian, she had major issues with organized religion. She didn't have a network of support or much of a family anymore. These days, her work associates filled that role. Even Nate was closer to her than her own brother. It was three years since she'd spoken to Lance, longer since she'd heard from her father. Her mother stayed in touch but loosely. Lita had left the church before Rachel—seven years before, when she ran off with their neighbor. After the divorce, Lita married the man for whom she'd deserted her family but never moved back to California. Neither she nor her new husband wanted to deal with Fredrick, a man consumed by his beliefs and by his need to impose them on others. These days, Lita lived in Montana, where she and Mitch had built a new life for themselves. One that rarely included Rachel.

"I can't believe you've never had a birthday party," Nate said.

"Rod threw me a party in January. He brought in a cake and everything."

"I know. I was there. I'm talking about while you were growing up."

"My father considered birthdays a pagan celebration. He says they foster feelings of self-importance."

They sped up as the road improved. "Yeah, well, you don't want to know how I feel about your father and *his* feelings of self-importance."

No doubt he thought Fredrick was off balance. Just like the majority of their neighbors had. Most of the time she did, too. But there were moments she felt she owed him some respect for remaining true to his faith and supporting her until she was almost of age. Maybe her mother hadn't been harsh, the way Fredrick had been, but neither had she possessed the strength to be the mom Rachel and her brother needed.

"Missing birthdays wasn't the hardest part." Sure, she'd been envious of kids who were free to enjoy the usual holidays. But going without presents at Christmas was nothing compared to being so different from everyone else. She'd had to be careful never to mention the name of a friend to her father or he'd march her over to that girl's house with religious literature. Maybe she wouldn't have minded "witnessing," as her father called it, if it'd been her idea, her choice, her conviction. But it never was. Her father had pounded his religion into her, sometimes literally.

Nate glanced at her. "What was?"

Lost in her own thoughts, she stared at him. "Pardon?"

"What was the most difficult part of growing up the way you did?"

She didn't want to talk about it. She wasn't willing to be pitied, especially by Nate. "Probably the divorce. But lots of children go through that."

"Not while living in such a warped world. But your experience with religion should help us," he said. "It gives you a unique understanding."

It also gave her a strong bias and too much rage. She knew what it was like to be held captive by hope and the desire to please, to be controlled by the fear that disobedience or disbelief might lead to expulsion from the family, as well as the church. Would that translate into an advantage or a handicap?

"Maybe," she responded. "If we can get in. Bartholomew's order not to come back could make it awkward to attend the meeting. We might not get any farther."

"I think it'll be okay. It's smarter for them to make friends with the people around here who might otherwise become enemies. I'm guessing Ethan's capable of figuring that out. That's got to be the reason for the Introduction Meetings." He turned on the radio, picked up nothing but static and turned it off again. "At least they'll have a frame of reference for our interest. They'll know how we came into contact with them, why we're curious."

"Since we've been in the area such a short time, it might actually be better than showing up at a meeting out of nowhere," she agreed.

"Exactly."

She wanted to free the Covenanters from whatever hold Ethan had over them, free them far more quickly than she'd been freed through education. But most of them probably didn't want their freedom or they wouldn't have joined Ethan to begin with. How could she or anyone else help willing captives? "I should've discussed it with you before I told Martha the truth. I'm sorry."

"You went on instinct. Sometimes we've got to do that in our line of work."

But she wasn't risking only *her* life. She was risking Nate's. She wasn't used to working in tandem; she'd have to be more careful. "Sometimes," she repeated.

"Stop worrying. It'll be okay. We're fine."

Now that the sun had disappeared behind the mountains, she removed her sunglasses. "I wish there was some way to know if Martha ratted us out."

The truck bounced and jerked as Nate maneuvered around the rocks, potholes and creosote bushes trying to overtake the road. "She didn't."

He couldn't know that. There was still a chance… and they certainly didn't need that working against them. Rachel already felt unsure of her ability to cope with this assignment. No matter how often she told herself the Covenanters were completely different from her father, that the religion he espoused wasn't what most people would call a cult, she heard echoes. And it was those echoes that made her uneasy. It'd been so difficult to escape the chokehold of her father and his religion, so painful to lose the relationships she'd had to sacrifice at the same time. Planning to become one of the Covenanters—even temporarily, even undercover— felt a bit like returning home.

12

The monsoon hit while they were at the creek. One minute, Nate was enjoying the perfectly calm weather and a nice view of Rachel's legs. The next, a gigantic black cloud rolled toward them, seemingly out of nowhere. It caught up with them before they could wade to shore.

"This is crazy. I've never seen anything like it!" Rachel yelled, laughing as the wind whipped her hair around her face and plastered her clothes to her body.

Nate was only an arm's distance away, yet he could hardly hear her. "We'd better run! It's about to rain!"

She increased her speed as she picked her way over the rocks, but she wasn't moving fast enough for his liking. Grabbing her by the waist, he hauled her out of the water and dumped her near their shoes so they could scoop up their belongings before dashing to the truck.

The rain didn't come down as soon as he'd expected. This monsoon seemed more like a tornado than any storm he'd ever seen. Not until they were in the driveway of the trailer did large fat drops begin to fall from the sky and spatter on the windshield—but those drops quickly turned into a deluge. As the rain pounded on the truck roof and instantly created puddles on the ground, they looked at each other in stunned surprise.

"Wow," Rachel breathed. "Hard to believe I could be cold after how hot I've been since we arrived, but I am."

That was apparent. Goose bumps stood out on her arms and legs—and her chest, which caused awareness to travel through Nate like a jolt of lightning.

At the creek, they'd been doing fine in their usual roles—work associates and friends. Other than a few glances at her various assets, reserved for when she wasn't watching, Nate had felt more comfortable than he ever had around her. And she'd seemed equally relaxed. Gone was the sarcasm she'd used to battle the attraction between them. They'd simply talked and laughed and enjoyed cooling off.

But they weren't talking and laughing anymore. They weren't relaxed, either. They sat staring at each other with such desire he knew he'd only look foolish if he tried to pretend he didn't appreciate her on a sexual level.

Fortunately, she tore her gaze away and wrenched open the door before he could do or say anything that might lead them down the wrong path. "Race you to the house," she cried. Then she was outside.

He didn't accept her challenge. He remained behind the wheel, telling himself exactly how he was going to behave once he reached the trailer. It didn't matter that they'd be alone, that he remembered how she felt beneath his hands and was dying to touch her again. He'd let her heat water for a bath and take his own after she was finished. No way would they bathe together the way he wanted to.

"That's it," he said, encouraged when his heartbeat finally slowed. "You can do this."

Rachel already had two large pans on the stove by

the time he stomped inside. As he stood in the entryway drying himself with the towel she'd put there for him, she didn't glance up. And he didn't speak to her as he removed his shoes, left them on the mat and trudged to his room. After peeling off his wet clothes, however, he stood completely still, remembering her bra hanging on his lamp, her panties on his doorknob....

Her tread made the floor in the hall creak. She was so close. Would she stop at his room? Why not? They'd been together before. What would it hurt to make love again? If they could get past that night in January, they could relegate this to the same "experiences to be ignored or forgotten" file in their brains. Spending this night more comfortably than the last wouldn't ruin anything. Would it?

He never learned the answer to that question. In the next second, he heard her bedroom door shut. Then the lock clicked.

He'd burned her once. She wasn't about to let him do it again.

Ethan reclined on a velvet pad in the pit with the men he'd chosen as Spiritual Guides sitting on their own pads in a circle around him. They'd been arguing for two hours. But once Ethan had brought out the meth, tensions began to ease. Even Bartholomew was docile. He became ultramellow when he smoked, but he didn't do it very often. Meth was really his only vice. He was impotent, so he didn't much care about sex. He hated being unable to think clearly, so he refused drugs more often than he accepted. And he had little use for money. He lived a simple, devoted life. All he cared about was Ethan, and Ethan knew it.

Grady Booth took a hit on the pipe and passed it to Harry Titherington. "So what have we decided?"

"To put an end to the trouble she's causing." Bartholomew's eyelids were heavy. When he was high, he looked even more like an Old Testament figure.

Harry rubbed his bald head, managing to muss what little hair he had growing on the sides. "The way you put an end to Courtney?"

"I don't know what you're talking about," Ethan said. "I let Courtney go."

"Sure you did," he muttered, but Ethan was so high he didn't react to the subtle challenge in that statement. With his sandals off and his knees pulled in to his chest, he was enjoying the relative cool of the dirt floor and walls that surrounded them. Several wall sconces held torches, which added a touch of the medieval and created a smoky haze that filtered through the cavernlike room, enhancing the effects of the drugs. Digging the pit had been one of his best ideas. Hidden down here beneath the Enlightenment Hall they had *real* privacy.

"She's gone. That's all that matters."

Wearing a scowl, Harry marshaled the energy to roll over and sit up. "To you, maybe."

"To all of us," Ethan said pointedly. "She found out about this place."

"The pit?"

"Umm-hmm."

"Are you sure?"

"Are you questioning my word?" Ethan countered.

Harry quickly retreated. "No. 'Course not."

It was Stan Whitehead's turn with the pipe. He sat cross-legged while he smoked. "I don't care if you killed Courtney. God wouldn't have wanted her to stop the progress of this great church. Far as I'm concerned, as long as you have the Lord's sanction, you can deal with Martha the same way."

"I agree," Grady said. "I've never liked her, anyway, ever since she gave me that venereal disease."

It was more likely that Grady had given chlamydia to Martha. When they were passing through South Dakota, searching for the perfect place to build their commune, half the church had been forced to get anti-biotics, and that was just a few weeks after Grady had joined. But Ethan didn't point that out. Although Grady used to frequent lowlife hookers, he was one of the Guides now, above reproach. What he'd done in his previous life was irrelevant.

"*There* was a woman who knew her place. She felt it was a blessing to pleasure any of us Guides. She never refused," Harry said. "Remember the first time we brought her down here?"

Stan nodded. "She loved it."

"I bet that kid of hers is mine," Ezra Mooney added.

Peter Marshall nudged him. "Looks more like me."

"Doesn't matter." Harry covered a yawn. "God's plan has provided for all the children born to this people. Every Covenant member is married, so every child has a mother and a father."

"How'd you dispose of the body?" This question was directed at Ethan and came from Joshua Cooley, who'd been unusually quiet all evening.

"What body?" Ethan refused to offer details.

Bart cut in before Joshua could answer. "We're not talking about Courtney. We're talking about Martha."

"But you took care of the problem?" Joshua said. "The…evidence won't resurface and ruin us, will it?"

"Courtney is no longer a concern," Bartholomew said.

Stan stretched out on his back. "You're a spiritual giant, Bart, you know that? Maybe God's deprived you of life's greatest pleasures, but He's given you the biggest balls of any man I know."

Ethan wondered if references to his impotence bothered Bart. They brought it up occasionally, but he never let on whether it upset him.

"We've already tried to find Martha and had no luck." It was Grady who steered them back to the situation at hand. "What makes you think we'll be able to find her now?"

"Have faith, Brother. As soon as she starts to feel safe, her guard will go down," Bart said.

"And once we recapture her?" Manuel Fry wanted to know. "What then? She disappears, like Courtney?"

"If that is God's will," Bart said. "We'll leave that up to His anointed."

"We could always use her for a celebration," Grady suggested.

Ethan wondered if that would appease them, make them forget about his blunder with Courtney. "What kind of celebration?"

"One that honors the procreative powers God has bestowed on us. Only this one could last for days."

Ezra Mooney squinted through the smoke. "So… what, Grady, you're saying we rape her until she's dead?"

The drugs were making their tongues too loose, but Ethan didn't chastise anyone. Grady's gaffe took the spotlight off him.

"Last I heard, raping a woman didn't kill her," Grady said. "I say we keep her in a cage and use her indefinitely. She's been cast out of the kingdom, so she doesn't count anymore. She's like garbage…to do with what we will."

Peter inhaled too deeply from the pipe and had to cough. "Might as well save Bart the trouble of disposing of another corpse," he said when he could speak.

"So we'd have a woman available whenever we felt the urge?" Harry smiled. "I could go for that. But what if she gets pregnant?"

"Bart will make sure she doesn't," Ethan said.

Dominic Studebaker, their resident medic, sat across from Ethan. They'd gone to the same college for a year but hadn't met until Joshua Cooley had brought Dominic to one of Ethan's meetings. He'd been listening and smoking but hadn't contributed. Apparently, the fact that Ethan hadn't relied on his expertise offended him and he finally broke into the conversation. "With a little surgery, I can make pregnancy impossible."

Ethan rose to his feet. "So we'll keep our options open and decide exactly what her punishment will be once she's back. Have we come to an agreement on that much?"

Everyone shifted as they prepared to vote.

"Will all those in favor of making sure Martha cannot harm the church say aye?" he called out.

Ayes resounded, without a single nay. But Joshua Cooley didn't seem enthusiastic, and that concerned Ethan. "Do you have something else to say, Joshua?"

All eyes turned on the twenty-eight-year-old father of three.

"Yeah. I say we get rid of her for good, like Courtney. We've got wives. And if that isn't enough to satisfy

every itch, we've got the Covenant women who participate in the rituals. We get all the sex we need."

Ethan arched an eyebrow at him. "You think our celebrations are about sex?"

"I think they're about honoring the procreative
power, just like you do."

"And yet you think it would be kinder to kill her?"

"I don't want to face her every time I come down
here. It's different with the other women. They participate willingly or we protect their innocence by making
it so they don't know what's going on and don't remember when it's over. As long as they aren't aware, I
don't see how it hurts anyone. But…a sex slave? You
have to look at this through the eyes of the outside
world. They won't consider that God's punishment.
They'll call it torture. And what if someone were to find
her? We'd all go to prison. It's easier to hide a body
than a live human being."

"Who'd find her?" Ethan asked.

Joshua stood. "Courtney stumbled onto this place,
didn't she?"

Ethan kept his gaze averted. Courtney hadn't stumbled onto it, exactly. He'd hinted, left her clues. He'd
wanted her to come here because he'd been excited
about having her participate. He'd thought Courtney
would offer herself to the group, become a partner in
their worship. She'd begged him from the beginning to
let her attend the most secret rituals.

But she hadn't understood the religious underpin-
nings of what they did in the pit. She'd used what she
knew and tried to blackmail him. And he'd had to stop
her. But suspicious though they might be, Ethan could

never admit to the Guides that he was directly to blame for her death. Allowing her into the pit without the usual precautions had been poor judgment on his part.

"I mean, if she'd gone to the police, we'd be awaiting trial right now," Joshua was saying.

Harry knew the truth, of course. He'd seen Courtney with Ethan before their big argument. But he had plenty of motivation to accept the lie. He didn't want to lose his place among the Guides.

"Forget Courtney." Ethan adjusted his robes so he wouldn't have to meet anyone's eyes.

Joshua pivoted to face the others. "So you want to do this? You really want to add torture to the list of things we do down here and call it sacred?"

No one responded.

"You're making a mistake," he said. "You're feeling untouchable, but you're not. None of us are."

"No one can hurt us," Ethan said. "Even if someone found Martha here, they wouldn't be able to get out of the compound before we stopped them. And God is the only power we answer to. If He provides her for our use, we will use her as we see fit."

Joshua wouldn't back off. "There's always a chance someone will find out," he said stubbornly.

"No, there isn't. You know how good Bart is at security. Trust him, as I do."

"It's not about trust. Courtney might be dead but—" he raised a hand when Ethan opened his mouth to interrupt "—but that doesn't mean we can forget how she got that way. I'm sure her parents and the police are searching for answers."

"They won't find anything," Bart said.

"They could," he insisted.

Ethan studied him. "Are you losing your faith? Are you beginning to doubt me, Joshua?"

With a scowl, he said, "Of course not. I understand why you feel entitled. I'm just saying the outside world won't."

"I will not be judged by the outside world!" Ethan thundered.

Silence descended. Finally Joshua cursed under his breath. "Fine. I'll go along with it, too. But…shit, Todd's my friend."

"Todd's getting a divorce," Ethan said. "He hates his wife."

"He doesn't hate her. He's a believer. He believes in *us*. And he's brokenhearted to think she could lose her faith. There's a difference."

Ethan accepted the pipe. "Don't worry about Todd," he said as he exhaled. "He will be rewarded for his belief. There are other women available to him. And, by your own logic, what Todd doesn't know won't hurt him."

"God willing, he'll never find out."

Handing him the pipe, Ethan patted him on the shoulder when he bent to accept it. "Relax. You like it here, don't you?"

"What's not to like?" he said grudgingly.

Ethan smiled. "God supports those who support Him. So stop worrying and remember who you are." Nodding toward the bong, Ethan waited until his friend had taken one hit and then another, and soon Joshua was sitting down again, talking about what he had planned for Martha, just like the rest of them.

At first, Nate fought the memories. He knew they'd only make sharing a trailer with Rachel more difficult.

But it was so hard to believe the woman sleeping in the next room had crept into his condo, *into his bed,* six months ago that he couldn't help replaying the incident. He couldn't sleep right now, anyway, so he let his mind wander back to that night as it so often did.

His unlocked door gave it away first. When he found the extra key on the kitchen counter, he thought his brother had come over. Randall was younger by eight years and did that sometimes. He raided the refrigerator or borrowed Xbox games. Sometimes he even brought a girl over to watch a movie or just hang out at his older brother's place. But Randall was loud. And he didn't smell of perfume.

Curious, Nate walked into the living room—and saw a lacy white bra hanging from a lamp.

His visitor definitely wasn't Randall. Was it some prostitute the guys at Department 6 had hired, thinking it would be funny to put him on the spot? The practical jokes usually ended when they got busy, and they were currently shorthanded. But…

No. He rejected the prostitute idea. The guys wouldn't bother unless they could be around to witness his reaction. And if they were here, they were doing a damn good job of hiding. So…who was it? He dated occasionally, but he hadn't been in a serious relationship for ages. Not since Susan had he brought a woman home….

The floor creaked as he followed a trail of discarded clothing down the hall to his bedroom. How had this woman, whoever she was, gained entry to his condo? It wasn't as if he kept his spare key above the door or under the mat like most people.

Then it dawned on him. Last week, he'd forgotten a

file at home and sent Rachel Jessop to get it for him. He'd given her his keys, so she could get into his place. Could she have made a copy?

No, this couldn't be Rachel. He'd never even asked her out. And yet...

The door to his bedroom stood partially open and had a pair of bikini panties hanging from the knob. He fingered the silky fabric, even brought it to his nose, imagining Rachel as he did so—and felt his body react. It'd been a long time since he'd been with a woman. And whether he wanted to admit it or not, Rachel appealed to him.

The door creaked as he pushed it wider. The room was dark, but in the light from the hall he could discern the color of the hair spilling across his pillow.

Blond, as he'd expected. Almost before that detail could register, she turned to look at him. Their eyes met, and he felt his knees go weak. It was Rachel, all right.

For a second, he was torn by indecision. She was taking a huge risk, doing something he couldn't imagine she'd ever done before. She was usually so *careful*. He didn't want her to be embarrassed but, after Susan, he'd sworn he'd never take a woman's love lightly again. Which meant he couldn't accept what she was offering.

What now?

"Hey." Her lips curved in a self-conscious smile.

Knowing he needed to do *something* before she felt even more uncomfortable, he crossed over to her. He'd simply talk to her, explain that he wasn't interested in a relationship with anyone at the moment, least of all someone he worked with. Having grown up without the usual teenage sexual exploration, she didn't fully understand the emotional complexity of what she was doing and how it might affect both their jobs. It didn't help that she'd become a police officer. Law enforcement had kept her circumspect. She'd seen too much but experienced too little. This was the first time he'd ever known her to cast all reservation aside.

God, what a way to go….

Without actually touching her, he sat on the edge of the bed. "What's…going on?"

"The panties didn't give it away?" Her smile suddenly faltered, which told him she was already losing her nerve. He *wanted* her to lose it, didn't he? He thought so—but he wasn't sure. He'd never been so much at war with himself.

"Rachel…we work together. As your boss…this probably isn't…" He struggled for the right words, the kindest words. But rejection sounded like rejection, which made this very difficult indeed, especially because, on a very base level, he didn't really *want* to turn her away. "…the best thing for us to do," he finished lamely.

"I guess I'm having trouble thinking of anything better," she responded, and then she guided his hand beneath the covers to her bare breast, burying all his good intentions beneath an avalanche of testosterone. He couldn't even remember what he'd said or where he'd planned to go with his little speech. He'd just been glad she hadn't really listened.

Stop now, his mind screamed in one final attempt to keep him out of trouble, but he didn't have the strength to withdraw. He willingly let go of sanity the moment their lips met. Maybe if he gave her as much pleasure

as she gave him, it would be an equal trade and everything would be fine.

He'd folded back the blankets, taken one look at
her and realized he'd willingly trade just about anything to have her. She was so beautiful, so soft, so
responsive. And it wasn't as if she wanted it polite
and easy. That seemingly unbreachable wall of caution she generally put between herself and the world
was gone. She'd gotten wild with him—sunk her fingernails into his back, bitten his shoulder and rode
him as hard as he rode her—which whipped him into
a frenzy unlike any he'd ever experienced. He was
confident he'd just had the best sex of his life. Until
morning. Then, as he slumped over her, exhausted,
he'd heard the softly uttered words that'd chilled him
to the bone: I love you.

A noise in the hallway brought Nate to a sitting position. Rachel was up. Judging by her footsteps, she was
adjusting the setting on the swamp cooler.

Rubbing a hand over his face, he willed himself to
relax. That memory had been so vivid his heart was still
slamming against his chest. The only way he could get
it to slow down was by focusing on the ending: *I love
you....*

No matter what happened, he *had* to keep his hands
to himself. Susan had taught him that *I love you* were
three very dangerous words.

The next evening Rachel had to take Nate's truck
and go to the first meeting alone. She'd known that
from the beginning. In a way, it was a relief to leave
Nate at the trailer and set off on her own. Since the

storm, the tension between them had only grown more intense. It seemed that he couldn't look at her without lowering his gaze to her lips or her breasts, and she wasn't faring much better. It didn't matter where he was, she felt compelled to seek him out. Even when he went outside to fix the air-conditioning in the truck, she'd gone to the window time and again, just to catch a glimpse of him.

They needed to infiltrate the Covenanters as soon as possible so they'd have something else to concentrate on—like guarding their true identities and finishing this assignment. Maybe, if they did, they could siphon off some of the excess energy that was putting them on edge.

But when the tall fence and barbed wire surrounding the complex came into view, Rachel grew nervous. That fence was a metaphor for what she'd experienced as a child, and her heart quailed at the thought that she'd be left to the mercy of another person's dictates. That she'd be cut off from the world she'd embraced since fighting so hard to establish her freedom.

Telling herself to calm down, she waited for the beat-up Volkswagen bus ahead of her to pass through security. The Covenanters were obviously very careful about who they allowed onto the property. They were checking IDs and vehicles as if this was a military installation.

Maybe the dossier Milt had created had been purposely vague, but he'd done his homework when it came to her ID. Department 6 had someone on staff who took care of that sort of thing. Someone good. Rachel wasn't worried that the Utah driver's license issued to Rachel Mott would be spotted as a fake. But she *was* concerned about what she'd learned from Thelma and Martha. She was also nervous about the sentiments expressed in the letters Ethan Wycliff had written to Charles Manson. Just how crazy was he?

Once the Volkswagen rattled inside the compound, she let Nate's truck move slowly forward until she came even with the two men working the checkpoint. "Hello," she said with a smile.

"Good evening, ma'am. May I see your identification?" One man, about twenty years old, peered closely at her face, comparing it to her picture. The other, a portly older gentleman wearing army fatigues like his younger companion, walked around her vehicle using a long-handled mirror.

As the younger man returned her license, Rachel tried not to stare at the crudely made *C* on his forehead. "Do you have any weapons with you?" he asked.

"Weapons?" she echoed as if bewildered. She felt naked without her gun, but was glad she'd left it at the trailer.

"It's just a precaution."

"I'm not a member or anything. I was told there's an Introduction Meeting here and that it's open to the public."

"That's true. It starts in a few minutes. We're only documenting who comes and goes and making sure no one brings any weapons into the commune. We are a nonviolent people."

"I see." Apparently the Covenanters didn't consider stoning to be violent. Continuing her act of innocence, she said, "I have nothing, nothing at all."

"How did you hear about the meeting, Ms. Mott?"

"*Mrs.* Mott. I met one of your members yesterday when I was out taking photographs with my husband."

His eyebrows slid up. "So you're the one."

"The *one?*"

"Yesterday evening Brother Bartholomew mentioned finding a young couple with a camera along the perimeter. Where's your husband?"

"He wasn't interested in coming. He...he doesn't feel any need for religion."

The young man rested his hands on her open window. "Maybe someday he'll change his mind."

It was a shame this boy had carved up his forehead. "I hope so."

His partner finished checking the truck's undercarriage and returned to their post, a small platform where he could take advantage of an overhang he soon wouldn't need. Dusk was settling in. And he certainly didn't have to worry about rain. Last night's monsoon had moved on as quickly as it had hit. By the time Rachel woke up at eight-thirty this morning, there were no puddles or even mud to show there'd ever been a storm—just some broken branches scattered by the wind.

Grateful that Nate had managed to fix the truck's air-conditioning, Rachel adjusted the closest vent and drove into the compound. There, she was directed by a third man, this one bald and wearing a T-shirt with ripped-out sleeves, to park near a large tent.

She did as she was told. Then she checked her cell phone. No service, as she'd suspected. This place was too remote.

"Damn." She couldn't text Nate to let him know she was inside. But it hardly mattered, since he didn't have service at the trailer, anyway. Not having a conduit to other people she trusted was as odd as it was uncomfortable. She was working without a safety net.

Despite its uselessness, she dropped her phone back in her purse and got out.

A woman wearing Islamic-style clothing—a green thobe and headdress with sandals—greeted her with a bouquet of wild flowers, one of which she slipped into Rachel's hair. "Hello, I'm Louise." Approximately thirty years old, the woman had a pretty face completely devoid of makeup and bore the same mark on her forehead as the men Rachel had met at the gate. "Welcome to Paradise."

Whether or not it was Paradise remained to be seen. "Thank you."

"Have you ever been here before?"

"No, this is my first time."

"I hope you enjoy your visit."

Rachel would've admired Louise's pleasant manner, except her vacant eyes and subdued behavior suggested she was on something, likely a sedative. Rachel was about to ask the woman where she was from and how long she'd been part of the group when a far more resonant voice interrupted.

"Sister Louise, you've made a new friend?"

Turning toward the sound, Rachel saw a tall man duck out of the tent. With his black hair slicked away from his face and his eyes shining like pieces of obsidian, she recognized him immediately. Ethan Wycliff was as well groomed as his picture. He walked toward her, wearing an expression of curiosity and avid interest.

Rachel was just as interested in him. She was also surprised. Although not everyone wore the Covenanter's mark, she'd certainly expected to see it on him....

13

"I don't believe we've ever met," Ethan said.

Intrigued as to the reason he wasn't marked with his own brand, Rachel plastered a smile on her face and tried to appear hopeful and genuine. Retaining that air of innocence took effort. She actually felt more comfortable, more in control, in the ghettoes of L.A. "My name is Rachel. Rachel Mott." She accepted the hand he extended.

From what she'd seen so far, most of those living in the commune, except the guards at the gate, dressed in Middle Eastern-style robes. Ethan was no exception. He wore a beige jalabiya with gold trim and sandals. His bare neck and forearms suggested he wasn't wearing a shirt underneath. Only a sash held the jalabiya closed. Considering the heat, Rachel could understand why he might forego a second layer of clothing. But there was something sensual in the way the loose fabric gaped open to reveal his tanned chest, as if he knew he was attractive and used it to his advantage.

His clasp was warm and dry, but he didn't shake her hand. He pulled her toward him and kissed her on each cheek. "I'm Ethan Wycliff, and these are my people. I'm glad you're here."

She let her gaze flick to his forehead. "You're the leader?"

"I am." He stared into her eyes. "Only I can offer you the living water you seek."

Rachel blinked. The statement was dramatic to the point of being corny. And yet he came across as sincere. She could imagine the women who might be taken in by such intensity, such conviction. If for no other reason, Ethan Wycliff was dangerous. "I'm not sure I'm seeking anything," she said with a laugh. "But I admit to being curious. Why is it that you don't have the mark on your forehead that I see on so many others?"

"Do they brand the shepherd as well as his sheep?" His mouth quirked, suggesting humor. Was it possible Ethan could still laugh at himself? Or was he laughing at the power he held over others, at their stupidity and weakness? Only a cocky man would be so bold as to call himself God's anointed and expect to be taken seriously. A cocky man—or a crazy one. Rachel was beginning to believe he might be both. But he certainly came in an attractive package.

Tilting up her chin to compensate for the difference in their heights—he was as tall as she'd assumed, based on his picture—she worked on controlling the subtle expressions that could label her as deceitful. A recent seminar she'd attended on body language had made her hyperconscious of what she might divulge without being aware of it. "I guess not."

"What brings you to Paradise, sweet Rachel?"

Sweet Rachel? The way he said her name brought to mind the sexual practices of this cult as explained by Martha. Ethan could have any woman here. And Rachel got the impression he availed himself of that privilege whenever it suited him. "A desire to see for myself."

"See what for yourself?"

"You, I guess."

"Honesty. I like that."

Someone else approached. Catching the movement in her peripheral vision, Rachel dragged her gaze away from "Alpha and Omega" long enough to see who it was and felt a jolt of anxiety when she recognized Bartholomew. She'd known she'd have to face him eventually; she just hadn't thought it would happen almost the first second she set foot on the premises.

No longer bare-chested, he was dressed in a jalabiya like his leader, except his was blue and had no trim. "Holy One. What have we here?"

"A guest," Ethan said.

Deep furrows formed between Bart's eyebrows. "I know this woman. She is the female member of the couple I caught trespassing."

Ethan remained unperturbed. "*Trespassing* is a harsh word, Bartholomew. She is welcome here. We are all friends, all family." Lifting her hand, he examined her wedding ring. "Where is your husband, Sister Rachel?"

"He wouldn't come."

"He's a skeptic?"

"He didn't feel the need."

"But you do."

Why? She needed a reason, something that might make him trust her. "I—I lost my mother not long ago," she said. "I just wanted...I don't know." She sought the empty spot inside her that made the pain real. Her mother had moved on so easily after the divorce, essentially abandoning her children, leaving them to a father who was too strict and controlling. Rachel probed that ache whenever she needed to tear up. It always worked, and it worked today.

Ethan lowered his head in apparent sympathy. "I'm sorry for your loss and am glad you were guided here," he said, then dismissed her by motioning to Bartholomew. "Seat her in the front."

Two women, also guests, had parked and were walking toward the tent opening. The moment Ethan intercepted them, Rachel heard a distinct purr in their voices as they responded to his questions and comments. Not only was he handsome, he was confident and powerful. That was a heady aphrodisiac among people who were lost and looking for a leader, searching for something to believe in or someone to save them.

Bartholomew waited for her full attention. "Why are you here?" he asked under his breath.

"I was invited," she replied.

"By whom?"

"By whoever posted a notice of the meeting at the Southwest Research Station."

That notice made this meeting open to the public, but the stiffness of his manner told her he wasn't any happier about her presence than she'd expected him to be. "Did you bring your camera?" he asked.

"Why would I? You said we had no chance of spotting an ocelot here."

He didn't have anything to say to that. Shooting a scowl at his leader, who had his back to them and was busy greeting more newcomers, Bartholomew whipped around and grudgingly led her to a seat right in front of the podium.

* * *

The meeting reminded Rachel of the tent revivals of the 1800s that she'd seen depicted in various movies— only it was so far removed from anything she thought the modern world would accept, she felt almost shocked that Ethan would be brazen enough to attempt it. But, like David Koresh and Jim Jones before him, his audacity knew no bounds. And especially in this setting, with no cell phones and no Internet, his presentation definitely spoke to a person's desires to receive unconditional love. It helped that he'd filled all the empty seats—about fifty—with believers. He was sufficiently rational to make himself seem sane, even though he was talking about the end of the world as if he had insider knowledge.

"It's my holy calling to identify those souls who will listen to Christ and believe. Believe in His power. Believe in His goodness. Let your faith start as a tiny seed, if that's all you can offer at this moment. Nurture it and let it grow within you until you can stand strong in love of your fellow man and do all that is right."

"Hallelujah!" the congregation shouted.

The sound echoed through the tent. The energy in his preaching, the response of the crowd and the music coming through speakers at opposite ends of the platform seemed to sweep even the visitors into a religious frenzy. All except Rachel. She could barely sit still for it. She'd heard too much of Ethan's rhetoric before, from her own father.

As she watched Ethan pound the pulpit and exhort them all to greater love and greater faith, she wondered if she'd be able to fake a conversion. How could she conjure up enough sincerity, when religion had lost its resonance for her in childhood? Her father had twisted his religion and its teachings to be anything he wanted them to be, and she suspected Ethan did the same. She had Martha's account of what went on here to prove it.

Then they started praying for those in the audience with special needs, and Rachel watched as more and more became seduced. She knew it was the unity they were experiencing as a group, the shared sorrow of pain and illness and the hope of becoming whole that affected them. And she had to admit Ethan had a gift for reaching people, one he exploited to the fullest.

Busy analyzing the show and everyone's reaction to it, Rachel didn't hear her name the first time it was called. Like the rest of the group, she was on her knees, swooning and praying aloud for Jesus to heal those who'd asked for His help. She didn't expect to be singled out, but soon realized why Ethan had wanted her near the front.

"Sister Rachel Mott, can you please come to the podium?"

The impatience in his voice indicated that he was repeating his request. Raising her head, she found Bartholomew standing nearby, ready to guide her to Ethan.

What was this? She wasn't sick or afflicted....

Ethan's voice boomed across the loudspeaker once again. "As I stood here, praying, it came to me that there is one among us who needs our help as much as these three who are suffering physically. This is one who has suffered in her heart. Let our combined faith heal her, too. Pray with me. Pray just as hard for those who need the Lord to heal their hearts."

"Hallelujah!" came the shout.

Rachel nearly stumbled climbing the stairs that led to the platform. Bartholomew was pulling her along; he was there to facilitate the proceedings and seemed determined not to be responsible for a loss of momentum.

"Sister Rachel." Ethan had her kneel in front of him. Then he cupped her face as if he were Christ showing mercy to those who worshipped at His feet. "I love you. God loves you. Do not suffer more because of your mother. Release the pain." With that he put his hands on her head and began to give her a blessing. And even though Rachel doubted he was anywhere close to being sincere, there was a part of her that could relate to the people who seemed taken in by the spectacle. Ethan had such charisma, and the others in the room chanted and clapped and stomped their feet. She *almost* wished she could let go of her cynicism long enough to feel what they felt....

Almost. But not quite.

"Love can conquer all!" they cried.

When Ethan drew her to her feet, she found herself in tears. But it had nothing to do with belief. The experience made her homesick, although she knew there was no going home. The home she craved didn't exist.

Ethan stood over her and tenderly wiped her tears. "Make sure you tell your husband that he is a very lucky man."

That line was for her ears alone, but she was glad to hear it. Because it meant Ethan couldn't see inside her soul the way he sometimes made it seem. It meant he didn't know that Nate was only pretending to love her. And that she was only pretending to believe.

"So what do you think?"

Nate sat on the couch in their trailer while Rachel

perched on the edge of the old recliner across from him. It was dark outside, nearly ten, so she'd turned on the lamps. "He's going to be formidable."

"How?"

The memory of the embrace she'd received from each and every Covenanter as she left the tent reminded her of the love and acceptance she'd felt at the meeting. It was part of the magic that held people, made them want to return and participate, to believe in healings that never really occurred. "He argues logically and boldly and he *seems* to have a clear basis for his beliefs. He's also a powerful speaker. He has a certain mystique that's very effective."

"Sounds as if you admire him."

"I don't *admire* him!"

"You were attracted to him?"

"Repulsed. But I recognize his strengths. He's definitely appealing in some ways. And his people seem very loyal. That'll make our job harder."

"Did you get the sense that he's dangerous? That he might've kidnapped the Sinclair girl?"

"I wouldn't put anything past him. Bartholomew was there, too," she added.

"How'd he treat you?"

"He wasn't particularly friendly. He kept his normal eye trained on me the whole time, watched every move I made. But it was hard to read what he was feeling. He's as coarse as Ethan is polished."

"If Ethan's the kind of cult leader I suspect he is, he needs someone to handle the dirty work." Resting his elbows on his knees, Nate let his hands dangle between his legs. "Did you see Martha's husband or son?"

"No, there were no children present. Todd might've

been in the congregation, though. A lot of the Covenanters showed up. I had the impression that's part of
the act, part of what makes Ethan's presentation so
moving. He fills every empty seat with someone he can
rely on to show the proper enthusiasm and support, and
it becomes infectious."

"You didn't ask anyone about Martha?"

"I didn't dare. I was afraid of creating suspicion."

"She's been in the news. I think it would've been
okay."

Once Rachel had met Ethan, she'd been asking herself if this person could be stopped—and if she was
capable of stopping him. "There wasn't room for me to
show too much skepticism. Not during this round."

Nate's eyebrows shot up. "What's that supposed to
mean? You were there as a visitor. Isn't some skepticism expected?"

"Of course. But I needed to come off as the interested party, the one driven by curiosity, or something
deeper, to seek the 'completion' Ethan supposedly of-
fers. That's what makes me a good target for him.
You're the hard sell, remember? I decided to wait and
let you broach the subject of Martha and her accusations when it's safe to bring you in."

"When will that be?"

"I have no idea. But not yet."

She toyed with some electrical tape covering a tear
in the vinyl upholstery.

The silence stretched on. "Does Ethan know you're
married?" Nate finally asked.

"Yes." The image of Ethan gently wiping the tears
from her eyes appeared in her mind. "He said to tell you
that you're a lucky man," she added with a chuckle.

Nate didn't laugh. He didn't even smile. He sat brooding for a few more seconds. "That meeting really made an impact on you."

"Ethan's as twisted as they come. But he really knows what he's doing."

"Let's hope we do, too," he said.

Nate pulled his truck around back, angling it so the headlights hit the outhouse directly. It was the easiest way to get the light he needed, unless he wanted to wait for the sun to rise, and he preferred not to do that. With the sun came the heat. Besides, Rachel generally woke early to jog. Doing it now gave him time alone to think. He always thought better when using his hands.

Grabbing a box of nails and a hammer from the bed of his truck, and some extra lumber he'd collected from around the property, he strode over to the badly listing outhouse. With some reinforcements, he could make the damn thing stand straight, no problem. He could even stop the creak of the door. But solving the turmoil inside him wasn't going to be as easy. This job seemed to be sliding sideways on them before they'd actually started.

Say they got in. How would they maintain a credible cover if they weren't even sleeping together? That wasn't usual behavior for a young married couple, especially a young married couple in a cult where free sex wasn't only condoned, it was promoted as part of their worship. He and Rachel would be living in a tent with eighteen others, for crying out loud. Their lack of intimacy would hardly escape notice. And what would he do if they were included in any type of ritual where he was expected to share her?

It seemed inevitable that he would make love to Rachel, too inevitable to continue fighting. But there'd be a cost...

Closing his eyes against the memory of what Susan had tried to do when he'd broken up with her, he cursed under his breath and hit the nail that much harder. Remembering the call he'd received from her mother still turned his stomach, and that would never change. *Susan slit her wrists, Nate. She's in the hospital....*

He'd never seen it coming. He'd gone along with the relationship even though he wasn't nearly as invested as she was.

Bam, bam, bam. The noise didn't soothe him, but he kept hammering long past the point where the nail head came flat with the wood.

There didn't seem to be any way to win on this assignment. If he took Rachel to bed, as he wanted to do, how would they make the transition back to being simply work associates after this was all over? Would he wind up breaking her heart, as he had Susan's?

He started on a new nail. *Bam, bam, bam.*

"What are you doing?"

Her shout made him whirl around. Rachel stood behind him in a tank top and panties. The unruliness of her long thick hair and the sleepy confusion on her face told him she'd just tumbled out of bed, not thinking about what she was or wasn't wearing. In this heat, a robe would be intolerable, anyway.

But she had no idea what the sight of her barely clad body did to him, especially in his current state. Tempted to close the five feet between them and sweep her into his arms, he felt his muscles tense. The sex would be good. It had been the last time. Until she'd ruined it by declaring her love.

They'd succumb sooner or later, he told himself. Why not sooner? He wanted it to be *now*. But he couldn't go through with it, knowing he'd only hurt her in the end.

Susan said she couldn't live without you, that she'd rather be dead.... "What does it look like?" he said, and went back to hammering.

"You've got to fix the outhouse at one in the morning?" she yelled above the racket he was making.

When he didn't answer, she moved closer. "Nate?"

He refused to turn. He didn't want to see her, didn't want her to realize he couldn't find an honorable solution in all of this. He couldn't leave Ethan to go on his merry way. There was no telling how many people he might hurt. Neither could he infiltrate the cult without Rachel. But if they managed to get in, he'd have to sleep in her bed night after night.... "It's too hot when the sun's up," he muttered.

"You were here all evening while I was at the meeting, weren't you?"

"No." He'd been in town for most of that time, having dinner at the café, talking to Thelma and setting up the fact that his "wife" had gone to Paradise to see what the Covenanters were all about. He'd even checked in with his parents, just to say hello, since it had been a week or more since they'd heard from him.

"Can you *stop*?" She took hold of his arm to keep him from swinging the hammer. "I'm trying to sleep."

Jerking out of her grasp, he threw the hammer to the ground. "Fine. I've stopped. Happy now?"

Confusion lined her usually smooth forehead. "I

guess. But…I'm at a loss here. What have I done to up-set you?"

"What do you think? I've told you before. Cover yourself up—unless you want me to take off what little you've still got on."

Her mouth formed a surprised *O*. But he didn't act on his words. He sidestepped her and jumped in his truck. Then he tore down the drive, heading to Rodeo.

Maybe he'd be able to find a damn bar.

14

Rachel sat on the bed, waiting. What was going on? Why had Nate been in such a terrible mood, how had she caused it and where had he gone?

She didn't have any answers to those questions. He'd made it perfectly clear in the past that he didn't want her. He'd never even called her after their night together, never mentioned it until the drive from California. And then he'd acted as if it wasn't a big deal. So why did what she wore or didn't wear bother him? She'd gone outside in a tank top and panties. But a bikini swimsuit revealed more. And she hadn't been *trying* to seduce him. She'd merely been trying to get him to quit hammering so she could sleep. Did he expect her to get fully dressed to come out for two seconds?

Whatever was bugging him probably had very little to do with her, she realized. He was worried about their assignment. And he had good reason. If Ethan was half as smart as he seemed, he wouldn't be easy to stop, even if he was abusing his power.

With a sigh, she got up to make herself some herbal tea, hoping it would help her sleep. She had no Internet access, no cell-phone coverage and no vehicle. She was stranded. There was nothing she could do but try to calm down and go back to bed.

* * *

After Nate Mott drove off, Ethan stopped worrying that he and Bart would be spotted watching the trailer. He was excited by the opportunity Nate's absence gave him and was tempted to reveal his presence by going to Rachel. She'd been rather cool during the meeting, tough to read and to reach. He could feel her resistance. But he was confident he could win her over and persuade her to believe in him. All he needed was enough time and personal contact. Maybe he'd say he'd been awakened in the middle of the night by a voice telling him her heart was aching. His ability to divine when she was upset or in trouble would go a long way toward establishing credibility.

But Bartholomew would never agree to it. Bart was the one who'd dragged him out here in the middle of the night, convinced that Rachel Mott should not be allowed to return to Paradise. He didn't trust her or her husband and was trying to talk Ethan into shunning them both. But Bart jumped at his own shadow. Ethan would never let a man so limited in his thinking stand in the way of what he wanted. Not for long. And after seeing Rachel at the meeting tonight, he was fairly sure he wanted *her*. She could bring back the excitement he'd felt with Courtney, would make up for the disappointment he'd suffered because of her and take his mind off Martha, too. Neither Martha nor Courtney could compare to Rachel. She was a prize far more worthy of his interest.

"It's like I told you, isn't it? They're not true candidates for conversion," Bartholomew whispered as they edged slowly and quietly away from the clearing and walked back to the Jeep. "They wouldn't be loyal."

Ethan didn't know what Bart meant. They hadn't been able to hear anything over the noise of Nate's hammer. How did witnessing a marital spat prove whether or not the Motts were candidates for conversion? Whether or not they'd be loyal? Even after the pounding stopped, their voices hadn't been loud enough to carry to the place where he and Bart were crouched behind some scrub oak. "It isn't the healthy who need a physician, my friend, but the sick."

Bartholomew gripped his shoulder. "Holy One, please. You must think of Martha and the trouble she's caused."

Ethan was still dwelling on the brief glimpse he'd gotten of Rachel standing in the beam of her husband's headlights wearing next to nothing. There was something different about her, something that stirred his blood in a very primal way. But it wasn't lust. It was challenge. The confidence in her bearing needed to be broken. Who was she, a mere woman, to think she could withhold anything, even her approval, from God's anointed? Before long, she'd be begging to spread her legs for him and would let him take her in the most degrading manner possible—him and all his Guides. The proud must be toppled from their worldly perch. They must be brought low, and women today needed to learn their place.

"Holy One?" Bart repeated, waiting for a response.

With effort, Ethan returned his focus to the conversation. "As long as Todd's heart remains true, Martha will be powerless. The police have already done all they can. It's over."

"It's not over. She's still in Willcox, filing papers for custody of her son." He used only the light of the moon to lead Ethan through the desert to their vehicle. Despite his bad eye, Bart was as sure-footed as a cat, even in the dark.

"If she takes it to court, we'll fight and we'll win," Ethan told him. "You've got pictures of her having sex with nearly every man in the compound. You also have pictures of her taking drugs." They had files on everyone. Such cheap and easy insurance made it possible to discredit any member of the group, if and when that was necessary. "Considering her background—all the times she ran away from home, the lack of even a high school diploma—she doesn't stand a chance."

"Todd's taken his share of drugs and had his share of lovers, too," Bart pointed out. "I've got as many pictures of him. One of them actually shows that he likes men almost as much as women."

Ethan suspected Bart liked men *more* than women but knew he'd never act on his homosexuality. That would get him expelled from the group. The scriptures were very clear on the issue. It was unnatural, an abomination before God. But Bart was impotent, so it didn't seem to matter what his preference might be. "Back when the church was still a secret group meeting out in the woods during the middle of the night, Cliff Winney came forward to say that Todd tried to have sex with him during an orgy," he said.

Bart stopped walking. "And you've forgiven him?"

Was his security adviser fishing, trying to see if Ethan had softened his stance? Maybe, but that kind of change was out of the question. He'd lose too many church members. Most of them came from a background of traditional Judeo-Christian beliefs, which preached against homosexuality. Reversing that would be too radical. Besides, mating with another man had nothing to do with procreation, so it couldn't be used in worship. "He came to me of his own accord and confessed. Unless he acts again, I will remember his sins no more." His robe snagged on a cactus and he waited while Bart jerked it free. "Besides, Martha doesn't have proof of what Todd's done the way we have proof of what she's done. Not only do we have pictures, we have witnesses. Anyone in Paradise would be willing to testify on Todd's behalf. They'll say she was an unfit mother while he's a devoted father."

"But these people—" Bart motioned toward the trailer, indicating the Motts "—they could be reporters or undercover police. If we let them in, we risk their interpretation of what we do. And we know the world's interpretation is not God's."

"The Motts could also be a married couple looking for the sexual freedom and spiritual fulfillment we offer," Ethan argued. "We live a better life. How can we not share what we've found with the rest of God's children?"

Stubborn to a fault, Bartholomew wouldn't give up. "They have no family or friends in this area. No history of ever having been here before. No previous association with Portal at all. How do you know they haven't been hired by Courtney's parents? The Sinclairs are looking for their daughter. They're not going to drop it."

Ethan remembered the tears on Rachel's face when he prayed for her. Part of him wanted to believe he'd reached her in that moment, but the other part wasn't so sure. There was that pride, that unwillingness to submit, which had flashed in her eyes immediately afterward…. "The Motts haven't been hired by Courtney's parents.

Portal is the birding capital of the world. That draws tourists and nature lovers, as well as photographers. Didn't you tell me Nathan is a wildlife photographer?"

"He *claims* to be a wildlife photographer. But I have no proof. They came out of nowhere. First they were caught snooping outside our gates. Then Rachel showed up at the meeting. They have too much interest in us too soon for it to have developed naturally. I think they're looking for Courtney."

Ethan wasn't pleased to be reminded of the grave outside his window. "You took care of Courtney. You said no one would ever find her."

"No one will."

"Then there's nothing to worry about." He paused to remove a rock from his sandal, which prompted Bartholomew to finally turn on the flashlight he carried. "I personally think their interest has developed naturally enough. Rachel's husband didn't even come to the meeting. He refused to attend."

Using his body to block any view of his light from the trailer, Bartholomew angled it at the ground ahead. "Something isn't right, Holy One."

"Didn't a guard check her ID at the gate?"

"Of course."

"And?"

"It's either real or a very good fake. But if she's with the police—"

"She could ruin everything," he admitted with a frustrated sigh. Why was he fighting Bart? Bart was only trying to protect him, to protect them all. Wanting to bring Rachel to her knees, to make her acknowledge his power, wasn't reason enough to risk destroying everything he'd created. He had to have patience, couldn't make the same mistake he'd made with Courtney. "Fine."

"Fine, what?" Bart bent close to get a glimpse of his face. "You'll shun them?"

"No, not until you bring me proof that I should. Just do whatever it takes to make sure they are who they say they are."

Stopping once again, Bart handed him the keys to the Jeep, which was a few steps away.

"You're not going back?" he said in surprise.

"No."

"But how will you get home?"

"If you'll send two members of my security staff with a vehicle and have them leave it here, I'll drive back when I'm ready."

It was so late…. "What do you hope to accomplish *tonight?*"

Bart turned to stare at the trailer, and Ethan glanced in that direction, too. When the light in the kitchen winked out, he imagined Rachel going to bed.

"I just want to poke around," Bart said. "And it's probably best to do it while Nathan's gone."

Nate was back. At least, Rachel thought he was. Something had awakened her.

Raising her head, she checked her cell phone for the time, which was all it provided in this part of the state. It had only been half an hour since he'd driven off.

He couldn't have gone far….

Yawning, she rolled over. God, what a night. It'd been hard enough getting to sleep the first time in this heat. Now he'd awakened her *twice*. What was wrong with him? Why was he so agitated?

Holding her breath so she could hear better, she thought he might be in the hall. But when she got up and peered out the window, she didn't see his truck. *Odd...* Could he have had a flat tire and walked home? Or, heaven forbid, wrecked the truck in a ditch or something?

"Nate?" she called hesitantly. "You home?"

There was no answer. Even the subtle sounds of movement that she'd heard before were gone. Was someone really in the trailer? Or had she imagined it?

Opening her door, she peeked out. The hall was dark and shadowy. She wanted to turn on a light, but the switch was too far away—another inconvenience with this particular rental. And she knew it wouldn't do any good to turn on the light in her bedroom. That would just make the kitchen and living room more difficult to see.

Getting her gun from inside the drawer where she'd put it when she unpacked, she inched her way down the hall. If Nate was home, he would've answered her.

Footsteps and the slap of the door against the outside of the trailer told her she'd definitely had a visitor. But was it Nate? She didn't think so. Whoever it was had heard her coming and taken off.

Determined to catch up, she started to run—only to stumble over an obstacle in the hallway that hadn't been there before. By the time she was back on her feet, the intruder had gone. She stood on the front stoop, gazing out into the desert, which seemed as quiet and empty as it had before.

What was going on? Thoroughly spooked, she sank onto the doorstep. She wasn't about to let this person, whoever it was, draw her out of the trailer, where it would be harder to defend herself. But she hated giving up the idea of catching him.

The intruder had cut the screen and jimmied open the living room window. Unless she or Nate had left it open. The swamp cooler wasn't much help, and she hadn't been worried about unwanted visitors. Not so far from civilization. And not with a gun at hand.

She had a different opinion about her vulnerability now. Closing the window, she locked it, then double-checked to make sure the rest were secure. She locked the door, too, all the while wondering what whoever it was had hoped to accomplish. Had it been a robbery attempt? There wasn't anything in the trailer worth stealing. Except, perhaps, the camera equipment or their guns.

Remembering the soft feel of the obstacle she'd tripped over in the hall, she turned on the lights and went back to see what it was.

Nate's leather duffel bag. Someone had dragged it from his bedroom and rummaged through it. His gun was gone, but she couldn't tell if it had been stolen. He generally had it with him.

Afraid her visitor might return, she sank onto the couch to keep a vigil until Nate returned but, eventually, lack of sleep began to wear on her and she dozed off.

Nate was carrying her to her bed when she woke again. "Someone cut the screen and broke into the trailer while you were gone," she mumbled, still half-asleep.

He froze. "Say what?"

"Someone broke in."

"Here?"

"Yep."

"Who?"

"Don't know."

"Did they take anything?"

"Do you have your gun?"

"I do."

"What about your computer, your tools and your other gear?"

His breath stirred her hair. "Locked in the toolbox in the bed of the truck."

"Good."

"You were here?"

"Where else would I be? You took the truck."

He cursed. "I'm sorry about that. Are you okay? They didn't hurt you, did they?"

"No. They ran away when I called out." She covered a yawn as he deposited her on the bed. "Who do you think it was?"

He pulled the blanket over her, but didn't answer.

"Nate?"

"Get some sleep. We'll talk about it in the morning."

The knock came just after Rachel got back from her morning jog. Since Nate was still sleeping, she left her coffee at the kitchen table and headed to the door.

"Who is it?" Nate stepped out of his bedroom, wearing nothing but a pair of basketball shorts.

"I have no idea," she murmured, opening the door.

A man stood on their small stoop dressed in the Middle Eastern robes the Covenanters liked so well. That would've given him away even if the brand on his forehead hadn't already proclaimed his affiliation.

After a formal bow, he handed her a note. "The Holy One sends his felicitations," he said, and walked back to a military-style Jeep idling in the drive.

Nate folded his arms and leaned against the partial wall that separated the kitchen from the living room. Rachel didn't know where he'd gone last night. She hadn't asked when he'd brought her to bed. But if he'd been drinking, it didn't show. He looked tired, as if he hadn't had much sleep, but he didn't seem to be suffering from a hangover. "Alpha and Omega is sending you something? You must've made quite an impression."

His sarcasm indicated that his mood hadn't improved since their argument. They needed to talk about what had set him off—and about the break-in—but first Rachel wanted to know what had motivated "the Holy One" to send her a note. She tore open the envelope, pulled out a card and immediately recognized the handwriting she'd seen in the letters to Charles Manson.

"It's from Ethan, all right," she breathed.

I had a dream you were unhappy and unable to sleep. My prayers are with you. Please feel free to visit me. I can help you. I can heal the hurt.

When she didn't read it aloud, Nate shoved away from the wall and took it from her. "He thinks he can heal your hurt?" he said, glancing up after reading it himself. "What, with a climax or two?"

"We need to talk." Reclaiming Ethan's note, she set it on top of the TV and gestured at the sofa. "Care to take a seat?"

"No." Frowning, Nate scratched his chest. "We don't need to talk. I'm sorry. I shouldn't have left you last night. It won't happen again."

"That's all you have to say?"

"That's it. We're fine."

"Then why aren't you acting like it? The fact that Ethan has noticed me and is going out of his way to include me is exactly what we want, isn't it?"

"It might be what *you* want."

"I'm pretty sure Milt would look at it favorably. You said yourself that I'm the bait. This note is an invitation to return, which means we don't have to guess when to make our next move. I can go up there right away and continue developing a relationship, which will make it easier for me to eventually pull you in. You should be excited."

"It's the *eventually* part I'm having trouble with," he said. "I don't like being left out, wondering what the hell is going on. Especially when this note leads me to believe it might've been the Covenanters who broke in. How else would Ethan know you had a rough night? Don't you think the timing of this note is more than a coincidence?"

"Yes. But at least you had your gun with you. They didn't find anything."

"Still, you've been to *one* meeting, one. And they've already broken in here? They're already asking you back? What the hell went on up there?"

"I told you."

"You told me he was dangerous."

"Information that first came from you! You said it when you showed me his picture in the conference room before we left California. We knew what we were getting into." That wasn't completely true. Milt had held out on them. But they'd known it wouldn't be easy.

"He's not all there, Rachel. He's trying to isolate you from me and I don't like it."

"What are you talking about? We're lucky he's interested in me." She waved at the note. "We always knew there'd be an initial setup period. That I'd be going in first. I'm just doing my job. Does it bother you *that* much to have to depend on me? Or is it the fact that I'm being more successful?"

"What kind of crap is that? Of course you're more successful. He wants to get in your pants!"

Remembering the way he'd reacted to her skimpy attire last night, she moved toward him. "Why don't you tell me what the real problem is, Nate?" A warning flickered in his eyes, but she ignored it and took a step closer. "It's not that *he* wants to get in my pants, it's that *you* do. Isn't that right?"

His hands whipped out to grab her arms, and the intensity in his expression made her heart race, told her he was running on the far edge of control. That was unusual for him, but she liked it. She *wanted* him to lose control. She'd wanted it ever since he'd lost control the last time.

"Is that what you want to hear?" he asked.

"Would it kill you to admit it?"

"No." He grinned. "It would just mean we'd get a later start on the day."

"You're saying I wouldn't refuse."

His eyebrows rose. "Are you saying you would?"

She shouldn't have challenged him. She realized that now. But she couldn't back down. Maybe if she faced the temptation he posed and overcame it, he'd lower his defenses and treat her like any other coworker. Something had to happen to release the tension between them. "That's exactly what I'm saying."

"Will you give me a few seconds to change your mind?"

The word *no* should've come out of her mouth right away. But shutting him down that quickly would only make her appear weak. And she knew better than to appear weak to a man like Nate. "Five seconds, ten seconds." She shrugged beneath the weight of his hands. "Twenty *minutes* wouldn't make any difference."

"I'm glad you think so," he said, then his fingers tightened and he bent his head to kiss her.

She braced for one of the passionate open-mouthed kisses they'd shared six months ago, the kind she'd craved from him ever since. But that wasn't what she got. The kiss he gave her was disappointing. Far too light. Too miserly. And far more effective against her than anything else he could've done. There was no question he possessed the ability to kiss her properly. He wasn't even worried about proving himself. He was putting a price on that kiss, demanding her capitulation before he'd satisfy her.

"Bastard," she whispered when he lifted his head.

He chuckled. "I'm not the one saying no."

She narrowed her eyes. "With that lousy kiss is it any wonder I'd refuse?"

"It gets better. I think you know that."

"If only I could remember." She mustered a cocky smile.

"So you *were* faking it in January when you begged me not to stop? When your nails scraped my back and I heard you gasp my name?" His voice, barely a whisper, conjured up the memories she'd been fighting ever since. And what he said embarrassed her.

She suspected that was as calculated as the disappointing kiss. She'd been so open with him that night in January, had given him all she had. And he'd walked away without a backward glance.

"I was just passing the time, playing around, like you were doing," she said. "Why didn't you send me home? I was there so you figured you'd go ahead and initiate the new girl?"

She'd managed to upset him. She could tell by the muscle that jumped in his cheek. "I've never slept with anyone else at Department 6."

"So *I'm* the only stupid one?" She managed a laugh. "Are you *that* angry I didn't call?"

Apparently, he could give as good as he got. "Not anymore. But neither am I interested in a second helping."

His gaze dropped to her breasts, which tingled beneath his intimate perusal. "If that's true, your body doesn't know it."

"Fortunately, it's my brain that's in control," she said, then she sashayed to her room, closed the door behind her and crumpled onto the grimy carpet.

Nate had no idea that raw lust could be so powerful. He stayed in the living room, feeling a bit shaken—but at least he didn't have a hangover. Last night, he'd found only a couple of bars within an hour's drive, and both of them had been closed at two in the morning.

He sighed. He'd known this would be a difficult assignment, but this was ridiculous. What the hell was wrong with him? They'd slept together six *months* ago and afterward they'd carried on as if it'd never happened. Why, after the passage of so much time, couldn't he forget and stop wanting her?

Because they were spending almost every minute together. There was no break, no distraction. And it didn't help that they had all the privacy in the world. They could make love for hours without fear of a single interruption....

Turning, he stared at her closed door. If they could keep their distance while they worked to bring Ethan down, they'd both be better off. He doubted that scenario was very realistic, but...

"Damn you, Milt," he muttered. Eager to escape the trailer, he grabbed the card Rachel had dropped onto the TV and went to bathe and dress. It was time he paid a visit to Paradise. Any husband would be incensed to have some cult leader sending notes to his wife. Nate saw no reason he should be any different.

But when he entered the bathroom, he saw his computer bag and realized he hadn't left his laptop in the truck's toolbox the way he'd assumed. He went out to be sure. Then he checked the living room, his bedroom and asked Rachel if she'd borrowed it. She said she hadn't touched it.

After searching the entire trailer again with no luck, he had to accept what he didn't want to face—it was gone.

15

Ethan glanced up from some architectural designs for the new school he'd been studying with Vince Gregory, the man who'd drawn them. "What did you say?"

Bartholomew stood just inside the large room where Ethan received visitors or listened to various complaints and requests. "Nathan Mott's here. The guards told him you were busy, but he says he won't leave until he talks to you."

The disapproval evident in Bartholomew's body language seemed to shout, *I told you that woman was trouble!* He'd shown up in the wee hours of the morning with Nate Mott's computer, but he hadn't been able to access the hard drive, which was encrypted. Knowing Bart, he was still trying, but he'd admitted himself that he hadn't uncovered any real proof that Rachel and Nate were anything other than what they claimed.

"Fine. Send him in."

"Holy One, I think maybe—"

He gestured impatiently. "Send him in."

With a stiff nod, Bartholomew walked out. Five minutes later, he returned with a man who was easily six feet four inches tall and two hundred and ten pounds of solid muscle. No wonder Bartholomew was worried.

Standing at the head of the conference table that took up one section of the room, Ethan told his young architect that they'd meet again later after lunch. Then he waited for the younger man to leave.

Bartholomew remained at the entrance; Rachel's husband stood slightly in front of him.

Smiling, Ethan came around the table to greet Mr. Mott with a handshake. He found it galling to acquiesce to a tradition that put them on an equal footing, but shaking hands would make him seem more respectable in Nathan's eyes. "Mr. Mott, welcome to Paradise. I'm Ethan Wycliff. To what do I owe the pleasure of your visit this morning?"

"Did you send this to my wife?" Nate held out the note Ethan had someone deliver earlier.

Bart wasn't happy to learn of the note; that was obvious. He preferred Ethan not to get involved until he knew more about the Motts. But as long as he was cautious, Ethan saw no reason he couldn't befriend them while Bart conducted the type of check that would keep the church safe. "That's the brief message I sent to Rachel, is it not?"

"You tell me. There's no signature."

"I apologize for that. I didn't intend to be cryptic. I felt so confident she'd know it was from me, signing it seemed pointless."

Nathan Mott's greenish-brown eyes were probing. "My question is *why?* What do you want with her?"

Ethan shrugged innocently. "Nothing of an inappropriate nature, I assure you. She came here last night seeking spiritual healing. As a prophet concerned with her eternal well-being, I merely wanted to let her know that she's been in my thoughts and is welcome to return at will.

"As a prophet."

"Yes." Ethan didn't qualify that statement. Doing so would compromise everything he'd accomplished so far. He had to present himself in the same way every time.

Nate's jaw jutted forward. "You have no other interest in her."

Excitement trickled through Ethan. He recognized a worthy adversary when he saw one, sensed the potential here and suddenly knew why he'd been so intrigued with Rachel. She could be the one. After months and months of careful searching, he might finally have found the Vessel.

"Only the same interest I have in you and every other man, woman or child." He kept his expression one of polite solicitation, but he told himself that there'd come a day when this proud man would gladly hand over his wife, even watch as Ethan rode her, and consider it a great privilege. "It's my job to see to the eternal salvation of all those who would be saved."

"You've hardly met my wife."

"I care equally about everyone."

"Even me?"

"Even you. So you see? You have nothing to be upset about. But I'm glad you're here." Ethan waved him over to the table. "You're a cement contractor, correct?"

"I'm a photographer."

"A cement contractor turned photographer."

Nate nodded.

"Wonderful. I was just going over the building plans

for our new school. Perhaps you could give me a bid on pouring the foundation."

Rachel's husband seemed reluctant at first, but it wasn't long before he gained some enthusiasm for the project. No doubt he could use the money to support his wife.

He stayed for more than two hours, figuring out the amount of concrete that would be necessary and writing an estimate. When they were finished, Ethan all but promised him the job, then walked him to the front gate. "We're having a celebratory dinner tonight," he said. "We'd love to have you and your wife join us."

"What are you celebrating?" Nate asked.

"One of our members has just learned she's expecting a baby." They were actually celebrating that this woman had given herself to all interested men via a ritual last month, which meant she had no idea whose child she carried and had therefore agreed to let it be raised by all. She would be no more than a regular "sister" in the child's life, in accordance with Ethan's vision of having all things in common.

Nate peered curiously at the people pouring out of the cheese factory. It was noon, when everyone took their lunch break. "Do you celebrate every pregnancy?"

"Some are more important than others," he hedged. "But yes, for the most part, we do. Children are a blessing, the future of our race and our religion."

"What about that woman I've been hearing about—Martha something? Is it true what she's telling people?"

Ethan had expected this question. "Not at all. She became disgruntled with her role in life and wanted to leave the commune. Her husband didn't wish to go with her, and he was the better parent so we supported him in keeping their child. Whatever happened was between them." Ethan lowered his voice as though taking Nate into his confidence. "I suppose it's possible he got angry and struck her, but I've never known him to be violent. If you want the truth, I personally think she gave herself those injuries. She's always had emotional issues."

"So she's simply a disaffected member."

"Every group has one or two, sometimes more." He patted Nate on the back. "Come tonight and speak to her husband. You'll see."

The simplicity of Ethan's lie was what made it believable. He had confidence in that. But Nate wasn't quite satisfied and it showed on his face. "What about the man who showed me in today? He stopped me and my wife when we were shooting pictures not far from here yesterday."

"You're referring to Bartholomew."

"Yes. He acted as if you have something to hide, as if you don't like strangers."

"Don't let Bart worry you. After hearing the wild accusations Martha's been spouting to the press, he's a little defensive, that's all. Surely you can understand. He's afraid outsiders will believe her. That they'll see what they want to see instead of the truth and cause problems for us."

Nate squinted against the sun. "I guess that makes some sense."

"All our beliefs make sense, if you'll allow me to explain them."

"Rachel and I don't have to give up our worldly possessions or get a tattoo on our foreheads to socialize with you folks, do we?"

"Of course not. Those who take covenants do so by choice. The brand is a symbol of their personal commitment, their faith."

"And you don't care that I don't have any faith?"

"Faith is something that has to be attained bit by bit. You are new to our doctrines." He smiled. "How can I convince you that an apple is good if I won't let you taste it?"

As soon as he'd said that, Ethan wished he'd chosen a different metaphor. But if Nate caught the inadvertent reference to Satan in the Garden of Eden, he didn't let on. "I just don't want to get involved in anything like that Jonestown massacre," he said.

Ethan laughed at his skepticism. "You are filled with fear of the unknown, my friend. Come to the dinner. You'll see. We will impose nothing on you that isn't of your own choosing. And you might enjoy yourself."

"I'll talk to Rachel about it."

"Good. I'm sure she can use some friendly neighbors."

At last, Nathan Mott nodded. "I don't want my wife to be miserable and lonely now that I've dragged her away from her family and friends." He motioned at some of the faithful who passed by. "But don't expect me to dress the part. I prefer pants to skirts."

"Not only is this the type of clothing best suited to the climate, jalabiyas are functional and inexpensive to make. But as I said, everything we do here is by choice." Ethan signaled to the guards to unlock the gate. "Thank you for coming."

Ethan watched Nate pass through. He wasn't sure what to make of him, but he was intrigued enough to want more contact—with him *and* his wife.

"Holy One."

Already, Bart was at his elbow. "What is it?"

"Did I hear correctly? Did you invite Mr. Mott to the celebration?"

"I did."

"But inviting these *outsiders*—" he spat the word with so much disdain that he might as well have said *infidels* "—could attract attention we don't want. It could encourage those who would see us disbanded."

Ethan turned to face him. "Have you figured out the password so you can get access to his computer?"

"Not yet."

"Take it to C. J. Howard. He's good at that sort of thing. I want to know what's on it."

"If you'll give me some more time I might be able to crack it myself."

"I'm in a hurry."

"Why?"

"Because—" he paused for maximum effect "—I've seen a vision."

Bart made no reply.

"Rachel Mott is the Vessel," he continued. "She's the one we've been waiting for."

"A *heathen,* Holy One? You would spill your seed in a heathen?"

Surprised, Ethan stiffened. "You'd call the mother of my son a heathen?"

As usual, Bart stood tall. He was nothing if not stubborn. But he also knew when he'd gone too far. "Of course not. I was…surprised, that's all. You know God's will better than me."

Slightly mollified, Ethan glared at him. "Oh, ye of little faith. No matter what she is now, she won't be a heathen when I'm done with her. She will become the bride of the whole church. Every man here will spill his seed in her." All those who were capable, at least.

"Yes, Holy One." Bart bowed his head. "I beg you, forgive me."

Ethan knew he was hardly repentant, but there was no point in punishing the one person he trusted above all others. Bart was only being cautious. "Do whatever you can to bring me reassurance that the Motts are what I hope they are and you shall be forgiven."

"Of course. I have done and will always do anything you ask. I think you know that."

Ethan squeezed his shoulder. "I do. Now get that computer to C.J."

Bart nodded and left. Maybe the man lacked refinement, as Ethan's father would say, but he was a valuable tool. Ethan had no doubt that once he felt reassured about the Motts, Bart would do everything in his power to deliver Rachel to the ceremonial platform they were erecting in the middle of the courtyard. There, everyone—including Nate—would witness the mating ceremony. The whole church would worship God, one another and the power of procreation every night until she was pregnant. Then they'd hold monthly ceremonies during which a new group of men would mate with her on the same platform. It would be a frenzy of sexual worship taking place in the dark of night with only the moon and stars and a few torches to give them light. But first, those who wanted to participate would mark their foreheads with charcoal, if they hadn't already made a permanent mark, and covenant to love and cherish Rachel. To die for her, if necessary—her and the holy child.

Ethan felt himself grow clammy with excitement. Of course the Vessel had to be an outsider. That was why he hadn't been able to find the right woman. He'd instinctively known what his conscious mind had not yet recognized—the group would never be willing to elevate someone with whom they worked on a daily basis to a position so far above them. But this…this was sheer genius. He'd notify the entire church of her calling before she came to the dinner. That would set the appropriate tone for how she should be treated. And it would allow everyone to court her in anticipation of the rituals to come.

The possibility that her husband might refuse threatened to dim Ethan's euphoria. But he quickly disregarded that idea. There were ways to persuade him. If he still refused, he'd be killed. It was that simple.

Rachel was angry when Nate returned, and he couldn't blame her. Once again, he'd left her without word of where he was going and without a car. Even though he'd promised not to. He should've clarified that he'd meant he wouldn't leave her at *night*.

She sat on the couch, watching a movie from a selection of DVDs that were almost as outdated as the trailer, and shot him a dirty look when he walked in.

"Hey."

She didn't respond, so he held out the bag he was carrying. "I brought you something." He felt a lot better. After his visit to Paradise, he was beginning to believe they might be able to stay in close contact with the Covenanters without having to live in their commune. It would certainly be easier to protect themselves if they weren't locked behind that gate with people who were convinced Ethan was a god.

A quick point of the remote muted the TV. "Unless you have news that you're heading back to California and sending Drake or someone else to replace you, I'm not interested."

"Sorry. All I have is a doughnut."

"That's your peace offering?"

"It was the last one they had. I saved it for you."

No comment from Rachel.

"Looks pretty tasty." He removed the apple fritter from the sack as if he'd eat it himself. "Okay, if you don't want it…"

She jumped up and whisked it out of his hand. "What'd Ethan say?"

He wadded up the empty sack, shot it at the wastebasket—and missed. "You know I went to Paradise?"

"Where else would you go?" She sampled a piece of the fritter.

"I thought about trying to find a place to develop my pictures. But I knew it would take too much time."

"And you would've brought me with you. Anyway, I don't think we're going to need those pictures. We're gaining direct access easily enough." She moaned at the taste of her doughnut.

"It's that good?" It really had been the last one, and fritters were his favorite kind. He'd bought it, hoping she'd share.

"Delicious. Too bad they didn't have another one."

"No kidding." After picking up the sack, he threw it away and went into the kitchen to get her a glass of milk.

"Are you going to tell me about your time in Paradise?" she called.

"I was treated okay. Ethan had me look at some building plans. He wants me to pour the foundation for a school."

"Isn't that kind of complicated?" She came as far as the partial wall and took a sip of the milk he handed her.

"Not really."

"You're sure? You'd know that?"

"Of course I'd know it. I grew up pouring cement with my uncle nearly every summer. I can handle it."

More interested in the doughnut than the milk—probably because he wanted it, too—she set the glass on a nearby table. "You could've told me that before."

He tried not to grin at the way she was lording her possession of that fritter over him. "I told you I could pour cement."

"You didn't tell me where you learned, or that you had extensive experience."

"That was important for you to know?"

"Of course! I would've been much more confident in your ability to pull off—" She rolled her eyes. "Never mind. Back to the Covenanters. You think we'll be around long enough that you'll have to prove your concrete-pouring skills by putting in the foundation?"

He watched her lick glaze from her fingertips. "I hope not, but the job gives us an excuse to establish a relationship with Ethan without having to join a religion that would be pretty tough to swallow."

"Not if you want to have sex with every woman you see," she said flippantly.

"True." He rubbed his chin as if he hadn't considered it from that angle. "Okay, on second thought…"

She slugged him in the arm.

"Hey, you know I'm joking." He rubbed his biceps, although it didn't hurt.

"No, I don't," she said, and slugged him again.

This time it did hurt. "What was that for?"

"For leaving me behind and being such a jerk last night."

He deserved it. He wasn't quite sure what had come over him, except a case of "I want what I can't have." But he didn't feel bad enough about his poor behavior to resist the opportunity to grab her wrist and shove her doughnut halfway into his mouth.

"Stop! That's mine," she cried, and the next thing he knew they were wrestling for it on the living room floor. She was stronger than he would've guessed, but she was trying to keep her doughnut from getting smashed so he pinned her quite easily.

As he was lying on top of her, breathing heavily from the exertion, he realized he should've quit while he was ahead. The sticky glaze that had flaked off during the fight was all over them. But that wasn't the only problem. Fresh desire slammed into him, sending blood rushing to his groin. He'd let down his guard, and this was what came of it. "Well, now we know who can take whom," he said.

She made a show of gulping down the rest of the doughnut. "You were worried I could take you?" she asked with her mouth full.

He was afraid she still might. But not in the way she meant. She seemed to have resigned herself to the fact that his feelings weren't what hers were—or had been—so she was better able to ignore the chemistry between them. All that did was make her more appealing because she seemed less fragile.

"Not really." He got up before she could notice that he wasn't feeling so playful anymore.

"What's our next step with the Covenanters?" She stood and dusted herself off.

"We go to a celebration there this evening."

She looked up, frowning. "You know their celebrations sometimes turn into orgies."

He shrugged. "An orgy's got to beat a stoning."

"What about your computer?"

"What about it?"

"If they're the ones who took it, we could be in trouble. The browser history alone will prove we have more than a passing interest in Paradise."

"Not necessarily. With the rumors flying around Portal and elsewhere in this part of the state, it's conceivable that we were curious enough to look them up."

"What about your work files? What if they get access to those?"

"That's what has me worried," he said.

16

That evening when Rachel rolled up to the gate at Paradise, she was riding in the passenger seat and she wasn't thinking about the height of the fence or the razor wire. She had the missing girl from Portal on her mind. She couldn't imagine that Ethan would socialize with locals if he'd kidnapped one. It would be far too easy to spot Courtney or pick up on some detail that would give away the fact that she was here. But the girl had to have gone *somewhere*. Maybe she was hiding in the compound of her own accord and didn't want her parents to know. After all, this was the ultimate counterculture. Maybe joining a cult seemed like a great way to punish her folks for whatever she held against them—like giving birth to her or living in Portal.

The security personnel were far more respectful than the ones she'd encountered during her first visit. They spoke in somber tones, barely glanced at her and Nate's IDs and waved them through without the undercarriage check. Bart himself came out to meet them after they'd parked at the big tent.

"Welcome back to Paradise," he said the moment they stepped out.

Rachel exchanged a furtive look with Nate.

Bartholomew's words were clipped, but at least he was making an effort. "Thank you."

"The Holy One is waiting for you in the dining hall. You're invited to dine with church leaders before the celebration begins."

Dinner sounded conventional enough, but knowing Ethan's support for certain kinds of festivities, who could say what might follow?

Bart led them to the largest of the permanent buildings she'd first seen through Nate's lens.

Nate put his arm around her as they climbed the steps and were shown into a room where Ethan sat at the head of a long table.

"The Holy One" turned immediately. "Ah, there you are," he said, and got up to greet them by kissing them both on each cheek. "We've been looking forward to seeing you again. Please have a seat."

There were twelve other men, most in their thirties or forties, around the table. They'd stood when Ethan had. Now they approached and embraced Ethan but not Rachel. As they turned to her, they bowed their heads, murmuring things like, "Your presence is a blessing" and "Thanks be to God, who sustains all life."

When she finally reached the table, Ethan had her sit on one side of him and put Nate on the other. "Friends bring much joy to an otherwise unremarkable day," he said. "Thank you for coming. Now, let us pray."

He prayed with his eyes open and his hands lifted toward heaven. The others bowed their heads and repeated his words. Rachel sat quietly, waiting for the prayer to end. She felt Nate's eyes on her but refused to look directly at him.

The meal consisted of marinated steak shish kebabs

and rice. She enjoyed the food but felt the others were paying her too much attention. Every time she looked up, she found one or another studying her curiously. Except for Bartholomew. Seated at the far end, he kept his gaze anchored to his plate. Was that because she was the only woman in the room? Was it unusual for Ethan to dine with a woman? Or was the problem that she was also an outsider?

She didn't know, but she felt as if she'd dropped through the rabbit hole in *Alice in Wonderland.* Here, anything could happen.

When Nate and Ethan began discussing the school and the other improvement projects Ethan had planned, Rachel started to feel more comfortable. But that didn't last. Soon Ethan was probing for information about them.

"So how long have you been married?" he asked.

Nate answered as smoothly as if he was telling the truth. "Almost three and a half years."

"Those first few years can be rough."

"If you don't get along." Nate took another bite of his food and talked through it. Rachel knew his manners were better than that, but he was playing up the blue-collar aspect of his character. "We haven't had any problems, have we, honey?"

"None," she confirmed.

Ethan grinned at her, implying he knew something she didn't, which bothered Rachel, but she resisted the temptation to try to convince him about her fake marriage. It was preferable to let Nate handle the web of lies this conversation demanded. She wasn't sure what Ethan and Nate had discussed when Nate came here on his own. Why risk contradicting him?

"Yours is a match made in heaven, then," Ethan said.

"More or less," Nate murmured.

"Where did you meet?" It was Bart who asked.

Nate gave him the spiel about the Jazz game and Rachel applauded the way he'd provided enough information to seem truthful but resisted the urge to embellish. Too much information could get an operative in as much trouble as acting too secretive. That was the first thing they'd been taught in their human behavior and psychology classes—to look anyone they needed to fool in the eye and to keep whatever had to be said to a minimum.

"So you're both from Utah?" Bart seemed eager to take over the questioning.

Nate pointed with his fork. "Rach is. I moved there when I was twelve. I grew up pouring cement with my uncle."

Bart picked at his food, as if he wasn't all that interested in eating. "What'd your father do?"

"He worked as a chiropractor until he retired a few months ago."

Rachel knew this part was true; she remembered when Nate had had to leave a staff meeting early to make his father's retirement party.

"How old is he?" Ethan asked, joining in again.

"What is he these days, Rach? Sixty-five?" He looked at her for confirmation, but being included in such a question almost made her laugh. She'd worked for Nate for six months but knew very little about his family. Like a lot of men, he loved them but talked about them only when there was a reason. From what she'd pieced together so far, he'd been raised in a middle-class home in Long Beach, where his family still lived, and he had grown up spending most of his time surfing. As a result his grades had suffered, so his dad had encouraged him to join the military because he was afraid his son would turn out to be a beach bum if he didn't get some discipline in his life. Turned out Nate was plenty ambitious; he was just a late bloomer. Nate's only sibling, a brother who was younger by seven or eight years, promised to give his parents far more trouble than Nate did. Randall had been going to SDU but was currently on suspension for his poor grades. Although Nate's voice was filled with affection whenever Randall's name came up, he usually called him a pain in the ass.

"Your dad just turned sixty-six," Rachel supplied.

"That's right." Nate nodded at her response and talked on as if they'd been helping each other answer questions like this for as many years as he claimed they'd been together. "But the way that guy eats, he'll probably last longer than me," he added.

Rachel had heard Nate jokingly refer to his father as Jack Lalanne, Jr., so this was probably true, too. Like her, Nate relied on the familiar when he could. It was so much easier to remember.

"And your mother?" Ethan asked. "Is she interested in health food, too?"

Rachel got the impression that Ethan was truly interested; Bart, however, was trying to trip them up.

"She worked with my father as a massage therapist," Nate said. "They ran the business together. When he retired and sold the practice, Mom stayed on, but in a limited capacity. She works ten or fifteen hours a week. Says she likes having the pocket change."

"Any siblings?" Bart asked.

Growing uncomfortable with Bart's level of interest in such specifics, Rachel searched for a way to change the subject, but Nate didn't seem to be concerned. "Just one, a younger brother."

Ethan offered them each more wine and poured it when they acquiesced. "What does he do?"

"Randy's still in school," Nate said. "He hopes to be a chiropractor like Dad."

"But you chose cement." Bart again.

"I was never that great a student. Working outdoors suits me better."

"And what about you, Rachel? What's your background?" Bart wanted to know.

Ethan turned expectantly, as though he was eager to hear her response, so Rachel gave a quick summary based on the rough sketch from the dossier—her family in Utah, her experience working in child care, her two years at a community college, her father's job as a supermarket clerk. Then, to avoid Twenty Questions, she asked about the Introductory Meetings they held and how many visitors came from week to week, and when they tried to bring the conversation back to her, she put them on the defensive by mentioning Courtney Sinclair.

These people knew something about the missing girl. Nate would bet his life on it. From the moment Rachel mentioned that a girl who'd attended one of their meetings had gone missing, and that her parents were frantically searching for her, the room grew quiet.

"We're aware of the situation, of course. It's a real tragedy," Ethan said, but he didn't seem particularly sincere.

Bartholomew spoke up immediately afterward. "Courtney's a nice young girl. She wanted to make her home here with us."

Nate swallowed the food in his mouth. "She said that?"

"Yes. She came to a meeting and asked to stay for the Preparatory, or initiation," he said, "but she wasn't old enough. She needed her parents' approval. She asked if I'd intercede for her, but that isn't my place. We welcome all who would be happy here, but we don't want trouble. I sent her home with a release form and—" he raised his bony shoulders "—she never came back."

"That she's gone missing is unfortunate, but not altogether surprising," Ethan added. "Her parents probably said no, just as she expected, and she's on her way to New York City or somewhere equally exciting to a young woman who's an adventurer at heart."

"How would she get there?" Nate asked. "Travel costs money."

"Believe me, she's very resourceful," Bart said.

"She was willing to do almost anything to get away from her parents. And since she left, I can see why. They're like other repressed Christians—afraid to experience the world for fear they'll fall into the hands of the 'devil,' so afraid of him they actually become just like him."

Nate found it ironic that Ethan, of all people, would say that. If his religion was like other religions, he, too, used the fear of hell to motivate his members. "So you think she's still alive?"

"I have no reason to believe otherwise." He closed his eyes and chewed with greater relish. "We must remember to thank Sister Maxine for this delicious meal. She has outdone herself, has she not?"

Just about every man there nodded and mumbled agreement. But Rachel ignored the change of topic and drew Ethan right back to Courtney.

"Her parents are claiming you've kidnapped her."

The enjoyment instantly fled Ethan's face. "I'm aware of that, too, but I have no idea why anyone would make such an unfounded accusation."

Once again, the "Guides" began to study their food as if they'd never seen steak and rice before.

"I talked to her mother a few hours ago," Rachel said. "I was looking at the flyer they have at the grocery store, when she came up and asked if I'd ever seen her daughter." She took a sip of wine. "When I told her I hadn't, she said, 'The Covenanters have her.'"

The encounter had never taken place. Nate knew that because Rachel hadn't had a car until he'd returned, and they hadn't gone to the grocery store before coming to Paradise. But she was selling the incident, making it believable—and making everyone uncomfortable.

"Did you tell her you were here for an Introductory?" Ethan asked.

"I did."

"And did you also tell her we have nothing to hide?"

"I told her that everything seemed perfectly normal and that you treated me well."

He raised his wineglass. "And what did she say to that?"

"She said things are not always as they appear."

He chuckled. "What a hag."

Rachel straightened in her seat. *"Hag?"*

"You'll have to forgive me. I don't care for the

woman. She doesn't even know me, yet she's pointing her finger in my direction. If she was a better parent, her child would probably be at home."

"I see."

"Some people will believe the worst no matter what," he added with a shrug.

"Maybe it would help if you allowed her to search Paradise," Nate suggested.

"No." Bartholomew shook his head. "We can't. We know Courtney's not here. Trying to prove it would only leave us vulnerable. What if Lynne Sinclair told the police that we mistreated her? Or that she saw some evidence she didn't see? She hates us. The prejudice we face almost everywhere is enormous. Nobody's willing to tolerate those who are different, who buck the status quo." He held up his own wine and examined the color of it. "Religious wars are often the bloodiest, most bitterly fought wars of all. And they've occurred throughout history. In some countries, they're happening today."

"Not in *this* country," Nate said quietly.

Bart put his wine back on the table. "This country isn't as tolerant as you might think. Staying away from mainstream society is really the only way to avoid the kind of opposition that could ruin what we have established. That's why there's a fence around Paradise. That's why we've chosen to live inside a cage in the middle of the desert. We don't want to bother other people, and we don't want them bothering us."

Rachel turned to Ethan. "Have you run into opposition in previous locations?"

"Everywhere," Ethan complained. "Opposition *and* persecution."

Nate wiped his mouth with his napkin. "Have you ever met Courtney's mother face-to-face?"

"Of course. She's been at the gate several times, demanding that we let her daughter go." He set down his fork. "Did you promise her you'd look for Courtney while you were here, Sister Rachel?"

Nate held his breath. Saying no wouldn't be believable. Anyone would agree to look for a missing child. But *yes* came with its own risks.

"I said I would, yes."

Waiting to see how "Alpha and Omega" would take this news, Nate held his next bite halfway to his mouth. But Ethan didn't seem upset. His lips, which looked more like a young boy's than a man's, curved into a smile.

"Then you'll have to live up to your word," he said. "I'll personally give you the grand tour as soon as we finish dinner."

"But the celebration—" Bart started.

Ethan silenced him with a glare. "Will wait. We have to do what we can to reassure the community, Bart. We don't want the poison to spread, do we?"

Bart didn't respond, but Ethan didn't seem to care.

"Now, are we ready for dessert?" With a clap of his hands, he signaled for the woman who'd been hovering near them to bring the final course.

Ethan watched his guests closely as he walked them through the compound. Because Bartholomew was ruining the illusion of openness he was trying to create, he'd sent him away to check on C.J.'s progress with Nate's computer. It was just the three of them now, and he liked it that way. They'd already been through the business, church and personal sections of the Enlightenment Hall, the temporary school Ethan planned to replace, various tents that housed his people, the beehives and chicken coops, and the garden and livestock areas that made the commune as self-sufficient as possible.

Ostensibly, he was taking them on this tour to prove he had nothing to hide, so he introduced them to everyone they encountered. He figured it couldn't hurt to generate some goodwill with the outside world, especially since that would undermine the support Courtney's mother was hoping to achieve. Besides, it gave him the opportunity to show off a little. Here he was, a college dropout, running an entire city.

"How many people work here?" Rachel asked.

They were standing on the cement floor of the cheese factory. A cinder-block rectangle filled with cheese presses made from pans, plates, mason jars, PVC pipe, wooden dowels, bicycle inner tubes and flour sacks, it wasn't exactly a state-of-the-art facility. But it *was* clean and well organized, and the people who worked here were getting very good at what they did. As of last month, the church had purchased a second refrigerated truck to bring in the milk they needed and to deliver their organic cheeses to distribution centers. "About forty."

Nate touched a can of salt. "Mostly women?"

Ethan remembered Nate's interest in those who'd exited this building at lunchtime yesterday. "All women, except the managers."

Rachel had wandered over to the racks where sack after sack of cheese curd hung so the whey could drain into collection buckets below. But hearing those words, she pivoted. "Why aren't there any women managers?"

It was the first time Ethan had felt irritated with her. Just because he was indulging her by showing her around didn't mean he had to apologize for the way he ran things. This was *his* church, *his* commune. The women here did whatever he told them to. "It isn't their place."

"Who decides what their place will be?"

She was challenging him again. Narrowing his eyes to let her know he didn't appreciate it, he folded his arms. "*I* do."

There was a pause, as if she thought he'd elaborate, but he didn't. Ultimately, it was Rachel who broke the silence.

"And if I were to join, what would *my* place be?"

The image that came to Ethan's mind dispelled his irritation. She didn't know how he expected her to behave. She was a feminist, like so many of the young women he'd known in college. But she'd learn her true calling. She'd fulfill her role just like his mother had. "I would make a very special place for you," he said.

The way Nate shifted toward his wife told Ethan this statement had been accurately identified as a threat. But it wasn't enough for Ethan to conquer Rachel. He wanted to subjugate Nate, too.

"I would love it if you both came to live here. There's no rent, no medical bills, no grocery bills. No rich or poor. We are all children of God, all equal in His eyes."

"And the work?" Nate asked.

"Is divided up just as equitably."

"With all the positions of authority occupied by men," Rachel said.

"Everyone does what's suited to him or her."

Nate's expression gave nothing away as he thrust his large hands into the pockets of his chinos, but Rachel was clearly displeased enough to frown as her husband changed the subject. "How'd you get into the cheese business? Is it what your father did?"

Ethan selected a reply calculated to make them admire him even more—one he hoped would strike a chord in Rachel. Along with hesitation and distrust, there was pain inside her. Ethan could sense it, but he wasn't sure where it was coming from. She'd mentioned losing her mother. Was that the only reason she kept the world at a distance? Or were there others?

"No, my father was an abusive alcoholic," he said. "He couldn't hold down a job."

"That's terrible," she murmured. "I'm sorry."

"Mine wasn't an easy childhood. But we can overcome our pasts. That's the chief message of my ministry. I am proof."

She stepped away from the racks of curd and peeked inside the refrigerators that held the wheels already formed. "You've done very well." Closing the door, she gestured around them. "You've not only established a new community, you've devised a way to provide for them."

"One of my first converts was raised by a chemist who was also a homesteader," he explained. "She'd been taught to make cheese and to do a variety of other things—garden, can, sew. She's been a great asset to the community."

"What's her job?" Rachel asked.

Ethan allowed himself a wry smile at her stubborn resistance to the concept that God intended women to be subservient. "She makes cheese like the others. That's what she's good at."

Rachel's lips thinned. "I'm sure she finds it stimulating."

Before Ethan could respond to her sarcasm, Nate opened the door. "Is this the end of the tour?"

Ethan hadn't shown them the hidden bunker where he stored the guns and weapons. Neither had he shown them the shallow grave that hid Courtney's body. But the tour was definitely over. "That's it."

"What about Todd?"

"Todd?" he repeated as though he didn't remember.

"Martha's husband," Nate clarified. "You said I'd meet him."

"And you will. I expect he'll be at the party." He clapped his hands to lend his words a note of finality. "Now, once the celebration is finished, I hope you'll feel comfortable returning to Portal with word that we are not kidnappers. That we have no idea where young Courtney could be hiding."

"I'll be sure to tell her mother," Rachel murmured.

"Great. I hear music. Let's not miss the fun."

Rachel slipped her hand into her husband's as Ethan led them back across the compound.

It was the first time Rachel had reached out to him. Nate wasn't positive why she'd done it, but he got the impression it was to show Ethan her preference for him. He liked that. He also liked the way her fingers slipped so easily through his. The physical contact gave him confidence that, as conflicted as they felt about each other, they were united against Ethan.

"Alpha and Omega" kept his back to them the entire walk. When they got to the large tent not far from the Enlightenment Hall, he paused to hold the flap for them. But once inside he became the center of attention and proceeded to play the part of God's anointed. Men and women alike flocked to him, kneeling at his feet and kissing his hands. He occasionally glanced over to make sure his guests were taking it all in, but Nate was glad when he and Rachel could drift away and get lost in the crowd. Many of the revelers were dancing to Bob Marley and other Jamaican music, enhanced by three men playing bongo drums at one end of the tent. Sometimes the people on the dance floor migrated to the edges to let a particular group of men or women perform.

"You okay?" he murmured to Rachel when he felt it was safe to speak to her without being overheard.

She released his hand and folded her arms, hugging herself. "I hate him," she said.

"I thought you were impressed by him, that you sort of admired him."

"I'm impressed by his ability to awe and inspire. But I'm revolted by everything he is and everything he does. Did you hear what he said to me about the women in the commune? Why do they put up with it? I don't know if I can fake acceptance of all this…crap."

"I'm not exactly an admirer myself," he responded. "That's part of the reason we've got to put a stop to it, right?"

"Right."

"Anyway, you told me you were good at faking it."

He'd been hoping to get her to smile, but she didn't. "My skin crawls at the thought of letting Ethan touch me and, even worse, pretending to like it."

"He won't touch you."

Rachel studied the crowd. "It's far tamer than I expected it to be."

"Tame? It looks pretty wild to me, for a religious group."

"At least everyone's wearing clothes."

He chuckled. "For now." Several women were serving beer at a makeshift bar, but as far as Nate could tell, no drugs were being passed around. Ethan probably saved that kind of worship for special occasions. Otherwise, it'd be too expensive. He needed to be careful with money if he was going to fulfill the big plans he had for Paradise. The school alone would be an ambitious project. "I wish we knew what Todd looks like," he said. "I'm still hoping to run into him."

"James might've been in the school."

"Maybe. But we couldn't possibly tell which little boy he was." Realizing that they'd instinctively gravitated toward an empty corner, he brought them back to the edge of the group. It wouldn't help them blend in if Ethan or any of his followers spotted them off alone, conferring as if they were doing exactly what they *were* doing. "We should introduce ourselves, start working the crowd," he said, nodding when he spotted the young architect he'd seen with Ethan earlier.

She opened her mouth, then fell silent.

"What is it?"

"Over there," she said with a subtle flick of her head.

Nate tried to be discreet as he cast a glance in the direction she'd indicated. "What is it?"

"That woman with the scars. The one in the turquoise." Then he saw her—and remembered that Martha had talked about a woman who'd been burned in a fire. What had Martha called her? Sarah. Martha believed Sarah had saved her life.

"It's got to be her," he whispered.

"You think so?"

"She's off by herself. She's the right size. And her face is heavily scarred. Burn victims aren't all that common."

"Not ones with such extensive skin grafts, anyway. Let's go talk to her." She began pulling him along, but he freed himself from her grasp.

"You make the contact. She might be less intimidated by a woman. I'm going to mingle."

"You mean, search for Todd?"

"I'd like to at least meet him while I'm here."

She hesitated, and he was tempted to promise he'd keep an eye on her, but he knew that would be the quickest way to offend her. "Is there something else?"

Glancing between Sarah, who was hugging one wall, and Ethan, who'd taken his seat on a raised dais, she frowned and leaned close. "One of these people must've come into the trailer last night and taken your computer."

She was right, of course. The Covenanters were suspicious, had doubts. But that was to be expected, wasn't it? He and Rachel were new and untried, and the Covenanters had reason to be defensive.

"If they have it, they haven't accessed my files yet or we wouldn't be welcome here," he pointed out.

"I agree. But the question is—what happens if and when they break the code?"

That depended on how much of a threat the Covenanters perceived them to be.

17

Rachel felt Bartholomew's eyes on her before she'd even reached Sarah. At first, she was afraid he'd intercept her, but he didn't. He watched from where he stood, like a sentry at the door.

Grateful for the crowd, which obstructed his view at least some of the time, Rachel got herself a drink and sidled over to Martha's friend. She tried to make it look like she was just searching for a place from which to see the festivities and hoped Bartholomew would believe she had no ulterior motive for choosing this particular spot.

After about five minutes of watching the dancers, she offered Sarah a smile. "Hello."

Sarah squirmed in shy discomfort, but responded with a softly spoken, "Hi."

"I'm new here."

Ducking her head as if to hide her scars, she muttered, "Yes, I know."

"How long have you been part of the group?"

"Three years."

"How did you first become interested in the Church of the Covenant?"

She smoothed her robe. "I joined when Ethan and four of the Brethren came through my village."

"Village?" Rachel had hardly ever heard an American refer to his or her hometown as a village.

"It's sort of a bedroom community outside Albany, New York," she said. "There are only six hundred residents."

"That's pretty small."

When she didn't respond, Rachel had to come up with another way to keep her engaged. "So the Holy One came to visit and you...what? How did you become familiar with him?"

"I heard he was holding an Introduction near the Appalachian Trail, so I attended to see what all the uproar was about."

"Uproar?"

"My father's an atheist. He thinks people who believe in God are weak-minded fools, that the stories in the Bible are merely that—stories, which have been handed down for centuries."

"I've heard his take on the Bible before." She gave Sarah a conspirator's smile. "I guess Noah's Ark and Jonah and the whale are particularly difficult to accept from a realistic standpoint."

"I guess, but...I believe anything is possible—with God."

Didn't Rachel believe that, too? Sometimes. She wasn't an atheist, despite what she'd been through. "So you went to hear Ethan even though you knew your father wouldn't be happy about it?" She definitely could relate to that.

"I wanted to make up my own mind about Ethan."

"You must've been impressed with his doctrine."

"He's a powerful speaker."

And joining his group offered her an escape from her

father. How much did that enter into it? "I'd have to agree. I attended the meeting the other night and was quite impressed."

Sarah's earnestness suddenly overcame her shyness. "You could feel the Holy Spirit so strongly at that meeting, couldn't you?"

"You were there?"

"I go to all the Introduction Meetings. I love spreading the word of God, I love bringing those who suffer in darkness into the light. I want to tell everyone about the peace I've found in Christ." She looked away, obviously embarrassed to have grown so passionate.

"I can see why you might like that," Rachel said. "But…what about all the rumors? They don't bother you?"

She shifted, instantly uncomfortable again. "What rumors?"

"You know, the ones in Portal and probably other places, as well, about some woman getting stoned out here. And I'm not talking about getting stoned by smoking pot," she added. "I'm talking about the biblical kind."

When she received no response, Rachel decided to press a little harder. "Those rumors aren't true, are they?"

The joy had fled Sarah's face. Now she seemed downright miserable. "I don't know what you're talking about."

She knew. She just didn't want to discuss it. But Rachel wasn't willing to let her off the hook. "From what I've heard, there was a woman who used to live here named Martha Wilson. She's been telling the press that your prophet ordered her killed and that everyone circled around her and began throwing rocks."

"Is that why you came to the meeting?" she asked sadly. "To satisfy your curiosity about some…baseless accusations?"

"I came because, like you, I have hopes of living a better life. But before I can join your church, I have to trust your prophet. I can't support a man who'd murder one of his followers."

"The Bible tells us that the wicked will be punished."

That was no answer. Rachel peered into her face. "But punished by God, right? Not by his people."

"By Him or His servants, it is the same."

"Then how do you know who's doing His will and who isn't? Anyone could claim to be His servant."

"'Ye shall know them by their fruits.'"

Rachel wasn't interested in quoting scripture or debating its meaning. That was an argument no one could win, or half the religious wars in history would never have been fought. "So you're saying it *did* happen?"

She seemed rattled. "I'm not saying that."

"What *are* you saying?"

"It didn't happen." Sarah spoke more clearly, but she was wringing her hands and had broken into a sweat.

"Did you know Martha?" Rachel asked.

"I—I'm sorry. It was really nice meeting you, but…I have to go. I—I promised to visit someone," she said, and hurried away. It wasn't until Rachel saw Bartholomew approaching that she realized it was probably more than just the conversation that'd chased Sarah off.

"Are you enjoying yourself, Sister Mott?" he asked when he reached her.

"I am. Are you?" she countered.

"For the most part, although I'm not much for dancing."

"Somehow that doesn't surprise me."

He seemed taken aback by her frank response. "I haven't seen you out on the floor, either."

"I've been hoping to get to know a few people, so I won't be such a stranger."

He waved toward Sarah's departing back. "And how did you like Sister Sarah?"

"Is that her name? She left before introducing herself."

"She's quite shy."

"What happened to her? To cause the scarring?"

"Her mother fell asleep in bed with a lit cigarette. Sarah, who was staying the night at a neighbor's, was still awake when the house started to burn. She spotted the flames through her best friend's window and ran home to see about her mother and her two siblings. But it was already too late. They were either unconscious or had already died of smoke inhalation. She couldn't get them out and got trapped in the process."

"That's terrible."

"Fortunately, the firefighters arrived soon after and were able to save her, but not the rest of the family."

"How sad—to lose so many loved ones." Rachel should know. She'd lost most of her family, too. Just not in the same way. "She was badly burned, then?"

"She spent months in the hospital, recovering. After that, she had to move across the country and live with her father."

Rachel could hardly imagine how terrible that would be. "Is she married?"

"She was for a short time, to one of our members. Alpha and Omega asked him to marry her and give her children, but he left her for a nonbeliever and was excommunicated. He's since died of cancer."

"That's a lot of pain for one person."

"The refiner's fire has made her heart very pure. She has a great deal of faith. That's what pulls her through."

Before Rachel could respond, the crowd parted and Ethan stood before her.

"Whenever we celebrate the blessing of a new pregnancy, we have a special dance," he said. "I was hoping you might do me the honor of being my partner tonight."

The rumble of expectation overtook the last strains of the previous number as the Covenanters cleared the floor. "I'm not sure I'll know how."

"Anyone can slow dance," he said with a far too innocent smile.

Rachel glanced around, searching for Nate, and saw him near the makeshift bar. He had a beer in his hand, scowling as if he didn't like what he was seeing. But he was the only one who seemed unhappy. Everyone else smiled brightly in anticipation of the ceremonial dance.

Although Rachel preferred to say no, she couldn't embarrass Ethan in front of his entire flock. Not if she hoped to gain his trust.

"I'll do my best to follow your lead," she said, and let him take her hand.

Nate felt the eyes of several of the people he'd just met resting on him as Ethan danced with his "wife." He got the impression that the Covenanters—especially those who'd been introduced as Spiritual Guides—

were watching his reaction. Knowing Ethan's background and what he was capable of doing, Nate was tempted to step in. He needed Ethan to take an interest in Rachel, but he didn't want that interest to become prurient or it could be difficult for him to protect her. It wasn't as if anyone else would help him stop Ethan, if necessary; the stoning suggested that much.

"You have a very lovely wife."

Joshua Cooley, a man about his own age with thick sandy hair and a Roman nose, whom he'd met a few minutes earlier at the bar, approached him.

"Thank you."

Joshua gulped some of his beer. "Are you a religious man, Nate?"

"Not particularly, no."

"You weren't raised Catholic? Protestant? Methodist?"

"No."

"Do you ever feel the need to seek God?"

Ethan was holding Rachel too close. It was an insult to Nate as her husband, and Nate felt compelled to stop him. "Excuse me." He was about to set down his drink when Joshua caught him by the arm.

"I wouldn't if I were you."

Nate felt his eyebrows rise. "Wouldn't what?"

"Interrupt."

"Why the hell not?"

"Because it's always better to be in Ethan's good graces."

The bitterness that infused that statement surprised Nate. "Why?"

"He's the prophet. He can bless you in ways no one else can."

Was he being facetious? No. Joshua was a Spiritual Guide. That meant he was a true convert—didn't it? "From what I can tell, Ethan's as human as you or me. I don't need the blessing of another man, someone who might be as fallible as I am. I'd rather trust my own instincts."

"Ah, ignorance is bliss," he said with a laugh.

"What does that mean?"

"It means you don't have to live under the same laws I do." He lowered his voice until it was barely audible. "It also means you might want to get out while you still can," he said, and then melted into the crowd.

Nate might have followed him and demanded an explanation, but he didn't want to draw attention to Joshua, not if there was any chance that he might become an ally. Besides, Grady Booth had already slipped into the spot vacated by Joshua.

"I see you've met Josh."

Keeping one eye on the dancers, Nate sipped his beer. "Yes."

"He's been with Ethan since the beginning."

Grady, older by at least fifteen years, was dressed like a farmer. He had the hands of a farmer, too—along with tufts of hair coming out of his nose and ears. Nate disliked him instantly, but since he'd barely met the man, he chalked that up to his bad mood. "The beginning of what?" he asked, as if he didn't particularly care. He did, but Ethan's hands were moving lower on Rachel's back, and Nate wasn't sure he'd be able to stop himself from causing a scene if "the Holy One" actually touched her ass.

"The beginning of the Church of the Covenant, my

friend. He was one of the original roommates who joined after Ethan had his initial revelation."

"His initial revelation," Nate repeated.

"That's right."

"What was the revelation? That he should start a new church?"

"Basically. He was told that the world had gone astray and he was to lead it back."

Ethan was smiling into Rachel's face—talking to her, flirting with her, laughing. He was putting on a performance, even though he had to know that her husband wouldn't enjoy it. He was testing Nate, almost taunting him.

Shoving his hands in his pockets so he couldn't curl them into fists, Nate made an effort to relax his jaw. "And how was this message relayed to him?"

"In a dream."

"Were narcotics involved?"

Grady blinked. A few seconds later, he chuckled. "You have a dry wit, you know that?"

"That's what they tell me," he said. "But I don't think anyone's going to find it very funny if I charge onto that dance floor and break Ethan's nose."

"Excuse me?" he said, obviously flustered.

Nate jerked his head in Ethan's direction as the "prophet" was giving Rachel a squeeze. "You might tell him to watch his hands."

Grady's expression went cold. "You mean…you don't like the way he's holding your wife?"

"That's exactly what I mean."

The other man's chest swelled with indignation. "You're jumping to the wrong conclusion."

"It's the same conclusion any husband would come

to. I'm afraid I'm not very understanding when I'm confronted by another man groping my wife."

Grady sneezed several times, then wiped his hand on his shirt. "Ethan doesn't intend anything untoward."

"Whether he intends it or not, he might be facing salvation sooner than he expects if you force me to deliver my own message."

The man's nostrils flared, but he stalked onto the floor with his cowboy swagger and whispered to Ethan, who turned to look pointedly at Nate. When their eyes met, he laughed and made a show of putting a few inches of space between Rachel and him.

Returning Ethan's smile, Nate gave him a little salute.

"Happy now?" Grady muttered when he came back.

"I wouldn't say *happy* is the right word, but I'm no longer having fantasies of bashing my fist into your prophet's face. I figure that's an improvement, don't you?"

Grady's heavy jowls blazed red. "Anger management issues?"

"No issues. I'm just determined to protect what's mine."

"How long have you been married?"

"Not very long."

"You might not be so protective in a few years," he joked.

Nate indicated the other man's forehead. "Why don't you have the mark?"

"Because I'm a shepherd, not one of the sheep."

Nate remembered Rachel telling him that Ethan had said the same thing to explain the absence of a brand on his own face. These men thought they were superior to the people who believed in them and supported them. And that really bothered Nate. He hadn't learned much about religion, but his father had introduced him to the concept of the strong serving the weak. To him, that was the real meaning of Christ's life. But that kind of humility only occurred when religious leaders were sincere, self-effacing. The very opposite of the men he saw here. Which told him as much as he needed to know about the Covenanters. "Bart has the mark. Isn't he a shepherd?"

"He has a slightly different role. He's…unique, in case you haven't noticed."

"Tell me, what happens if a lamb wanders off?"

"It's my job to bring it back into the fold."

Nate mimed the use of a shepherd's crook. "Right around the throat, huh?"

Grady stared at him for several seconds. "I do it with gentle persuasion." His lips curved into a grim smile. "But when it comes to keeping out the wolves, I can be ruthless."

Nate had just established himself as a wolf, a danger. But that was *his* role. They were testing him, pushing him, trying to figure out what they could or couldn't get away with. He had to play the heavy, the grumpy disbelieving husband, or things could get out of control very fast. In this situation, Rachel was supposed to be the helpless lamb.

He just had to be sure she wasn't led to the slaughter.

18

The first song ended, but another slow one came on immediately after, and Ethan made no move to let Rachel go. She guessed he was prolonging the dance as some sort of payback, since Nate had taken exception to it. Ethan seemed to enjoy making him angry. Perhaps Nate provided a challenge, something he wasn't used to encountering these days. At least, not now that he'd become the be-all and end-all to his followers.

"Your husband is a jealous man," he said as Nate continued to watch them closely.

"He can be."

"He doesn't trust me."

She tried to keep things light. "He can be a bit skeptical. It takes time to win him over."

"Did it take time for *you* to win him over?"

She'd blown any chance of that the night she'd offered him everything she had, including her love. But this was just pretend, so she played it as if her "husband" really felt something for her. "As a matter of fact, it did."

"And now you know he's completely devoted."

"As devoted as any man could be, I suppose."

Ethan threw back his head and laughed. Rachel suspected he was exaggerating his reaction for Nate's benefit. He wanted Nate to think they were having more fun than they were. But she didn't care how their dance might be affecting her boss because she knew his jealousy was all part of the act.

"You have issues with men?" Ethan asked.

"Only when they try to control me. I'd had enough of that by the time I was seventeen."

"And who has tried to control you, beautiful Rachel?"

"Mainly my father, who was formidable."

Ethan's suit smelled of expensive cologne, which wasn't a wholly unwelcome scent. "He was strict?"

"Militant."

She hadn't gone into much detail at dinner.

He seemed to think that over. "At dinner, you said you were from Utah."

"That's right."

"Mormons can certainly be…rigid."

The music swelled and the volume of voices around them crescendoed with it. "A decent guess, but I've never been Mormon."

"What religion were you, then?"

The dossier Milt prepared hadn't covered this, so— like Nate at dinner—she went with what she felt would be convincing, and the truth was the most convincing of all. "A break-off from the Jehovah's Witnesses."

"A break-off?"

"When my father was in his early twenties, he met a man who was heavily involved in a faith that his brother had founded, one even stricter than the original. It's only been around for about thirty years. It isn't large."

"What's it called?"

"The Church of the Witness of True Faith."

"I've never heard of it. I don't know much about Jehovah's Witnesses, either. My own family was agnostic."

"Then it's ironic you became so religious."

"We all worship something."

"What did your family worship?"

"Money."

Hadn't he told her earlier that his father was a dissolute alcoholic? "And booze, right?"

His grin slanted to the side. He didn't seem to care that he'd just given away his lie. "Right."

"Definitely not *my* father's problem," she went on. She didn't want the conversation to focus on anything remotely close to the fact that she'd already known his background.

"What was?"

"Control, of course."

"The True Faith was more restrictive than most religions?"

"You could say that."

He turned her so she could no longer see Nate, only the faces of the many strangers looking on. "I've heard that Jehovah's Witnesses can't get a blood transfusion or donate blood," he said. "Was that also a belief in the True Faith?"

"That and more."

"For instance…"

"I wasn't allowed to attend a school dance. Or any school activity, for that matter." Her father had refused to permit her to join such activities. She could spend very limited time with girls whose beliefs differed from his, which put her on the outside of about every group or clique there was.

"Now I understand why you were reluctant to come out on the floor with me. You're not accustomed to this type of celebration."

"*Any* type of celebration."

Sobering, he rubbed her back lightly. "Poor baby. Tell me, what else did you miss?"

She hid a grimace at the endearment but had to admit he seemed genuinely interested and even somewhat sympathetic. "We didn't celebrate any holidays, including Mother's Day, Father's Day, Valentine's or our birthdays. I couldn't join the Girl Scouts, become a cheerleader, run for class president or play any sports. I wasn't supposed to salute the flag or sing the national anthem. And I couldn't date without supervision. I couldn't even say 'bless you' when someone sneezed, although I can't remember the reason for that."

He turned her yet again. "I'm guessing the worst sin of all would be marrying an unbeliever, correct?"

"Correct."

"But you did just that."

Not yet. However, it was exactly what she planned to do if she ever found the right man. Never would she marry someone who was ultrareligious. "Yes. I walked out when I was seventeen and haven't looked back." That was a bit of a stretch. She looked back all the time. But she couldn't *go* back. Only part of her ever wanted to.

"What a little rebel." Using one finger, he tilted up her chin. "How'd you get by?"

"I lived with another member who'd left the church until I graduated from high school. Then I put myself through college. College would also have been off-limits if I'd stayed at home, by the way."

"What about sex?"

She arched her eyebrows. "What about it?"

"With restrictions that limit everything else that's enjoyable in life, I would expect your religion to have strict rules regarding intercourse."

"'Neither fornicators, nor idolaters, nor adulterers, nor men kept for unnatural purposes, nor men who lie with men, nor thieves, nor greedy persons, nor drunkards, nor revilers, nor extortioners, shall inherit the Kingdom of God.'"

"I've read that somewhere," he said with half a smile.

"First Corinthians."

A nod told her he knew as much. "You're well versed."

"I had no choice. It was memorize the Bible or get a whipping."

"Spare the rod, spoil the child."

"Something like that." She noticed Sarah watching them from behind a knot of men and couldn't help wondering what she was thinking.

"We as Covenanters have no need to control the minutiae of another person's life. We offer freedom, patience, love." He motioned at everyone around them. "You'd like it here."

"You don't agree with the Bible?"

He turned her again, and she lost sight of Sarah. "Of course, when it comes to homosexuality and other issues. We just have a different definition of adultery."

"What's your definition?"

"Adultery is making love to a woman without the consent of God."

"Isn't marriage how you get that consent?"

"Not necessarily. It requires honest prayer and petition and a responsible plan for any children that might be created as a result."

"Doesn't the commune take care of that?"

"As a matter of fact, it does."

"So wouldn't a man be likely to get whatever answer he wanted to his prayer?"

"The woman also prays. It has to be agreed by both."

"I see."

"The prophets of old had many wives and concubines," he said.

"You're making a case for polygamy?"

"Not polygamy as you might know it." His breath fanned her cheek as he leaned toward her. "That's illegal, isn't it?"

"Technically."

"Contrary to what some outside these walls might say, we believe in upholding the laws of the land."

She saw Nate again and tried to ignore his displeasure. "I'm sure the locals will find that very reassuring."

"Especially Courtney's mother," he said with a theatrical sigh. "Are you still planning to vouch for me?"

"As long as you don't suddenly grow horns and a tail and prove to me that you're as evil as she claims you are."

He clasped a hand to his chest. "Ah, Rachel, your doubt wounds me. You think I'm evil?"

"I think you like to flirt. With temptation, that is," she added.

He dropped his voice. "Even a prophet has desires."

"Every human has desires."

"Exactly." He whispered his next question near her ear. "So what did your religion teach you about behaviors not mentioned in the Bible?"

"Such as…" she murmured.

"Oral sex."

He must've been hoping to titillate her with this talk. He had no other reason to address such an intimate subject in the middle of the dance floor. But she refused to act flustered. "Completely off-limits."

"Along with masturbation, I presume."

"Of course."

He grimaced. "How narrow-minded to curtail the enjoyment of God's greatest gift."

This time she couldn't help laughing. "You can be quite irreverent, for a prophet."

"Sometimes I meet someone who makes me wish I was just a regular man." He drew her hand inside his jalabiya and placed it over his heart. "See? I, too, am made of flesh and bone."

The smooth skin of his hairless chest took her off guard. Instead of pulling her hand away, she stared up at him, astonished by how easily he could manipulate people's emotions. One minute she hated him and everything he represented. The next she felt…almost attracted to him, in the same way one might peer over a cliff and be tempted to jump. Was it the siren call of letting go?

Then it dawned on her. He was the man every other male in the room admired, the man every female wanted. His sphere of influence might be limited to Paradise, but inside this microcosm he was everything. He had looks, money, power. And he wanted *her*. She was

no longer the idiot who'd confessed her love to Nate.
Neither was she the outcast she'd been growing up, the
girl usually left out, the one everyone whispered about.
"Why won't her father let her color that picture? It's
just a witch on a broomstick." "She can't sing Christmas carols? How sad." "She's the only one who didn't
bring valentines for the class. We'll have to send her to
the library during the party or we'll be hearing from her
father." "Look at her clothes. She wears a dress *every*
day...."

Maybe Ethan was no Prince Charming, but the adoration of everyone in the room helped create the illusion
that he was. And the way he was looking at her right
now, as if she was all he'd ever wanted, made her feel
strange.

Fortunately, whatever spell she was under broke as
soon as Nate strode up and dragged her away.

"You were *touching* him. You had your hand in his
freakin' Jesus robes."

Nate was driving too fast. Rachel wanted him to
slow down, but didn't ask. She felt foolish, didn't know
how to explain what had come over her while she was
dancing with Ethan. "The Holy One" was a poor sub-
stitute for the kind of man she really wanted, as different as Cain was from Abel. But in that moment, Nate
hadn't mattered, and her father hadn't mattered, and it'd
been such a relief to forget them.

Keeping her face averted, she gazed up at the moon.

"You don't have anything to say?" he prompted
when she didn't respond.

"I was playing a part, Nate. I have to seem...open to
him, right?"

"You have to be careful. If he decides he wants you, Rachel, we're going to be in trouble. It could blow the whole operation."

"Everything will be fine."

"You don't know that."

"Stop worrying."

"I can't help it, damn it!"

Taking a deep breath, she finally faced him. "Why not? If Ethan gets...out of hand, it's my problem, not yours."

"Are you kidding? It's my problem, too! If he tries to take his interest too far, we'll have to head back to California just to keep you out of his bed—and that leaves him in power."

"We won't have to take off," she grumbled. "I can look after myself."

"You can?"

If she could establish some emotional equilibrium... "Yes."

He thumped a hand on the steering wheel. "So what are you saying? That you're willing to sleep with him if it comes down to it?"

She didn't even attempt a response.

"Just how far are you willing to go?"

"I don't have to answer that."

He took a turn too fast. "Why the hell not?"

"Because it's none of your damn business, and it shouldn't matter to you one way or the other!" She hadn't meant to raise her voice, but she had, and he came right back at her.

"It's my job to keep you safe, for God's sake!"

"No, it's your job to infiltrate the cult and stop any abuse that's going on—the same as my job. You're not my babysitter, you're my partner, Nate. While we're here, anyway. You wouldn't care if Drake or...or Roderick slept with someone in that commune in order to maintain a cover or get information. You'd consider their choices to be their choices. Why should I be any different?"

He opened his mouth as if to make a quick retort, clamped it shut, then reconsidered. "I don't condone operatives using anyone."

"But you'd leave it up to them. That's all I'm saying."

"It's not my job to be everyone's conscience."

"Exactly my point!"

He fell silent until they reached Portal.

"Does this have anything to do with that night in January?" he asked as they came into town.

"It has nothing to do with that." At least, she didn't think it did. But there was always the possibility. Was she assuaging her wounded ego by reveling in Ethan's apparent interest?

"You're not trying to prove to me how desirable you are to other men?"

"No! I'm not trying to prove anything."

"But you think I don't see how attractive you are."

She pressed her palms to her eyes. "Stop it. That's not my problem at all."

He punched the gas pedal again once they'd passed Portals few buildings. "Then what is?"

Her problem was that she wasn't acting this time, couldn't slip into another persona, be someone else, like she did when she went undercover on drug deals. She had to cope with her feelings for Nate; not only that, the religious aspect of this assignment forced her to confront her resentment toward her father. The combination was awkward, uncomfortable, upsetting. She was undercover, but she was playing herself, the one person she usually tried to escape. "I don't know. I think it's all the echoes from my past. It just makes me so…angry that anyone could use religion as a tool against others."

"You didn't look angry when you were staring into Ethan's eyes," he muttered. "You looked like you were thinking about a completely different kind of tool."

"That's crude."

"Is it true?"

As far as she was concerned, that didn't deserve an answer. "Listen, not everything I do is going to please you, but I'm trying my best, okay?"

"If that was your best, it's not good enough. He ordered his followers to stone a woman, Rachel. Plus, a girl not even eighteen years old went missing shortly after visiting the compound, and I got a very uneasy feeling during dinner that Ethan knows more about it than he's willing to say. Then there's the drunk-driving accident that killed one of the Spiritual Guides who was, by all accounts, growing disenchanted with the Church of the Covenant."

She loosened her seat belt a little. "You think I've forgotten our purpose here? I'm in this to bring him down, not to get off! If all I cared about was getting off, I'd have plenty of other options."

His voice dropped. "You're not on the beach now."

"So? What are you trying to say?"

"I'm one of those options, Rachel. Under the circumstances, I'm your *best* option."

She blinked. "You're offering me sex? You can't be serious."

He met her gaze but didn't answer, so she let out a laugh to cover the embarrassment—he really believed she might be desperate enough to accept his ridiculous offer? "You *are* serious. Well, thanks for being willing to make such a big sacrifice, but you can relax. I wouldn't sleep with you again if you were the only man on earth. Not after last time."

"I thought you couldn't remember anything about last time," he said as he parked in their driveway and shut off the engine.

"Because I didn't want to hurt your feelings by admitting the truth."

"Which is…"

"You were lousy, okay? You're no good in bed, and I'm not interested." Jumping out of the truck, she headed for the trailer.

19

Nate knew he hadn't handled that very well. The only way to put an end to the tension between them was to seduce Rachel. But his conscience wouldn't allow it. He hadn't taken Susan's devotion seriously, and look what had happened there. She was okay now and had since married and had a daughter, but things could have ended very differently. For a moment they almost had. A relationship with Rachel could go just as wrong. She'd been on her own for too many years, was lonely and disillusioned and searching for the love she'd been denied by her father. And he wasn't the right man to give her that. They were worlds apart. But it bothered him that, after the ceremonial dance, Ethan was probably as aware of her need as he was—not the need for religion she was trying so hard to feign but the need for love she was trying so hard to hide.

Leaning his head against the back of the chair he'd dragged into the front yard as soon as he thought Rachel was asleep, he gazed up at the stars. What should he do? He was going crazy out here. All he could think about was touching her, regardless of the damage he might cause.

Thanks for being willing to make such a big sacri-

fice.... He laughed softly to himself. She had no idea. If he wasn't working so hard to protect her, she would've been in his bed the first night they'd arrived and every night since.

Movement in his peripheral vision made him turn toward the trailer. Rachel was up. Thanks to the moonlight, he could see her at the kitchen window, peering out toward the driveway, checking for his truck.

With a sigh, he pushed himself up and headed inside. He wasn't out here to worry her or punish her. The situation between them was tense enough.

As soon as he walked in, she folded her arms over the tank top she wore to bed each night. Obviously, she hadn't been expecting to run into him. She hadn't even turned on the lights. She'd merely tiptoed out of her room to see if he'd left.

Because of what had happened the last time he'd seen her like this, he expected her to dart into her bedroom and not come out again. But she held her ground.

"You have something more to say to me?" he asked from the entrance to the kitchen.

She cleared her throat. "As a matter of fact, I do. I— I owe you an apology for—" her eyes lowered "—saying what I did about that night in January. I... What happened at your condo was my fault, not yours. I realize that." He couldn't see her clearly in the dark, but he could imagine how flushed her cheeks were. The embarrassment she felt made her voice sound a bit strangled. "So it's not fair for me to be unkind about it. I got what I asked for, and when it was all over I got what I deserved."

He winced. "Rachel, I wasn't trying to hurt you. I—"

She broke in. "I know. I understand. I put you in a

very awkward position, and I'm sorry. I can't believe I was so colossally stupid. I don't know what I was thinking."

He knew exactly what she'd been thinking. She'd overheard the guys at work talking about how great it would be to come home and find a beautiful woman in bed and she took a risk to give him that. It would've been fine, except that she was expecting more than he could offer in return. He wanted to explain, but she was determined to get through her spiel.

"Anyway, I want you to know that you...you're not lousy in bed. That's a very mean-spirited thing to say to a man."

"You don't have to apologize." He hated that she was. It made him feel worse. But she had such an exacting conscience. She couldn't stand the thought that she might've hurt his feelings or damaged his ego when she was the one who'd instigated everything in the first place.

"Let me finish," she said. "You had every right to kick me out, *and you should have.*"

She'd spoken with enough chagrin to tell him that she wished he'd done it. But he'd tried. She'd be surprised to learn he hadn't been able to refuse her, that he'd wanted her too badly.

"I was...upset when we left Paradise," she went on. "Upset with myself and not you. And that's why I lashed out." Her eyes finally met his again; he could see the reflection of the moonlight in them. "But you also need to understand that I'm completely over you, so you don't have to be afraid that I might...misinterpret what you say or do, okay? I won't put you in another terrible situation."

That night at his condo had been anything but terrible. At least, until the sun rose and they'd had to confront reality—and each other. "Rachel—"

"Please, I don't want you to say anything. I...I need you to trust me the same way you'd trust anyone else at Department 6." Her voice dropped. "Trust me to do my job."

He stepped toward her, but she backed away, keeping the same amount of space between them. "Can you do that?"

Shit. She had everything all wrong, had no idea how much he'd enjoyed the night they were together, how many times he'd replayed it since. But what good would it do to explain? What he had to say wouldn't change the bottom line. "Sure, I can do that."

She managed a smile. "Great. I appreciate it. And now that I've apologized, I'd be really happy if we could forget my little blunder." Her expression turned sheepish. "Er, *huge* blunder."

He couldn't forget. He'd tried. "No problem."

"Great," she said again. "You haven't told any of the guys, have you?"

The intensity of her regret bothered him. "Come on, I'm not like that."

She sighed in relief. "We're good to go, then. It's in the past, I've finally apologized and now we can *both* forget."

"Sure."

"Shall we start over? Be friends?"

He shoved a hand through his hair. She was saying all the right things but, damn, he liked it better when she was yelling that he was lousy in bed. At least then he knew she was as rattled by whatever was going on between them as he was. "Of course."

"Thanks." She stuck out her hand to shake on it, but the second he clasped her fingers he felt as if he couldn't let go. Maybe it was those big eyes of hers. Or that wide, expressive mouth. It could even be her chest, which was rising and falling too rapidly to make him believe he was the only one whose heart was beating in his throat.

"Rachel?"

Her tongue darted out, wetting her bottom lip. "Hmm?"

"You talk too much," he said. Then he kissed her. It made no sense. He was doing the exact opposite of what he should be doing, especially now that they'd agreed to start over, but sometimes he couldn't think straight when he was around her.

Her mouth was as pliable and warm as he remembered it. She tasted like the wine she'd drunk at the party. He slid his thumbs under the flimsy lace of her panties as he brought her hard against him.

When she molded to him, and her tongue met his, he moaned. He thought he was home free. But then she stiffened as if she suddenly realized what she was doing and pushed him away.

"Ha, ha. That was…that was a clever test," she said with a breathless laugh and fled the kitchen.

"I think it would be a mistake."

Ethan scowled at Bartholomew. They were in his room, where they could speak freely. But it wasn't often that Bart disagreed with him so strenuously. "*Why?*

You had no argument with what I wanted before."

"I had the chance to observe her husband tonight."

Ethan pulled off his jalabiya and gave it to Bart, who turned to hang it up for him. He handed over the less formal robe Ethan wore when lounging in his rooms, but Ethan tossed it aside. He liked being naked, liked knowing how it affected Bart. "And?"

Bartholomew's eyes swept over him, his appreciation obvious and far more gratifying than it should've been. "He'll never go along with it."

"So?" Ethan shrugged. "Who is he to stand in my way?"

"I'm afraid he's more formidable than you think."

Letting Bart look his fill, Ethan struck a provocative pose. He wanted another of Bart's massages. Bart used to offer them all the time, but lately it'd been Ethan who instigated the contact. He didn't want to be the seeker tonight. "He's got a nice physique. But that doesn't mean he's got a brain."

Bart seemed transfixed. It was the first time Ethan had ever been so open with him, and he was definitely taking note. "No, he's intelligent. And more determined than a lot of men." He stepped forward as if drawn by an external force. "Damn, I love you."

The words slipped over Ethan like a silken sheet, confirming what he'd long suspected. And, oddly enough, he didn't mind hearing it as much as he'd always told himself he would. On the contrary, he found Bart's passion reassuring, even *thrilling*. Of all the Spiritual Guides, he had the most respect for Bartholomew. "I don't plan to challenge him," he said, ignoring the personal declaration.

Bart moved to the nightstand, where he withdrew the

massage oil just as Ethan had hoped he would. They were inching closer to what had been coming for months, maybe since they'd met. "Naming his wife the Vessel, the bride of the whole church, will challenge him, make no mistake."

"Which is why I'm not going to name her the Vessel." Ethan stretched across the bed. "Not right away. First, I'll give Nathan any woman he wants, let him choose several a night if it makes him happy. Once he accepts our ways, once we have enough pictures that he wouldn't want her or the outside world to see, he'll become more pliable, I promise."

"Pliable? That's not a word I'd ever associate with him."

"He's a man, isn't he? He won't be able to resist what we have to offer."

"There are some men who could."

Ethan propped himself against the pillows. "Men like yourself?"

"Men like your father."

"You mean, a rigid bastard?" he said with a grimace.

"I mean, a man who prides himself on honor and control. That's what Robert's like, isn't it?"

Ethan shrugged. He knew he didn't have as much honor in his whole body and soul as the old man had in his little finger. He had even less control. And he hated the contrast. "But Nathan's young and hot-blooded. He's not so different from me. You could see the way he watched Rachel when she was in my arms. He's as sexual as I am. I just have to convince him that I'm his friend so he'll let down his guard and indulge. Grady was hesitant at first, too, remember?"

"Grady will hump anything that moves. I don't think

he's a good comparison." Bart rubbed the oil between his hands, warming it before touching Ethan's skin.

"We could throw a few temptations his way, gauge his level of interest, then decide. Rachel's worth fighting for."

"You thought Courtney was worth fighting for, too. And she's now in a grave under that window."

Ethan shoved the pillows aside and moved onto his stomach in preparation for his massage. "Thanks to your lousy plot selection."

"Closer is better. Trust me."

He did, which was why he'd allowed it.

"I'm merely making the point that there'll be others," Bart continued, smoothing the oil up and down Ethan's spine. Bart knew every muscle, every sore spot. He'd given Ethan at least a hundred massages, more in recent weeks than ever before.

"That feels good," he moaned.

"Good enough that you'll leave Rachel alone?"

A year ago, Ethan would've thrown Bart out for trying to persuade him to change his mind. But he'd been growing more and more dependent on Bart and his opinions. What had started out as tolerance in exchange for devotion had grown into a bond he preferred not to classify, primarily because it called his sexuality into question. That was something he'd never doubted before. He'd always been heterosexual, and he still was.

Except, perhaps, when it came to Bart.

"Don't make me angry," he said.

Bart laughed. "I'm not. I'm giving you exactly what you want, aren't I?"

"How do you know it's what I want?"

"Because no one else can take care of you like I can."

Ethan couldn't argue with that. "Why do you do it?"

"I just told you."

"You love me."

No response.

"How much?" It was the first time Ethan had ever asked. He'd never really wanted to hear it spoken aloud before. But tonight… There was something different going on, something titillating.

"More than life," Bart admitted.

Ethan rolled to his right, once again exposing himself. "How does that translate into action?"

Their eyes met, but Bart didn't answer.

A tremor of fear and excitement ran through Ethan. "No reply?"

"You already know my answer. I'll do anything to have you."

Clasping his hands behind his neck, Ethan gazed at his own quickly growing erection. He could have any woman in the compound, yet he wanted *Bart?* He almost couldn't believe it, but he couldn't deny it, either. The lust was as real as it was powerful. "Why don't you show me?"

The strength of the emotion that flickered in Bart's eyes took Ethan's breath away, yet Bart hesitated. "Once you cross that line, there's no going back. Are you sure you're ready?"

Bart acted as if it had been coming to this all along, as if he'd expected it. Ethan arched one eyebrow. "How can you be so sure I'll enjoy it?"

"Because I know you."

That was true. Bart was the only person in the world

who loved him for who and what he really was. "Sounds like it's a good thing we're alone."

"You won't be able to tell anyone about this, not even the Guides."

Bart was *still* protecting him. He finally had a chance to share his feelings in a physical sense and yet he was holding back because he feared for Ethan. Had anyone else ever cared about him this much? "You think I don't know that?" he said. "The Covenanters won't abide homosexuality, even if it's just a little fling."

"This isn't a fling, Ethan. Or I'm not interested."

Ethan narrowed his eyes. "What are you talking about?"

"I'm talking about an ongoing relationship."

"No way! My people would see that kind of relationship as a threat to the traditional family on which I've founded this church!"

"That's why they can't ever find out. Do you think I've waited this long for a momentary thrill? I could've taken that secretly with Todd and let him repent afterward."

"Except that you're impotent."

Bart didn't seem the least bit ashamed. "An unfortunate medical disorder. But there are a lot of ways around that, and you know it."

Ethan considered the man with whom he'd spent much of the past five years and realized that Bart's impotence might actually be an advantage. For him, anyway. Ethan had never been particularly adept at giving pleasure. He preferred to be the recipient. With Bart, he wouldn't have to give anything. He'd only have to let

Bart express his love. "You're saying you're good with your hands?"

The smile Ethan expected didn't appear. With Bart they were rare. But the conviction in Bart's voice made his blood simmer. "You have no idea what I could do to you."

Somehow, taking this step seemed like an extension of what they'd already been doing. Bart had been taking care of Ethan for a long time. He was just offering to take care of him on a sexual level, as well. It was as natural as…as courtship leading to marriage, he told himself. But secrecy wasn't his only concern….

"We've promised the people a Vessel. Nothing can interfere with that."

"Nothing will," Bart said.

"I want it to be Rachel. I won't have you come between us."

"Have I ever denied you anything?"

No. That was why they got along so well. "I still enjoy women. Lots of women."

"You think I don't know that?"

"I'm wondering if it'll start to bother you."

"Not at all. You will need to show your appreciation of women as often as possible. Otherwise, rumors would overtake us and destroy everything we've created."

We. Ethan didn't correct him. The church had been a joint undertaking. Bartholomew had been there, looking out for him, covering for him, almost from the beginning. Without his support and calm, steady influence, the Church of the Covenant would not have developed into what it was today. "So life will go on as usual."

"Except, perhaps, in our most private moments. There it will change a great deal because I will always want you to come home to me. That's all I ask."

"You already live in the same suite."

"Now I will move into your bed and you will no longer sleep with anyone else in this room."

The domination in that statement made Ethan even harder. "And if word of our…involvement leaks out?"

"It's a risk. That's why I'm asking you to think, to be very certain, before you make this decision. Are you willing to take the chance?"

Why not? He was Ethan Wycliff. He could get away with anything he tried, have anything he wanted. And right now he wanted Bart.

"You worry too much," he said. Then he guided Bart's hands to his straining member, closed his eyes and sank back onto the bed.

Rachel wasn't ready for morning. Not after last night. She lay in bed, ignoring the disciplined part of herself that ordered her to get up and jog. She could miss a day, couldn't she?

No, she couldn't. Then Nate might know he'd gotten to her with that damn kiss, left her rattled and craving what she claimed she no longer wanted. And she couldn't allow that. She had to convince him she was as over him as she'd said she was or this assignment would just get more difficult.

God, why hadn't Milt sent Roderick with her?

Because he knew she could never pull off a pretend marriage with Rod. He was like a brother to her.

Forcing herself out of bed, she put on a pair of jogging shorts and her track shoes. If she and Nate stayed in the trailer many more days, they'd have to find a Laundromat somewhere because she was quickly running out of clothes. No way would she use the washboard she'd found in the utility room! Not unless Milt was forking over hazardous-duty pay. Considering the outhouse, she thought she could make a case for that already.

A knock at her bedroom door startled her just as she was pulling her hair into a ponytail. "Rachel?"

Damn. Nate was up. She'd hoped to have an hour of solitude before she had to face him again. "Yes?"

"Ready to go jogging?"

"You're coming?" she asked in surprise.

"I need to work out. Figured I might as well join you."

"Great." She tried not to let her voice go flat, but knew she'd failed when he spoke again.

"I can tell you're excited."

"I *am* excited. About as excited as I'd be to meet a rattlesnake on the trail," she added under her breath.

"Think of it this way. If you do meet a snake, I'll be there to sacrifice myself on your behalf."

Apparently, he'd heard her. "So if I'm thinking really positive, you might have to be airlifted back to civilization?"

"Yeah. Then you and Ethan can have all the time alone you want."

"Listen to us. We're putting each other down like pros. *Now* people might actually believe we're married." She opened her door to see him wearing a pair of shorts and a T-shirt. "It's going to be too hot for that," she said, indicating his shirt.

"I could take it off, but I'm not sure you'd be able to

keep your hands to yourself." He grinned, and she rolled her eyes. Before she could respond, she heard another knock, this one at the front door.

"Sounds like you might have another message from Alpha and Omega," he drawled.

She pushed past him. She thought it might be another message, too, but it wasn't. A woman stood there, clutching a picture of the girl Rachel had seen on the Missing flyer they'd taken from the restaurant in Portal. "Hello?"

Tears streaked the woman's face, smudging mascara that looked as if it had been applied yesterday. "Mrs. Mott?"

"Yes?"

Short and round, their visitor had permanent eyeliner and hair dyed a harsh black. Unless Rachel was mistaken, she'd had a face-lift, as well as cheek implants. She looked like an aging Hollywood starlet who'd lost her way in the desert. "Thelma Lassiter told me about you and your husband," she said. "I...I'm sorry to bother you. I know it's too early to be out callin' on folks. But...I'm getting frantic. No—" she rubbed her face "—not *getting* frantic. I *am* frantic."

Rachel felt nearly singed by the radiant heat of Nate's body as he pressed close behind her. She stepped to the side so he wouldn't crowd her. "You're Courtney's mother."

"Yes. Lynne Sinclair."

"Would you like to come in?"

"No, my husband's waiting for me." She motioned at the car idling in the drive. Then her eyes shifted to Nate, but she didn't speak to him. She'd choked up again. "I'm here because Thelma told me that...that you've been visiting the Covenanters," she eventually said.

"I've been there twice. But I haven't seen anybody resembling your daughter. I've looked."

"She *has* to be there," she insisted, her voice cracking. "I just...found this last night. It—it was hidden under the house where she liked to go to be alone. She made herself a little hideaway of sorts, and we...we let her because she seemed to need her own space so badly." She held out a plain black book with an elastic band around it.

"Is this a journal?" Rachel asked.

"Part scrapbook, part journal. She cut out things from magazines and taped them in here. She included e-mails from international pen pals and so on."

The worn cover suggested it had been well used. "Did she write about the Covenanters?"

"Yes." She dashed a hand across her cheeks. "In the last few entries."

Mrs. Sinclair seemed to expect Rachel to read it right then and there, so she turned to the passages marked with Post-it notes.

No letters or e-mails from Texas again today. Everyone's gone on without me. Last I heard, Lola tried out for cheer and took the spot I would've had if I was still there. Now I've got nothing. It wouldn't have happened if my parents hadn't dragged me to this hellhole. How could they? What am I going to do?

There was a space and then some more writing.

If I get pregnant with Ethan's child, they'll have to let me live with the Covenanters. They won't be able to keep us apart. And I like it out there. Everyone's cool, so different from my bossy parents. They smoke weed and everything. Ethan and I actually got high together. Then he kissed me....

The smiley face after that last line said almost as much as the rest of it. With a grimace at the mental picture that conjured up, Rachel showed Nate, then handed the book back to Lynne. "You should take this to the police."

"I'm on my way. I wanted you to see it so you'd believe me. It's not safe up there. I don't want anyone else to get hurt. But...if you do go back, will you ask the other Covenanters if anyone's seen her? *Someone* must have. I'd go there myself, but Ethan won't let me in."

"I will," Rachel promised. "I'll go back and I'll talk to everyone there and let you know what I learn. But...please don't mention that I'm trying to help. The Covenanters won't talk to me if they don't trust me. And if they find out after I'm already inside, well...I could disappear, too."

"Right. I understand. Thank you." She turned away, hugging the journal to her chest, but didn't make it more than a step before pivoting to face them again. "I'm afraid...I'm afraid it might be too late for Courtney. Despite the trouble we've had, I'm positive she would've come home by now if she could. Or at least told us that she's okay. She was angry at us, but she had to know that we—that *I*—love her."

The qualification raised a hint of alarm, but Nate reacted before Rachel could. "Her father doesn't love her?"

Lowering her voice, she turned her back to her husband waiting in the car. "Richard isn't her real father.

Her real father lives in Texas. She wanted to stay with him when we moved, but he wouldn't take her. He's a lazy, irresponsible loser who's never lifted a finger to support the poor kid. Richard adopted her a few years ago, so he's her legal father, anyway. But…they've never really gotten along. She's been a difficult child." She sighed and shook her head. "They were always putting me in the position of having to choose between them."

Rachel could tell she was beating herself up, feeling responsible. "It's difficult to be in the middle," she said sympathetically.

"I thought—" more tears "—I thought I should back up my husband. I didn't want another divorce. But now I've lost my daughter, and he won't agree to pay for a private investigator because he's deep in denial. He keeps saying she'll come home when she's ready."

"You don't believe there's a small chance that's true?" Rachel asked.

"No. In my heart I know—" she covered her mouth as if trying to hold in the sobs "—I know she *can't* come home."

20

"I got a funny feeling when you mentioned Courtney at dinner last night," Nate said while they ran.

"What kind of funny feeling?" Rachel asked.

"There was some sort of emotional current between the Spiritual Guides. Did you pick up on it?"

"I noticed they got awfully quiet."

"It was as if everyone in the room knew what had happened to her but not a soul would say."

"Is it possible they're all in it together?"

"Anything's possible."

She struggled for the breath to continue speaking. She normally ran at a decent speed, but she was afraid she'd unconsciously stepped it up too far today. She wasn't sure if she was trying to run away from Nate, or simply show him that he couldn't leave her in the dust. "Bartholomew seems to be the…designated spokesperson. I think they've…been told to let him handle…all inquiries."

"He certainly has more power than he likes it to appear."

"What—" she drew another breath "—makes you say that?"

"Something about the way he and Ethan look at each

other. The rest of the Spiritual Guides aren't as close. Bart's the one Ethan trusts. I suspect they make a lot of decisions together and the rest have to put up with what they decide."

It bothered Rachel that Nate didn't seem to be the least bit winded. Why did he have to have *every* advantage? "So we need to get to…some of the Guides, see…if they'll talk."

"Yes. I want to start with Joshua Cooley."

"Joshua who?"

"Cooley. He was at dinner."

"The youngish guy…with the sandy-colored hair?"

"Yes. He said something very strange to me at the celebration."

Rachel was getting an ache in her side, but she was determined to fight through it. She wasn't about to reveal any weakness to Nate, not now, not ever. Those days were over. "Which was…"

"He said we should get out while we can."

The surprise of hearing that remark took her mind off her fatigue. "As in…get out of Paradise?"

"Yep."

"But he doesn't…seem to be there…against his will. He's almost as revered as Ethan…. Why would he… have any complaints?"

"There are other ways to feel trapped. Maybe he's in too deep. Maybe he wants out but he's afraid to leave the compound or tell anyone what he knows for fear Ethan and Bart might retaliate."

"Or maybe—" she fought for breath "—he's just as guilty as they are and knows—" another breath "—he'll go to prison along with them if the truth ever comes out."

"It could even be a warning that we'll be in danger if we stay," he said. "We were definitely treated differently than everyone else, and I got the impression it isn't just because we're showing interest in their religion."

Although the sun was barely up, its heat already seemed to be baking Rachel's skin. "You don't think… they've cracked the code on your computer?"

"It's possible—if they have it."

"It's also possible that Martha's opened her mouth about us."

"That's true."

Did Ethan know they were undercover? Was he playing them as much as they were trying to play him? She wished they could make faster progress. "I think we need to…head back to Willcox and…talk to Martha again. See what she has…to say about…Joshua and…the others we've met so far."

"What did Sarah tell you?"

"She's pretty defensive—" *puff, puff* "—of the religion and—" *puff* "—the whole way of life."

"Did you ask her about Martha?"

"She claimed…the stoning never occurred. She—" Rachel squirted water from the bottle she carried in a pouch at her waist into her mouth to buy some time before finishing her statement. "I could never get…her to say whether or not…she knew Martha. She got spooked…and excused herself right before…Bart approached."

"Bart, the enforcer."

"He's a…a very dominant figure."

Nate finally seemed to realize that her breathing was more labored than his. "Do you want to slow down?"

Sweat rolled from Rachel's hairline, down her back, everywhere. "No. I'm...fine," she lied, and he didn't question it. He was too engrossed in the conversation.

"Do you think Bart's more dominant than Ethan?" he asked. "Maybe he's the one who's really pulling the strings. It could be that Ethan's merely a figurehead."

"Bart's...smarter than Ethan...but Ethan's...the spoiled brat. The pretty...boy. He gets...his...way."

"If Bart's smarter, why doesn't he take over?"

"He can't." Her burning lungs begged her to stop and rest. They'd been running hard for three miles, but she had to win this battle. She wasn't sure why it was so important to her. It just was. "He doesn't have...the looks or...the charisma."

"And Ethan doesn't have the caution or the intellect. They need each other."

"Together...they might be...unstoppable."

He squinted against the bright sunlight. "Everyone slips up. We have to play our parts and remain watchful."

The stitch in her side grew worse, but she kept up the pace. "I didn't have...a—a chance to ask...Sarah about Courtney."

"That's too bad."

"Did you ever...find Todd?"

"No."

"It's weird...that Ethan didn't follow through...with his promise...to introduce you."

"*Ethan's* weird."

"Should we...contact the local...police? See what...they're doing to find...Courtney? Maybe let them know...we're here?" God, how much longer before they reached the trailer? Her lungs were on fire.

But they still had quite a distance to go. They'd turned around to head for home only a few minutes ago.

"I'm afraid to do that. The way word gets around in a small town I think it's better to work independently of anyone who actually lives here."

She agreed. When a leak could endanger their lives, she'd rather be cautious—and safe. "It doesn't feel...as if they're doing...enough."

Suddenly he scowled at her. "Are you okay? Your face is beet-red."

"It's...hot...out."

"Not that hot. Maybe we should slow down."

"I'm fine," she insisted, but when she increased her pace, he grabbed her arm and forced her to stop running.

"What the hell is wrong with you?" he demanded, glaring down at her.

She was slightly mollified to see that he was sweating, too. "I don't know—" she struggled for enough breath to speak "—what you're talking...about."

"You don't have to compete with me!"

Her chest heaved. "I'm not...competing with you."

"So what are you doing? *Trying to kill yourself?*" There was an edge to his voice that proved he was really upset.

"I was just overdoing it...a little, that's all." Bracing her hands on her knees, she bent forward, praying she wouldn't throw up in front of him.

He stood, watching her. "Every time I think it's possible to get past what happened, I discover it's not."

She assumed he was talking about that night in January, so she forced herself to straighten despite the nausea. "Why not? It couldn't have been...that bad...

for you. It was an easy lay, one I'm taking full responsibility for."

"You don't know anything," he snapped.

"You're upset because…I've been running too fast?"

She was confused, but he didn't explain. He took off at such a quick pace she knew she didn't have a prayer of catching him even if she wanted to. And she didn't. In her current state, she wasn't even sure she could finish the run.

"Show-off," she grumbled, and sat down on the warm earth. This assignment was a disaster, and the worst part was that she couldn't blame it on anyone else. *She* was the problem. She couldn't regulate her emotions, stay on an even keel.

Frustrated, she pulled her knees to her chest and leaned her head against them.

When she figured Nate was gone, she took a deep breath, leaned back and stared up at the widest expanse of cloudless sky she'd ever seen. "Why can't I stop loving him?" she whispered.

"I know who helped her." Bart stood in the bathroom while Ethan showered.

Letting the water pound his back and neck muscles, Ethan yawned. They'd been up late, but it'd been one of the best nights of his life. He was excited that Bart had returned. He'd hated waking to find him gone. He wasn't sure whether to believe last night was for real. "Who helped who?" he yelled above the water.

"Martha. I know who helped her escape."

Ethan opened the shower door and poked his head out. "You're kidding. Who?"

"Sarah Myers."

That surprised him. "The burn victim?"

"One and the same."

"That isn't like her. She's too passive and faithful and...I don't know, cowed."

"Apparently, those still waters run deeper than we'd guessed."

"That's a pity." He flung his dripping hair out of his eyes. "I always liked her. How'd you find out?"

"Scott Renson was at the gate."

"Didn't you check with him before?"

"Of course. He lied to me."

When he noticed Bart's fixation on his nudity, Ethan straightened. Last night was real, all right. "For *Sarah?* How do they even know each other—more than casually, I mean?"

"They don't. But her scars affect people."

"He feels sorry for her?"

"That's what he told me. He said he didn't want Sarah to get in trouble, because she's been through enough in her life. He saw her shielding Martha during the commotion, pushing her toward the gate, and let her through so Sarah wouldn't fight him over it and wind up getting shunned."

"Does Sarah realize he knows it was her?"

"Of course. But she hasn't spoken to him about it. She didn't stick around to thank him, either. She just shoved Martha toward the gate and, once she saw her slip through, ran back to the group."

Ethan leaned against the cold tile. "Well, what do you know.... What finally made him come forward?"

"We had a staff meeting this morning. I told all the guards that they'd be given only bread and water until I learned the truth. Someone with keys, or access to keys, had clearly let her through, right? Knowing that others would be penalized for his mistake, he cracked almost immediately."

"You do know how to get what you want."

The smile that curved Bart's lips made Ethan smile in response. He felt like a kid experiencing his first crush.

"I can be patient when necessary, but my patience in this matter was growing thin."

"What did you do to him?" Ethan asked.

"I banished him to a tent of his own and put him on bread and water rations for a week."

"He accepted that?"

"He endangered the whole church with his actions. Of course he accepted it. He even thanked me for being forgiving and for not making his punishment worse. So did his parents."

Ethan adjusted the water temperature. The air-conditioning pumping through the vent above Bart's head made him cold. "What about Sarah?"

Bart's bad eye drifted. "I have a different plan for Sarah."

"Which includes…"

"I'll explain later. Right now I need your permission to have Sister Maxine call her to the Enlightenment Hall to clean up or something."

"Clean up? How is that punishment for helping Martha?"

"It isn't. I'm going to speak with her but I want the contact to seem like a coincidence. I don't want her to suspect I know the truth."

Ethan scowled. "You're being very clandestine."

"You trust me to do my job, don't you?"

"Are you going to punish her?"

Bart's eyebrows went up. "What do you think? She put you at risk. That means she's going to pay."

Nate fixed the broken skirt on the trailer while Rachel bathed. He didn't want to be inside when she had her clothes off. But tinkering in the hot sun probably wasn't the smartest thing to do. He'd washed up before she'd returned from her run, but now he needed to bathe again.

Letting the door slam when he went inside, he stood directly beneath the swamp cooler.

"We're out of water," she called. "I barely had enough to get my hair washed."

She'd heard him come in, as he'd intended. But he wasn't too pleased to learn they were out of water. He'd have to go to town without washing up. And knowing they didn't have any more water immediately made him thirsty. "I'll throw the cans in the back of the truck. We'll have lunch at the café while we're in town and pick up some fencing material, too."

"Why do we need fencing material?"

"For the dog pen."

"The what?" she called in apparent confusion.

"The dog pen. It's broken."

"And you plan to fix it."

"Why not?"

"Because we don't *live* here, Nate."

"We do for now."

"But we don't have a dog!"

"So? I enjoy fixing things." Inanimate objects were certainly easier to patch up or improve than people. He spent most of his days sending bad guys to prison, but most of the offenders he dealt with returned to a life of crime once they got out. What he did was necessary, but not always effective in the long term.

"Whatever," she grumbled.

He shot a dark look at the bathroom door. "Quit trying to make it sound as if what I want to do doesn't make sense."

"It doesn't make sense. You're nuts."

"Yeah, well, you like me that way."

She came out of the bathroom wearing nothing but a towel. She was walking to her bedroom to dress but paused to frown at him. "No, I don't."

Desire coiled in his groin as he studied the cleavage showing above the knot in her towel. One tug and that towel would be on the floor.... "You're sure?"

"No question."

She started for the bedroom again, but he caught her and pressed her against the wall with a hand on either side of her head. "You said you loved me, Rachel." The reminder made her flush a bright red, almost as red as when they were running earlier, but he didn't care. He needed to be clear.

"I didn't know you well enough to make that decision," she said with a scowl.

"And now you do."

"Now I do."

"Then I could take you to bed and it wouldn't be any big deal."

"I wouldn't go to bed with you. I've told you that already."

"I don't believe you."

"Because you're a cocky son of a bitch." She was suddenly angry, frustrated.

He knew the feeling. "Here's your chance to prove me wrong." When he tugged on her towel, she didn't stop him. She let it fall, and that was when his anger and frustration coalesced into a desire more powerful than he'd ever felt before.

"Wow," he murmured.

There was a stubborn resistance in the tilt of her chin but he chose to ignore it. Bending his head, he took one perfect nipple into his mouth.

Gasping, she writhed beneath him, but she didn't push him away. By the time he looked up, her eyes were closed, her lips were parted and her body quivered whenever he touched it. He should stop. He was making another mistake. Everything inside him screamed that he was taking this too far. But he couldn't seem to pull his hands or his mouth away. He'd been craving this, craving her, for too long.

"I hate you," she murmured as his lips moved up her throat and his hands slid over the contours of her body.

"I don't blame you." He found her mouth, kissed her deeply. He wanted her to pull at his clothes, help him remove them. He could feel the tension inside her, but she refused to act on it. She refused to be the aggressor in any way. That would've told him something, had he been thinking. But he'd quit thinking the minute he'd seen her in that towel. The only thing going through his mind right now was the acute pleasure it gave him just to touch her. And the fact that he had a condom in his wallet.

Sweeping her into his arms, he carried her into the bedroom, where he did everything he could to get her to the point they'd found so easily back in January. She responded but wouldn't fully engage, wouldn't let go long enough to be able to enjoy their lovemaking to the same degree. And when it was over, she wouldn't touch him as a lover might, wouldn't curl into him so they could sleep, didn't have anything to say.

"You okay?" he asked, suddenly unsure of the logic that had brought him here.

"I'm fine." She sounded indifferent and, as soon as he slid off, she got up.

"Rachel?"

She stepped into a pair of lacy panties. "What?"

He'd gotten what he wanted, and yet he wasn't satisfied. Something was missing, and it gnawed at him. "I'm sorry if I…I mean, I feel like maybe…I owe you an apology." Had he misread the signs? He was pretty sure she'd wanted to be with him when they started. She certainly hadn't said no or tried to stop him, and yet…he was afraid he'd crossed a line he shouldn't have.

"You don't owe me anything," she said. "It was nothing, right?"

"So you're okay with what happened?"

"Of course. Now we're even."

Leery, he got out of bed. "Even in what way?"

She kept dressing, didn't deign to glance at him. "You gave me what I wanted in January. And I gave you what you wanted just now. Like I said, we're even."

"That's all there is to it?"

Her wedding ring flashed as she pulled on a T-shirt. "That's all there is to it," she said. Then she walked into the living room, where he could hear her taking the cans to the truck.

21

While Sarah polished silver in the large conference room that doubled as a dining hall, Ethan met with various committee chairmen in charge of new construction. Bart was with him. Whenever Ethan was alone, they talked about some computer; it sounded as if they'd lost the password. She didn't know what that meant but they were both acting…odd. Almost…intimate in a way she'd never witnessed before.

Bart was gaining too much power, Sarah decided. And that worried her. She didn't care for Bart. Unlike Ethan, he had no passion for life, for God, for people. As much as she would've liked to feel a certain kinship with him—he, too, had a very obvious physical defect—he seemed devoid of the more tender emotions. He had a job to do and he did it well. She couldn't picture Ethan without him. But why was he inside today? He had his own office not far from the front gate.

She blinked as she realized Bart was staring back at her and bowed her head over her work. She'd heard him mention Martha's name, so she knew at least some of his business had to do with her old friend. Was Martha causing trouble on the outside? If so, it was probably because she was trying to get James back. Any mother would want her child, wouldn't she? Sarah had often wondered how Martha was coping without her family.

She didn't have to look up to know that the footsteps drawing close belonged to Bart.

"Sister Sarah."

Swallowing hard, she kept polishing. "Yes?"

"You were talking with one of our visitors last night, were you not?"

"Yes."

"What were you saying?"

"I was doing my best to testify of Christ and His Word."

Placing a finger alongside his nose, he propped up his elbow with the other hand. "And was she receptive to the Word?"

Sarah remembered Rachel's uncomfortable questions but focused instead on her statement that she, too, wanted to live a better life. "She said she was."

"Did she ask about Courtney?"

"No."

"What about Martha?"

Sarah felt caught. She couldn't lie to the Lord's anointed. Not again. She'd already lied to Bart when she pretended not to know about the unflattering statements Courtney had made before she left. Sarah had read her scriptures for an hour a day ever since, hoping to make amends for that sin. *By me or my servants, it is the same.* Bart wasn't Ethan, but he was anointed as a Spiritual Guide.

"I asked you a question," he said when she didn't reply.

"No, Brother." Sarah winced at her reflection in the silver. Another lie. Was she making herself as ugly inside as she was out? Possibly. But she was fairly sure she'd feel worse if Bart got angry at Rachel because of what *she* said, although she had no idea why that might be true. Rachel was an outsider. It was Rachel she shouldn't trust.

"What did she say?"

Sarah couldn't tell if he believed her or not. "She said she could feel the spirit of the Lord at the Introduction."

"She did."

"Yes."

"It was there in abundance." He started to walk away, but turned back unexpectedly. "Have you heard the good news?"

"Good news?" Aha! Something *had* changed. She'd sensed it.

"We're planning to announce this in the general assembly tonight, but I think I can trust you to keep it secret until then."

She was surprised he was even tempted to confide in her. Unless she approached him, he usually ignored her. Some of the other Guides pressured her to take the Covenant—and to show it with the brand—but Bartholomew had never mentioned it to her. Still, she wanted to comply, to display proof of her faith as others had, but every time she planned to go through with it, she backed out at the last minute. *Do you swear absolute allegiance to the Church of the Covenant and to Ethan, as the Lord's anointed, so help you God?* She couldn't make a commitment to what they asked, not unless she was completely sure it was right. She'd always reserved that loyalty for Christ alone. "I won't breathe a word." Keeping her mouth shut was never a problem for her.

"Last night the Holy One had a vision."

"He did?"

"Yes."

"And…were you there?" He acted as if he was, but she couldn't imagine anything that sacred coming to the prophet when he had others around him.

Bart thought for a moment, then nodded. "Actually, I was."

"Is it about the Vessel?"

"It is."

Sarah felt her stomach tense. They'd been waiting for Ethan to name the Vessel for three years, ever since it was revealed to him that he was to select a very special woman to deliver him a son. Was Bart giving her advance warning because—she covered her heart with her hand and lifted her gaze to meet his—*she* was the one? She'd secretly been praying for such a privilege, but after helping Martha escape and now lying for Rachel who was a stranger, she doubted she was worthy. Besides, she hadn't taken the Covenant of Brotherly Love and she expected him to choose from the women who had.

"The time has come," she breathed.

"Yes."

She licked dried lips. "Who is it?"

His good eye seemed to look right through her while the other one drifted off. "The guest we were just discussing."

"Rachel Mott?" Although Ethan had told them it could be anyone, this came as a shock.

"Why not?"

"She—she's married," Rachel stammered.

"That shows God's wisdom. Ethan is so busy with

the church he can't be expected to fulfill the role of father. This way, the Vessel will have a partner to help her raise the child."

"But Rachel's not even a member. She's from the devil's flock."

Guilt overwhelmed her the moment those jealous words escaped. Maybe Rachel lived in the outside world because she didn't know any better, because she hadn't had the opportunity to receive the Lord's gospel in its fullness. Who was she to judge?

"Not for long," he said. "She will soon become a convert. And that will make her our equal, will it not? We are *all* converts in one way or another."

"Yes, Brother."

"You're excited, then?"

Tears she didn't understand and couldn't explain welled up, but she blinked them away. How could she expect to be named anything special? Maybe she was a member, but she was a doubting Thomas. "Yes."

"Bart? Shall we have lunch?" Ethan stood at the entry to the much smaller dining area he used when he wasn't entertaining guests.

"Coming," Bart said but didn't move.

"Is something wrong, Brother Bart?" Sarah asked.

"You were friends with Martha Wilson, were you not?"

The horror of the stoning rose in her mind. "Yes."

"And you like her a great deal."

"Yes." She hoped she didn't sound as frightened as she felt. She knew it wouldn't go well with her if Bart discovered that she was the one who'd helped Martha escape. Especially if Martha was causing problems on the outside.

"You don't know how she managed to get away that night, do you?"

She went back to polishing. "No."

"What did you say?"

She cleared her throat. "No."

"You didn't see anyone help her?"

Sarah thought her heart might knock a hole in her chest. "No."

Kneeling beside her, he took her hands. "You're aware of the penalty for rebelling against God, aren't you?"

She was. But she kept finding herself in the same quandary. Was a sin against Ethan a sin against God? Or would God want her to help her friend? "Of course."

"You've made Paradise your home."

"Yes."

"You wouldn't want to lose what you have here."

"No."

"So you'd tell me if you knew anything about Martha, how she got away, where she might've gone, if she's tried to make contact with you since?"

"I haven't heard from her." At least that much was true. Sarah was glad Martha hadn't tried to contact her. She was frightened enough about what she'd done. She didn't want to carry on a secret relationship with a fallen angel, a captive of the devil.

"Bart?" Ethan was growing impatient. "Can't you deal with this later? She's not going anywhere."

"One second." He clamped a hand on her shoulder. "I need to take you on a little errand," he told her.

"An errand?" she repeated.

"As soon as I finish lunch, we'll go to Willcox. If

you need to do anything to prepare, I suggest you handle it now."

"What's in—" she swallowed to keep her voice from shaking "—Willcox?"

"Martha, of course."

Now Sarah *knew* she was in trouble. "I—I'm not supposed to leave the compound. I've sworn never to do so."

"It's fine if you have the blessing of one of the Guides. I give you that blessing. And you have Ethan's blessing, as well."

Ethan seemed to be watching them with interest. Self-conscious under his perusal, she twisted the rag she'd been using. "But I—I don't want to leave. Why would I? Martha's been shunned. I want no part of her."

"We need to find her."

"I would help you if I could." She cringed at yet another lie. "But I have no idea where she might be."

"Maybe not. But it's your job to help us reclaim her, since you're the one who let her escape."

Her breath caught in her throat.

"Well?" he asked calmly. "What do you have to say? Will you make amends to those you have wronged?"

Swallowing hard, she managed a nod. He didn't seem angry, but his calm, calculated reaction frightened her more....

"Restitution is a necessary part of repentance. You believe that, don't you?"

Sarah couldn't bear his disapproval. It scorched her like the hot sun beating on the desert soil. "Yes, Brother."

"What did you say?" he prompted at her soft reply.

She spoke up. "Yes, Brother Bart."

"Good. Do not worry. God is a god of mercy," he said. Then he released her and hurried over to Ethan.

The dirty dishes were still there, with the dried-on food. The cigarette smoke that had clouded Martha Wilson's apartment still hung thick in the air. But she was gone.

Nate stood in her kitchen and frowned at the mess. He'd never considered himself compulsively neat, but it was all he could do to stop himself from bagging the garbage spilling out of the trash can. It wasn't healthy to live in these conditions. He might've hauled it outside, except it would no doubt frighten her to come home and find it gone.

"Where do you think she is?" Rachel called from the living room.

It was a simple question, nothing personal, but he was just glad she was speaking to him. She'd said hardly anything all day. After they'd made love, she'd eaten with him at the café, spoken to Thelma about their visits to Paradise and gone back to the trailer, where she'd insisted on bathing again. He'd gotten the impression she wanted to wash away every trace of what had happened between them earlier, which should've encouraged him. He didn't want that encounter to mean anything to her, right? So why did it leave him feeling so unhappy?

"I don't see her purse." He'd looked for it first thing. "Maybe she went out to get some cigarettes." Since there wasn't a pack lying around and he knew she couldn't survive an hour without smoking, a trip to the store sounded reasonable. "Or maybe she went to dinner. It's about that time."

Rachel seemed hopeful when she came to the entrance to the kitchen. "Nothing looks disturbed—not as if someone *bothered* her here—so maybe you're right."

"*Someone* meaning Ethan or one of the Covenanters?"

"I don't know anyone else who'd want to intrude."

"Having Ethan on your ass is more than enough." He followed when she disappeared from view and watched as she rummaged through the first closet she came across. "What are you hoping to find?"

"Notes. Letters. A journal. She's been spending a lot of time here. Maybe she decided to put down her feelings about Paradise. If so, it might tell us more about Todd, Joshua, Ethan, Bart, Sarah. Who knows?"

"Good point."

She didn't raise her head. Was she mad at him? Part of him wished it could be as simple as "mad."

Heading down the hall to the only bedroom, he poked his head in the bathroom, which was in even worse condition than the kitchen, and checked the cabinet. Nothing. When he reached the bedroom, he saw a black plastic garbage bag pushed under the bed. Once he'd pulled it out and started to dig through it, he realized it contained things Martha was hoping to keep, not things she intended to throw away. Mostly, it was filled with letters that had never been sent. There were also some legal papers regarding her custody suit and a commitment from an attorney, agreeing to work pro bono.

I'm sorry for your grief and want to assure you that
I will do all that I can to help you regain custody
of your son. I know it will be difficult for you to

establish a regular life, but I honestly believe you'll
be happier in the long run for leaving Paradise.
I'm willing to provide this work without charge.
And the owner of the apartment building I mentioned over the phone has agreed to let you stay for
at least six months. He told me to have you come
to the office at the following address.

The address in that letter corresponded to their current location.

"You finally got a lucky break," Nate muttered to
Martha even though she wasn't there to hear him.

"Did you say something?" Rachel came up from behind.

"Her attorney—a Mr. J. H. Haddock—is providing
the apartment. Or, at any rate, he's the one who made
arrangements for her to stay here."

"Who says all lawyers are greedy bastards?"

"Lots of people say that." Nate held up several sheets
of lined paper, which had been torn out of a spiral-
bound notebook and folded into thirds. "I found some
other letters, too."

"Aha! I knew it."

He shuffled through the stack. "This one's to Todd.
Here's one to someone named Margaret. And this is to
Sarah."

"Sarah from Paradise?"

"I assume so."

"What does it say?"

"I haven't read it yet. Looks like—"

A knock interrupted them.

Rachel's eyes widened and met his; then they both

stood perfectly still, waiting to see what would happen next.

"Martha? Martha, are you in there?" It was a female voice, one that sounded worried and slightly unsure.

"Should we try to bluff, pretend we're a couple of friends?" Rachel whispered. She always wanted to approach everything head-on. Nate suspected that was because she had something to prove to the world, that she felt she had to outsmart or outwit everyone else, just like she'd felt she had to outrun him this morning. But why resort to a lie unless they were forced into it?

"No, we stay put and hope she goes away," he breathed.

The woman didn't leave. A second later, the creak of the door suggested she'd let herself in, and the sound of her voice, clearer and louder now, confirmed it.

"Martha? I—I thought I heard you come home. Hello? Can you hear me? It's Jean."

Okay, now they didn't have a choice. They couldn't get caught cowering in the bedroom. Nate was about to make a move when Rachel nodded for him to stay put and walked out. Since it would seem less threatening to encounter a woman than a man, he was glad she'd taken the initiative.

"Excuse me. Are you looking for someone?"

He edged close to the open door so he could peer down the hall.

A slightly overweight redhead, wearing cutoffs and a baggy T-shirt, was partially visible—once Rachel stepped aside. "I'm sorry," she said. "I didn't realize Martha had company."

To her credit, Rachel didn't act flustered. "Who are you?"

"Jeannette Winters. I live in the apartment next door."

"I'm afraid Martha isn't home right now, Jeannette."

"She's not back?"

"No."

She'd left the door open. The way she glanced back at it implied that she'd noticed the slight damage he'd done when he jimmied the lock. "But…she's okay, isn't she?"

"Why wouldn't she be okay?" Rachel asked.

"It's been a while since she went out." Worry clouded the neighbor's face. "Are you…a friend of hers, or—"

"I'm not a friend, no."

Where was Rachel going with "no"? Nate wondered. But he had confidence in the self-assured tone of her voice.

"I'm a professional acquaintance of her attorney's," she continued. "I have some experience counseling abused women, so he asked me to stop by and look in on her, see how she's doing. He told me she never leaves the apartment, so when I got here and she didn't answer, I was concerned enough to enter on my own. You came right after I did."

Nate silently applauded her. Rachel hadn't volunteered a name with that story, but she'd spun the lie so well the other woman didn't ask for one.

"You're a social worker, then?"

"A psychologist."

"Oh, I'm sure the poor thing could use a good psychologist."

"You two have become close?"

"Not close, really. I just feel sorry for her so I've

tried to reach out a little. But I'm afraid I might've done the wrong thing—with the best of intentions, of course, but still…"

Rachel moved closer. "What did you do?"

Jeannette's expression was sheepish as she gnawed on her lip. "I told her about the woman at the grocery store, and…maybe I shouldn't have."

"What woman?"

"I don't know her name. She was wearing a wrinkled brown skirt and a beige blouse with a pair of sandals, and she had wispy brown hair. She was maybe this tall—" she brought her hand up to her shoulder, indicating someone about five foot five inches tall "—and twenty to thirty pounds thinner than me."

A quick calculation from her description put this woman at around one hundred and twenty-five pounds.

"I'd never seen her before," she was saying. "I'd recognize her if I had because she had all these…scars on her face. You know, from burns."

The image Nate was building in his mind immediately came into sharp focus. *Sarah.*

"Did this woman speak to you?" Rachel asked.

"No. She kept her head down, wouldn't look at anyone. But she was standing at the entrance handing out a flyer that said, Don't Be Deceived. When she gave me one I realized it was denouncing the Covenanters in Paradise, so I got one for Martha."

Had Sarah left the Covenanters? Nate supposed that was possible, but it seemed too sudden and a bit odd that she'd go from defending the religion one night to attacking it the next day.

"I brought the flyer home to show her she wasn't the only one who'd become disenchanted with those people," Jean went on. "I thought it might comfort her to see she wasn't alone. I also thought she might know the burn victim and be able to get some emotional support from someone who really understands."

"And how did she react?"

"She got very excited and wanted to go there right away, but I couldn't take her. I was expecting a repairman to fix my washing machine at two-thirty. I have three kids and couldn't survive another day without it," she added in an exasperated aside. "I told her I'd take her as soon as he was finished, but she said she couldn't wait."

"So…she left?"

"Yep."

"When was this?"

"About three hours ago."

"How'd she get there?"

"Walked, I guess. I've been watching for her ever since. I would've driven over to the store by now but my baby's down for a nap, and…I keep telling myself there's no need to wake him, that I'm worrying about nothing. Martha's scared of the Covenanters, but I know very little about them. Maybe she's afraid for no reason. Besides, it sounded like the burned lady was an old friend. They're probably catching up or having a meal together or…or something, right?" She ended on a hopeful note.

"Anything's possible."

She glanced back at the door. "Was the knob broken when you arrived?"

"You're saying the damage is recent?" Rachel asked.

"I'm pretty sure it is. I would've noticed it otherwise."

"I'll look into it. But for now, maybe it'd be best if I drove to the grocery store to see if Martha's still there or if someone knows where she went."

"That'd be great." The woman sagged in relief. "And once you find out what's going on, will you call me?"

"Of course. Which store was it?"

"Safeway. It's just a few blocks away, on Bisbee Avenue."

"I've seen it."

"Thanks a lot." Jean gave Rachel her number, which Rachel stored in her phone.

After the neighbor left, Nate came out of the bedroom. "What would Sarah be doing here in Willcox?"

"I'm almost afraid to guess. But something's wrong. I know Sarah's committed to the Covenanters. So why would she be passing out flyers criticizing their beliefs?"

"And how did she get down here? The Covenanters don't have any vehicles for personal use, only the Jeeps they use for the Guides and to bring in supplies. I saw that for myself when we were there yesterday."

Rachel scowled. "Even more to the point, why Willcox? Why would she come *here* to pass out flyers unless—"

"Unless Ethan was using her as bait."

With a curse, Rachel shook her head. "She told us they'd be looking for her. We should've come sooner."

Instead, they'd been making love in that tin can of a trailer. His attraction to Rachel had made him lose focus—but he hadn't realized they were up against a deadline.

"Maybe it's not too late," he said, and they hurried from the apartment. Whether the next-door neighbor saw him as they were leaving, Nate didn't know and he didn't care. The only thing that mattered now was getting to the grocery store before Martha could disappear—possibly forever.

22

There was no one passing out flyers at the entrance to Safeway. The locals went in with empty baskets and came out with full ones, but the scene Jeannette had described had changed.

"They have her. We're too late," Rachel said. Just as she'd feared.

Nate shoved his fists in his pockets and made another pass through the produce section, even though they'd already walked the whole store—twice.

Rachel watched him from near the registers. When he returned, she asked, "What do you think Ethan will do to her?" She had a pretty good idea; she was just hoping Nate might have a more optimistic view.

"If I were him, I'd get the job done quickly and efficiently."

So much for hoping he'd be optimistic. "No more public stonings."

"No."

"Then we may never find her."

Before he could respond, a man in his fifties with white hair and a goatee strode by, wearing an employee's smock. Nate's gaze flicked over his name tag, which indicated he was the store manager. "Excuse me," he said, moving to intercept him.

A beaming "customer service" smile replaced the man's previous look of absorption. "Yes? What can I help you with?"

"A woman was here earlier. A burn victim. She was passing out flyers by the door?"

"I remember. I chased her off once, but she came back. When I saw what she was passing out, I turned a blind eye. I think that cult in Paradise is dangerous. You've heard about the woman they tried to stone, haven't you? She lives here now. So I didn't mind that someone was trying to warn folks."

He might have minded if he'd known Sarah had an entirely different agenda. "Was she alone?"

"For the most part. Although—" he stroked his carefully trimmed goatee "—now that you mention it, I did see her talking to a gentleman at the far edge of the parking lot. She got in with him for a few minutes. Then she got out and he left."

"What was he driving?"

"A Jeep. Why?"

Nate didn't answer. "When was this?"

"About an hour ago." Confusion formed a deep V between his eyebrows. "Is there some reason you're so interested?"

"There is. You know that woman you mentioned? The one the Covenanters tried to stone?"

"Yes."

"Would you recognize her if you saw her?"

"Maybe. There was a picture of her in the paper not long ago."

"She's gone missing."

He dropped the hand that'd been stroking his goatee. "You're kidding."

"I'm afraid not. You haven't seen her in the store today, have you?"

"No."

"She didn't leave with that burn victim who was at the door?"

"She might have. One minute that woman was there. The next, she was gone. I figured she ran out of flyers, or the heat became too much for her."

"You didn't notice the Jeep in the lot other than that one time?"

"I didn't. But I wasn't looking for it. Even when I'm outside on break I'm usually collecting carts, picking up trash, talking to customers. And it's been a busy day."

"I understand." Nate gave him a nod. "Thanks for your help."

"Sure. I'm sorry to hear about that woman—what was her name?"

"Martha Wilson."

"I hope she turns up, and that she's okay."

"Me, too," Nate said, but Rachel could tell he didn't think she would be.

"You're guessing it was Bartholomew out in that Jeep," Rachel said as they walked to the truck.

"I'm guessing it could've been. It was one of the Covenanters. I'd bet money on that."

She paused when they reached the front fender. "So what do we do now?"

"We go back to Paradise."

"But we won't have much of a chance if we go together. You're too protective, too defensive. Just having you around insulates me from Ethan and slows my progress."

His eyebrows shot up. "You're not going without me."

A woman walked past. When she was gone, Rachel said, "Yes, I am. If we hope to save Martha, I have to."

"There's got to be another way."

"Nothing quicker than this. Hit me."

He scowled at her. *"What?"*

"Hit me! I'll tell Ethan we had a fight, that you were angry about how close he held me when we danced last night. He'll believe I left you if I show up injured."

"No! I'm not going hit you."

"We have to make it believable." She slugged him in the arm. "Come on."

"Stop it." He grabbed her wrists so she couldn't do anything more to provoke him. "I won't hit you."

"It's the only way to get in without raising suspicion."

"Even if I was willing to do it—which I'm not—we're in a parking lot. I could get arrested."

"Not unless I pressed charges."

"Someone could see us."

"No one's going to see behind this van." She patted the carpet cleaner's vehicle that blocked sight of them from the store. "What else can we do?"

He scowled. "Just *say* I'm abusive!"

"I won't have the same level of credibility. Our marriage is a match made in heaven, remember?"

"That came from me, not you."

"We have to come up with something that shows a real rift."

His frown told her he couldn't think of a better idea, so she continued to press him to follow through on hers.

"I'd have instant sympathy, especially after the way you acted at the celebration."

"There's one problem. I *can't* hit you. Not even to make it look good."

How else could she get banged up? "It'll be harder if I have to do it myself," she said, considering her options.

"Let *me* go up there," he said.

"And say what?"

"Maybe I wouldn't be embraced as readily as you, but..." He scratched his head, shook it, then sighed. "Yeah, that won't work. But...you'll have to go in uninjured. You could say we had an argument. It doesn't have to be a damn fistfight."

"An argument won't be as dramatic. I have to be able to convince them you're dangerous so they'll invite me to stay."

"Do you realize—"

"Don't argue with me on this, Nate. We may have only one shot. A woman's life is on the line. Hit me. Please."

"No!"

"You'd do it if I was a guy."

"Probably. But you're not a guy." Boy, didn't he know it....

"Quit being so damned sexist! I *want* you to hit me. And make it visible. A black eye, a bruised cheek, a split lip. Otherwise, you'll just have to do it again."

"You've got to be kidding me!"

"I'm not."

His scowl deepened. "I really have to do this?"

"We're running out of time!"

"Son of a bitch." He doubled his fist and pulled back to swing, but when she flinched, he lowered his hand. "It's no use. Even if I were angry, I couldn't hit you."

"Nate, Martha's counting on us! We're all she's got." Tears gathered in her eyes. She knew what it was like to be alone, to have no one when she needed a friend. She wouldn't abandon Martha or anyone else. And she wouldn't risk her own life without a cover she could sell. "Pretend I'm a man. Come on, you big pussy. Hit me! Or maybe I'll *really* fall in love with you. Then where will you be?"

"I can't!" Shaking her off, he started around to the driver's side. He wasn't going to do it. If she wanted the evidence of injuries, she'd have to make it happen herself.

Taking a deep breath, she squeezed her eyes closed and yanked the door open, hitting herself in the face so hard it knocked her to the hot pavement. She lay there blinking up at the sky and saw stars even though it was only midafternoon.

"Shit," she muttered. That door had felt like a sledgehammer. She shook her head, trying to clear it, but the pain radiating through her skull made it difficult to think.

Nate was beside her in a second. He helped her to her feet, then pulled her into his arms. "You're one crazy chick," he whispered, holding her tight. "Are you okay?"

She'd split her lip, just as she'd wanted. She could taste the blood, feel it begin to swell. "I'm f-fine." She was tempted to laugh at how rattled she was. She'd been involved in some fights but, thanks to her martial-arts training, she'd never taken such a direct hit. "Thanks for n-nothing," she teased.

"I never dreamed you'd… Just hang on. The fog will clear in a minute."

She tested her jaw and, fortunately, found that it worked. "Wow. Maybe I was a little too determined." She added a weak laugh but her head was still spinning and her stomach threatened to rebel.

"Are you going to be okay?"

"Yeah." But she no longer had the strength to stand on her own. So she stayed where she was, her face against his chest. She was bleeding on his T-shirt, but he didn't seem to mind. He actually brushed a kiss across her forehead.

"I knew I shouldn't have brought you out here," he said. Then he tilted back her head to check the damage and cursed again before helping her into the truck.

The bumpy ride jarred Sarah to the bone. She sat rigid in the passenger seat, trying not to think about Martha slumped over behind her. To the casual observer, it probably looked as if her friend was sleeping. But Sarah knew better. After she'd led Martha around to the back of the store, Bartholomew had grabbed her and covered her mouth with a handkerchief. A few seconds later, Martha's eyes had rolled back in her head and she'd sagged to the ground. Obviously, there'd been some chemical on the white linen. Sarah guessed it was the chloroform they used to fumigate the grain in the storage bins, which worried her. Chloroform was dangerous. If Bartholomew had used too much, Martha might never wake up....

"When will she come around?" she asked, nibbling at her bottom lip while watching the minute hand on her watch move slowly toward seven.

Bartholomew paid no attention. He pulled off the

highway and tied Martha up. Then he started driving again.

"Bart?" For some reason she couldn't call him "Brother." He didn't feel like her brother. Right now, she couldn't respect him at all.

"What?" He acted as if he hadn't just ignored her.

"When will she come around?"

"It doesn't last long. Ten or fifteen minutes."

"It's been nearly twenty."

"She'll be fine."

He didn't seem to care one way or the other, which increased Sarah's panic. This didn't feel like God's errand as he'd said it was. This felt like the bitterest of betrayals. "How do you know?"

"I just do."

"What if she's *not* fine?"

"If God has taken her, that's His will."

But it wasn't God who'd done this.

"That was even easier than I hoped," he muttered with a glance at Martha's prone body.

It wouldn't have been easy without her, Sarah thought. Martha's hair and clothes were unkempt, and she'd lost weight, suggesting she'd been severely unhappy since the stoning. Most people would be unhappy after being torn from their loved ones. But the second Martha had spotted Sarah, her eyes had lit up and she'd rushed forward to clasp Sarah in a tight hug—

What have I done? Sarah asked herself. But deep down, she knew. Being part of the Covenanters was no longer about faith and testimony and building a unique and wonderful place. Somewhere along the line they'd lost all that, if they'd ever had it to begin with. This was a farce, the greatest lie she'd ever been told. She had to figure a way out—not only for herself but for Martha.

She studied Bartholomew. With both hands firmly on the wheel and his gaze fixed on the highway, he didn't react, even when Martha began to regain consciousness. But the moment Sarah heard her friend stir, she went weak with relief. At least Martha wasn't dead. At least it wasn't too late to correct this terrible mistake.

Martha groaned and Sarah reached back to put a hand on her leg. She hoped to extend some comfort, to communicate that everything would be okay. She was going to do something about this, something she should've done long ago and would have, if she hadn't been wearing religious blinders. She'd wanted to believe in the ideals she admired—wanted to believe so much she'd ignored the fact that Ethan was using religion to manipulate her and everyone else.

But she wouldn't let him get away with it anymore. She'd leave Paradise and take Martha with her.

Fleetingly, she thought of the good people who'd been misled as she had. She wished she could tell them about her experience in Willcox, explain that Ethan couldn't be a prophet if he allowed Bart to do things like that.

Maybe if she told them she was leaving, some of the other Covenanters would go, too. They deserved to be warned. But there was always the chance they'd think her wrong. How many times had she heard someone say that Martha had been seduced by Satan? They'd likely say the same about her. Maybe one of them would even turn her in.

No, if she expected to get Martha out alive, she

couldn't tell *anyone*. She had to work in the utmost secrecy.

As they got close to Paradise, Bartholomew used his CB radio to contact the compound. He spoke to the guard at the gate and asked him to convey a message to Ethan that must've been in code, because Sarah couldn't understand a word of it. She didn't think much about that at first. She was too consumed with her plan to slip out of the compound after dark and go to the authorities. But once they arrived and there wasn't a soul around, not even at the gate, she knew the message had been a cue for Ethan to call everyone inside. That way, no one would see Bart driving through Paradise with Martha bound and gagged in the backseat.

Then it occurred to her: If Bart planned to keep Martha's recapture a secret, he wouldn't want someone who knew the truth walking around.

Rachel was dedicated; he had to hand her that.

Nate looked over to see her leaning against the door, bracing every time they hit a bump. He'd offered to stop and get her some Tylenol but she refused to let him take the extra time. She'd said she didn't want it to dull the pain, that the pain would help her behave in a more believable manner. But he didn't think she was going to have any problem convincing the Covenanters that he'd beaten her. Anyone who saw her face looking as it did right now would readily accept the story they'd concocted.

"How are you feeling?" he asked as they approached Portal. He'd tried to get her to lean on him. But she wouldn't.

"Like I've been decked," she mumbled through her swollen lip.

"Maybe you should've given yourself a black eye."

She didn't lift her head. "Do black eyes hurt less?"

He thought about it for a second. "No, not really. And they take longer to heal. The lip's better."

"That's comforting."

He winced, remembering when she'd hit herself with that damn door. "I hope Martha appreciates this."

"I hope she's around to appreciate *anything*."

Rachel's resistance to him bothered him even more now than it had earlier. He didn't know why. "So what will I do while you're up there?" he asked. He already knew he'd drive himself crazy wondering what the hell was going on and whether or not she was safe. They probably had his computer. The moment they were able to access his files, they'd know she was a cop.

"The dog pen's still broken."

He sent her a dirty look, and she tried to laugh but groaned instead. "Ow! Why'd I have to hit myself so hard?" she complained, and sat up to examine the damage in the rearview mirror.

"Because you wanted to leave a mark, remember?"

She wrinkled her nose at her reflection. "This is Martha's best chance of survival."

"I need something to use for transportation while you're gone," he said. Before leaving Willcox, he'd found an electronics store and bought himself a new laptop. He'd also considered renting a car, but they couldn't look as if they'd prepared for this split. It had to seem spontaneous.

Shoving the mirror away, she slumped in her seat. "Why won't you have the truck?"

"Because you'll have it. I don't want you up there without transportation."

"But taking the truck won't help. If they accept me into the group, they'll only confiscate it."

"Maybe not immediately."

"There's no way to be sure. I'd rather you have it than risk losing it. If they take it, we'll both be on foot."

The idea of Rachel being on her own and without wheels in this situation made Nate even less thrilled with their current plan. He wanted the assignment to hinge on *him,* not her. But he couldn't figure out how to manage it. The Covenanters, especially Ethan, were far more receptive to her, although Nate didn't really want to dwell on the reason for that.

"So how will you get up there?" he asked.

"I'll have to beg a ride from someone besides you."

They were just coming up to the café. He jerked his head toward it. "What about asking Thelma?"

"She's my best bet. It's not like I could ask Courtney's mother."

"That *would* look a bit strange."

She adjusted her seat belt. "I'll drop you off at the trailer and drive back to the café. Then I'll leave the keys in the ignition as if I was so upset I just ran in. You'll have to walk over to retrieve it, but you can handle three miles. Then you'll have the truck, I'll have my ride and—"

"And Thelma will think I'm a son of a bitch for pounding on you," he broke in. "I've had to play a lot of parts, but—" he rubbed his neck "—I gotta tell ya, I prefer the role of a drug dealer, even a murderer, to a wife beater."

She grinned, despite the pain, and it did him some

good to see her bounce back from her injury. "You've got the self-esteem to handle it."

Maybe he could tolerate ruining Thelma's good opinion of him. But it killed him to think that Abby would also see and believe the worst. "You know how to hot-wire a Jeep, right?"

"Stop worrying."

He couldn't, but he drove the rest of the way in silence. As soon as he parked, she opened the door, hopped out and came around to replace him at the wheel.

"Aren't you going to pack?"

"No. I can't act as if I had all day to do this. I'll say that after fighting for most of the night, we got into it again at dinner, things got out of control and I grabbed the keys and ran out."

He remained where he was.

"Hurry up! I've got to go," she prodded.

"You okay to drive?"

"I'm fine. Well…considering."

He climbed out and she made a move to slide past him, but he caught her by the shoulders. "You don't have to put your life in danger. We could go to the police."

"You'd never suggest that if you were going with me."

"I'm not going with you."

"The police will take too much time and you know it. They'd have to investigate, get search warrants."

That didn't change his reluctance. But she had a point. With a sigh, he picked up her left hand and studied the wedding ring he'd given her.

"What is it?" she asked when he didn't speak.

Raising her chin with one finger, he brushed his lips across the uninjured side of her mouth. "Don't do anything I wouldn't do."

Her smile was lopsided but endearing. "No problem, since that leaves my options wide-open."

"Not as wide as you think."

"There's something you wouldn't do?" she teased as she slid behind the wheel.

"I wouldn't sleep with Ethan."

She started the engine. "Yeah, well, as you know, beefcake is tough for me to resist."

"That's what you like? Beefcake?"

"Yep." She fastened her seat belt. "I only want you for your body."

He'd been telling himself he preferred a shallow encounter. But making love to Rachel hadn't lessened the frustration he was feeling; it'd made it worse. "You didn't act as if you enjoyed it too much this morning."

"This morning wasn't about me. It was about giving you what *you* wanted."

"A willing partner?"

"Cheap and easy, no strings attached."

Nate wasn't so sure about that anymore. "Thoughtful of you."

"I owed you one." Closing the door, she drove off.

Nate stood where he was, but it wasn't easy to let her go. It felt like he was tossing her, bleeding, into shark-infested waters—and walking away.

23

Abby's hands began to move the minute she saw Rachel standing in the entrance of the café.

Thelma noticed her granddaughter before spotting Rachel. "What is it?" she asked. Then she turned and saw Rachel and rushed over. "Rachel! What happened? Are you okay?"

Rachel summoned tears. "It—it's Nate."

Doubt and confusion appeared on Thelma's face. "What do you mean it's Nate? He—he didn't...*hit* you, did he?"

Thelma obviously didn't want to believe it. Rachel could tell she liked Nate and that made her feel even worse about ruining his reputation, especially because hitting a woman was so far from anything he'd really do. She hadn't been able to goad him into it, even with the knowledge that Martha's life could depend on the credibility of her lie. "We had an argument."

"Do you want me to call the police?"

"No." Rachel grabbed her arm before she could move away. "No, I—I provoked him." That made her feel a tiny bit better. "But he's probably on his way here right now. I need to leave, hide. And I can't take his truck. Could you possibly give me a lift to Paradise?"

Thelma stared at her. "You don't want to go to the Covenanters, honey."

"They're not as bad as everyone's making them out to be. You've said so yourself. And...and they've got guards with guns. They're the only ones who can keep me safe."

Abby was following the conversation with eyes as big and round as silver dollars. She shook her head at this and began signing. When her grandmother didn't notice, she nudged Thelma to get her attention.

Rachel wished she knew what Abby was saying. "What is it?"

Thelma signed to Abby but didn't answer Rachel.

"What is it?" Rachel asked again.

"She can't believe Nate would do this. I told her that nice people sometimes do bad things."

Guilt created more anxiety. But Rachel had to get to Paradise, and she had to do it in a way that meant they'd accept her and welcome her in. This was her best shot. "I need a ride," she said frankly.

Thelma wrung her hands. "What do you think the Covenanters can do for you that the police can't?"

"A lot! They can hide me and provide a safe place until...until I decide whether or not I want to end my marriage."

"Has he done this before?" Thelma asked, her voice sad.

When Rachel went undercover she had to lie about all kinds of things, but it wasn't easy to make someone she cared about look bad. "We need some time apart," she said. "Will you take me? Please? I know what I'm doing. I promise."

"I—" Thelma glanced over her shoulder. "Rob's

here and the dinner rush is over. I guess I could take you. If you're sure this is what you want to do."

"I'm sure."

She left to get her keys, but Abby stayed.

"Don't hate him," Rachel said to her. "Okay?"

Thelma returned a moment later. "Let's go."

Rachel pivoted, but Abby stopped her. She patted her chest, pointed to her grandmother and then to Rachel.

"She wants me to translate for her."

The pressure Rachel felt to get going made her reluctant to take the time. "What is it?"

Thelma watched Abby speak, then frowned. "No, Abby. That doesn't make sense."

"What doesn't make sense?" Rachel asked.

Abby's motions let Rachel know she was encouraging her grandmother to explain.

With a sigh, Thelma relented. "She wants me to warn you about the pit."

"The pit?" Rachel echoed.

"She insists that someone was talking about some sort of pit when we attended one of the meetings."

Rachel wasn't willing to discount this as easily as her grandmother was. "What about the pit?"

Abby signed again, but her grandmother acted as if she didn't need to watch her hands, as if she already knew the answer. Probably because she'd heard it before. "'Imagine what we could do to her in the pit.'"

The muscles in Rachel's stomach tensed. "Who said this?"

"A man named Grady. He's one of the Spiritual Guides."

Rachel squatted in front of Abby, enunciating as clearly as she could. "What else did he say?"

Thelma interpreted her response. "Nothing. The man standing next to him—she doesn't know his name—told him to keep his mouth shut, and he laughed and said, 'What does it matter? It's not like she can hear me.'"

"They didn't say any more about the pit?"

Abby shook her head.

Did the words Abby had read on Grady's lips mean anything? Martha hadn't mentioned a pit. She'd been stoned in the courtyard. If there *was* a pit, why hadn't they used it for the stoning? "Do you think they put Courtney in the pit?" she asked Abby.

The child nodded sagely.

No wonder she was frightened of the Covenanters. Whether this pit existed or not, hearing about it would be unnerving, especially considering the absolute privacy in Paradise. "I'll be careful," she promised, and started to get up.

Abby took hold of her hands long enough to detain her. Then she pointed at her face.

"She wants to know what happened," Thelma said.

Rachel wasn't immediately sure how to respond. She'd already given them the story she and Nate had concocted. "I told her."

Eyebrows knotted in frank refusal, Abby shook her head.

"She doesn't believe you," Thelma said, and Rachel wasn't surprised. Abby was too adept at reading body language. And Rachel's body couldn't lie, not when it came to telling a lie she found so repugnant.

Standing, she caught Abby's chin and tilted it up so their eyes met. "Trust me, okay?"

"Trust you?" Thelma repeated. There was uncertainty in her voice, but Abby was already nodding.

The gate loomed larger than ever as Thelma came to a stop a few feet from the guards' station. This time there were no other cars passing through, and any activity inside the compound was taking place behind closed doors. Probably due to the weather. Dark clouds rolled across the sky and the wind whipped up the dirt and the dust, promising another monsoon. But until now, Rachel had barely noticed. She knew she had to sell her lie more effectively than she had at the café or, if there was a pit, she might become far too familiar with it. That was all she could think about on the drive over.

The young man on duty spotted their vehicle and passed through a small gate in order to approach them. "May I help you?"

Rachel climbed out of Thelma's van to meet him. "I'm here to see Ethan."

His eyes zeroed in on her swollen lip. "Is he expecting you?"

"No. But...I hope he'll see me, anyway. Will you tell him I'm here? My name is Rachel Mott."

A brief hesitation ensued, but as soon as Thelma started to turn the van around, he hurried to the station and made a call. Rachel could hear only a few words above the blustery wind. "...Mott...no, he's not with her...that woman with the deaf child...van...yes, I'll tell her."

His lips were pinched as he walked toward them again. "I'm afraid you'd better not let your friend leave. The Holy One is busy right now. He can't see anyone."

"Did he say that? Was he the person you just talked to?"

"It was Brother Bartholomew, but—"

"I can't leave," she interrupted. "I *won't* leave. I—I have to stay here. It's the only place I'll be safe."

The *C* on his forehead wrinkled as he raised his eyebrows. "You need to go home."

"No! I won't! I can't go back to him!"

"Ma'am, there's nothing we can do for you here. Please, get in the van."

Tears streamed down Rachel's face. Something was going on in the commune. The Covenanters weren't generally all that friendly, but they were even less friendly tonight. They had their hands full with some problem, and she was pretty sure she knew what problem that was.

"Ethan!" she called, going to the gate. "Ethan, let me in! I—I have nowhere else to go. Please!"

The appalled guard didn't seem to know what to do. "Ma'am, I don't want—"

"Call him," she broke in. "Call him and tell him I need him. Bart hates me. Don't talk to Bart."

"But he's head of security."

Ignoring him, she began to yell. "Ethan! Ethan, come out! You said you'd help me!"

The guard grabbed her arm, trying to peel her away from the fence. Poor Thelma sat in her van, looking horrified, no doubt unsure whether or not to proceed.

"Go!" Rachel told her, waving in her direction. "I'm staying. I'm staying no matter what!"

The brake lights flickered, but the van didn't move.

"No, don't leave! She's going with you!" the guard called.

Rachel's arm was beginning to hurt from the young man's fingers, so she jerked away and slapped him when he tried to grab her again.

Clearly surprised that she'd resisted physically, he scrambled away and headed back to the guards' station. He was probably going to place another call, but he didn't get that far. Bart came charging out of the building where they'd had dinner.

And Ethan was right behind him.

Nate was waiting for Thelma when she returned. Considering what she believed about Rachel's injury, he expected her to look at him as if he were pond scum, but as he watched her climb out of her van, she seemed more shaken and confused than anything else.

"Is Rachel okay?" He figured that question was general enough. It certainly wasn't as revealing as, Did she get in?

"I think so. But her face…"

"I feel bad about her face," he admitted, which was true, even if he hadn't caused the damage.

In an obvious attempt not to respond to the contrition in his voice, Thelma leaned in to get her purse. "You should."

Rachel must've gotten inside the compound. She'd still be in the van if she hadn't.

He stepped between Thelma and the café. "Where'd you take her?"

She studied him, apparently trying to determine whether or not she could tell him the truth. He sensed that it was as difficult for her to lie as it was to be rude. "I'd rather not tell you," she finally murmured.

"I'll find out, anyway." He cringed to think his

behavior—his persistence and his questions—would solidify Rachel's story and convince Thelma that he was an abusive husband. But he wanted to hear as much as she'd say about what had occurred when they reached Paradise, and that meant playing along.

"She's safe. That's all you need to know."

"Thelma—"

"I don't want to talk to you, Nate." With that, she marched around him and into the restaurant.

Nate remained outside, braving the storm and wondering if he should drive to Willcox. He needed to get on the Internet and check in with Milt. He hadn't done that since letting their boss know they'd arrived safely. But Willcox was an hour and forty minutes away, and he didn't want to put any more distance between him and Rachel. Although service was slow and sometimes erratic, the Internet worked here in Portal. Besides, he was starving since this had all erupted before they could have dinner.

Deciding to brave Thelma's displeasure a little longer, he retrieved his new computer and headed inside.

He stood near the Welcome, Please Wait for a Hostess to Seat You sign, but Thelma didn't reappear. Maybe she knew he was waiting and didn't want to seat him.

Her husband, Chaske, came out from the kitchen instead. "Just one?"

His expression didn't reveal whether he'd heard about Rachel's fat lip. "Yes."

Chaske led Nate to a table in the corner, handed him a menu and left without further comment.

Thelma showed up a few minutes later. She was

wearing lipstick and a clean apron, as if she'd freshened up to prepare for any late stragglers, but her smile wilted the moment she saw him. Ignoring two parties who'd come in after he had, she hurried over.

"Nate, I won't tell you where Rachel is, so it's not going to do you a bit of good to camp out here."

He was just opening his laptop. "I understand. I won't ask you again."

She seemed taken aback by his capitulation. "Then why are you here?"

"The trailer feels too empty without her," he said, which was true. He couldn't stay there, all the while imagining what might be happening in Paradise. He'd started walking to Portal the minute she'd left. "I just want something to eat, okay?"

She pursed her lips. "I still can't believe you'd hurt her like that."

"Neither can I."

"You gotta control your temper. You're gonna lose her, you know that? You might have already."

His muscles tightened at the thought of how permanent "losing" her could be. He was coming to care about her, much more than he wanted to. After Susan, he wasn't eager to take the risks associated with a relationship, but he couldn't let that stop him from ever getting close to a woman again, could he? "I sincerely hope not."

"What were you thinking?" she asked. "You—"

"Food, Thelma," he cut in. "I haven't had dinner."

"Fine," she snapped, and moved off to take care of her waiting customers.

"Hi, Joanie. How's the new horse?" Her voice carried, but he didn't listen for long. Abby appeared with his water, then lingered near his table, staring at him.

"I suppose you're mad at me, too," he said.

She gave no indication. She didn't have much of a chance. Her grandmother tugged on her sleeve as she passed by and pointed toward the table she'd just seated, and Abby hurried off to get those people some water, too.

With a curse of frustration, Nate shoved his menu aside. He'd order a burger. It wasn't as if he cared what he put in his stomach.

After two botched attempts, his Internet connection held well enough for him to access his e-mail. His computer was as slow as a damn snail, but he had time—too much of it now that he was resigned to waiting a few hours before driving up to Paradise. He hated feeling so helpless.

There were a number of e-mails in his in-box. Some were from friends and family. Most were spam. He began by opening one of two messages he'd received from Milt. The first had been sent the day after they arrived.

That was the briefest check-in on the planet. What's going on? Have you busted this asshole yet?

Nate would've chuckled except he felt pretty far from having the upper hand where Ethan and the Covenanters were concerned. If Rachel got in—and he was fairly certain she had—they'd turn him away. He knew that already. She'd spend the night in the commune…alone.

Milt's next e-mail was longer and had been sent just this morning.

Hey, why haven't you checked in? I send you away with a beautiful woman and you disappear? Call me. I have something you need to hear.

"What now?" Nate exited his e-mail program, left his laptop on the table and took his cell phone outside.

Milt answered on the first ring. "It's about damn time!" he complained instead of saying hello.

"Whatever you do, don't say anything to piss me off," Nate said.

"Wow, you *are* in a shitty mood."

"What do you want?"

"What do I want?" he repeated. "How about a fucking update?"

"Martha's gone missing, and Rachel is in the compound, trying to find her."

"Where the hell are you?"

"Taking a nap, Milt. What do you think? I'm biding my time until I can go bang on the gate and get in there with her." He hated the fact that he couldn't do anything until then.

"Things aren't going well, huh?"

They weren't. Nate kept thinking about the stoning and the girl who'd gone missing and the way it all tied back to Ethan and Paradise. Rachel thought she could handle everything so she didn't shy away from anything. It was a bad mix, a dangerous mix. And then there was that business with his computer. "Could be better."

"If that's the way you're feeling, this probably won't help."

Bracing for more bad news, Nate paced in front of the restaurant. "What is it?"

"I hired a private investigator to do some checking, had him go to several of the places the Covenanters lived or visited before settling in Paradise."

"And?"

"He stumbled across a woman who met Ethan. This was outside Cincinnati when the cult passed through there. They only stayed two weeks. They weren't welcomed by the locals. And they couldn't get enough money together to buy the land they wanted. So they moved on, searching for greener pastures. But this woman, she felt badly about the discrimination they faced, so she tried to extend the hand of fellowship, as she put it."

"And that means…"

"She went out to visit them. She wasn't interested in joining. She just wanted to make up for some of the bad treatment they'd received."

"What did that bad treatment include?"

"From what I could gather, it was just your basic antagonism—heckling, throwing rocks, spray-painting unflattering messages on their tents. Jesus Freak, Remember Jonestown—that sort of thing."

"So she stepped in, trying to do a good deed."

"Right. She struck up a friendship with Ethan and his cronies, whatever he calls them."

"Spiritual Guides." Which were more like the blind leading the blind, in Nate's opinion.

"Yeah, that's it. They invited her up for dinner and

various celebrations. The last time she visited was the night before they bugged out."

"And?" Surely this had to be leading *somewhere*...

"She woke up the next morning in her own bed. Her car was in the drive, but not where she normally parked it. And she doesn't remember driving home."

"Had she been drinking?"

"She'd had a little, so she chalked it up to that and purposely ignored a few other signs that things weren't quite right. She was afraid that if she made any accusations, the community would turn on her and say, 'I told you so.'"

"But..."

"A few weeks later she learned she was pregnant."

Nate came to a dead standstill and lowered his voice. A family of five had just parked and was heading for the door. "You're saying the two are related? You're saying she was, you know, *forced?*"

"She suspected it."

"And the baby wasn't her husband's."

"She wasn't married, Nate. According to her, she hadn't slept with a man in two years."

The way Ethan had been holding Rachel while they danced leaped into Nate's mind. "They must've given her something, a roofie or another drug."

"That's what she believes. She says it's the only way to explain what happened to her."

Nate's hand tightened on the phone. "Did she have the baby? If so, we might be able to do some DNA testing and prove that—"

"No baby," Milt interrupted. "By the time she realized she was pregnant, she'd met the man she ended up marrying and was too afraid to tell him about the baby.

She thought he wouldn't understand how it had happened. Even *she* didn't understand. So she acted to protect the relationship."

"You mean, she ended the pregnancy."

"Yes."

A hard lump formed in the pit of Nathan's stomach as he realized what this could mean for Rachel. "Is there any chance she could be making this up?"

"From all indications, she's reliable."

Nate dropped his head in his hand. "Rachel's up there, Milt," he said. "She's up there without me."

"She's a good agent. Smart. She'll be fine."

Sometimes even the best agents didn't make it. The fact that Milt seemed to discount Nate's concern made him angry. He was tempted to tell his boss that if anything happened to Rachel, he'd personally make him pay for sending her down here. But he knew that was irrational. He was blaming Milt for Rachel's being in jeopardy, but it had been Rachel's decision all along.

A flutter of movement caught his attention. It was Abby. She'd come out of the restaurant and was hugging the pillar not far away, watching him.

Knowing that anything that shot out of his mouth right now would not be something he'd want her to read on his lips, he told Milt he'd check in later and disconnected without an explanation. Then he stalked back and forth, waiting for the adrenaline to subside. But it didn't seem to decrease and, a moment later, Abby clutched his arm.

Startled that she'd approach him so boldly, he glanced down, and she let go so she could use her hands to communicate.

"I don't understand." Too impatient to manage

social niceties just now, he tried to shrug her off. He
didn't want to deal with her, not after what he'd just
found out from Milt. For all Rachel's talk of sleeping
with beach bums, she had very little sexual experience.
He couldn't imagine how being raped by Ethan, and
maybe other members of the cult, would affect her.
Couldn't imagine how her sensitive heart would be
able to recover.

But Abby was undeterred by his gruffness. He was
struggling to make sense of what she was trying to tell
him when the door opened behind them and her grandfather stepped out.

"I thought you might be here," he said. "Come on,
your grandmother's looking for you."

Shaking her head to let him know she wasn't ready
to go in, she made the same signs as before and beck-
oned for him to translate.

"What is it?" Nate asked.

"Abby says she shouldn't be there."

Obviously, she was talking about Rachel and Paradise.

Nate didn't bother pretending he didn't know where
Rachel was. "I'd like to go after her, but I can't," he explained. He had to give Rachel time to convince the
Covenanters to accept her, had to trust Rachel's ability
to take care of herself. That was what she'd asked him
to do. Besides, he'd destroy everything they'd set up so
far—could cost Martha her life—if he jumped in too
soon.

The girl looked confused. She signed again, then
nudged Chaske to translate.

"She says, 'If you don't go now, you don't love her
as much as I thought.'"

Love was a powerful word. He cared about Rachel. But…did he love her? He was almost afraid to ask himself that. "You can't judge a relationship by a diamond ring," he said. Abby had no idea that was a charade.

"She says the ring has nothing to do with it," Chaske said.

"Then what does?" Nathan demanded. What did a young girl know about love? About a fake marriage?

Abby responded instantly, and Chaske passed on her message. "'The way you look at her,'" he said, then he drew his granddaughter back inside, leaving Nate staring after them.

24

Rachel sat across from Ethan; Bartholomew stood at the door. She'd been in the Covenanters' Enlightenment Hall a few times now, but never in this particular room, which was small and intimate, paneled in dark wood and furnished with bookshelves and an elegant desk. She guessed it was Ethan's private office, perhaps where he wrote his sermons. A photograph of him and his twelve Spiritual Guides hung on the wall but noticeably absent was a picture of Christ. As far as she was concerned, this church talked a good talk but seemed to be uncertain about whom they really worshipped.

"You realize what you're asking of us," Ethan said.

"I—I do." She conjured up tears again, then wiped them as they fell. "I'm sorry. But…I have nowhere else to go. And this place…it just seems so safe and protected. Peaceful."

"Which is what you want."

"Yes. I want peace more than anything."

"We can't take you in," Bart said from his sentry position. "We've had too much trouble with the locals already. They've accused us of everything from kidnapping to stoning." He acted as if those were false accusations and that it was his duty to stop them.

Rachel sniffed and focused her entreaties on Ethan, who seemed inclined to let her stay. She *had* to get in: It was now or never—at least for Martha. "I agree you haven't been fairly treated. I'd go back to Nate while I continue to learn what you teach here, but I'm scared. Next time...who knows what he'll do?"

Ethan studied her carefully, particularly her swollen lip. "Continue to learn what we teach here," he repeated.

Bartholomew interrupted. "We're not a shelter for abused women."

"I understand that," she said.

"So what are you asking?" Ethan leaned forward, his eyes bright with interest. "If you're merely searching for a place to hide for a few days, you need to look elsewhere, as Brother Bartholomew says. We can't be drawn into the fight between you and your husband. And we can't risk the anger and suspicion of the community, should they side with him. If you don't plan to stay permanently, you have to leave."

She crumpled the tissue in her hands. "I do plan to stay. I mean, I don't know everything about your religion, but I've felt God's spirit here. I want to be part of what you're building. I've wanted something more in my life for a long time. Something important's been missing. It's time to reconcile with God."

Ethan glanced at Bartholomew and Rachel thought he was asking his security chief to stand down. "So you'd be willing to join us? Officially?"

Would they believe her? She prayed they would. "Yes."

Bartholomew left his post to approach the desk. "Holy One, a woman in this situation might be tempted to say anything. Look at her. She's just been through a horrible ordeal and I'm sure she'd like to avoid a repeat performance. No other place probably seems as safe as Paradise, where we can shelter her behind a fence with a guard. But that doesn't make her a prime candidate for conversion."

"Maybe the Lord has prepared her heart. Who are we to say what humbles a person enough to make her receptive to the gospel? Maybe this is it, Bart. Maybe she *is* a prime candidate."

Rachel sensed a standoff between them. Bart was voting she be kicked out; Ethan was voting she be allowed to stay.

"And what of her husband?" Bart challenged.

"He has to worry about the welfare of his own soul," Ethan replied and ended the standoff by turning back to Rachel. "You are welcome here. We will make you one of our own. The ceremony will take place tonight."

"Holy One—" Bart began, but Ethan broke in.

"It's over. I've decided. Now take her to a room where she can have a nap before dinner."

There was a marked delay, but Bart eventually acquiesced with a bow. "If you'll come with me…"

Bestowing a grateful smile on Ethan, Rachel got to her feet. "Thank you," she said. "I want to be a better person."

"And you shall be. I have great plans for you, lovely Rachel." He remained in the office while Bartholomew guided her to a room on the second floor. Decorated in brown and green, it looked very much like a hotel room and had a bathroom off to one side.

"Thank you," she murmured when Bart turned to go.

He hesitated at the door. "Ethan is more trusting than I am," he said. "Don't disappoint him."

Rachel didn't know how to respond. Was her acting up to par? She hoped so; it'd been a long time since she'd been this frightened. She'd promised to go through some type of initiation and had no idea what that entailed. But Martha had to be in the compound somewhere. Sarah had been at that grocery store, passing out flyers; Bartholomew was most likely the man in the Jeep. And yet, as far as she could tell, nothing had changed in Paradise. If Martha was back, nobody knew it....

What had Bart done with her?

Whatever his plans, he wasn't making them public.

That meant anything could happen. To her. To Martha. Even to Sarah.

This was the first time Bart had ever revealed any disappointment or frustration with him, and Ethan was alarmed by how much it upset him. "Stop acting like my father," he snapped.

"Someone has to be the adult, Ethan." He glanced at the door to their suite, which was closed, but lowered his voice, anyway. "You've got Martha and Sarah caged in the pit. You can't afford to attract any attention."

"No one even knows Martha's in Paradise!"

"The Guides do!"

"The Guides have shown themselves to be trustworthy in the past."

"It's still a risk we don't need to take. But you've been so coddled and protected your whole life, you think you can have anything you want the instant you want it."

Ethan stalked to the window. "It's true. I *can* have whatever I want." The grave outside that window served as proof. Or did it? Maybe it was proof that he *couldn't* have everything. He'd wanted Courtney, hadn't he?

Bart spoke before he could decide. "Not if I stop providing it."

"You believe you're the one who made me a prophet? That you gave me my power, my wealth, all these worshippers?" He waved his arm to indicate the tents beyond the glass.

"No, but I'm the one making sure you keep what you've got, aren't I?"

They glared at each other. Bart wasn't referring only to recapturing Martha and burying Courtney. He was talking about the way he had to cover for Ethan when he was on dope. Ethan couldn't live without it. Not anymore.

"You're overstepping your bounds," he said.

"My bounds as what?" Bart asked. "Your security adviser? Your pupil and follower? Or—" he lowered his voice "—your lover?"

"As all three!"

"Fine. If you want me to leave, I will." He started for the door, but Ethan caught his arm. He knew Bart was testing him, knew he should let him go. But he was too aware of how much he needed his new lover.

"Stop it," he said. "You're overreacting. You know how I feel about you."

"And how is that, Ethan? I've declared myself to you, but you haven't declared yourself to me. You take what I have to give, you enjoy it, and then you ask for more. Why don't you try giving something in return?"

"Like what?"

Bart grabbed his face. "Kiss me. Kiss me like you want me, like you're in love with me."

Ethan could allow Bart to pleasure him, but he couldn't reciprocate, couldn't make a *commitment* to homosexuality.

Jerking out of his grasp, he turned back to the window. "Not now."

"Why not? Are you too good to be gay, Ethan?"

"I'm *not* gay. I like sleeping with women and you know it."

"Quit lying to yourself. You're just as gay as I am. You're in love with me but you're too cowardly to face it, to act on it, to embrace it."

The scorn in Bart's voice made Ethan cringe. How had an argument over Rachel veered so far off course? "Stop it! We're not fighting about *us*."

"But that's at the root of it. I want to know when you're going to grow up and accept yourself for who and what you are."

"I like women!" he insisted.

"You like to *degrade* women. That's not the same thing. You use them for rituals. You drug them and tie them up and share them with as many men as possible. You *want* to like women, but you don't. You hold them in contempt merely for *expecting* you to want them."

Bart's words evoked a strange fear, one that left a metallic taste at the back of Ethan's throat. He couldn't be gay, not really. He enjoyed experimenting because he liked knowing his father would writhe in embarrassment if he ever found out. A lot of people tried making love with someone of their own sex at some point or other. His secret relationship with Bart didn't mean

anything; even Bart had agreed that their sexual inter-
ludes wouldn't preclude Ethan's normal activities. But
to actually embrace an alternative lifestyle? To commit
himself to another man as a man might commit himself
to a woman? Regardless of how secretive they tried to
be, that would eventually lead to public awareness, and
Ethan couldn't have that. He was excited that Rachel
had returned; he wanted *her,* not Bart.

"I've told everyone she's the Vessel, Bart. And now
she's here and willing to be baptized. She's left her husband. The situation's too perfect not to take advantage
of it. This will show our followers that God has provided the perfect woman to bear my child, just as I've
promised. There are too many who are beginning to
wonder, who are growing doubtful because of Martha
and Courtney. This will bring them back. They'll forget
their doubts and their questions and once again be in
rapture with me, with what I can do."

"Another mercy session would do the same thing.
Let me gather those who are ill or otherwise afflicted
and you can call down the powers of heaven to heal
them."

He didn't want to go to all the effort of making
people sick—using just the right poison—so he could
"heal" them. He was too afraid he'd get caught. As
powerful as mercy sessions could be, they were risky.

"That only works in the presence of great faith, and
I just told you their faith is weak."

"But her husband won't let her stay. We've talked
about this. You saw how possessive he is. He hit her out
of jealousy! That proves he won't give her up. I bet
he'll be banging on our gates before nightfall."

"Don't talk to me like that."

"Like what?"

"Like I'm a child. There's nothing he can do if she wants to stay. We'll make sure she's happy here, well taken care of. She'll be the one to tell him to go, not us."

"Which means…what? We put off the mating ceremony everyone's expecting? Or do you plan to keep her drugged from her baptism on?"

"We'll wait as long as we need to, until you're comfortable with proceeding."

This concession seemed to mollify him. But the stiffness of his posture told Ethan that Bart wasn't ready to yield completely. "Then we should kill Martha and Sarah and be done with them."

"Fine. We'll kill them. In a few days. Until then we'll enjoy what they have to offer while I'm courting Rachel. It'll keep us occupied and happy in case we get impatient. And it'll be a good distraction for the Guides, who might watch us too closely otherwise."

"Too closely for what?"

"Too closely not to realize something's changed."

"You're talking about us."

"Of course I'm talking about us!"

Bart pivoted and began to pace. "Sometimes I wonder why that would be so terrible. Maybe there's some way we could get them to accept it."

"You know what it says in the Bible. You know what I've taught."

"We might lose some followers. But we could rebuild our numbers. There's no reason we shouldn't be able to love each other. No reason you shouldn't be able to accept me as an equal before the whole world."

This was getting out of hand. "Someday, perhaps. But the timing isn't right. We've worked too hard to build what we have. We can't let a single person turn on us, not now."

"Ethan—"

Whirling, Ethan took two long strides toward Bart and grabbed his hands, the hands that had touched him so intimately only hours before. Although he didn't want to acknowledge it, even now the contact made his heart race. "Listen, we have to focus on the here and now and save everything else for later. And the here and now is this—I've already promised the Guides Sarah and Martha. We can't take that away from them. Not yet. We'll let the eleven of them play until they're bored. Meanwhile, we'll invite Rachel to a few ceremonies but escort her to bed before anything happens that she might object to. She'll slowly become one of us and, as time passes, her husband will move on, the rest of the world will forget about her, and we'll have the freedom to do as we please."

"You have to have the Vessel *now?* With so much else going on?"

"Yes. If we don't, and people find out we have an ongoing sexual relationship, it'll all fall apart. Let me give them a Vessel. A bride for the whole church will be something strong and powerful to worship. It'll unify us at a time when we're threatening to self-destruct."

"But what about the practicalities, Ethan? Do you really want a child?"

"Sure," he said with a shrug. "Why not? It'll be *our* child." Telling himself he was only doing it to appease Bart, he leaned forward to kiss him, to prove he could be demonstrative. But the second their lips touched he realized Bart was right. He was as gay as a man could be. His partner was impotent, but he was in love with him, anyway. And he hated women, especially attractive women like Rachel, because even *she* couldn't tempt him, and that made it impossible for him to be anything his father would admire, approve of...or envy.

Sarah had never dreamed there was a secret room beneath the Enlightenment Hall, let alone a damp hole in the ground that looked and felt more like a medieval dungeon. She'd participated in some rituals inside the hall's main assembly room and knew there were other rituals for those who'd taken the Covenant—a few lasted all night long. But she'd assumed they occurred inside the hall, too. Now that she'd seen the altar, the ring of stones, the candles, the torches and the thick mats lying all around, she knew that probably wasn't the case. Whatever Ethan's most devoted followers did down here was accompanied by the burning of incense. The scent was so strong she could barely breathe. Having smelled the same scent on Ethan's clothing a number of times, she connected it with him.

"What goes on during the Covenant of Brotherly Love Celebration?" she asked Martha.

Martha didn't answer. Maybe she couldn't. She was lying in a heap in the next cell, hardly moving. Once they'd passed through the gates into Paradise, she'd begun to squeal for all she was worth. She couldn't actually scream because of her gag, but she was making enough noise that Sarah had used the diversion to jump out of the Jeep. She'd hoped to get help, to alert someone to what Bartholomew was doing. But she hadn't succeeded. As soon as she'd landed on the ground, Bart had been on her. And he'd used chloroform to make quick work of her defiance. She couldn't remember anything from that moment until she woke up here, in a cage down a wide hall off the main cavern, where the altar was located. She could see that there was at least one other cell, an empty one, on the far side of Martha's. Perhaps there were more; it was difficult to tell. There was only one torch burning, and it was near the altar.

"Martha?"

She heard movement, a groan, but nothing she could make any sense of. Chances were Martha couldn't think straight. If Bart had used chloroform on Sarah when she jumped out, he might have used it on Martha again, too.

The possibility of an overdose, of Martha dying down here, made Sarah anxious. Although they were only eight feet apart, they were separated by metal bars. Sarah couldn't even get close enough to check.

Hugging her knees to her body, she shivered against the chill. The temperature was much lower than on the surface, but it wasn't cold. She was having some sort of reaction to the chloroform, the fear coursing through her, or both.

Glumly, she stared out at the altar, the top of which resembled a giant phallus. Sarah wished it was the flickering light that made it look that way, but she knew it wasn't. The Covenanters embraced sex as the greatest life-giving source there was. Sarah had no problem with that. But the altar had a white marble base that was covered in velvet cushions—with manacles in each corner. Did they restrain women? Maybe even rape them?

She hoped not. She'd planned to take the Covenant of Brotherly Love next month. It was a goal she'd been working toward since she'd joined the church. She would've done it long ago except she'd wanted to be sure she approached it with the proper gravity and respect. Ethan had made very clear that there was no going back.

She thought of all the time she'd spent reading the Bible and praying that the Lord would purify her soul so she'd be worthy. What she was seeing now turned all of that on its head. It seemed so sacrilegious, an absolute mockery of all she held dear.

"Help me," Martha mumbled. "Please…help me."

Sarah scrambled over to the bars. "Don't worry," she said. "You're going to be okay. You're not alone. I'm here."

"Who are you?"

"Sarah."

"Sarah, the one who…who saved me from the stoning?"

"Yes." But she was also the one who'd betrayed her at the grocery store. Did Martha not remember?

"I don't feel so good. I'm…sick."

"It's the chloroform. Try to relax and let your body recover."

"What happened?" she asked, but seemed to get her bearings before Sarah could explain. "Oh, God…we're in the pit! I can smell it."

"What does that mean? What goes on down here?"

Martha dragged herself closer, until she could lean against the bars between them. "Rituals, supposedly."

"What kind of rituals?"

"A celebration of the procreative power." She rubbed her face, drew in a deep breath. "At least, that's what I used to believe when I participated. Now I realize that it's nothing more than an orgy for the benefit of Ethan and his Guides."

"An *orgy?*" Sarah echoed. Already disillusioned, she almost couldn't grasp such a base concept in conjunction with the church she'd once loved. "So the rumors, what outsiders are saying about us, it's all true?"

"Ethan describes it in a more…positive light, but—" she laughed bitterly "—it's all to satisfy his own lusts."

Orgies were bad enough. But…what about the manacles? Sarah swallowed hard. "Everyone who participates…they—they're willing to be involved, right?"

"They were when I was down here. It was only the covenanted few."

Sarah cast another glance at that ominous altar. "So why would anyone need to be restrained?"

Martha rubbed her temples. "It's just…part of the show. It's more powerful if the woman seems completely dominated."

"And these *cages?*"

Martha lifted her hands to the bars. "I was told they're symbolic, too. Ethan frees those who are kept here as he will free the souls who accept the truth of his church."

"That's what the Covenant of Brotherly Love involves?"

"No, but you're required to have taken the Covenant to participate. Only a select few are chosen."

Sarah had been weeks away from making the initial commitment. Did that mean she would eventually have been invited down here? "So Ethan locks up men and women and then—"

"Just women," Martha interrupted. "Once a month,

he puts a virgin in here who is then offered to him on the altar as restitution for Eve's sin. That kicks off the so-called celebration. And then the rest of the Guides take a turn with her, too."

Bile rose in the back of Sarah's throat. "But where would he get a virgin? Any virgin in *this* compound is just a girl. She hasn't taken the Covenant."

"Well, everyone except her has. He takes whoever's the oldest."

Sarah tried to calculate how many unmarried women lived in Paradise. "But there aren't more than a handful over eighteen. Does that mean he takes *young* girls?"

Martha sagged against the bars. "Don't worry. The girls don't even know what's happening. They're drugged before they're brought down here and are no worse for wear afterward."

That made it okay? Sarah was shocked by how the religion she'd embraced had been twisted into something sordid and wrong and frightening.

"I can't agree with that," Sarah said. "It's not right. The girls don't have a say in what's happening to them. Even their parents aren't included in the decision." But the parents she knew probably wouldn't disagree. Not believing as they did. She'd been like that, too, hadn't she? To a point, anyway.

Martha laughed again. "You don't get it, do you? Ethan is the Holy One. What does it matter what some girl's parents have to say? Any decision he makes over-rides all other considerations, or he'll simply claim that whoever's opposing him has lost the faith."

But Ethan's word alone wasn't enough for Sarah. Not anymore. The potential for abuse was too great. No

man should have so much power, not when power cor-
rupted human hearts the way it did. "And you don't
have a problem with rituals like this?"

Martha's laughter suddenly switched to tears. "Not
until he turned on me."

Sarah had never felt so much contempt for another
woman. And yet, could she really judge Martha? If
more time had passed, and she hadn't learned what
she'd learned, would she have followed along as
Martha had and gotten swept away by it all?

"What will he do to us?" she asked dully. She was
thinking about her father and his admonishments to
stay away from the Covenanters. In her efforts to find
God, to rise above the violence and decay of normal
society, she'd turned a blind eye to danger signs she
should've heeded. But Ethan pressured them to sacrifice reason and common sense to faith and obedience;
he made them feel they weren't worthy to be chosen if
they relied on their own thinking. Every time she was
inclined to trust her judgment she suffered guilt. Choosing between the two had been a constant tug-of-war,
which was partly why she'd put off taking the Covenant
of Brotherly Love.

"He's going to kill us," Martha said. "Why else
would he risk bringing me back here? If the police find
out, it'll put an end to the church."

"Then why hasn't he done it? Bart could've killed us
both."

"They plan to have a little fun first."

Fun… Sarah studied the phallic symbol above the
altar, wondering if that would be the last sight she ever
saw. Then she remembered Courtney. Had her friend
been brought down here?

Hoping to find the girl in the cage that appeared to be unoccupied, she strained to see past Martha, but could make out nothing. "Do you think he murdered Courtney Sinclair?"

"The girl who disappeared after I left?" Martha asked.

"Yes."

"If she's not down here, there's no question."

25

She'd found Todd. At her request, the woman sitting across from her pointed him out to Rachel while they were eating in the dining hall.

"I feel so bad for him," Rachel murmured as a way to explain her interest. "He must be heartbroken over losing his wife."

"Don't worry," the woman, who'd identified herself as Cori, responded wryly. "Around here, one woman is as good as the next."

When Rachel allowed her confusion to show, Cori lowered her voice. "As long as we cook and clean and spread our legs, what does a man have to complain about?"

"You're unhappy here?"

She sighed. "I don't know. Sometimes I am. Other times I realize the outside world isn't any better. Anyway, Todd's okay. He's already seeing Penny Platting." She nodded toward the buxom woman with thick black hair sitting beside him.

"Doesn't he have to wait until he's divorced before he starts seeing another woman?" she asked.

"Martha's been shunned. That means she no longer exists. He can't be married to someone who doesn't exist, right?"

"I guess not." Rachel feared Martha's lack of existence had become more real than everyone thought. In the few hours they'd left her to "nap," she hadn't been able to discover anything new about Martha. She'd wandered around the compound, hoping to get a sense of any impending action, but so far she hadn't heard or seen anything to indicate that Martha was back.

Maybe she *wasn't* back. Maybe she'd been killed en route, and Bart and Ethan, noticeably absent all afternoon, were out burying her. Anything was possible….

Wishing she could talk to Nate, she stole another glance at Todd. Did Martha's husband know she'd been seized? He certainly didn't act as if he'd just learned that his wife was in Paradise—or dead, for that matter.

Catching sight of her, he smiled. She quickly dropped her gaze, but he got up to make his way over.

"Hello."

She tried to smile despite her swollen lip. "Hi."

"I hear you've come to stay."

"Word travels fast in Paradise."

With strawberry-blond hair, golden lashes and skin so pale she could tell he'd once had a face full of freckles, he wasn't the most attractive man in the world. "That's true," he said. "You can't take a dump around here without someone knowing about it."

He didn't seem to realize how vulgar that statement was, especially at the dinner table. "Goes with living in a small community, I suppose."

"I suppose. Anyway, I think you're going to like it here."

She straightened her silverware. "I hope so."

"It's got to be better than living with that bastard who busted your lip, right?" he said with a lame chuckle.

Rachel took exception to his superior tone. He'd joined in when *his* wife was being stoned. But she nodded. "True."

He thrust hands that were still freckled in the pockets of his jeans, which were far too tight to be stylish. "I saw your husband when you came here yesterday."

"You did?"

"Yeah. Looks strong."

She pretended to test her jaw. "He is."

"But he must be stupid."

"Excuse me?"

"He'd *have* to be stupid to lose a woman as beautiful as you."

Uncomfortable with his frank admiration, she cleared her throat. "Your wife's the one who left the commune, claiming you tried to kill her, isn't she?"

He rocked back, instantly defensive. "Yes, but I didn't. That's a lie."

"People will say anything to justify their own behavior," she said with her own lame chuckle.

"Exactly. She *knows* she was in the wrong."

"She does?"

"Deep down."

"What'd she do?"

"She broke her covenants. And there's nothing worse than that."

Rachel feigned confusion. "Which covenant is that?"

"She disobeyed a prophet of God."

Didn't Todd participate when she disregarded Ethan's mandate that they not sleep together? "Do you have to do *everything* Ethan says?"

"Of course. You can't pick and choose. What kind of follower would that make you?"

"But…Ethan's only human. Maybe he made a mistake. You two are married, after all."

"He didn't make a mistake. Prophets don't make mistakes. God would never allow it."

From her recollection, the Bible warned of false prophets, but no one here seemed to question whether Ethan might be false. "I see. So…if he told you to jump off a cliff, you'd do it?"

"Sure. There could be no greater test of my conviction."

"My father has faith like yours," she said.

He took it as a compliment. "You can develop it, too. I'll help you learn, if you like."

Fortunately, the woman he'd been sitting with sauntered over and slipped her hand in the crook of his arm. "Come back," she whined. "Before you miss dessert."

"I'm just saying hello to our newest member."

Penny's eyes weren't nearly as friendly as Todd's. "Hi. Sorry to hear what your husband did to you. He's *so* handsome. I never would've expected it from a man like that."

"He's not that handsome," Todd muttered, but Rachel ignored him. Evidently, Penny had seen Nate last night, too. "Sometimes it's the people we trust the most who surprise us."

"True." Penny dragged Todd away. "Talk to you later," she called back.

"I heard there was a child involved," Rachel said to Cori after they were gone. "Where is he?"

"With a family who takes good care of him."

"Todd hasn't tried to get him back?"

"He can see him whenever he wants, but he knows it's better for James to be raised by both a mother and a father."

Which James had before everyone turned on Martha. "Maybe James will have a new mother soon," she said, once again eyeing Todd and Penny.

"Looks that way," Cori grumbled. "But I think Todd's going to realize Martha wasn't such a bad wife."

"Penny can't measure up to her?"

"I've always found her a bit vain and silly. But Ethan's given them his blessing to see each other. So who am I to say they shouldn't?"

Rachel had the impression that Ethan wasn't paying as much attention to business as he used to. "I met someone else at the party that I don't see here tonight."

"Who's that?"

"Sarah." Did anyone else know she'd gone to Willcox to find Martha? If Ethan and Bart knew, or even suspected, that she'd been the one who'd helped Martha escape...

Cori half stood to see over the heads of everyone at the tables. "That's odd," she said. "I don't see her, either."

"She usually comes to dinner? I mean, she's not working in the kitchen or anything?" Rachel asked.

"No, she works at the cheese factory, like I do, and she's usually here." With a frown, Cori settled back in her seat. "Maybe she's not feeling well."

Or maybe she was dead.

Ethan was on top of the world. C.J. hadn't been able to crack the password on Nate Mott's computer, not yet, but that seemed less and less important. They had too many other things going for them. Courtney could never threaten him again. Martha was back. Sarah, the only person who could link Martha's abduction to him, would never see the light of day. And the woman he'd named as the Vessel was in the compound of her own free will and planning to join them. All those terrible feelings of foreboding he'd had over the past several weeks had been wrong. Life couldn't be better. It was as if every problem had disappeared in one day. Not only that, the clandestine nature of his relationship with Bart was more titillating than anything he'd experienced thus far. They couldn't keep their hands off each other. After Bart had returned with Martha and Sarah, they'd had the raunchiest sex imaginable—in his office, of all places. Ethan could still smell Bart's cologne on his jalabiya.

He was in love for the first time. And the person he loved felt just as strongly about him. It was so different to have that bond, to respect the person he was sleeping with and to care what that person felt or thought afterward. In some ways it seemed to Ethan that he hadn't truly lived until he and Bart had come together.

Seeing Bartholomew from across the crowded assembly hall, he curved his lips into a faint smile to tell his lover that he was thinking about the passion they'd shared. Then he focused on the crowd waiting to hear him speak. It was showtime. Rachel sat in a place of honor in the front row. She looked a bit uncomfortable, but he wasn't worried that she'd back out. The welcome ritual was powerful and moving and would make her feel instantly connected. He'd seen it work time and again.

"Tonight we have a new member in our midst," he

said into the microphone, and the crowd fell silent. "Sister Rachel." He nodded in her direction but didn't bother with her last name. He didn't want to mention anything to do with her husband. She belonged to him now, to the Covenanters. She was his gift to his followers. "She's been sent to us to nurture and strengthen us by adding her talents to our talents, the work of her hands to the work of ours. And we, in turn, are to guide her as a loving parent, to protect her as a loving husband and to accept her as a loving friend."

"Amen!" came the response.

"From this time forward, she will belong to us and with us. She will share all her worldly goods, her heart and her knowledge, and we will do the same. We will have all things in common. Let there be no poor among us."

"No poor!" the crowd shouted.

"And now, we will welcome her through the gate of acceptance." His eyes sought Bart again; he found him standing in the far corner. "Brother Bartholomew, will you escort Sister Rachel to the front, where she will receive the robes of righteousness?"

Bartholomew straightened in obvious surprise. He generally remained in the background while the other Guides helped with the initiation. But Ethan wanted Bart to do the honors tonight. This action symbolized and confirmed their private bond in a public setting. He was asking Bart to give him Rachel, to give him the Vessel he'd promised their people.

And, as usual, Bartholomew didn't disappoint him. He bowed with respect before making his way to the front, where he offered Rachel his hand and escorted her up on stage.

"And now, my lovely Rachel, you will disrobe."

Her eyes shifted from him to the crowd. "I will… what?"

"Disrobe. In this ritual you lose all shame in your nakedness. You are created in God's image, as the rest of us are. You must pass through the same gates, stripped as bare as the day you arrived on this earth." He waved, and the two women he'd designated before the opening prayer appeared with the white robe he'd had them make.

Rachel saw it and seemed to relax a little.

"This is symbolic," he explained for her ears only. "You take off your worldly clothes and you don the robes of righteousness. But we baptize you first. Then rub you with oil. After that, you'll be ready to become bride to the church."

He knew the others recognized, from the expense and style of the robe and from the subtle changes in the ceremony, that this ritual was different than any they'd witnessed in the past. This was special, modified for the Vessel. Rachel was the only one who didn't understand the magnitude of what was happening.

But she'd find out soon enough.

Rachel could count the number of people who'd seen her naked on three fingers. Her mother, when she'd walked in while Rachel was showering at ten years of age. That guy she'd slept with to punish her father—she couldn't remember his last name and preferred to forget even his first. And Nate. But as she stood in front of the Covenanters, gazing out at their expectant faces, she knew this was one of those compromises she'd have to make for the sake of some greater good, although it required a sacrifice of her comfort, her ideals and her dignity.

With shaking hands, she pulled off the tank top she was wearing and unbuttoned her cutoffs before sliding them over her hips. With so many people in the same room, it'd been too warm a moment before. Now it seemed downright cold. Goose bumps jumped out on her skin as she stood before them in her bra and underwear. She hoped that would suffice, but she suspected it wouldn't. That fear was confirmed when Ethan leaned forward to whisper, "Take it all off."

Rachel attempted to calm her nerves by telling herself that this was something everyone in the room had been through in order to join. She even tried to distract herself by continuing to search the audience for Sarah. But she couldn't find her, and the level of interest in what was taking place didn't seem commensurate with a common ritual. That bothered her. Of course, she'd never participated in or even seen a ritual involving nudity, so maybe she was wrong and they were all like this.

Steeling her nerves against the self-consciousness and embarrassment that came with stripping in front of an audience, she unhooked her bra and let it fall. Then she stepped out of her panties.

"Beautiful," Ethan murmured, but the compliment made her feel even less comfortable. Especially when the women with the robe didn't come forward as she expected. Wondering what was taking them so long, she turned to see, but Ethan drew her in the opposite direction—to a table that held two tall but unlit candles in silver candlesticks and a decorative basin of water.

When Ethan motioned to someone at the side of the

room, all the lights went out, except for a spotlight directly over her head. Then Bartholomew lit the candles, chanting as he did so. The crowd picked up the chant, and the sound crescendoed as Ethan dipped his hand into the water.

"You're about to be purified," he told her, "so that you enter the church untainted by the sins of the world."

What did that involve? She would've asked except Ethan was now saying something theatrical into the microphone, something that sounded like Latin. As he moved away from the mic, he withdrew a sponge from the decorative basin and brought it down over her right breast and then her left, making the shape of an *X*.

Gasping at the cold water, she nearly bolted. She wanted to put on her clothes, wanted to be gone from this place. She'd already sacrificed more for the sake of religion than most people; she couldn't bear to submit her will again. But the hope of saving Martha kept her standing resolutely on stage, even as Ethan knelt before her and ran the sponge down each leg.

Rachel longed for the robe, but Ethan wasn't done yet. He made another motion and each person in the congregation came up to run the sponge over her bare skin. They were chanting and wearing hoods. She had no idea where the costumes had come from. They made it impossible to see whether it was a man or a woman touching her, but she could sometimes tell by their hands. Not surprisingly, the men tried to touch her more intimately.

Closing her eyes, she struggled to endure the intrusion. *It'll be over in a second. Hang on. For Martha. You can beat Ethan at his own game....*

Suddenly, the touching stopped. She opened her

eyes to see that the people were gone—probably back to their seats. Blinded by the spotlight, she couldn't tell whether they were still wearing hoods, but the thought of them staring at her through the eye slits made her feel as if she'd been thrown into a Ku Klux Klan meeting.

Ethan dabbed her forehead with a drop of water, and did the same over each of her closed eyelids and her heart. He spoke again—in Latin, if it *was* Latin—after which he had her kneel at his feet and gave her a morsel of bread and a sip of wine. "Praise the Lord," echoed through the hall.

"And now, Brother Bart and I will do the anointing," he said.

There was a rumble in the crowd, as if this was somehow unusual, but Rachel had nothing to judge by. She curled her fingernails into her palms and pictured Nate—the way he'd kissed her, the way he'd made love to her. It'd been the most difficult thing in the world not to give him everything she'd given before, but she was proud of herself for showing some restraint. He didn't want her love, only her body.

"Rachel?"

She raised her eyes to see Ethan and Bart, the light above their heads creating an imperfect halo. "Yes?"

"Do you covenant to love us as we love you?"

Another sacrifice for the greater good. "Yes."

"The Great Alpha and Omega opens his arms and his heart to you," he said, and he and Bart smoothed hot oil over her whole body.

The chanting started again. This time Rachel could make out the words. "Bring me your heavy-laden, and I will give you rest... Bring me your heavy-laden, and

I will give you rest… Bring me your heavy-laden…"
The words and the motions seemed to blend and swirl.
Bart's hands no longer seemed as calloused as before.
His strong fingers, together with Ethan's smooth ones,
swept up the muscles along her spine, over her buttocks
and down her legs in rhythm with the chanting.

Her goose bumps were gone by the time this portion
of the ceremony was over. She was almost relaxed
when Ethan told her to kneel so he could pray over her
again. Some of his words were in English. Others
seemed to be taken from some foreign or historic ritual
she didn't recognize.

When he'd finished, he drew a *C* on her forehead
with a stick that'd been charred in the candle flame. It
wasn't hot enough to burn her, but it was sharp enough
to scratch. As he etched the letter into her skin, everyone called out, "God be with you." Then the lights went
on and, at last, the women with the robe stepped
solemnly forward to dress her.

"You make the perfect bride," Ethan breathed as they
belted her robe. He took her wedding ring off her finger, dropped it in his pocket and presented her to the
crowd.

"I give you the High Vessel of the Holy One!"

26

When Nate finally allowed himself to drive to Paradise, he was angrier than he could ever remember being. It was the helplessness and the worry that were getting to him. He wanted to storm Paradise, kick the Holy One's ass and take Rachel home. But even if he could figure out how to succeed against two hundred, he couldn't make the attempt, and that put him on edge. He was approaching the compound, knowing he might get his own ass kicked instead, and that pissed him off even more.

But it had to be done. And there was a bright side. He'd been looking for a target ever since he'd watched Rachel leave, and the man at the gate gave him one. Nate met the twenty-something guy halfway to the guard's station and left him on the ground, out cold. He could've taken the second guard, too, but he purposely hesitated long enough to let the man set off an alarm. He couldn't fight too well or he'd reveal his training.

When the bell sounded, people poured out of the Enlightenment Hall like ants. Nate could hear them coming, the pounding of their feet, the shouts that rang through the air. "It's Rachel's husband!" "There's a fight!" "Get Bart!"

Nathan knocked the second guard down and turned

to face the two men who reached him first. It was a relief to be active, to discharge some of the anxiety that'd built up over the past hours. He managed to plow his fist into someone's nose and to land a jab with his left hand, but after three or four punches they swarmed him. They were kicking him and hitting him from all sides, so he really let loose, but it was no good. There were at least forty—far too many.

"He's a tough son of a bitch," someone grunted as his foot connected with one body part or another.

Nate tried to draw his arm back to throw another punch but couldn't move. They had a tight hold on every limb and were forcing him to the ground.

"He's drunk. I can smell it on his breath." This came from a man who shoved a knee in Nate's gut. But Nate wasn't drunk. He'd had a few beers and intentionally spilled some on his shirt, just to make his actions and demands appear authentic. The better he played his part the safer Rachel would be. Or so he hoped.

"Get my wife!" he shouted. "I want my wife. Rachel!" He sounded drunk, even to his own ears. Drunk and enraged. But only the enraged part was real.

"Where's Ethan?" someone called. "If this guy gets loose…"

"He won't get loose," another man said. Then white-hot pain rocked through him as a fist slammed into his jaw.

Rattled, Nate shook his head to clear away the stars that burst across his vision, but the faces crowding around him, staring down at him, didn't immediately come into focus.

"Rachel!" Nate called again, his voice growing hoarse. "Get my wife!"

"Why? It won't do you any good to see her," someone said. "She's one of us now. You're not getting her back."

So they'd accepted her. That was a positive development for the mission. But it caused a fresh trickle of fear to pour through his blood. He didn't want her here, with these people.

"Ethan's on his way," someone cried.

Another person began pressing the onlookers back. "Make room."

"What's going on?"

Nate recognized the voice even before he saw the face that went with it. Bartholomew. Gazing up at the man he'd first met in the desert, he noted the unmistakable determination.

"Get back," Bart said to the onlookers and, a second later, Nate realized he'd been making space for Ethan, who was the next to peer down at him.

"He's come for her, just like I told you he would," Bart told his leader.

Ethan's lips pressed into a thin line. "So? We'll throw him out, just like I told *you* we would." He nodded to the men surrounding them. They started to drag Nate toward the entrance, but he wasn't ready to go. First, he wanted to see Rachel.

"Wait! I'll leave on my own," he said. "Give me a second. I promise I'll go in peace if you'll let me talk to my wife."

"She has nothing to say to you," Ethan responded.

"Then let her tell me that. Rachel!"

"Go home," Bart snapped.

Nate wasn't willing to make it that easy. Not when he'd come this far. He wasn't leaving the compound until he caught at least a glimpse of Rachel. But he was too restricted to be able to fight. So he went limp, hoping to convince them he'd given up.

While some let go, four men continued to drag him to the gate. The rest followed behind. But even the ones who'd hung on relaxed their grip when they thought they'd won. And that was when Nate poured every ounce of strength he had into getting free.

He almost managed it. He slammed one man into another, decked the third and felt the fingernails of the fourth scrape deep in his arm as he tore out of his grip. Then he found his feet and made a mad rush toward the Enlightenment Hall. But the crowd that had been following swarmed him again, and he was soon lying facedown in the dirt.

"This guy's dangerous!" someone yelled.

"I want my wife!" His words were muffled from the pressure on his back as they pushed him into the ground. "Tell her I'm here. Tell her I'm sorry. Let me see her. Please."

"She's no longer your wife," Ethan said. "She belongs here now. Don't come back."

She belongs here…

As they yanked Nate to his feet, he was considering the wisdom of another attempt at escape. But then he heard exactly what he'd been hoping to hear.

"Wait! Don't hurt him! I can calm him down. Just…let me explain to him."

It was Rachel. Suddenly exhausted and in more pain than he'd previously realized, Nate sagged.

"He's drunk. He won't listen." Ethan tried to keep her from approaching, but she jerked away.

She was a more skillful actress than Nate had given

her credit for. The distress and concern on her face seemed real. "Oh, God, are you okay?" she asked as she knelt at his side.

He blinked away the dirt and sweat in his eyes. "They…they wouldn't let me see you."

"I'm here." She glanced at the men surrounding him. "Let go of him."

They wouldn't, but she cupped his cheek, and her cool hand on his skin made him feel instantly better. "I—I'm sorry I hit you," he said.

"I know. You're always sorry but…I can't come home. I—I know it'll happen again."

It wasn't easy to pull his eyes away from her. She was wearing a white robe with gold embroidery, and it looked as if she was naked beneath it. He wanted to know what they'd done to her, if she was truly as okay as she seemed. But he couldn't stop acting just because he'd been somewhat reassured of her safety. He shifted his gaze to Ethan. "What's she wearing?"

Ethan's eyebrows went up. "That's none of your concern." He put his hand on Rachel's shoulder, the movement as authoritative as it was proprietary. "Go back to your room, Rachel. I'll be there to speak with you shortly."

Tears streaked down her cheeks. "But you've hurt him."

"He got what he was asking for. He'll be fine."

Her quick embrace made him wish he could use his arms. He wanted to clasp her to him, if only for a second. But his captors didn't trust him; they weren't giving him another chance to break free.

He caught the scent of some oil or perfume just

before he heard Rachel whisper, "Upstairs in the Enlightenment Hall, second room on the right."

She'd told him where she was staying. Smart girl.

Satisfied, Nate stopped resisting and soon found himself tossed outside the gate.

Rachel waited in her room as Ethan had instructed. Because she'd come to him for refuge, he had more power over her than he otherwise would. The way he'd acted when Nate showed up proved he'd take full advantage of it, too. He was behaving more like a father or husband, someone who had greater control than a prophet or spiritual leader. And there were even some indications that he was treating her differently from regular church members. As far as she knew, she was the only one ensconced in the Enlightenment Hall, under his direct supervision. And what was that business at the end of her initiation, the part about being the "high vessel" of the Holy One?

Elevated status or not, she wasn't sure how long she could last here. She was still nervous about Nate's missing computer, wasn't sure if that was a problem or not. And even if she couldn't find Martha—and she'd seen no sign of her since arriving in Paradise—she had to get close to Ethan to figure out a way to stop him. Or get close to those who knew him well. She'd been hoping to spot Sarah tonight, but Sarah hadn't attended either dinner or the initiation, at least as far as Rachel could tell. The fact that she was missing made Rachel anxious, eager to slip out and do some investigating. But Ethan had promised her a visit and she dared not leave until he'd said what he wanted to say and gone for the night.

With a sigh, she paused by the mirror. She was still wearing her new robe but only because she had nothing to change into. She wasn't sure what had happened to the clothing she'd been wearing when she arrived but her tank top and shorts hadn't been returned to her. And of course she hadn't packed anything else.

Already she regretted that decision. What she had on made her feel as if all freedom—and the confidence she'd developed since leaving her father's home—had been stripped from her. It didn't help that the lack of underclothing made her feel so vulnerable.

A brisk knock told her Ethan had finally deigned to make an appearance.

Battling a sudden case of nerves, she crossed to the door and opened it a crack. It was Ethan, all right.

"How are you feeling?" His pupils were dilated, and his eyes looked glassy and almost entirely black. She could tell he was on something.

"Tired. It's been an emotional day."

"Yes, but one that's ended well. I hope you understand you're safe here. We've already proved that once, have we not? Your husband will never be able to hurt you again."

He didn't mention that seeing Nate's face bloodied and bruised had obviously upset her but that concern had been too genuine to hide. Just the thought of Nate being kicked and hit by all those people made her willing to do *anything* to stop it.

Nate shouldn't have staged such a big scene. He could've come to the gate, demanded to talk to Ethan and been sent away without getting hurt.

But then she wouldn't have seen him.

"I appreciate the safe haven," she said. "But being

here, leaving Nate, doesn't mean I want to see him injured."

"Of course not. And he's not injured. Not really."

"You're sure?"

"I'm sure."

"Where is he now?"

"How should I know? Probably at home, sleeping off the alcohol."

She hoped that was the case. She could survive this much better if she knew he was safe.

When she said nothing, Ethan glanced into her room. "So…are you comfortable for the night?"

"I'd like my old clothes back, please."

"Don't worry about them," he said with a dismissive wave. "You need to dress in clothes more befitting your station."

"My station?" she echoed.

He swayed on his feet but retained his balance by catching hold of the doorjamb. "You're a Covenanter now."

She'd seen Covenanters dressed in a mismatch of styles and clothing. Why was Ethan so picky about *her* wardrobe? "But I have this—" she indicated the new robe "—and nothing else." She hesitated to mention her lack of underwear. She was nervous about Martha's assertion that orgies were quite common here. After the parade of people who'd watched her disrobe and then the many hands that'd helped "cleanse" her, she could believe it. Such intimate contact could easily mow down the typical barriers to that kind of behavior. She didn't need a psychologist to tell her that.

"Everything you need will be provided."

"When?"

"Tomorrow."

"And tonight?"

He lowered his voice. "Sleep naked, beautiful Rachel. Sleep naked and think of me as I'll be thinking of you."

"Ethan!"

The sharpness of Bartholomew's voice surprised Rachel. Apparently, it surprised Ethan, too. He gave her a guilty "I've been caught" expression, then chuckled softly as he twisted around to see his head of security. "There you are," he said. "I was wondering when you were coming to bed."

"I was just about to retire to my room," Bart responded. "But I had an important matter to discuss with you before you retire to yours."

"Of course. I'm coming." With a nod exaggerated in its politeness, Ethan left.

Rachel shut and locked her door, then pressed her ear against the panel, trying to hear what was being said in the hall. Bart kept his voice too low, but Ethan wasn't as careful. "I don't know what you're talking about," he said.

There was more rumbling from Bart. Although Rachel couldn't make out the specific words, she sensed he was upset. Was it Ethan's visit to her room that had spurred his displeasure? Or was it her initiation? Or the fact that she was staying in the Enlightenment Hall? Or did his annoyance have something to do with Martha and Sarah?

"Of course I know that," Ethan said. "I'm fine. I'll be careful. You're such a killjoy."

Bart spoke again as they moved off. Then she heard a door close farther down the hall.

What did their interaction mean? She'd assumed Ethan was in control of Paradise, but the exchange she'd just overheard sounded as if Ethan had been trying to cajole a strict parent.

Maybe it was about the drugs. Martha said Ethan took drugs, and he'd obviously been tweaking tonight.

Either way, something was different from even a few days ago, something that gave Bart more power than before. Was it somehow related to Martha's recapture? What else could've happened?

Rachel knew she wasn't going to find out by cowering in her room. According to an alarm clock on the nightstand, she waited an hour, maybe longer. Then, when she found the hall dark and empty, she slipped out.

27

It wasn't going to be as difficult to get in as Nate had thought. The fence was high, was topped with razor wire and appeared to go at least a foot deep into the ground. But it was regular chain-link, and there were only two guards on duty, both of whom sat in the station most of the time and rarely walked the perimeter. If he came upon Paradise from the opposite side, over by the mountains, he'd place himself behind the Enlightenment Hall and out of sight of those guards. He'd also be close to where he wanted to end up. All he had to do was cut the fence along the ground, slide beneath it, bend it straight and throw a little dirt to hide where it'd been cut.

Supposedly, Ethan had weapons, which meant that Nate risked more than getting his ass kicked again. Although he'd been sorely tempted, he hadn't brought his gun. He figured he'd have a better chance of convincing them he was simply a vengeful husband bent on getting his wife back if he wasn't armed. Then, if he did get caught, it might not blow the whole operation.

But he didn't plan on getting caught. This time he wasn't here to put on a show. He wanted to talk privately with Rachel, make sure she was okay, find out what she'd learned so far and decide how he could best support her—but mostly, he just wanted to see her.

Making a wide arc, he stopped to take a look at Paradise through the night-vision goggles he'd brought in his backpack. Two dogs trotted back and forth in a cage not far from the Enlightenment Hall. He'd seen them when he was here before but had forgotten about them. Although he was far enough away that they didn't seem to notice or care about him, that wouldn't be the case as he got closer, and he couldn't have them barking and making a fuss.

While checking for other problems, he decided to change his point of entry. He'd come through the fence by the garden area. There were no dogs there. That meant he'd pass through the largest number of tents but he'd soon reach the cheese factory, which should be deserted at this hour. Most people were going to bed. If he acted as though he belonged, maybe anyone he met would assume he was one of the guards. Many of them wore camouflage, too.

If that didn't work, he'd have to start acting belligerent again.

Stretching his sore jaw, he winced at the thought of playing it that way.

After gathering the items he'd need, he hid the rest of his gear behind some boulders and hiked down. He was pretty sure his clothing was thick enough to protect him when he slid under the fence. But he'd have to shed his jacket once he got through. No one wore a jacket in the middle of a night as warm as this one, and he couldn't afford to stand out.

How he'd get into the building once he breached the perimeter, he had no idea. He was hoping it wasn't locked. It probably wasn't. They lived behind a tall fence patrolled by armed guards. Why would it be necessary to lock the doors?

If the place *was* locked, he'd just have to break in.

He could do that.

Maybe…

The ground was as hard next to the fence as elsewhere in the desert. Silently cursing the rocks jabbing into his knees as he knelt, he used wire cutters to create the opening. Then he bent the fence and slid underneath on his back so he wouldn't get snared on a piece of sharp wire.

Once he'd made it through, he saw that the damage to the fence was more obvious than he'd expected. He considered repairing it, at least superficially, but the fact that it was nearly eleven o'clock and most people were in their tents satisfied him that it was safe to wait.

He bent the fence back as far as he could, donned the ball cap he carried in his pocket and took off his jacket and gloves.

Movement and voices from inside the tents reached Nate's ears as he passed. Keeping to the shadows as much as possible, he put his head down and moved with purpose, and no one seemed to notice him—until he rounded the corner of the cheese factory and started across the open courtyard. Then he encountered a man and a woman, holding hands as they strolled. He attempted to walk right past them, but the man stopped and caught his arm. "Hey, do we know you?"

The Enlightenment Hall was completely empty. Rachel had already tiptoed through the kitchen, which had been cleaned and abandoned for the night, plus the room where they'd performed her baptism and initiation, the conference/dining room and Ethan's office, all without running into a soul. Now she was back on the second story, standing in a suite of rooms that could only be Ethan's private chambers. The scent of his cologne was stronger here, and one of his robes had been tossed over a chair.

Hesitating near the door, she listened to make sure no one was coming. Then she shored up her nerve and moved farther into the suite, which consisted of three bedrooms and two baths. The first bedroom, obviously Ethan's, was the grandest. The second looked lived in, as well, but she wasn't positive it was Bart's room until she spotted his blue jalabiya in the closet.

Ethan kept his head of security very close, closer than she would've expected. But maybe he was paranoid. Maybe he'd done enough horrible stuff that he *should* be paranoid....

Beneath the various garments Bartholomew owned was a guitar. She hadn't thought of him as someone who'd be interested in music.

There were other surprises, as well. The boxes stacked on the shelves above the clothes rail contained photo albums from when Bartholomew was a child. Although Rachel was curious and wanted to look through them—she couldn't imagine Bartholomew ever being a child—she didn't dare take the time, not when he and Ethan could return at any moment.

She shoved the albums back where they belonged and poked her head into Bart's bathroom, but there wasn't even a washcloth to suggest he'd used it recently. If this was his bedroom, why didn't he use the bathroom?

"Interesting arrangement," she murmured, and visited the third room, which was obviously unoccupied.

Once she had an overview of the suite and knew for sure that it was empty, Ethan's room became her main focus. She went through his closet and drawers and quickly found drug paraphernalia—a pipe and what appeared to be a dime bag of meth. She wished she could turn him in for possession, but that wouldn't put him out of circulation for very long. She had to come up with something bigger.

The entrance to Ethan's bathroom was right next to his dresser. It had elegant washbasins, marble floors and a gigantic shower made of clear glass. It was unusually large, almost as big as his bedroom, but the bathroom drawers held the same toiletries found in most bathrooms.

Then it occurred to her—there were *two* toothbrushes in the holder.

She fingered the bristles. They were both wet.

I was wondering when you were coming to bed....

Ethan's words had sounded a bit like one married partner speaking to another, but she'd shrugged them off. Bart was Ethan's bodyguard. Of course they'd stay close. But...those toothbrushes made her wonder just *how* close.

"Hiding a few more secrets than I expected?" she breathed. If Ethan was gay, it would be quite ironic that he led a church that followed most other Judeo-Christian religions in condemning homosexuality.

A noise caused Rachel to freeze. She'd put Ethan's meth in the pocket of her robe. Having discovered *some* evidence of wrongdoing, she was reluctant to give it up, even though it wasn't the kind of evidence she needed.

But now she wished she'd left it. She didn't want to be caught in his bathroom with his drugs. They proved she'd been snooping and made it impossible to use the excuse that she was merely seeking him out so they could talk about her conversion or her situation with her husband or whatever.

Listening for the sound she'd heard a moment earlier, she tiptoed through the bedroom and peeked into the hall. The noise wasn't repeated, but she was fairly sure someone else was in the house. Had Ethan returned? Was he on his way to bed?

A creak broke the silence, coming from the stairs, but it was too dark to see anyone. Should she return the dope or get the hell out?

The second creak convinced her. Someone was climbing the stairs. If she didn't get out, she'd be trapped.

Swallowing hard, she moved as quietly as possible into the hall. Snippets of her conversation with Nate played in her mind as her heart rate spiked. She didn't want to be Ethan's next target. *Help me make it. Please help me make it,* she prayed.

She breathed more easily once she got to her room. Whatever she'd heard must've been a product of her imagination, reinforced by nerves, because as far as she could tell she was still alone. At least, she *thought* she was alone—until she closed the door. Then someone grabbed her from behind and clapped a hand over her mouth.

Bart was surprised to find their housekeeper, Maxine Maynard, waiting for him at the door to the pit. They'd held no public rituals tonight. They'd had a private meeting for the Guides alone. So why hadn't she left at ten, as usual? What was she doing here at nearly two in the morning?

"Holy One!" An expression of relief swept over her face the second she spotted Ethan in the crowd coming up the metal staircase, but Bart quickly intercepted her. Ethan wasn't in his right mind. He wouldn't be able to respond coherently. If they had a problem on their hands, Bart didn't even want him to know about it. When he was like this, there was no telling how he might react, how difficult it might be to get him to go to bed and leave the important decisions to Bart.

"Is anything wrong, Sister?" he asked, steering her off to one side.

Obviously disappointed that he hadn't given her an opportunity to address her beloved leader, she frowned. "I saw something that troubled me."

"What's that?"

She seemed reluctant at first. Bart didn't have Ethan's charisma, his way with people, and they often showed their preference for Ethan. But Bart had a better mind, made better decisions. Slowly, the Covenanters seemed to be accepting the duality of leadership. And Maxine served as proof. As soon as she started talking, she lost her initial reluctance.

"At first I thought she was just restless or that she was looking for Ethan, but...the way she went through the place...I know she was snooping around."

Fortunately, Brother Titherington had engaged Ethan on the landing just inside the metal door.

The Guides were laughing, probably at a joke that had to do with the punishment they'd just dealt out to Martha. Ethan had framed this evening's activities as an exorcism. He said the devil had taken possession of her soul and caused her to act as she had, which gave them license to be more violent than usual. It had been exceptionally impressive—until the drugs began to hamper Ethan's performance. When sober, he was magnificent. But he was sober less and less of the time. Bart wasn't sure what, if anything, he should do about that.

Hoping to prevent Ethan from noticing Maxine, he pulled her farther off to the side, between the racks of food. After the other Guides had filed past, he closed the pit door, keeping Ethan and Titherington inside, where they were still talking, but the dampness of the pit from which they'd emerged clung to his clothes, making the air in the storeroom musty and heavy. "You're not making sense," he said, his voice barely a whisper. "Who's snooping?"

"The Vessel!"

"Rachel Mott?"

"Yes. I couldn't sleep so I wanted to do some knitting. But then I realized I'd forgotten my knitting bag. I was just returning to the Enlightenment Hall to grab it when I saw her slip into Ethan's office. I almost went to the guards. But…I was afraid the Holy One would be angry if I involved someone else. So I hid in the corridor, where I waited. And watched."

"And?"

"She went through the drawers of his desk. I could hear them opening and closing. Then she came out and went upstairs and into the suite."

"*My* suite? The Holy One's chambers?"

"Yes."

"What was she doing in there?"

"I have no idea. I didn't dare go close enough to listen. There's no alcove outside that door like there is near the office."

He immediately thought of Ethan's drugs. What else would Rachel find in the bedroom? Evidence of their involvement? Maybe. But he didn't understand why she was even looking. What was she up to? Had he been right about her all along? He'd pressured C.J. to hack into Nate's computer but the man wasn't half as good as they'd assumed, or Nate's encryption was more complicated than most. "Is she still there?"

Someone pushed on the door from inside, but he didn't react. He had a few seconds before Titherington or Ethan realized it was blocked.

"Maybe. As soon as I saw her go in, I came here."

Bart's blood ran cold. If someone like Maxine had a funny feeling about what was going on, he knew there was reason for concern.

"Hey!" Ethan called from inside. "Open the damn door."

Shocked when he didn't immediately jump to obey this command, Maxine stared at him.

"The Holy One hasn't been sleeping well," Bart explained. "I don't want him to hear about this tonight. It'll only upset him. We both know he'd want me to handle it, anyway."

She nodded. "So should I go see if she's still up there? Confront her?"

"Bart? Did you leave me?" Ethan called. "Where are you? If this is a joke, it's not funny."

"Hey!" Titherington joined Ethan in yelling. "Anybody there? Let us out!"

"I'll tell you what I want you to do." Taking Maxine by the elbow, Bart drew her close so he could whisper his instructions in her ear. Even though they hadn't been able to access Nate's damn computer, maybe there was another way to figure out exactly who the Motts were and what they were after. If he was clever enough, maybe he could do it without alerting Ethan or the two Guides who were too shit-faced to return to their tents and were planning to stay in the extra rooms on the third floor.

Only after Maxine was gone, did he open the door.

"What the hell is wrong with you? Why'd you shut us in?" Ethan snapped.

"Serves you right for taking so long," he said. "I'm tired, and it's my job to lock up and walk the perimeter."

Had he been less stoned, Ethan might've been angry at this retort, but he was flying too high to let his irritation last. And Titherington knew better than to complain about anything. He was Bart's least favorite of the Guides—other than Joshua. Joshua was as young and attractive as Ethan. But his conscience was beginning to get the best of him. That would eventually make him a security risk.

There was so much to consider when you were running a compound of this size, Bart thought with a sigh. It was the most intriguing game of chess he'd ever played. But whatever move he made against Joshua would have to wait. Tonight, he had the chance to take the queen.

28

Once Rachel realized she wasn't being attacked, she calmed down. "You scared the hell out of me!" she whispered. "How'd you get in here?"

Nate stood in the middle of the room, only a foot away from her. The lights were off and had to stay off, but he could see her outline in the moonlight pouring through the window.

"It wasn't easy. I ran into a couple who stopped me—"

"No!"

"Yes. I thought for sure it was all over. But they must not have been part of the crowd earlier. They didn't recognize me. I told them I was a cement contractor Ethan had invited to stay while I worked on the bids for the new school."

"And they bought it?" she asked incredulously.

"They bought it. Wished me luck and everything. Said they hoped I'd be here for the next Introduction Meeting."

She whistled. "That was lucky."

"We were due for a break. What's been happening around here?"

"I had to swear loyalty to Ethan and his church." She

held out her arms and turned, displaying the robe she was wearing.

"What's with the new threads?"

"They took all my clothes."

His gaze dropped to where the robe parted at her cleavage. "So you're not wearing anything underneath?"

"Not a stitch."

His body reacted to the image his mind so readily supplied, but he tried not to show it. "So this is what they wear after they join up?"

"Following baptism. But they did some other rituals, too. Too bad you had to miss the big event. It was...-quite interesting."

"Looks that way." It *still* looked interesting....

"It was also a little disconcerting."

He studied what he could see of her, but it was difficult to identify nuances of expression. "Ethan didn't...touch you, did he?"

"*Everybody* touched me—while I stood in front of the entire group."

"*What?*"

She held up a hand. "Not the way you think."

"I'm waiting for the details."

When she gave them to him, he wanted to bash Ethan in the face for making everything so sensual. But Rachel distracted him by putting a gentle finger to his bruised cheek. "How badly are you hurt?"

"I definitely got the worst of it." He chuckled at the memory. "But I'm okay."

"You *had* to get yourself beaten up? You couldn't trust me to handle this?"

She sounded upset. Was she assuming he'd shown

up because *he* wanted to be the one to take Ethan down? That he was afraid he'd be upstaged by an underling? A woman? She'd accused him of being sexist. But that wasn't it at all. It was her. He'd come for her.

"You wanted me to sit in that trailer and let you do all the heavy lifting?" he said.

"Not necessarily. I just didn't see the point in you getting hurt."

"I never would've known which building you were staying in if I hadn't done that."

"That might not have been a bad thing. I'm not so sure having you here is a smart idea."

"Why not?"

"Because I don't want to watch what they'll do to you if they catch—" She stopped. Voices, coming from downstairs, filtered up to them. When it became apparent that Ethan and Bart were coming, her eyes latched on to his and widened until he could see their whites, even in the dark.

"What should we do?" she murmured. "One of them, or both, might come in here. You've got to get out *now*."

Nate brought a finger to her lips. They weren't going to move. They were on the second story with only one door and one window. He didn't have time to escape through the window, and he couldn't get out through the door. Their only option was to remain absolutely still—and hope for the best.

Rachel held her breath as she listened.

"That was amazing." Ethan's words were slurred as he climbed the stairs. "Didn't you think it was incredible? I could've gone on all night, especially when she started to beg. That's when I spread her legs and rammed that—"

"Shut up!" Bart cut him off.

"I'm just enjoying the aftermath. When did you turn into such a bitch?"

"We have company. I shouldn't have to remind you of that."

"She's got to be asleep by now."

"She doesn't *have* to be anything. Exercise some caution for a change."

Nate's fingers slipped between hers and Rachel hung on to him. Ethan had mentioned begging. He'd also begun to describe something that sounded very ugly. Had he been talking about Martha—or some other woman? What had he done tonight?

"You're getting on my nerves, you know that?" Ethan said. They were on the landing. Rachel could tell by the volume and proximity of their voices.

"I have a feeling that won't last long," Bart replied dryly.

"What's that supposed to mean?"

"You know what it means."

"That you're going to make it up to me?"

"Be quiet!" Bart snapped.

"I don't want to be quiet. Kiss me here. In the hall."

"Ethan, stop. You don't know what you're saying."

"I know exactly what I'm saying. And I know exactly what I want."

"Come on, into the room."

"I want to do it here, on the landing, right by my wife's door."

At this, Nate felt for the wedding ring he'd given her and didn't seem pleased when he found it missing.

The sudden quiet made Rachel believe Ethan was getting his wish. It also made her hesitant to speak. Bart and Ethan were so close. But Nate risked it.

"What the hell?" he whispered, the words barely audible as his lips made contact with the rim of her ear.

She moved closer, so he could hear her response. "I was getting to that."

As she came up against him, his hands slid around her waist, anchoring her to the spot. "Please tell me they're not doing what I think they're doing."

"They might be…"

"Let's get you to bed," Bart said, and he must've walked away because the next time Ethan spoke he seemed to be trailing after his lover.

Soon, Rachel could hear the murmur of voices but not the individual words.

"Ethan's *gay?*" Nate whispered, but he didn't let her go.

"I'm beginning to get that feeling." She told herself to break off the embrace. Now that Ethan and Bart were in their suite, she and Nate could separate and still hear each other. But she couldn't seem to make herself act. Seeing him beaten by the crowd had upset her. Being able to feel him against her, to reassure herself, was too gratifying.

He didn't step away, either. "Wait…I'm confused. Doesn't he teach that homosexuality is an abomination? Or did I just assume that because—"

"I don't think it's merely an assumption, or he wouldn't have to hide his involvement with Bart."

"What a hypocrite." He settled her against his hips, and it became apparent that she wasn't the only one suddenly reacting to their closeness. "I *hate* hypocrites."

She shivered with the longing that welled up inside her. She'd made love to Nate recently, but she hadn't let her heart participate along with the rest of her. She'd limited her emotional involvement and, therefore, her enjoyment. She regretted that now. Somehow, everything she'd been worried about didn't seem quite as important when they could be dead before the next sunrise. Maybe she should've thrown caution to the winds as soon as they hit Arizona and taken whatever Nate was willing to offer. It could've been an exciting week. A casual relationship was better than nothing, wasn't it? She doubted they'd ever work this closely together again, which meant she'd never have another chance.

"Ethan's full of contradictions," she said. So was she. She knew there was no point in giving Nate her love, but she couldn't overcome what she felt. When the Covenanters had held him on the ground and were coming at him from all sides, and she hadn't been sure she'd be able to stop them from doing him serious harm, she'd realized it was futile to fight her feelings for him. Whether he cared about her or not, she was in love with him, and there was no changing that.

"How do you explain the orgies?" he asked. "Martha said he participates, with women." His mouth was an inch from hers. She could feel his breath fan her cheek. She tried not to remember the sensuality of his kiss or how much she enjoyed the softness of his lips and the way they moved on hers.

"She also said he sleeps with other men's wives when he visits the various tents at night." Wrestling with the magnetism she felt whenever she was in Nate's presence, she took a deep, steadying breath. "My guess is there's no limit to his depravity. When Abby was here, she picked up on something that suggests they have a pit of some kind, where certain rituals occur. What they are, I don't know. But a pit doesn't sound like a place you'd want to be, does it?"

"Definitely not."

When the roughness of his chin touched her jaw, she tilted her head so their lips brushed. She wasn't sure if she'd initiated the contact or he had. He certainl hadn't avoided it. But the way her heart slammed against her chest set off a warning bell in her head. She couldn't make love to him again and expect to act indifferent afterward.

Pulling back, she reached for the door handle. "You should go."

He grabbed her hand. "I'm not leaving. Not yet."

"But if they catch you here—"

"They won't. We'll wait until they're asleep, or so preoccupied we could tramp through the place without being heard. Then we'll look for Martha."

"I can do that by myself."

"I'm going to help you. The sooner we find her, the better. For her, and for you. I want to get you out of here."

That sounded so protective, as if he cared about her. But he didn't. Like any good leader, he was simply concerned about his team. "It'd be better if you left."

"Why?"

She had plenty of reasons, but the one she mentioned wasn't the one uppermost in her mind. "If I'm caught snooping around, I can make up some excuse and maybe Ethan will believe me. If we're caught together, any chance of finding Martha and Sarah or gathering evidence against Ethan will be lost."

"Then we won't get caught."

If he wouldn't go, they needed to get to work—or do something else to stop the terrible longing. "Why won't you *ever* cut me a break?"

"What?"

"You heard me."

"You want me to go."

"Yes." She didn't bother to conceal the frustration boiling up inside her. One way or another, she had to get out of this dark bedroom. If she stayed another second, she'd throw herself at him and lose what little self-respect she'd managed to recover since she'd let herself into his condo and given him the surprise of his life.

"Even if I was willing, I can't do that now."

"Why not?"

"We have to wait, make sure they're asleep."

She swallowed hard. "How long?"

His lips were at her ear again, teasing, tempting. They were all she could think about. "Fifteen or twenty minutes."

And what would they do in the meantime? Fifteen minutes sounded like an eternity. She couldn't hold out much longer. She felt as if she were clinging to the side of a cliff and quickly losing her grip.

Succumbing to a fatalistic impulse, she considered letting go. Maybe she'd fall to the rocks beneath, but what a way to go....

"Nate?" she murmured.

"What?"

"What would you do if I kissed you?"

"What do you think?"

"You'd kiss me back." She just wished it could mean something....

He didn't wait for her to make the first move. Cupping her face in his large hands, he touched his lips to hers.

She didn't want it to be as good as it was. But the pleasure that surged through her confirmed what she'd already guessed. All her efforts to fall out of love hadn't worked. As his tongue slid against hers and his hands parted her robe, she began spinning hopelessly and completely out of control.

29

Afraid to use the bed or even a wall for fear they'd make too much noise, Nate urged Rachel down on the carpet. But he was pretty sure she didn't mind. The way she was tugging at his pants told him she was just as desperate, just as eager, as he was.

The rough spontaneity of their actions created the perfect outlet for the emotions that had been raging inside him all day—the worry, the concern, the fear, the anger, even the jealousy. How dare Ethan remove Rachel's wedding ring? How dare he tell Bart she was *his* wife? Ethan had no right. Maybe she wasn't really married to Nate, but Ethan didn't know that.

The relief he felt at being with her, at seeing her so animated and responsive, like she'd been that first time in January, made the pleasure more intense than ever before. This wasn't Susan; Rachel wasn't anything like Susan. He should've realized that long ago. Rachel was tougher than he'd given her credit for, one of the toughest women he'd ever met.

The moan she attempted to stifle as he pushed inside her made him realize he had less control than ever before. They were just getting started and already he was on the edge. It was because he'd been so afraid he'd

never see her again. Yet here she was, wrapping her legs
around his hips and pulling him deep.

"You feel so good," he muttered, but he couldn't
think about that or their lovemaking would be over far
too soon. He definitely didn't want it to be like it had
been at the trailer. This time, she was going to enjoy it
as much as she had the very first time they'd been together.

"That's it," she gasped as he struck a rhythm they
both seemed to like. "Don't stop." As she arched into
him, gripping his buttocks, he begged his body not to
let him down. *Hang on. Not yet…*

Soon they were both breathless and slick with sweat,
but he continued to thrust into her, gripping the corner
of the dresser for leverage as her hips rocked up to meet
his. He thought he didn't have a chance of holding out.
But then she gasped and he knew he'd made it. She was
there, right where he wanted her to be. They were *both*
there.

Throwing back his head, he abandoned his self-
control and pleasure ripped through him in a series of
bone-melting spasms.

"Tell me you love me," he said as he sank, exhausted, onto the floor beside her.

Judging by the sudden stiffness of her body, she
didn't trust him. "Quit being a jerk," she said.

Summoning what little energy he had left, he rolled
over and caught her chin so she had to look at him. "I'm
not being a jerk, Rachel. I *want* to hear it…if it's still
true."

She seemed about to say something but he never got
to hear it. Almost before he realized what was happening, he heard a key in the lock.

Grabbing his clothes, he made a dash for cover—and barely reached the bathroom before the door swung open.

Rachel's heart never stopped pounding. Pleasure turned instantly to fear as her visitor snapped on a flashlight. She wanted to react immediately, to sit up and demand to know who was entering her room without permission. But she hadn't managed to get into bed. She'd barely had time to belt her robe. At this point, she thought it was smarter to pretend she'd had a crying jag and fallen asleep on the floor. She was so confused about Nate that she *felt* like crying, so it was actually close to the truth.

The beam of the flashlight lingered on the bed before continuing around the room. It stopped the moment it landed on her.

Pretending it was the light that had awakened her, she squinted and blinked and raised a hand to block the glare. "Who—who is it?"

A snap returned the room to darkness, but not before Rachel saw a person dressed in one of the Klan-like robes she'd seen the audience wear at her initiation ceremony. This person seemed tall, but from her position on the floor, almost anyone would.

"Wh-what do you want?" she asked when her previous question went unanswered.

The intruder lunged at her and clamped a hand over her mouth, pressing so tightly she could hardly breathe. Because Nate was in the bathroom and already knew someone had come in, she didn't scream. But the intruder's actions caused a brief squeal of surprise.

"Shut up!" The words were a harsh whisper. "I'm

not going to hurt you. I'm here to warn you. You're not safe. Do you understand? Get out of Paradise before you wind up like—"

That was as far as the masked intruder got before Nate yanked him off Rachel. She tried to stop what came next, but it happened too fast.

The sound of fist on bone made her wince. Then the costume-draped intruder crumpled onto the floor beside her and Nathan stood over them both, shaking his hand.

"Did you break your hand?" Rachel asked.

"I don't think so. Did he hurt you?"

"No. He wasn't here to hurt me. He was trying to warn me. At least, that's what he said."

"Warn you about what?"

"I didn't get the whole message. He said I needed to get out of Paradise before I wound up like… And then you smashed his face in."

Nate cursed. "He had to warn you by coming to your room in the middle of the night? By attacking you?"

"Maybe he's afraid of Ethan. Maybe he didn't dare come at any other time. And he wanted to make sure I wouldn't scream."

"Who is the bastard?" he asked.

At this point, Rachel wasn't even sure the "bastard" was alive. It was rare to be killed with one punch, but the adrenaline surging through Nate's body had likely amplified his strength, and he was strong already.

Picking up the flashlight from where it had fallen, Nate turned it on while she removed the man's hood. But it wasn't a man at all. It was a woman—Ethan's housekeeper.

"Oh, no…" Rachel whispered.

"Tell me she's only out cold…" he responded.

Rachel searched for a pulse at the woman's neck. She was alive, but she wasn't moving. They had to get help.

Nate pinched the bridge of his nose as he tried to figure out what to do. He'd had no idea the person he'd hit was a woman, but he doubted that would've stopped him even if he'd known. He couldn't tell whether the intruder had entered with a knife. He'd acted instinctively to protect Rachel, and he didn't regret that. Depending on their visitor's intent, this could've gone very differently.

"We have to get her to a hospital," Rachel said.

He bent to scoop up the limp body, but when the woman moaned and began to turn her head from side to side, Rachel touched his arm.

"Wait, don't move her. Let's see if she's okay." Crouching over her, they peered into her face.

The housekeeper squinted. "Who—who are you? W-what happened?" Her voice sounded more like a croak as if she'd been suddenly awakened from a lengthy sleep. But it didn't take long for the confusion to clear. "The Vessel," she muttered. "You're the Vessel."

Nate sent Rachel a questioning glance. "She means you're a *possible* vessel, right? By Ethan's definition, every woman in the compound is here for his pleasure—a possible vessel."

"I'm not sure. I might have a slightly elevated status. I *am* living in the Enlightenment Hall."

"I thought that was temporary protection from me."

"So did I, but there were a few things said at my initiation that made me wonder—"

The housekeeper interrupted her. "You—you have to get out." She gingerly prodded her cheek, where she'd taken the blow. "You're not safe here."

"Why do you say that?" Rachel asked.

She shifted her attention to Nathan. "You—you're her husband."

"Yes."

"Take her away. Tonight."

"Why?"

"I can't say."

"Sure you can."

"No. I can't trust you." She tried to get up, swooned and Rachel caught her as she fell back. "You hit me."

"I'm sorry. I'm not used to people sneaking into my wife's room in the middle of the night, especially people wearing hoods."

"But you weren't supposed to be here. How'd you get in?"

"I made my own entrance," he admitted.

Closing her eyes, she continued to moan quietly.

"Do you need us to take you to a doctor?" Rachel's voice was filled with concern.

"No, I—I'll be okay. In a minute."

They waited until she could sit up. Then Nate squatted in front of her. "Tell us why you came here."

"To warn your wife," she said.

"Warn her about what?"

"Nothing. I have to go." She managed to get up but wobbled on her feet.

Nate blocked her way to the door. "Why did you feel

it was necessary to tell my wife to leave the compound?"

"It's dangerous here. You heard about the woman who was stoned, didn't you?"

"It's true, then?"

"Of course. I was there."

Nathan's heart began to race. Had they just found an informant? A witness? That could make a huge difference. "What about Courtney Sinclair? Can you tell me anything about her?"

"I don't want to talk about Courtney. It's not safe for me to be here."

"If you know about the stoning and you don't agree with it, if you're so scared, why haven't you gone to the police?" Rachel asked.

"Because they can't protect me. They couldn't protect Martha, could they?"

Nate grabbed her arm. "You know Martha went missing? Is she here? Did they bring her back?"

She didn't answer. Jerking away despite her unsteadiness, she reached for the door, but Nate wouldn't let her open it. "What if I told you we could offer you protection? *Real* protection? Would you tell us what you know?"

"No one can offer me real protection." She touched her injured cheek. "Least of all you."

"That's not true. We work for a private security company. We have people who are trained in that sort of thing, and they're damn good at it. I promise you we'll provide the manpower. All we need is your testimony."

"You're not who you said you are?"

Rachel cut in. "We're colleagues—not husband and

wife. We were hired to figure out what's going on here. We're going to stop Ethan, for the sake of Martha, Courtney, Sarah and anyone else who might be at risk. Will you help?"

"You know Sarah's missing, too?"

"We know she helped recapture Martha. Then she disappeared. Help us find her? Can you do that?"

Her eyes shifted between them. "What about my family? My friends?"

"They'll be protected, too. The sooner we put Ethan away, the better off everyone will be."

Her hair, brown streaked with gray from what Nate could remember, fell forward as she bent to pick up the hood Rachel had removed. She turned it over in her hands, staring at it. "Okay. Meet me downstairs in the storage room off the main laundry. It's just past the kitchen. But give me fifteen minutes to make sure it's safe. If Ethan or Bart find us, we're all dead."

A Covenanter who'd talk. Now they were getting somewhere. "What's downstairs?" Nate asked.

"Something you should see."

Rachel sat on the bed in silence. Nate was beside her, but she didn't touch him. Not after the frenzy that had consumed them before Ethan's housekeeper had let herself into the room. He'd asked her to say she loved him, but her emotions had been the problem before. He didn't want a commitment. So why he'd said such a thing she had no idea. She needed to push what had occurred between them out of her mind, avoid the confusion. She couldn't deal with it right now.

"What are you thinking about?" he asked.

"Sarah," she lied.

"What about her?"

"I'm wondering why she betrayed Martha."

"You know the brainwashing people in cults go through. You went through something similar. Ethan probably told her it was God's will. Or she'd be shunned by her family and friends if she didn't do what he said. Some damn thing. Maybe he even threatened her life. You never know. Not with Ethan."

Rachel said nothing, but her thoughts turned to her father. Why did he insist on living in such a small world? Why couldn't he allow others some freedom of choice, have respect for their decisions?

Nate startled her by taking her hand. "What we were talking about before…?"

Her heart skipped a beat. "Before what?"

"When we were making love," he said pointedly.

It took effort to sound nonchalant, but she managed it. "What about it?"

"I want to discuss it again. After this is all over."

She pulled away and clasped her hands together in her lap. "I think we should leave it alone."

"Maybe. But we're going to talk about it, anyway," he said. Then he checked his watch. "It's time. Let's go."

30

The pit was real. Nate had guessed it would be. They stood at the top of some metal stairs that extended into a dark, cavernous void, which resembled a kind of cellar. Except that it was bigger than any cellar he'd ever seen. The air billowing up from inside smelled of fire and incense. But it seemed to be empty.

"This is where Ethan performs his rituals?" he asked.

The housekeeper, who'd just told them her name was Maxine, had turned on a light in the pantry, making it possible for them to see her clearly for the first time tonight. Her hair was mussed, disheveled by static from the hood she'd worn, but her makeup was mostly intact. Obviously, she hadn't been to bed this evening. The swelling where Nate had hit her was beginning to close her right eye, although she seemed to be thinking coherently. "If Martha and Sarah are alive, they'll be in the pit," she said, and motioned for them to go down ahead of her.

Nate made no move to do so. Something about Maxine was making him cautious. He couldn't figure out exactly what. She had reason to be nervous, and she was. She also had reason to sympathize with Martha and Sarah, if not Courtney, and she acted as if she did. That was why she was helping them. He even found it believable that she'd kept quiet about the stoning for fear of reprisal. It all made sense.

So...why did he feel uneasy?

Maxine motioned toward the stairs again. "Don't you want to look in the pit? Martha might still be alive. Maybe we can get her out while Ethan's sleeping. The Brethren are finished in there for the night. We might not get another chance."

Then they'd have to force an entrance later, Nate thought, because he couldn't go in that hole, couldn't put himself and Rachel in such an indefensible position. There was only one way in or out—a single door that could easily be controlled by Ethan, should he become aware of their presence.

Catching Rachel's arm as she brushed past him, he shook his head. She had guts; he had to give her that. She was so eager to find the women who'd gone missing she would've marched down those stairs regardless of danger. But that pit could become a prison. Or a grave. They couldn't help anyone if they compromised their own safety. "We'll go for a warrant and come back," he said. "Let's get the hell out of here."

"You don't want to check?" Maxine asked. "You don't want to find out if Martha's down there? There are cages. I've seen them with my own eyes."

He studied the *C* carved on her forehead. She'd seen a lot; she'd also participated. Which meant she had convictions he wouldn't understand. Even after everything she'd been through, Martha had maintained some loyalty when it came to the religion, wouldn't share certain details about the rituals. She wasn't upset about the orgies, the use of women for pleasure or the everyday abuse of power. She'd liked it here and would probably have remained if Ethan hadn't turned on her personally.

"Like I said, we'll be back. You can come with us if you want."

Her uninjured eye widened and her nostrils flared. She seemed frightened, confused, as if she didn't know what to do, and that was Nate's cue to get out even faster than he'd planned. Clutching Rachel's hand, he pulled her along with him as he navigated the narrow walkways in the pantry. They were just entering the kitchen when he heard something that made his heart seize in his chest. His instincts had been on target. Maxine, the housekeeper, had told them what she knew they'd believe, had used that information to persuade them to reveal who they really were, and had drawn them right into a trap.

Dealing with crack dealers, whores and pimps, Rachel had had a lot of guns shoved in her face, generally semiautomatic pistols. It wasn't as if she scared easily. That constant threat was part of the job, part of the adrenaline rush that made her feel alive even though she was "dead" to her family. But seeing a group of Bartholomew's guards standing in a circle around her and Nate, holding various guns, most of them banned weapons that must have been purchased on the black market, frightened her more than usual. Because they were cut off from help, had no backup in place.

She felt Nate go rigid at her side, felt his hand tighten on hers and knew he was thinking, as she was, that this could be the end.

Focusing on a boy no more than eighteen or nineteen

holding a .22-caliber rifle with a sawed-off barrel, he said, "You really plan to use that, kid? You want to be responsible for blowing someone away?"

The boy never got to answer. Bartholomew came up from behind him, placed a fatherly hand on the young Covenanter's shoulder and spoke first. "Mr. Mott, apparently you're willing to go to great extremes to reclaim your wife." He chuckled. "Or should I say partner?"

"Where's Ethan?" Nate asked.

"Asleep in his bed, where he should be. This isn't his problem. This is my domain."

Ethan probably didn't even know what was going on. From what Rachel had overheard earlier, he was tweaking on meth again.

"If we go missing, you'll have hell to pay," Nate told him. "There will be no confusion about whether or not we were here."

Maxine came around to stand by Bartholomew, her uninjured eye narrowed with the hate she'd previously hidden, and a triumphant curl on her lips.

"Last I checked, the police still have to prove guilt beyond a reasonable doubt," Bartholomew said. "And that takes evidence, does it not?"

Rachel counted men and weapons while searching for the closest exit. "You never know what they'll find," she said. "They'll come and search every tent, every building, turn over every rock. If nothing else, they'll discover your cache of guns and maybe some of the drugs floating around this place."

He shrugged. "Not if I don't want them to."

"With two hundred people in the compound, there's got to be at least one person who has a conscience," she insisted. "The police could come across someone who's ready to talk."

"You mean, like Maxine was ready to talk?" Bart laughed and, with a wave of his arm, directed them back toward the pit.

The men with guns moved in. Rachel could feel Nate trying to decide whether they should make a break for it now or allow themselves to be shepherded into the pit. They didn't have much of a chance either way. She preferred to make their move now and knew he'd come to the same conclusion when he jerked her behind him, grabbed the gun of the closest person and used it like a bat to knock down two of Bart's guards. The element of surprise was on their side. But only for a few seconds.

Trying to reach Bart, to capture a hostage who'd matter, Nate fought his way through two more men. But Bart wasn't taking any chances. "Shoot them!" he yelled, and his men didn't hesitate.

The blast deafened Rachel. She tried to push Nate to the ground, away from the bullets, but he was too busy trying to shield her. He managed to pull the trigger of the gun he'd stolen—twice. Rachel heard the screams of those he'd hit and felt a small glimmer of hope. They'd already gotten farther than they should have.

As more shots rang out, she kicked a man coming up from behind and turned to fight someone else when Nate fell into her. He'd been hit.

"No!" She grabbed for his gun as he collapsed. She wouldn't let them kill him. She'd shoot them all if she had to. But that was only wishful thinking. Someone struck her from behind and down she went, right on top of him.

* * *

Rachel woke to the sound of water dripping. *Drip… drip…drip…* Steady, monotonous, but by no means reassuring.

At a complete loss, she lay perfectly still, listening for any clue that might bring comprehension. What had happened? Where was she? It was so dark. More than dark. Black. And the smell! It turned her stomach. Mildew, damp earth, fetid water, incense…

Incense! That triggered the memory she'd been searching for. She'd been standing at the door of a pit, a pit that had the same smell. Only she was no longer at the door. She was inside, sprawled on bare earth….

Had Bartholomew buried her alive? Left her alone down here to die?

Claustrophobia welled up like bile. She would've screamed if she hadn't heard movement. "Hello? Anybody there?"

No answer.

She began to wonder if an animal had made that noise. She could easily imagine rats scurrying around down here. The mere thought made her skin crawl. But this was more of a dragging sound. "Hello?" she said again, her voice shaky and as uncertain as her rioting stomach. She tried to sit up but couldn't. Whoever had hit her had really clobbered her. The pain was so bad she felt as if her head would explode.

And then she remembered. *Nate.* They'd shot him.

A sob caught in her throat. Was he dead?

More movement.

"Nate?" She was afraid to even hope. But she couldn't refrain from calling the one person she wanted more than any other.

The dragging sound started again. Someone or something was trying to reach her. Although she knew it might cause her to pass out again, Rachel was about to scramble to her feet so she could evade what was coming, if she had to, when she finally received an answer. "It's…me."

Nate was alive. But he was also in a great deal of pain. She could tell that crawling over to her was taking every ounce of energy he possessed. Recalling the hail of bullets that'd cut him down, she was almost afraid to learn the extent of his injuries. She didn't want him to die but, even more than that, she didn't want him to suffer.

Her concern for him somehow muted her own pain. She'd been struck, but she hadn't been shot. She needed to bear up, be tough. "Are you okay?" she whispered.

He grunted, but she didn't know whether that grunt signified yes or no.

"Don't move. Stay where you are. I'll come to you." Wincing against the dizziness and nausea that descended when she rolled onto her hands and knees, she paused to brace herself against her body's revolt. Then she began to feel her way across the dirt floor in the direction of his voice.

She found him a few feet away. His breathing was labored, and he was sweating despite the cool air. Or…no. The dampness on his shirt wasn't sweat; it was blood. "Where'd they hit you?"

"In the chest."

Carefully modulating her voice, she snuggled close. "Do you know if…do you know if the bullet's still inside?"

"I have no idea. The way…my chest burns…you'd think so."

Warning herself to remain calm, to sound unafraid, she took a deep breath. "You—you're still bleeding, then?"

"A little. It's more of a…a slow leak or…I'd already be dead."

Squeezing her eyes closed, Rachel said the humblest prayer she'd uttered in years—and felt tears roll down her cheeks despite her best efforts to stifle them.

"What about…you?" he asked. "You…okay?"

She didn't see any point in mentioning her wound when he was in far worse condition. "I'm fine." Locating his arms, she traced them to his fingers. He was applying pressure to the wounds in his chest.

Rachel could tolerate a certain amount of blood and gore, but the thought of Nate bleeding out almost made her faint. She couldn't distance herself from what it might mean; she cared too much about him.

"You—you're going to be fine," she said. "I'll take care of you." She didn't know how she'd do that, but she wanted to bring him all the comfort and reassurance she could.

"See if…if the bullets came out."

Carefully rolling him toward her, she felt along his spine, then worked in a grid pattern over his broad back. She wasn't sure whether to hope for exit wounds or not. It would've been comforting to think the bullets were out of his body. But more holes meant more blood.

When her fingers encountered a large wet spot on his shirt, she knew she'd found where one bullet had made its exit. "One's gone."

"And the—" his gulp was audible as he struggled to speak "—other?"

She finished her search without finding a second hole. "Must be inside."

"Am I bleeding…very badly…back there?"

"No, but I'm going to apply some pressure, just in case."

She felt his muscles bunch when she did, knew it hurt like hell and couldn't stop herself from bending to kiss his forehead.

"Rachel?" He forced her name through gritted teeth.

"What?" She was praying again, praying as hard as she could, begging God to forgive her if her father was right and she was wrong. But not for her own sake. For Nate.

"For what it's worth…I love you," he said. "I'm… pretty sure I've loved you since…that night at my condo. I just didn't want to…to let you down if…I wasn't ready."

"God, now I know you're really hurt," she said with a sniff.

He attempted a laugh, but it came out as more of a rattle. "No…I mean it, okay?"

Wiping her nose with the back of her hand, she eased herself out from under him. "Don't move," she said. "I'm going to find a way out of here. I have to get you to a hospital."

"It's a…a pit, Rach. Only…one door."

"There's got to be *something* I can do."

"You could…tell me you love me…too," he said. "I threw those words…back in your face…once. I'm sorry about that."

Swallowing against the hard lump in her throat, she rocked onto her behind. "Stop it. You don't need to hear it, because this isn't goodbye. You're a tough son of a bitch. So prove it, okay? Hang on until I get back."

He seemed to be trying to speak, but the effort was too much. He went limp and silent.

Afraid that he'd died, Rachel scrambled to find a pulse—and almost collapsed in relief when she felt one beating softly in his neck.

He wasn't gone yet. But unless she could figure a way out of this place, it wouldn't be long.

Rachel was curled around Nate when he regained consciousness. She'd been holding her hands to the bullet wounds in his chest while trying to keep him warm. She couldn't let his body temperature drop, couldn't let him slip into shock.

"Hey," he mumbled. "We home yet?"

"Not yet. But don't worry. I—I've got it all worked out," she lied. She couldn't tell him the truth, couldn't admit that they were in a ten-by-ten-foot cell without so much as a blanket or a bowl of water. He'd know that meant they had no chance whatsoever.

"Sooner would be better…than later," he breathed.

She kissed his neck, held him tighter. "You're never satisfied."

He must've known she hadn't found a way out or anything that might help them, because he drifted off to sleep again without making any attempt to move.

Rachel lay in the tomblike silence, holding him with a desperation she'd never experienced before, listening to the water drip, wherever it was, and praying. Again.

She'd realized something about herself in the past few hours. She and God weren't enemies. Maybe her faith wasn't like her father's—but it was every bit as real.

31

Rachel was awakened by someone crying. At first she thought it was a dream or the echo of her own sobs. Had Nate died? Maybe so. She didn't see how he'd hung on this long. Maybe he'd died and she'd cried herself to sleep or been crying *in* her sleep.

But that couldn't be. Nate was in her arms, and he was still breathing. So who else was down here? And why hadn't whoever it was responded when she called out earlier?

Trying to slip away without disturbing Nate, she crawled to the edge of her cell. It was a woman. But which woman? Martha? Sarah? Courtney? Someone else?

"Who is it?" she called.

The crying stopped. Then an unsteady voice said, "Martha?"

Rachel could tell by the speaker's uncertainty that this was considered an unlikely guess.

"It's Rachel Mott." She used her fake last name because she knew that was the only one anyone from Paradise would recognize.

"Rachel?"

"Yes."

"You—you're locked up, too?"

"I'm in a cell with my husband. Who are you?"

"Sarah. I met you at the party, remember?"

Rachel grabbed the bars of her cell as if she could get closer. She wanted to see Sarah, wanted to find out what condition she was in. "Where's Martha?"

"I don't know." Her voice broke. "I think they killed her. They were doing such awful things to her. I—I don't know how she could survive it. She wasn't moving when it was over. I saw her lying there, on the altar…." She sniffed, then cried some more. "There was blood."

Rachel recalled that fragment she'd heard from Ethan when he was on the landing. *I could've gone on all night, especially when she started to beg. That's when I spread her legs and rammed that—* Wincing, she tried to block out those words and what they'd meant for Martha. "How long have you been down here?"

"I don't know. I just…I just woke up. They must've given me something. Wait, yes, I know they did." She seemed to recover a bit. "I remember. After what they did, I was hysterical. Beside myself. Couldn't quit screaming or crying. Dominic gave me a shot. He said it would make me sleep. I think he felt sorry for me."

"Not sorry enough to let you go."

"No."

"Did he rape you?"

"Not me."

"Martha, then?"

"Yes. Him and the rest of them."

Was that what she had to look forward to? Gang rape? And what did the Covenanters have in store for Nate?

"But Dominic wasn't as cruel as the others," she added.

"That doesn't make him a friend."

There was no response.

"What kind of shape are you in?" Rachel asked.

"I'm bruised and sore. That's all. And hungry."

"What about Courtney?"

"I haven't seen her since I've been down here."

"But you saw her before?"

"Not recently. She was in Paradise for a while. Probably longer than Ethan admitted to anyone who came here looking for her. But all I really know is that we accepted her, and then she was gone."

Gone…and yet she hadn't shown up at home. What had Ethan done to her?

Suddenly, there were other noises. The creak of a door some distance away. Footsteps. Light reached the dark corners of the pit and, eventually, two men passed Rachel's cell, carrying a limp body. The shadows made it difficult to recognize anyone, but the men moved as if familiar with the pit and its cages, and Rachel could hear keys jingling.

"Martha!" Sarah cried.

Martha didn't respond, but Rachel hadn't expected her to. She was obviously unconscious. The men who'd brought her didn't speak, either. They laid her in a separate cell, closed the door with a clang and rattled it to make sure it was locked. Then they passed Rachel once again on their way out.

"Dominic? Dominic, wait!" Sarah called.

He didn't even pause. "I've done all I can for you, Sister Sarah."

"What about Martha? Is she dead?"

"No."

"Why'd you take her away?"

"She was hemorrhaging. But I got the bleeding stopped." He sounded tired. "I did everything I could for her. Try to get some sleep."

"Dominic?" Rachel called. She'd met him at the dinner she and Nate had attended in the Enlightenment Hall with all the Brethren.

He came to a halt. "What the— Is someone else down here?" As he and his companion walked up to the bars of her cell, she recognized the man who was with him, too. It was Joshua Cooley.

"My husband," she said. "He—he's bleeding to death. Will you help him? Please? I'll do anything, anything at all."

"I can't." He rubbed a hand over his face. "It's almost morning. If Bart catches me interfering—"

"It's not as if you'd be letting him escape," she argued. "You'd just be doing what doctors are trained to do, what they're supposed to do. You'd be saving his life. *Please.*"

He shook his head and would've left if Joshua hadn't stopped him. They murmured to each other. Then Dominic returned to her cell and, with a sigh, opened it with a key on the ring he carried.

Rachel wanted to fly at him the moment he opened the door. Her first impulse was to kick and claw her way to freedom. She didn't trust these men much more than she trusted Ethan or Bart. But she knew that if she didn't succeed in escaping—maybe even if she did— her actions would guarantee Nate's death. She'd told them she'd do anything if they'd save him, and she meant it.

"Get back in the corner," Joshua warned, and she scrambled to obey.

Dominic bent over Nate, obviously struggling to see his injuries.

"He's been shot in the chest," she volunteered. "Twice."

"Who did this?" Joshua asked.

She opened her mouth to reply, but Dominic beat her to it. "I'll give you three guesses."

Joshua clicked his tongue. "Bart's out of control."

They didn't ask her to confirm what they'd guessed or to explain how it had happened. They were in too great a hurry. Together, they dragged Nate from the cell. Rachel could hear them grunting, laboring to manage his weight. But they seemed to make it up the stairs.

After a few minutes, the light went off, a door opened and closed, and they were gone.

It was easy to tell that Ethan wasn't in a good mood.

Bart watched him eat the grapefruit Maxine had sectioned for him. He had to have half a grapefruit every morning, with sugar on top. He also had to have his favorite spoon to eat it with, the one with the jagged edge. It didn't matter that today was fast day for the rest of the compound. Ethan never went without. Unless he was tweaking. Meth killed his appetite.

"Look at her." Ethan used his spoon to indicate Maxine's black eye as she brought his boiled egg to the table.

"I told you," Bart said. "It got ugly."

"He must've hit her hard." Wearing a dark glower, he

finished the grapefruit and began squeezing the leftover juice onto his spoon.

"He's strong."

Ethan gestured for Maxine to leave them. When she was in the kitchen, he said, "I can't believe they're cops."

"They're—"

"I know, but cops all the same. I feel so betrayed, so angry, so—"

"We'll have the last laugh," Bart cut in.

"How?" Ethan demanded. "Now we have another mess to clean up."

"You liked last night's ceremony. We could have more. It might even be fun to use Nathan Mott—or whatever his name is—in a few."

He didn't immediately catch on. "Which ones?"

"The *private* ones."

This drew Ethan at least partially out of his black mood. "Now, *there's* an idea."

"The sky's the limit."

He ate his egg, which Maxine had already peeled. "I can't believe the gunfire didn't awaken me."

So that was it. He was sulking that he'd missed all the action. "I preferred to let you sleep in safety, Holy One. What if you'd been hit by a stray bullet? He shot two of my men."

"Flesh wounds, you said."

"It could've been worse."

"What will you tell their families?"

"That's been handled. I told them Rachel's abusive husband broke in to the Enlightenment Hall and they were injured fighting valiantly to protect the Vessel."

"They must be proud."

"They are."

Ethan sniffed. "You're good at your job."

Bart lowered his head. "I try to be." Bart hadn't been this solicitous in several days. Since they'd become a couple, there'd been high points, but some discontent, too. It wasn't easy to redefine a relationship.

"So where do we go from here?" Ethan asked.

"Anywhere we want, Holy One. We have Martha, Sarah, Rachel and Nathan. All our known enemies are gathered in one safe spot. I don't understand why you're so upset."

He seemed to consider this. "I don't understand, either. It just felt strange to wake up to such news, to feel so...out of the loop."

"If I'm involved, you're not out of the loop. I always look after your interests."

"And what are my interests when it comes to Rachel and her husband?"

"They have to disappear."

"The Vessel can't disappear!" Ethan stabbed the air with his spoon to punctuate that sentence. "The whole church is looking forward to the mating ceremony I've promised them. What will it say about me if my own bride disappears? Everyone will assume she ran away, like Courtney. Or they'll wonder if I murdered her, and that'll make them rethink their beliefs about Courtney, too."

"What if we hold the ceremony tonight?" Bart asked.

Ethan dropped his spoon and drummed his fingers on the table. The *ba-ba-bump* irritated Bart but he schooled his face to show no sign of it.

"It would make more sense than waiting," Ethan said at length. "Consummation follows close behind the vows."

"Exactly. So we do it now and get it over with. And if Nate survives the day, I say we make him watch. Maybe he isn't her husband, but he cares about her. He took two bullets trying to protect her."

"What happens after the ceremony?"

"We finish him off when we're good and ready. And we lock her up in the pit so we can trot her out every now and then for special functions."

Ethan stroked his freshly shaved chin. "What if she escapes?"

"Don't worry about that. I'll keep an eye on her."

Ba-ba-bump. Ba-ba-bump. Finally, Ethan smiled. "I like it. She can be our little show pony."

"And tonight will be your first ride."

He slapped the table. "Go tell the Guides."

When Dominic and Joshua brought Nate back, Rachel was aware that they'd given him something for the pain. He wasn't conscious, but she was relieved to know his wounds had been cleaned and dressed.

"Did you get the bullet out?" she asked as she hovered at the back of the cell. Again, she didn't dare come too close to the door. They'd brought a third person this time, a man she didn't recognize, who carried a torch. She didn't have a chance against all three. She couldn't leave Nate, anyway.

"I did. And I gave him several pints of blood. He's a lucky man. One of those bullets went right past his heart."

She thought of the hole beneath Nate's left shoulder

blade. Was that the one? "Thank you. Thank you for helping him."

After putting Nate on the ground, Dominic straightened. "I don't know who you are, some housewife from Portal or Utah or someone else, but you signed your death warrant when you came here. I hope you know that."

"You could let me go," she said. "Let us both go."

"And have you bring the police?" He shook his head. "No, thanks. I'm not going to prison. Not for you, not for anyone."

"If you turn state's evidence, prison could be avoided."

"You don't know that."

"It's a possibility."

He and Joshua headed for the door, where the third man was waiting. "I'm not willing to take that risk."

"So why'd you save him?" she asked.

The door clanged shut with a finality that made Rachel want to cry. Dominic obviously didn't plan on answering, but Joshua did. "There's good in bad people, just as there's bad in good people," he said.

She shook her head. "There's no good in Ethan."

"There is when you compare him to Bart."

"Brother Joshua?" Sarah had been standing at the bars of her cell, watching, waiting, ever since they'd arrived. "Will you let me out? Please?"

Ignoring her, he started to leave.

"Brother Joshua!" she yelled more loudly.

"Don't call me 'Brother,'" he said over his shoulder. But then he grabbed Dominic's arm, and the three men conferred, heads bent and voices low. A second later,

Joshua walked back but he stopped at Rachel's cell, not
Sarah's.

"What is it?" she asked, surprised.

"This won't be a good day for you. Do you want
something—for the pain?"

Her breath seemed to be stuck in her throat. "What's
going to happen to me?"

"The worst nightmare of your life."

Icy tentacles of fear curled through Rachel's veins.
But if Ethan had plans for her, they'd be taking her out
of her cell. That meant she had to keep her wits about
her, had to work out how to escape.

"Do you want it or not?" he asked when she didn't
respond.

Her life depended on her ability to get away. So did
Nate's. "No."

Whatever Ethan had in store for her didn't take place
right away. In an attempt to learn more about the Covenanters and to direct her mind from the fear, the worry,
the darkness and her hunger, Rachel spent hours talking
to Sarah. She also tried to get Martha to respond—
without any success—and did all she could to keep
Nate warm.

"Do they ever feed you down here?" she asked as her
stomach growled.

"They fed me once."

"What did you get?"

"Meat loaf. I'm guessing it's what they served in the
dining hall. I've had it plenty of times before."

That was hopeful, at least. "What will they do to
me?" she asked.

Sarah didn't respond. Until now, Rachel had purposely not requested the details of the "nightmare" Joshua had mentioned. She was afraid that knowing would wipe out the small amount of courage she'd been able to reserve. But as the hours and minutes dragged on, and Nate and Martha continued to sleep, her fear of this unknown fate grew steadily worse. It hadn't taken long for her "better not to know" approach to reach a point of diminishing returns.

"Sarah?" she prompted.

"You're the Vessel," she said simply.

Sarah clearly didn't want to discuss this, but now that Rachel had asked, she couldn't let it go. "What does that mean, Sarah? Torture? Rape? Murder?" She hoped it wouldn't be that bad. The Vessel was supposed to bear Ethan's next child. She'd have to be alive and in reasonably good health to do that.

"You've been named bride to the whole church."

Rachel checked Nate's pulse, which she did every few minutes. "That doesn't answer my question."

"You'll be put on an altar."

Her breath caught, even though she'd expected something like this. "Here in the pit?"

"No, in the courtyard."

"Why the courtyard?"

"It's the only area large enough."

"For what?"

"To hold the whole assembly. Besides, this place is secret to everyone except a select few of those who have taken the highest vows."

Rachel's nails cut into her palms. "The entire church is going to watch Ethan rape me?"

"They're going to form a line."

Gang rape. As she'd thought. "And what's the purpose of that—from a religious standpoint?"

"As every man spills his seed inside you, the marriage is consummated and you'll be made holy like
Ethan, bride to the whole church."

"But I'm not even a believer."

"I know. That means it'll be a mockery," she said.

Struggling to compose herself, Rachel tried to imagine how she might handle what was to happen. "There
are women who'd be willing to do this?"

"For a female Covenanter, this is the greatest honor
Ethan could bestow."

"And he's chosen me."

"I'm sure he's realized his mistake."

"Which means…"

"You might not survive the experience."

"Why doesn't he just kill me now? Choose a different Vessel?"

"Because *he* didn't choose you. *God* did."

"God did," she repeated.

"He claims it was divine inspiration. Now he has to
deliver what he promised or he'll look like a fool. And
the prophet can never be wrong, can never be pegged as
a fool."

"I see. And Nate? What will they do to him?"

There was a long silence. "I have no idea."

Rachel sat without speaking. Then she said, "You
know Ethan is gay, right?"

"What?" Sarah cried.

At Sarah's apparent shock, Rachel mustered a bitter
smile. "He and Bart are lovers." She wasn't sure why
she divulged this information—probably because it was
her only form of revenge.

"That doesn't make sense," Sarah said in a bewildered voice. "He teaches that—that the *devil* delights in homosexual practices."

"It would take a devil to know."

32

Nate had never felt so weak or so uncomfortable. "What...happened?" His voice sounded raspy from disuse; he had to clear his throat to be heard. "Was I hit by a train?"

"Nate? Thank God!"

He'd already known he wasn't alone. He had his head in a woman's lap, could feel a cool hand on his face as he came around.

It required a massive effort just to lift his eyelids. But even after he did, he wasn't sure they were open. He couldn't see a thing. "Am I blind?" he asked.

"No. You're in a dark hole, a pit."

This time he recognized the voice. Rachel. From work. From the trailer. From Paradise. From his bed. The information was coming—but not fast. "What's going on?"

"You were shot. Twice."

Testing his ability to move, he shifted an inch or two. "That would explain a few things."

"How do you feel?"

"Like shit," he said, falling back with a groan.

"At least you're alive."

"I'm half-alive. Maybe."

Her fingers combed through his hair, distracting him from the pain and easing some of his discomfort.

"Most people who get shot wake up in a hospital," he said. "In one of those beds that adjust."

"Sorry to disappoint you," she said with a soft laugh. "We're currently being held captive by a cult leader, who's a complete psychopath."

"Damn. No Jell-O, either."

"Not until I can get us out of here."

"What are the chances of that?"

"Not good." ·

The underlying dejection in her voice concerned him because he couldn't be much help to her, not like this. "Well, the pillow's nice," he said, trying to keep it light. "How serious are my injuries?"

"I can't say for sure. You seem a lot better. You were staring death in the face."

He let his eyes slide shut. "I probably wasn't as close as you think."

"You told me you loved me," she said, as if that proved her point.

"I must've been delirious," he teased.

Her fingers slipped through his hair again. "There is some good news."

About time. "What's that?"

"We've found Sarah and Martha."

"Where?"

"They're in the pit with us."

"That's the *good* news?"

"Depends on how you look at it."

"How are they?"

"Sarah seems fine. She's in the next cell. I think she's asleep because I haven't heard from her in the past hour or so. Martha's in the cell beside hers, but she might be in worse shape than you. They brought her back unconscious and she hasn't stirred since."

"And Courtney?"

"No sign of her."

He tried to figure out what he could do to improve the situation, but his thoughts were too jumbled and sleep was already pulling on him, dragging him down…. "Is Ethan really having an affair with the reincarnation of Moses?" he mumbled. "Or did I dream that?"

Maxine the housekeeper left torches when she brought food. She had to make two trips, but she delivered four trays, which she pushed through a gap in each door. Rachel was as grateful for the light as she was the food. It was a relief just to be able to see.

After finishing her own chicken and rice, she woke Nate and fed him as much as he'd eat. She hoped the food would help him regain his strength. Sarah ate, too, but she'd grown morose since her nap and didn't speak during the meal. When she was done, she tried to rouse Martha again, got worried when she couldn't and slumped against the bars of her cage.

"I think she's dead," she whispered with fresh fear.

"They gave her something to knock her out," Rachel said, determined to remain optimistic. "Maybe it hasn't worn off."

"It's been hours."

"I know." But hope was the only thing Rachel could offer.

Curling up beside Nate, she laid down to rest—and to wait. Earlier, Sarah had told her the Guides would probably come for her at midnight. The hour was symbolic, she said. She also said the ceremony would be performed at night, partly for effect and partly so it couldn't be observed by any outsiders who might be nosing around. Rachel didn't know exactly how much longer it would be, but the hour had to be drawing close.

"I'm doing better," Nate told her.

He was lying in an attempt to boost her morale; she could tell. She'd never seen him so drawn and pale. And the way he moved indicated he was in a lot of pain. How was she going to get them both out—alive?

She'd thought about it all day but still had no answer. Without resources, allies or help from the outside, it seemed hopeless.

Suddenly, footsteps pounded the dirt floor.

Rachel got up as several of the Brethren approached. Brady, a man she recognized from when she'd met the twelve at dinner, led the small group.

"We've come to prepare you for your big night," he announced when they arrived at her cell.

She eyed the group—Harry, Grady, Ezra, Peter and a guy whose name she couldn't remember. "*My* big night?" she said. "From the eagerness on your faces, this is *your* big night."

Nate had never dreamed he'd be sitting in a front-row seat for anything like a mating ceremony. He'd expected to be left in the pit with Sarah and Martha during the ritual. But from what he'd been told by the men who'd brought him out here, Bart had demanded he watch.

It wouldn't be an easy thing to see. He knew that.

But he had a greater chance of helping Rachel here than he did in a cage underground.

Slumping in his chair to make it seem as if he couldn't sit up, he kept track of what was going on from beneath half-lowered eyelids. A burning sensation radiated through his chest—the slightest movement felt like someone was sticking a red-hot poker in those bullet holes—but he had more strength than he was letting on. He wanted the Covenanters to discount him as a possible threat and, so far, they seemed willing to oblige. They'd tied his hands and feet and shoved him into a chair. Then they'd become caught up in the anticipation and excitement of the festivities and forgotten about him.

He could see why they might be distracted. Rachel was in the center of the square fastened to an altar, and she wasn't wearing anything except a filmy negligee. She'd been allowed to bathe, or someone had bathed her, and her hair was arranged in a fancy braid that wrapped around her head. A sheer white veil covered her face.

Nate was close enough to smell the oils that made her skin gleam, but he didn't think she'd noticed him. She didn't seem to be paying attention. She was somewhere inside herself, probably bracing for the degradation she was about to suffer. Or, more likely, she'd been drugged.

Except for Ethan and the Brethren, the Covenanters wore hoods like the one Maxine had donned when she visited Rachel's bedroom. The faithful crowded behind a single row of chairs reserved for the Covenant elite— the Guides and their wives, Maxine and a few others Nate couldn't identify. Ethan stood on the raised dais that held the altar. As he called the assembly to order, Bart took his seat with the rest of the Brethren.

"Brothers and Sisters, welcome to the night we've long been waiting for," he said.

With everyone's attention riveted on their leader, Nate began to work at the ropes that bound his hands and feet.

"God has smiled on us," Ethan went on. "He has provided the Vessel for which we've all prayed. Tonight we will join with her and become one."

"We will be one!" the crowd shouted.

Bart stared over at Nate, as if to make sure he was taking it all in. Nate kept his feet still so his efforts wouldn't be obvious, but he knew he was working against the clock and continued trying to free his hands, which were bound behind his back. When he let his head loll onto his shoulders, Bart finally returned his gaze to Ethan.

"Look at her!" Ethan was saying. "Is she not a goddess? Is she not fit for the seed of a prophet?"

Wild cheers showed the Covenanters' enthusiasm and approval.

"She will bear us a child, my brothers and sisters, a child who will one day become prophet in my stead."

There was a crescendo in the cheering as Ethan parted the filmy gauze and exposed Rachel to the crowd. She turned her head away, to hide at least her face, and Nate's stomach twisted with agony. He couldn't let this go on. Somehow, some way, he had to put a stop to it.

Already the men were lining up. The Brethren would go first, of course. There was a man at the head of the line telling the others to make room.

Ethan started talking again, about the sword of power embedding itself in the sheath of virtue. He lifted a golden phallus, but Nate couldn't listen to what he said. Not anymore. Blood was rushing through his ears, blocking out the noise as his hands strained against the rope and his mind searched frantically for a solution. If only he could get free and grab a weapon…

He thought of the guns Ethan supposedly had. But even if he could find where they were hidden, they'd probably be locked up.

Maybe he could relieve some guard of his rifle—a guard more interested in watching the rape of a beautiful woman than in doing his job. But Nate couldn't spot anyone on security patrol. Bart seemed to be concentrating all his forces along the perimeter of the compound. The Covenanters couldn't risk letting someone from the outside see or hear what was going on….

And then it occurred to him. The guards' station. This late, he couldn't imagine they'd man it. Most likely, all the guards would be walking the fence. The gate was part of the fence, of course, and they'd be watching it carefully. But no one would expect a threat to come from *inside* the compound. If he could sneak into the guards' shack, he might be able to find an extra weapon….

He checked to see what Bart was doing. Ethan's right-hand man was up out of his seat, holding back the men waiting for their chance at Rachel. He was also organizing the Brethren in the line, as if order was important. For the moment, he seemed to have forgotten Nate. Maybe he was thinking about the fact that his lover would be the first to "spill his seed" into the Vessel "God had prepared."

As the crowd pressed closer, some of the Covenanters moved in front of the chairs and, at that point, Nate couldn't see Bart at all. But neither could he get free. He was too tired, too weak.

And then someone came up to him. "You're a fool for losing a woman like that."

Everyone looked the same in a hood, and Nate couldn't place the voice. "Who're you?"

"My name's Todd."

"Todd who?"

"Todd Wilson."

Martha's husband? New hope flowed through Nate. "I have to tell you something, Todd," he said in a low voice.

"What's that?"

"I know where your wife is."

Todd had to fight the crowd just to remain stationary. "So do I. The Brethren called me in, told me she's in Willcox. They want me to try and get in touch with her. I sent a letter to the post office there, hoping they'd deliver it. But there hasn't been enough time to hear back."

"Your letter won't reach her. Bart took Sarah to Willcox yesterday and used her to gain Martha's trust."

Todd braced against two people who shoved past him. "So what are you saying?"

"I'm saying your wife's in a pit under the Enlightenment Hall. And she's dying."

"That's a lie!" The incredulity in his voice said he refused to believe it. Nate had to convince him.

"No, it's not. Last night they raped her with everything imaginable. She's been passed out on the floor

of her cell ever since. We couldn't get her to respond
to us."

"Raped her? No. She lost her testimony. The Guides
were just…" His words fell off as if the excuse sounded lame even to his own ears.

Beads of sweat rolled down Nate's back. "It's murder," he said. "And what's happening here isn't right,
either. Untie me so I can protect my wife."

The eyes showing through the slits in Todd's hood
darted between him and the altar. "It's a privilege to be
the Vessel. What we'll be doing, it's an—an act of
love."

"Ask her if she *wants* your love," he spat. "She's
drugged out of her mind and yet she'd still refuse if she
could."

"Is your love any better?" Todd shot back. "You beat
her. I saw the evidence."

He didn't have much time. They were about to start.
"She did that, I didn't. We're both undercover agents.
And if you don't help us, you'll be as guilty as Ethan
and Bart."

"Undercover agents?" he echoed.

Nate brushed off his surprise. "There'll be plenty of
others who'll come looking for us. If you want to stay
out of prison, I suggest you let me go before Rachel is
raped. If you do, I'll make sure you have a second
chance at a good life, one that doesn't include hard
time, so you can raise your little boy."

Todd wrung his hands but made no move to help.
They hadn't touched Rachel yet. Ethan was whipping
the crowd into a frenzy of excitement.

"Todd!" Nate snapped. "Now!"

The chanting grew louder. "But…what if you're lying? I'll be kicked out, shunned."

"You're wearing a hood. No one'll know it was you who set me free. If it comes to that, I'll say I did it my-self." Had he possessed his usual strength, he probably could've freed himself.

Still, Todd hesitated.

"For God's sake, untie me so I can help her," Nate hissed. "Or, if I ever get out of this, I swear, I'll kill you myself."

With a frightened glance around to make sure no one was paying attention, Todd moved behind him. While feigning interest in the ceremony, he loosened the knot at Nate's wrists.

When he was free, Nate had Todd come around in front to hide him while he untied his own feet. Then, struggling to retain his equilibrium and his footing, he got up and slipped into the crowd, which was humming and swaying along with the cadence of Ethan's voice as he prayed.

Closing her eyes to avoid seeing the crowd, Rachel focused her thoughts on Nate. They'd given her some-thing, a drug, that made it difficult to remain lucid. The noise around her seemed so loud, deafening, the move-ment dizzying. What was happening? *I love you.* Nate had said that. *I'm pretty sure I've loved you since that night at my condo….*

Or was it Ethan? Ethan stood next to her, spreading her legs and anchoring each ankle to a separate corner of some weird bed. Rachel fought him, but it was no use. She had no strength left. She began to shake.

* * *

Ethan was at the height of his glory. He'd never felt so powerful. This wasn't a ritual he was performing in the pit for the pleasure of a few trusted members. He was giving the entire church a spiritual experience they'd never forget, one he'd long dreamed about. He'd once idolized Charles Manson, but this was far beyond anything Manson had been able to accomplish. It was on a whole new scale.

"Praise the Lord!" he cried, and relished the echo that came back to him. The religious fervor was electrifying.

He looked to Bart—his lover, his best friend, the one person who knew him better than anyone else—and believed he saw admiration in his normal eye.

Lifting his robe, Ethan tied it above his waist, proudly displaying his manhood to the cheering and whistles of all. He'd taken Viagra an hour ago, just in case he ran into any problems on the performance end. But he was so pumped up on adrenaline, the precaution had no doubt been unnecessary.

Still, he was the Holy One, the first to consummate this sacred marriage. He had to put on a good show.

It was time to bury the sheath of power he'd preached about. And he didn't plan to be gentle. The more degrading this was for Rachel, the more he'd enjoy it. The more Bart would enjoy it, too.

The crowd was ready. Bart could barely hold them back. There was even one man, wearing the hooded robe, who was too eager to wait. He'd worked his way around to the side and was approaching the altar.

Ethan would've yelled for Bart to make the man take his rightful turn, but he didn't want to break the momentum. Why ruin this climactic moment? Let the over-eager bastard watch the action up close. It wouldn't hurt anything.

"And now I mount the Vessel!" He started to climb onto the altar, only to be yanked back by the man he'd thought so harmless a few seconds before.

"What are you doing?" He tried to push the hooded figure away but couldn't. Knowing the ritual would be ruined if he got angry, he fought to wriggle out of the grip that held him so tightly.

It was no use. He stopped trying when he felt the man's arm go around his neck and the barrel of a pistol nudge his left temple.

"Drop your skirt before I put a bullet in your head."

Nathan Mott! But Bart was supposed to have taken care of him. According to Bart, he'd been shot twice last night!

Fingers shaking, Ethan untied the knot in his robes and let them drop, and the crowd went silent. Everyone was beginning to realize something was wrong. The Covenanters stared at him through the slits in their hoods as if they couldn't believe what they were seeing. Even Bart didn't speak. Or move. That frightened Ethan as much as anything. It meant Bart had no idea what to do, which was completely unlike him. Bart had an answer for everything.

"Tell your gay lover to untie Rachel." Nate's voice growled in his ear.

Gay lover. He *knew*. How? And what now? How did he get out of this? Nate didn't seem to be doing well. He was hurt and sweating profusely; the dampness came through his robes. But it didn't take much effort to pull a trigger. Not for a man as determined as Nate.

As far as Ethan could tell, there wasn't any way out of this. All he could do was buy time until Bart came to his rescue.

"Who—who are you?" he asked. "What do you want with me?"

"You heard me. Do it now or say goodbye to your people."

Finally, Bart stepped forward, but he stopped well short of them.

"Untie…" Ethan's voice failed him. Pretending it was because Nate had too tight a grip, that it was choking him, he tried again. "Untie the Vessel."

The one eye of Bart's that focused correctly cut between him and his captor. "Mr. Mott, put the gun down," he said coolly. "Even if you shoot Ethan, you won't be getting out of here. Neither will Rachel."

That wasn't the response Ethan had expected. Had he heard correctly?

"Unless you want your prophet's brains blown all over your bathrobe, I'd untie Rachel," Nate responded. *"Now."*

Ethan could feel Nate's tension and his struggle to remain coherent. He was afraid Nate might get confused or panic and fire, anyway. He could hear how hard Nate was breathing. "He'll shoot me, Bart! Don't mess around. Untie her!"

When Bart continued to hesitate, Ethan's panic escalated. Bart didn't seem particularly concerned about whether or not Ethan was going to die. This was the man who supposedly loved him? What was going on?

"What are you waiting for?" Ethan cried. "Do you want me to be murdered, for God's sake?"

"Of course not," Bart replied. "But there are other considerations."

It wasn't until that moment that Ethan realized the frenzied thoughts that had passed through his brain a second earlier were actually right on target. Bart didn't care if he died. Bart had played him, had known from the beginning that he had issues with his sexuality and had set out to seduce him. He'd been using Ethan the whole time. "You bastard," he shrieked. "You said you loved me."

"I love all God's children," Bart murmured, and Ethan immediately recognized it as something he might've said himself.

"You love no one but yourself!"

"Are we so different? You have to understand, Ethan— this might be the only way for the church to survive."

"You think you'll take over?" How could he have missed such overwhelming ambition? It would never have occurred to him that someone as homely and easily overlooked as Bart would ever aspire to so much. "You'll never make it without me."

A half smile curved Bart's lips. "I knew the time was coming. You're not the man you used to be. You let the drugs win. And now I have no choice but to step up and lead our people. I can't give in to Mr. Mott's demands. He'll take the Vessel and bring the police." He lowered his voice so that only a select few could hear. "And you know what'll happen then."

"Nothing will happen!" Ethan cried. "We could be long gone. Together. What if he had this gun to *your* head?"

"That's what I *am* wondering," Bart said. "Would you sacrifice what you want most—for me?"

Growing impatient, Nate jerked Ethan to the left and fired. Pain seared Ethan's foot. He screamed, thought he might pass out and began to beg. "Let me go. Please. I haven't done anything to you. It was Bart. It was all Bart. I wasn't even there last night!"

The disgust in Bart's sneer didn't matter to Ethan. Bart had betrayed him first.

"Look at what you're afraid of." Bart pointed at Nate. "He's so injured he can barely stand, yet *you* start sniveling? I hope he sends you to hell," he said, and parted the crowd as he left, head held high.

Despair settled in as Nate put the gun back to Ethan's temple. He wasn't going to get out of this. He couldn't believe it. All his life he'd been able to avoid any consequences he didn't like. There'd always been someone to bail him out, some way to escape. Frantically, he searched the crowd for another savior. But there was no one.

"Tell your people what you've done with Martha," Nate said. "Tell them what you've done or the next bullet I fire will be fatal."

He had to comply. Nate knew the truth. "M-Martha's in the pit."

"Louder!"

"Martha's in the pit," he screamed. "But she deserved it! I was only meting out God's justice. She failed us all!"

"Is it God's justice to rape her until she hemorrhaged?" someone else shouted. It was Todd, Martha's husband. He pushed his way to the front, carrying his wife's lifeless body. A bedraggled Sarah followed closely behind. "You raped her and then you left her to bleed to death! Sarah will confirm it," he announced to everyone else. "Sarah, who's never told a lie in her life, will explain how our prophet holds secret meetings beneath the Enlightenment Hall, where he and the other Guides drug our wives and rape them at will. Look at her! She's dead," he sobbed. "You can see for yourself!"

"It's true," Sarah added, also crying. "They killed Martha in the vilest way imaginable. I watched them myself."

One by one, the hoods came off, revealing dumbstruck faces as, one by one, each Covenanter came to see or touch Martha. It was almost too much for Ethan. A few minutes earlier, these people had been chanting in unison with him. He could do no wrong in their eyes. How could they gaze at him with such abhorrence now?

"And Courtney?" Nate asked.

Ethan scrambled for the lie he'd been telling since Courtney's disappearance. "She's—"

The gun nudged him harder. "Don't do it," Nate said. "Tell them the truth or I will. Either way I'll search until I find her body if it means I have to dig up the whole compound."

"She's d-dead," he said with a sob. "Bart killed her!"

"No!" Joshua's wife gasped and looked to her husband for a denial. But Joshua said nothing. He didn't have the chance. Bart had returned with the armed guards who'd been walking the perimeter.

"Ethan Wycliff is a fallen prophet!" he shouted. "Take him into custody for crimes against us all."

The security staff moved to respond, but Todd and Sarah and several others intervened. "No! Bart, the twelve, they're all just as guilty. They've lied and used every one of us."

Those words rang in Ethan's ears. *They're all just as guilty.* There would be no Armageddon, no final battle.

They'd lost their strength because they'd lost their unity. Because of Bart. The one person he'd loved and trusted above everyone else had betrayed him....

Weak-kneed, Ethan no longer felt capable of supporting himself. When he sagged against Nate, Nate let him sink to the ground. It was over. With Martha's corpse there for all to see and her husband crying over her, Paradise had fallen into upheaval, a melee of blame and recrimination. This was the end, and no one could change that. Didn't Bart realize? Didn't he know what he'd done? The covenant of secrecy had been broken, and Paradise depended on the covenant. "This is your fault," he wailed at Bart. "You caused this!"

"No, *you* caused this." Bart appealed to the guards again. "All are guilty—except me. Arrest them! Arrest the Brethren, along with the unbelievers. They're the devil's own. I have no doubt they had a hand in all of this."

The guards, young men Ethan had prayed over and led, put their rifles to their shoulders. They were turning on him, just like Bart. Ethan couldn't watch. His end would be as ignominious as Manson's.

Refusing to see the scorn in their faces, he looked away, but soon saw that he wasn't the only one in whom they'd lost faith. At Nate's insistence, and with Todd and Sarah's support, two members of security forced Bart up against the altar—beside Ethan. Others went after the Guides who'd slunk off, hoping to get away in the confusion.

When Nate released her, Rachel felt as boneless as a rag doll.

"You okay?" he whispered, covering her with a Covenanter's robe.

Was she? She didn't know. Her thoughts were spinning. But she understood that Martha was dead. Martha and Courtney. She tried to speak, to express her sadness, but the words wouldn't come. How would they ever break the news to Courtney's poor mother?

At least Mrs. Sinclair would have some closure, Nate said, which made her wonder if she'd managed to express herself after all. She'd been right about her daughter—Courtney would've come home, despite their differences, if she'd had the chance. Ethan had taken that opportunity away from both of them. But he'd never be able to hurt anyone again. Nothing else seemed to make sense, but that did. He'd finally fulfill his dream to be like Charles Manson because he, too, would spend the rest of his life in prison. So would Bart and all the other Guides. Even Maxine, the housekeeper, would have to answer to the law.

The rest was confusing to her, a kaleidoscope of swirling colors and sounds. "You're going to be okay," Nate told her. She must've asked about Sarah, because he said that, in time, she'd be fine, too.

Feeling stronger as Nate led her away from the crowd, she allowed someone she didn't even know to help her into a Jeep. Nate was getting in, too. That was all that mattered. She was going where he was going, and the man behind the wheel said that was the hospital.

Epilogue

This diamond was the real thing. Rachel had been wearing it for three days, ever since Nate had surprised her with it in Prescott, but she still couldn't believe he'd actually proposed. As they drove away from the cabin where they'd spent the previous two nights, she kept glancing down at the large solitaire as if it might disappear. A lot had changed in the past two weeks. Not only were they engaged, they'd taken time off to visit tourist sites in Arizona; in fact, they'd been on the road ever since Nate's release from the hospital. Rachel thought she'd never had more fun. The Grand Canyon had been the final stop on their list. They were on their way home now. But she didn't mind. Nate was planning to move in with her once they hit L.A. They were looking forward to sharing the rest of their lives with each other.

"What are you thinking?" Nate asked.

The thrumming of the tires had lulled her into a mellow state. Or maybe it was the way Nate had made love to her before they'd left the cabin…. "I'm thinking I'm glad that you fixed the air-conditioning. It's hot out."

He gave her a mock scowl. "That's *not* what you were thinking."

She arched her eyebrows. "It's not?"

"You were thinking how much you like that ring," he teased.

She laughed. "True. And I was reliving what we did in the shower this morning."

"Don't remind me, or I'll have to pull over. I was hoping to be at least two hours down the road before I was dying to get in your pants again."

"Such willpower." Smiling, she laid her head on his shoulder, and he shifted to put his arm around her.

"What do you think Milt and everyone else at Department 6 will say when we tell them we're getting married?" he asked.

Rachel hesitated. She wasn't sure Nate was ready for the answer that sprang to her lips. But she was so excited she couldn't keep her news a secret any longer. She'd almost told him a dozen times already. "Not as much as they'll have to say when we tell them we're going to have a baby."

Suddenly slamming on the brakes, he pulled to the side of the road and turned to give her his undivided attention. "What are you talking about? I mean…are you saying you wonder how they'll react when we *decide* to start a family? Or are you saying that we're *already* starting a family?"

Butterflies rioted in Rachel's stomach. She didn't imagine Nate would have a problem with the pregnancy. It wasn't as if they'd been able to use any birth control when they'd made love in the Enlightenment Hall. He hadn't even mentioned birth control since then.

But he'd never said he wanted a child, either.

"I'm saying I took a pregnancy test after we got back from the grocery store yesterday."

"And…"

Unsure whether he was excited or upset, she licked her lips in an effort to calm her nerves. "And it was positive."

"Really?" He gave her a goofy smile. "Wow."

Wow was good. His expression confirmed it. Rachel knew in that moment that she'd never loved anyone more. Maybe Nate had once been reluctant to return her love, but he hadn't shown any sign of that since he'd made a commitment to her.

"So…you're okay with it?" she said.

"Are you kidding me? Come here." Pulling her closer, he kissed her gently, but it wasn't long before those gentle kisses turned into hungry ones and his hand found its way up her blouse.

"There's just one problem," he said as he unsnapped her bra and raised her shirt so he could gaze down at what he'd uncovered.

Rachel felt her pulse pick up. "What's that?"

"We'll have to get another motel room."

"Why?"

He gave her a lopsided grin. "I'm not going to make it two hours."

She laughed. "We could do it in the desert…."

"Now you're thinking," he said, and drove to the very next turn, which led them to…paradise.

* * * * *

REQUEST YOUR
FREE BOOKS!

2 FREE NOVELS
FROM THE SUSPENSE COLLECTION
PLUS 2 FREE GIFTS!

YES! Please send me 2 FREE novels from the Suspense Collection and my 2 FREE gifts (gifts are worth about $10). After receiving them, if I don't wish to receive any more books, I can return the shipping statement marked "cancel." If I don't cancel, I will receive 3 brand-new novels every month and be billed just $5.74 per book in the U.S. or $6.24 per book in Canada. That's a saving of at least 28% off the cover price. It's quite a bargain! Shipping and handling is just 50¢ per book.* I understand that accepting the 2 free books and gifts places me under no obligation to buy anything. I can always return a shipment and cancel at any time. Even if I never buy another book, the two free books and gifts are mine to keep forever.

192/392 MDN E7PD

Name _____ (PLEASE PRINT)

Address _____ Apt. #

City _____ State/Prov. _____ Zip/Postal Code

Signature (if under 18, a parent or guardian must sign)

Mail to **The Reader Service:**
IN U.S.A.: P.O. Box 1867, Buffalo, NY 14240-1867
IN CANADA: P.O. Box 609, Fort Erie, Ontario L2A 5X3

Not valid for current subscribers to the Suspense Collection or the Romance/Suspense Collection.

Want to try two free books from another line?
Call 1-800-873-8635 or visit www.morefreebooks.com.

* Terms and prices subject to change without notice. Prices do not include applicable taxes. N.Y. residents add applicable sales tax. Canadian residents will be charged applicable provincial taxes and GST. Offer not valid in Quebec. This offer is limited to one order per household. All orders subject to approval. Credit or debit balances in a customer's account(s) may be offset by any other outstanding balance owed by or to the customer. Please allow 4 to 6 weeks for delivery. Offer available while quantities last.

Your Privacy: Harlequin Books is committed to protecting your privacy. Our Privacy Policy is available online at www.eHarlequin.com or upon request from the Reader Service. From time to time we make our lists of customers available to reputable third parties who may have a product or service of interest to you. If you would prefer we not share your name and address, please check here. ☐

Help us get it right—We strive for accurate, respectful and relevant communications. To clarify or modify your communication preferences, visit us at www.ReaderService.com/consumerschoice.

MSUS10R

BRENDA NOVAK